"Catheryn, my shoulders [...] any weight you see fit to [...] husband, and as long as I w[...] you need carry alone."

The tears she wanted to shed earlier slipped past her closed eyes and down her cheek. Oh, how she longed to believe him. To know she was not alone. To have someone she could trust without doubts would be a dream realized. But dreams were for children and never came true. Never. Or they came true as nightmares.

And yet...The image of a dark knight thundering toward her raced through her mind. An oft-repeated promise rang in her ears.

Thou pretty herb of Venus's tree, thy true name is yarrow...

Denise Lynn

Dream Knight

Brezden's Love Spells ~ Book 1 (Yarrow's Promise)

DREAM KNIGHT
First Published 2000 by Starlight Writers Publishing
Copyright © 2019 Denise Lynn

NOTE: This is a work of fiction. Names, characters, places and incidents either are the product of the author's imagination or are used fictitiously. Any resemblance to actual events, locales, business establishments or persons, living or dead, is coincidental.

ISBN: 978 1 091 80998 7

Award Winning Author Denise Lynn lives in Ohio with her husband. She loves sharing her tales of brave men and strong women with others. When not tapping on the keyboard, she can be found doing one of her favorite hobbies—sleeping, researching, hiking, sewing, or tending her herb garden.

OTHER BOOKS BY DENISE LYNN

The Falcons (Harlequin Historical)
    Falcon's Desire
    Falcon's Honor
    Falcon's Love
    Falcon's Heart (RT Reviewers Choice Nominee)
Commanded/Bedded (Harlequin Historical)
    Commanded to His Bed
    Bedded by Her Lord
    Bedded by The Warrior
The Warehaven's (Harlequin Historical)
    Wedding at Warehaven (Novella currently unavailable)
    Pregnant by The Warrior
    The Warrior's Winter Bride
    At the Warrior's Mercy (The final Warehaven AND first Warrior Wolf)
Warrior Wolves ~ The Rouls (Harlequin Historical)
    At the Warrior's Mercy
    The Warrior's Runaway Wife
The Drakes of Dragon's Lair (Harlequin Nocturne)
    Dragon's Lair (Currently unavailable)
    Dragon's Curse
    Dragon's Promise

For more information, visit:
www.denise-lynn.com

Dedication

For Tom ~ my "Dream Knight"

Prologue

"No!"

Her terrified scream failed to stop the advancing horror. Mail-clad warriors astride Satan's own destriers raced through the fog toward her.

Armor as black as the starless sky covered each from helmed head to leather-booted foot.

The mighty warhorses drew ever closer. Paralyzed and unprotected on the open moor, she could only tremble at their onslaught.

Ironclad hooves pounded in perfect unison with the heavy thudding of her heart. Swords, pikes, and axes raised, the demonic army neared. Its leader ensnared her gaze. Dark eyes held no sign of mercy. There would be no quarter given if she were captured by this unforgiving force.

A cloying smell of death permeated the air, broken only by an acrid scent of smoke and destruction. The vile stench seared her nostrils. She shuddered with revulsion, then fought to calm her racing heart and force her trembling limbs to still. She would not cower before her enemies, nor would she kneel in the cold mud and beg for mercy. With a hushed voice she prayed, "Lord, give me strength."

The leader of this pack of armor-clad wolves stopped before her as the remaining warriors raced past. A thunderbolt lit the sky. Raindrops rolled down the mailed arm reaching out for her and shimmered over an emerald and gold ring on an ungloved hand that grasped her shoulder.

Lifting her hands before her face in a feeble attempt to ward off a *brutal end to her life, she begged, "Dear God, have mercy on my——"*

Lady Catheryn bolted suddenly awake, looking frantically for her enemy. A draft of air blew across her naked body, creating gooseflesh on sweat-soaked skin, and she blinked away the last traces of her dream. She sighed with relief at the familiar view of her own chamber. She was safe. At least, as safe as this chamber ever made her.

The sight of the crumpled bed curtain still entwined in her tightly clenched fingers almost made her laugh with disbelief as she remembered what had caused such a nightmare. She retrieved the yarrow-filled dream bag from beneath her pillow. The words of the sachet's intent came back to her. *"Thou pretty herb of Venus's tree, thy true name is Yarrow. Now who my brave, true love must be, pray tell me by the morrow."*

A chill not caused by the night breeze sent a shiver down her spine. In a moment of desperation and amusement, she'd asked for a dream of true love. Instead, she'd received a vision of terror and death.

Sadly, that seemed her lot.

Chapter One

"He is out there," Catheryn, Lady of Brezden, whispered into the empty darkness.

It had been three nights since her dream began. Each night, during her fitful slumber, she'd witnessed the deadly attack. The destruction of her home and the deaths of her people at the hands of an unknown warrior. Only then did he turn his ferocious attention toward her. But tonight…tonight the dream—nay, the nightmare—seemed not just a vision of her sleep, it seemed more a portent of the future.

Between the castle walls and the forest, nothing moved. Cold spring rain fell on the surrounding terrain, yet the blustering wind carried the scent of a man bent on destruction, a destruction that she herself had unwittingly called forth. Perhaps her own destruction. But she would not regret it. One simple charm, meant to give her a glimpse of the man who would be her life's love, had worked well. Far too well. She felt his nearness in the chill of the night air.

The rustle of the trees vibrated with his strong, steady heartbeat. Catheryn shivered—not from the cold or the rain, but from the knowledge that, no matter his true form and visage, her vision would soon come to life. What exactly had she summoned? To trust her dream, a helmeted demon with hard, unforgiving eyes. She would meet her "true love," and surely not in the manner or shape she had imagined. Not that she had encountered any such gentleness from men. Not for many years.

"My lady, you should be abed."

"He has come, Agnes." Catheryn despised the alarm she heard in that simple declaration, a fear she would never voluntarily show to anyone. But she could never successfully hide the emotion from her nursemaid. Since the murder of Catheryn's mother, Agnes had been more than just a servant. The older woman had become the very strength that kept Catheryn from falling into an abyss of despair.

"Who is here?"

"My *true love*." Catheryn almost laughed at the thought. She turned the sachet over in her hands one more time then relinquished it. "The dark knight of my dreams has arrived."

"Fie," Agnes said, examining the pouch. "That isn't possible."

"You think I don't know that?" Catheryn peered deeper into the night. Her dark intended's heartbeat drummed in her blood. "But regardless of what was *supposed* to happen, I cannot deny what I know without doubt *will* happen." And she did know. At least part of it. She resisted the urge to give in to the hysterical laughter threatening to bubble forth, turned away from her chamber's single window and lit the tallow candles ensconced on the wall.

"This is impossible. Mistress Margaret said—"

"I don't care what the midwife said." Catheryn pulled a gown from the clothing chest and tossed it atop her bed. "All I know is that the good mistress's charm must be stronger than we thought."

Agnes grabbed the gown before Catheryn could slip it on. "What are you doing?"

"Preparing to meet my destiny."

"But you said he was leading an assault. You are not going to meet him at the gates!"

"What else can I do? He will find me regardless." Catheryn retrieved the dress with a gentle tug and slipped it over her head. "And shall I let Brezden's people be attacked without giving them notice? Shall I stay here in my chamber quivering like a coward?"

"Pike is the master here. Let him deal with any invaders."

This time Catheryn did laugh—with disdain. Months after her father's death, a little over four years ago, King Stephen had appointed Pike her family's guardian and steward of Brezden. Her two sisters had been sent away when Catheryn's mother received news regarding the man's appointment. Rumors of Pike were plentiful, and they confirmed what her mother already knew, so she wanted the girls as far away as possible to keep them from his reach. She'd sent them and a couple of her father's older, trusted guards to France to live with distant relatives until she could find a way to get rid of him. She never had. Catheryn had adamantly refused to go, and her mother had been unable to sway her. Catheryn was glad she stayed. She'd been able to offer at least a little comfort to her mother, especially in those final days. No matter the cost to herself.

"Pike? What do you think he will do? He will consult his minion, de Brye." A shiver coursed down her spine. "Then the two of them will save their own hides, using whatever means they can." It was a shame. She'd like to see the pair try to meet the oncoming assault.

"But what about—?"

"No!" Before Agnes could say anything more, Catheryn strengthened her resolve. "I must do this. Don't you see? A man comes to sack Brezden, a man who will surely succeed. No one else is aware of his presence, except me. It is my responsibility to warn what few loyal soldiers we have left to seek safety."

Without allowing her nursemaid another word, Catheryn opened the door to her chamber then walked out into the dark corridor beyond. She'd resisted the urge to soothe the worry lines from the woman's brow and now fought the need to return to Agnes and provide reassurance. Not that she could. How could she ease the concerns of another when she didn't know herself what this night would bring?

ᙅᙁ

Brezden Keep was almost invisible through the curtain of rain falling from the sky. A bolt of lightning gave a glimpse of the massive stone walls surrounding it. From his vantage beneath the shelter of trees, Baron Gerard of Reveur noted the few men pacing up top. How many more would be concealed in the towers?

Gerard knew the castle's defenses were sadly lacking. For more than a year he had waited and planned, gathering every piece of information he could about Brezden and its lord.

In a time when brother fought brother and nothing was as it seemed, paid spies came easily. They had supplied him with details he'd not have been able to garner on his own.

At last, fate had smiled on him. His overlord, William, the Earl of York, called for help to secure his land from traitors. Pike ignored that call to arms, adding Brezden to the list of those disloyal to Earl William and King Stephen. Gerard had immediately volunteered to capture the stronghold. As long as Brezden fell into loyal hands, no one would care if his own schemes found fulfillment.

DREAM KNIGHT

The sound of wheels clattering over a stone road gave Gerard cause to smile. He reached out and patted the thick, wet neck of his destrier. The twitching ears and bulging muscles of the black warhorse informed him that the beast had also heard the wagon's approach. A wagon driven by his men.

"Not yet. Can you not be patient just a little longer?"

The animal bobbed his great head up and down. Gerard rolled his eyes at imagining the horse had done so in answer to his question.

The wagon rolled past, and shouts could be heard. As the outer castle gates groaned slowly open a frown replaced Gerard's smile. Brezden's guards had allowed the hay wagon entrance without so much as a second glance. At the very least he had expected its driver to be stopped and questioned. His spies hadn't been totally accurate. While the castle was lightly guarded, they hadn't mentioned it was garrisoned by fools.

A drop of cold rain found its way through his mailed coif to trickle down the back of his neck. Who was he to call the men sitting warm and dry behind those walls fools? Any sane person would think the knight preparing for battle in the middle of a storm was the real fool.

They would be wrong in their assumption.

He'd played the simpleton once. And his misjudgment had cost him a beloved wife and a newborn son.

Gerard glared up at the steady downpour of rain and wondered if the bad weather was an omen of things to come. The storm had been with him and his men for the three days it had taken to ride southwest from Scarborough. For each of those long days he'd relived his wife's horrible death.

Crossing himself, he cursed his apprehension. He cursed life and cursed God. He cursed the man who had turned his idyllic world into a nightmare. Gerard closed his eyes against the sickening memory of Edyth's twisted and broken body and swallowed his pain before vowing, "I swear to you, beloved, I will satisfy our need for revenge this night."

Riding down the line of mounted soldiers, Gerard joined his captain Walter at a break in the forest. "The fires will start slowly tonight. This rain has surely soaked the thatched roofs," he muttered to the older man.

Blue eyes encased by a weather-beaten face lifted briefly to the dark sky. "Aye. But we expected little else."

Gerard snorted at his captain's disgruntled tone. He knew Walter disliked this northern climate more than he did and had cautioned against fighting in this weather. Nodding toward the castle, he said, "The wagon gained entrance."

"A little too easily."

Glancing back at the walls, Gerard weighed his options. There was but one choice. By now his men already inside would be anxiously waiting for their signal.

"If anyone decided to stop the wagon after its entry, we would have seen more guards attend the walls." Taking one last look up at the keep, Gerard made the final decision. "Go. Take your men and proceed as planned. As soon as I hear your commotion, I will lead my group to the wall."

Walter and his men moved forward as Gerard watched through the blackness. Lightning split the sky like a whip, and in its eerie light Gerard thought he felt someone watching him in return.

The stare fell upon him with a certainty he could hardly fathom. It was as if someone inside eagerly awaited his arrival and the salvation they thought it would bring.

How would they feel once they realized he offered only death?

He shook the strange thoughts from his mind and the

dripping rain from his helmet's nasal plate. Peering back at Brezden, he reassured himself that his flight of fancy was just that. Then he shouted for his men to advance.

☙

From the walls of the keep, Catheryn watched a hay wagon enter the bailey with little interest. Her *beloved* would not enter concealed in a wagon. No. *He* would ride a warhorse as black as his armor through Brezden's gate. *He* would charge murderously forward, brandishing a sword before him and striking down all who stepped in his path.

A bitter satisfaction fell upon her soul to accompany her fear. Men would die this night.

Her own soldiers, Brezden's faithful few, were safely away through the tunnel entrance hidden in her chamber. They had challenged her, and she laughed in triumph at the memory—a small victory. It had come down to her will against theirs, her orders against their pleas, and at last, they had gone grumbling to safety. Now, somewhere along the river gliding silently past Brezden, her men watched and waited. She'd ordered them to hide far away, but Catheryn knew they would disobey. Her only hope was that they weren't found and eventually might return.

She glanced around at the remaining men stationed on the wall-walk. These were Pike's men—and de Brye's. She cared little what happened to them. They were scum, the dregs of the earth, and they deserved whatever fate this night held in store. How many times had one or more of them held her arms pinned, making her unable to escape de Brye's crude, taunting threats, stinging slaps and childish, twisting pinches?

It had been obvious by his sickening smirks the next day that he took great pleasure from seeing her bruises—the visible ones. Only she and Agnes saw the ones concealed beneath her clothing. How many nights had her cries gone unanswered while these men drank and played cruel games with her maids? And while the torment inflicted on Catheryn had been humiliating, terrifying and painful, their torments had produced bastard children and the deaths of two young, innocent women barely out of childhood. Her own men had been forced to look on in helpless horror as de Brye's raped defenseless maids with no regard to their age. They'd seen early how any challenge was rewarded—with execution.

Not one pleasant evening had been spent in this keep since her father's death over four years ago. After her mother's death last year, the days and nights had become even worse.

Cease. Catheryn silently bade the memories vanish. She needed to remain in control. Having held off her grief and terror this long, surely one more night would not make any difference.

From the far edge of her vision, she saw Raymond de Brye for less than the blink of an eye before he grasped her arm. She jumped and tried desperately to yank free of his hold. How ironic, that this was the minion of her guardian.

"That's right, sweeting, fight me. You know how I so enjoy your struggles." He smiled and nodded at the wagon now rolling towards the stables. "You have been out here watching the gate far more than normal of late. Are you waiting for someone?"

She silently shook her head while cursing herself for being too obvious.

"Only crude knaves command that wagon. Do you think they would deal with you more gently than I? I could easily give you to them."

Catheryn refused to rise to his bait. She would not give him the pleasure. Then he grazed her cheek with his mouth, and it took every ounce of willpower not to scream at the feel of his lips touching her skin.

"No, my darling," he continued. "I will not share you." Jerking her with him, de Brye dragged her back down the stairs and toward her bedchamber. "Anyone who thinks to take what is mine need be prepared to pay with his life."

She was not *his*, nor would she ever be, but she had no choice except to follow where he led. Something was different in his manner. He was more determined, his steps were quick instead of sauntering, and this movement seemed urgent.

Catheryn felt a level of fright she had never before experienced. When he pulled her into her chamber and tossed her on the bed, she gasped and rolled to the floor. Raymond de Brye was a cruel, sadistic brute, but this outright forwardness was new. He had never attacked her in her own chamber before. Landing on her hands and knees she scrambled toward the door, but her attempted escape was cut short as de Brye grabbed a handful of hair and dragged her backward. He quickly loosened his leather belt and waved it before her face like a whip.

"Move again, and your tender skin will feel my wrath."

Without turning her head, Catheryn frantically searched the room. Agnes had hidden well, and for a moment that brought a measure of relief and gratitude.

It was short-lived. Reaching into the curtained alcove, de Brye grasped Catheryn's maid by her hair, dragged her to the chamber door and pushed her out into the corridor. "Keep yourself beyond my sight, else you'll watch your lady die."

Catheryn froze. She knew his threat to be true. Something had definitely changed. He had repeatedly belittled her, taunted her and caused her harm, but he'd always done so with as large an audience as possible in attendance. His excitement—and torment—increased in proportion to the number of people gathered to watch. And while he'd boasted to others about what he'd done to her in private, in truth he had never touched her physically when she'd accidentally been in his vicinity alone.

This attack suddenly seemed more personal, and she greatly feared that he *would* kill her with only Agnes as witness. She urged her maid, "Agnes, go. Do as he says."

While Agnes scrambled to obey, de Brye swung back to glare at Catheryn. "Open your mouth again and I'll close it for you permanently."

Still believing in her vision, still believing that a dark horde brought death to her castle—death and perhaps reprieve—Catheryn bit back a scathing retort. If pressed too far, this monstrous man would kill her. She needed to gain enough time for her dark knight to attack. Anything would be better than this.

A sly smile twisted de Brye's face into a mask of pure evil. "That's right, sweeting, do as you are bid, and it may go easier for you."

He turned to the door and shouted for Pike. Waiting for Pike, her captor simply stood across the room and stared at her. His hooded gaze sent shivers down her spine. Catheryn averted her attention and silently prayed for her avenging angel to hurry.

Angel?

When had that dark-eyed demonic form become a celestial being?

Pike arrived before she had time to sort out her confused thoughts. Chainmail askew, helmet held in one shaking hand and a wavering sword in the other, the man's disheveled appearance belied his authority. This was no true commander of men and most certainly no steward for Brezden.

12

"What do you want?" Pike spared but a glance at Catheryn. "I have no time for your games at present, Raymond. There are strange reports from—"

"Games?" de Brye's voice held a note of sick humor. "I play no games, my lord." Had she been anywhere else, Catheryn would have laughed at the tone of abject disrespect de Brye used. But she wasn't anywhere else, and she was well aware this was no game.

Pike grimaced. "I ask again, what do you want?"

Pulling off his tunic, de Brye said nothing. He slowly approached the bed.

The fear that had kept her limbs frozen now propelled Catheryn from the mattress. Pike and de Brye blocked any escape through the door, so racing toward a long thin arrow slit in the wall she hoped to scream and capture someone's attention. Anyone's. Perhaps her dark knight, or one of his men, was close enough to hear and come to her aid.

Her hope was irrelevant. Before she could make a noise, de Brye wrapped his hands around her neck, effectively cutting off her cries. She clawed at his fingers, but the act did little to loosen his vise-like grip and de Brye only laughed before squeezing harder. Catheryn's vision clouded. Her lungs burned with the need for air. Finally, de Brye released his grasp and tossed her back on the bed as if she were little more than a child.

Catheryn's chest heaved with the effort to breathe. She had to get away.

As if reading her thoughts, de Brye wound her hair around his hand. He looked at Pike and smiled before stating, "I thought perhaps you'd enjoy being witness to your ward's first bedding." Then, before she could free herself, de Brye launched himself atop her. He moved with an agility she had not realized he possessed.

"Really, Raymond, do you think now is the time to be satisfying your urges?" Pike shifted from one foot to the other. "There are reports that—"

"*Urges?*" De Brye's face was so close that Catheryn could feel his sickening hot breath on her cheek. "Not urges, my lord." He grasped the back of her head. "It seems our dear Catheryn is awaiting someone. Have you not noticed her odd visits to the main wall of late? She stands there as if she's expecting someone to appear."

Catheryn shuddered. She heard Pike approach the bed.

"Is this true?"

"No. For whom would I be waiting?" It wasn't as if she could have sent for someone. She wasn't even allowed to send a brief missive to her sisters in France without Pike reading it and giving permission.

De Brye tightened his grasp on her hair. "I do not trust her." He looked at Pike. "And I am sick of waiting for the king to respond to your request for my marriage to her." Turning his attention back to her, he added, "She and Brezden will be mine this day. Now."

Had that been their plan all along? For her to wed de Brye, giving him legal right to her and all she possessed? She'd rather die. Catheryn kicked and twisted. "Let me go. Dear Lord," she addressed the heavens, "do not allow this to happen."

"Raymond is correct. You will belong to him once King Stephen sends his decree. It makes little difference if happens today or a week from today."

The sounds of battle suddenly drifted in through the window. Catheryn twisted, and Pike sighed then patted her cheek before turning back to his crony. "It seems the reports were accurate and there are indeed intruders at the gate. So, Raymond, I must make an appearance as lord. I'd suggest you come with me but…Well, I don't believe it's a very large force. Try not to be too unpleasant, though. You'll want her willing later."

De Brye smiled. "Close the door on your way out."

Pike did. Catheryn heard his exit while she stared at the man above her. She had not the physical power to stop him, but she'd not be a willing victim. Keeping her voice steady she ordered, "Get off of me." Imperiousness seemed her last weapon.

Releasing her hair, de Brye rolled to one side, grasped the front of her gown and rent the fabric to her waist. "I only want to prepare you for the night to come."

Horrified, Catheryn tried to scoot away. She slapped his hands then yelled, "You are worse than a swine! You have no right!"

"I have every right." De Brye pulled her back and stopped her accusations with a stinging slap to the cheek. Her mind screamed with pain as his fingers squeezed and prodded an exposed breast, and her soul cried out when he shredded the rest of her gown. She tried desperately to close her mind to what was about to happen, but something, either fear or anger, kept her from escaping inside herself.

She spat in his face and swore, "Regardless of what you do, I will kill myself before becoming your wife. Do what you want with my body. There is no way you can keep me prisoner forever. Someday I will escape. Somehow. And God will punish you for all that you are. I curse you with everything I am."

Stark, insane rage covered de Brye's features. Then his fist closed in on her face.

☙

Men on horseback rushed from the woods, surprising the defenders stationed behind and atop Brezden's thick stone walls. Swords drawn, Gerard's men poured through the open gates. As the unsuspecting guards fell from the castle's outer walls and towers, their screams of astonishment and pain mixed with those of the surprised animals stabled in the outer bailey.

"Remember the Lady of Reveur and leave no traitor alive!" Gerard shouted. Then he remembered his promise to a broken and battered Edyth as she took her last breath in his arms. He cried a final order to his men, "Brezden's lord is mine!"

His soldiers quickly crossed the outer courtyard. With heavy swords and two-headed battle-axes they dispatched anyone who offered the slightest resistance.

Reaching the wall that separated the inner and outer yards, Gerard offered a silent prayer of relief and gratitude as he watched the iron-shod portcullis rise. His advance men had performed their duties to perfection and gained control of this last barrier. Certain that his men were capable of taking possession of the inner ward, he tightened his grip on his sword and turned to look up the motte toward the keep itself.

He sucked in his breath with a hiss when a bolt of lightning streaked across the sky and outlined Brezden at the top of the earthen mound.

Gerard swallowed the bitter taste of iron and urged the destrier up the man-made hill. The metallic taste of blood before a battle was nothing new. It only served to strengthen his resolve to be victorious.

At the base of the keep, Gerard dismounted and slapped his horse on the rump. "Go."

He shook his head at the departing animal, knowing there was no need for concern over its welfare. Its iron-clad hooves and strong teeth could easily maim, if not kill, anyone who came within reach.

Gerard turned and raced up the stairs leading into the keep. The narrowness of the stairway permitted only one person at a time to try to hold him back, and none could. Each slash of his sword and every contact he made with an enemy fueled his desire for battle. By the time Gerard reached the Great Hall, he could hear his heart pounding in his ears. He could feel the blood course through his body. He wanted to take Pike now, while he was primed and ready.

Entering the hall, Gerard stopped. He quickly scanned the Great Hall for the lord of the holding. Edyth had described two men before she died. One was old, fat, balding, and cowardly—Pike. Her description of the other had been brief. *Satan. The devil.* Gerard had little doubt which had been the one to send her to her early grave.

Spotting a portly older man in chainmail on the upper level, Gerard ran up the steep, curved stairs at the side of the hall. "Pike!" When the man stopped and turned, Gerard added, "The time has come to pay for your act of villainy."

"Come, pup, whomever you may be. Try to wrest Brezden from my hand." The man extended his sword and beckoned Gerard forward. "You, some nameless scum, think to challenge *me?*"

"Nameless scum?" Gerard lifted his own weapon and swung, striking Pike's blade. "It was my wife you killed a winter past. My infant child whom you slaughtered." When the man appeared unable to remember the act, Gerard stepped back and bowed. "Baron Gerard of Reveur at your service."

Pike blanched and tossed his sword over the railing to clatter on the stone floor far below. Smiling, he spread his arms. "Your reputation precedes you. While you may truly be one of Earl William's warriors, it is said you are as

17

honorable as you are fierce. Would you prove those claims false by killing a defenseless man?"

Gerard chose the spot on Pike's chest where his sword tip would do its final work and smiled back. "Yes, I would."

But in that same instant, he remembered the oath he had sworn when knighted four years ago after the Battle of Standard. He was to be a paragon of valor. Of honor.

Pike spun around and raced down the long corridor. Gerard charged after him.

Pike reached an alcove, ducking in to seek what Gerard instinctively knew would be another sword. At the same time, Gerard heard footsteps behind him. Turning, he rammed the tip of his weapon into the treacherous knave who thought to take him unawares. The enemy soldier died with a gurgle.

Before Gerard could fully turn back, his opponent slashed at him. Had it not been for his double-linked chainmail, he would have lost a limb. He grasped the hilt of his sword in both hands and plunged the weapon into Pike's chest—exactly in the spot he had chosen only moments before. The single-link chainmail burst, and the older man fell to his knees, dead. A soothing peace flowed through Gerard's veins. Closing his eyes, he saw Edyth grant him one of her sweet smiles.

Yet, his pleasure was brief. He'd only accomplished one of the two vows he'd made to her. He still needed to find the other man, the one she'd called Satan.

Forcing himself away from the image of his wife, Gerard jerked his blade out of Pike's unresisting flesh and wiped the bloody sword on his tunic. Looking down, he crossed himself then resisted the urge to do the same for the dead man on the floor. The fiend deserved no such blessing.

Gerard strode back to the landing and glanced over the

railing to see that his men had all but finalized their victory. He yelled down, "Secure the rest and gather the survivors in the hall." As an afterthought, he added, "Make sure they see their previous lord's fate."

There would be no mercy. None had been shown to Edyth.

ᘓ

Having given his order, Gerard paused long enough for his pounding blood to slow, but only slightly. Then he began searching the remaining chambers. Each room proved dark and empty, all save the last. It was a sleeping chamber. His eyes adjusted quickly to the dim light provided by the wall candles, and entering cautiously, Gerard saw a bed. White and pale blue shredded curtains draped its length. A figure lay within.

"Show yourself," Gerard demanded. Receiving no answer, he proceeded around the perimeter of the room. "The keep is lost. You have no choice but to surrender."

Gowns were carelessly discarded nearby, lying half out of a chest against the wall. A light scent, spicy and floral, wafted up from the rush- and herb-covered floor.

Gerard clenched his jaw. No one, not one of his many spies, had said anything about a female residing in the keep. They'd not mentioned Pike having a wife or a daughter. But, then, he had to admit that he'd never cared enough to ask.

He slapped his leg impatiently, he didn't have time for games. Using his sword to part the frayed curtains, Gerard wasn't sure if he should laugh or roar, so he simply stared, dumbfounded. This couldn't be happening.

Sleeping? A battle takes place outside her very door and she sleeps?

Then he noticed something else.

A gut-wrenching pain twisted his innards. As a warrior he'd killed many men for his king and overlord. He'd destroyed keeps and manors without second thought. The sounds and sights of blood and death were familiar to him, but never an image like this. In the unsteady glow from the candles, he realized this woman lying on the bed had faced her own battle—and lost.

Grasping the hilt of his sword tighter, Gerard stepped away from the bed. It would take a vile miscreant, much like the one he'd just dispatched to hell, to beat a woman in such a manner. Had it been Pike, or had the spineless cur responsible been the other black-hearted knave he still sought?

Only one person could provide the answer.

Chapter Two

Would death claim her this night?

Catheryn sought frantically for a way to escape the advancing terror, but she stood in the open, outside the walls of Brezden. There was no place to hide, nowhere to run as Lucifer's horsemen charged forward. They were so close now she could see the gleaming whites of the riders' eyes. The nasal plates of their helmets glittered with each crack of lightning. Puffs of steam plumed from the horses' nostrils. She could feel the animals' warm breath on her bare flesh.

Fighting to calm a racing heart, Catheryn forced her trembling limbs to still. She would not cower before her enemies, nor would she kneel in the cold mud and beg for mercy. With a hushed voice, she prayed, "Lord, give me strength."

The leader of this pack of death-hungry wolves stopped before her as the remaining warriors raced past. A thunderbolt lit the sky. Raindrops rolled down the mailed arm reaching out for her. These tears from heaven shimmered over an emerald and gold ring on the naked hand that grasped her shoulder with a bruising hold.

Slowly, the fog began to clear. Her breath caught in her throat. She felt the grasp on her shoulder and realized she was not dreaming. Catheryn opened her eyes and stared warily into the burning gaze of her nightmare come to life.

Her heart stopped. Reality crashed in around her. The

events of the day flooded her with fear as cold as a mountain stream. It flowed up her body and clouded her mind with its icy grip. Unable to form any coherent thoughts or words, Catheryn remained still.

The man released his hold and backed away. His instant retreat helped to both ease her fear and prompt her into action.

Keeping a close watch on him, she moved to sit up. Bruised muscles cried out with pain. The cool night air brushed against her naked breasts. Lifting a hand to her throbbing face, she groaned with the rush of recent memories. One was worse than the rest. *Sir de Brye.* Had he fulfilled his evil threat? There had been no one here to prevent him from doing so.

Catheryn swallowed a sob and took a deep breath to steady herself. While she ached from being beaten, she felt no pain that claimed she'd been violated sexually. She was certain that, had de Brye raped her, he would not have been gentle about it and she'd have no doubts that he'd done so. She sighed with relief before darting her gaze to the man in her chamber.

He was trying hard to avoid staring at her exposed flesh. She thought it odd that a stranger would show such restraint. *Ah, but he is no stranger, is he?*

She tried to clasp the torn remnants of her gown together but was unable, so Catheryn gingerly reached for a blanket. She flinched when pain accompanied her movements.

The intruder stepped close, his spurs clinking softly as he came near. "Here, let me." He made quick work of covering her and then lightly touched her swollen face. Before moving back, he asked, "Who did this?"

Catheryn looked up at him. After asking his barely audible question, the stranger had removed his helmet and pushed back his mailed coif. Etched cheekbones, straight nose, and square jaw looked as if they had been carved in marble, but the artist's hand must have slipped with the chisel, leaving a small jagged scar running crosswise over his temple. Damp hair fell to just above his immense shoulders. Those unruly raven locks had matched the color of his eyes in her dream. While his hair was actually as inky as a raven's, his deep sapphire-hued eyes were far from black.

Even though he didn't appear as frightening in the flesh as he had in her nightmares, he still caused terror to lift the hairs on the back of her neck. This dark knight was supposed to be her promised love. What if her trust in a charmed dream was wrong and her worry of his arrival justified? What would he do with her?

He suddenly glared at her, and she realized he must have asked her a question. Quickly finding her voice, she said, "Pray, forgive me. I did not hear."

"Who did this?" he repeated in a clipped tone. He didn't sound like he was used to repeating himself. "Where is the vile knave?"

His eyes were piercing. Catheryn studied his arrogant face and decided this was a man who expected to be in complete control of every situation. Her first impulse was to throw herself on his mercy. Except, he did not have the look of a man who knew what mercy was.

Taking a deep breath, she clutched her cover tighter to her neck before whispering, "De Brye. Sir Raymond de Brye." It was all she could do not to gag as the words left her lips.

Pity and disgust flitted across the intruder's features, but Catheryn would accept neither. Nor did she wish to discuss the man who had made her life little more than a living hell. Ignoring the pain flooding through her, she sat up straighter

23

on the bed. Squaring her shoulders, she lifted her chin and asked, "What have you done with my people?"

The stranger stepped closer to the bed. "What soldiers we found have been dispatched along with their lord."

"I care little what happened to Pike or his men." She ignored the burning of her throat when she tilted her head back to look up at him. "What about my *people*?"

"Your people? Was not Pike the lord here?"

Catheryn choked out a short, bitter laugh. "Pike, the true lord of Brezden?" Shaking her head, she fought the unladylike urge to spit on the floor. "The usurper Pike was only here due to King Stephen and Earl William's well-intended, albeit misguided grace."

"You lie."

Her head snapped back up. "No. I would never lie about my keep. Nor about my people."

She watched disbelief and confusion cross his face before a look of bland unconcern won out. "So, you are the Lady of Brezden?"

If it had been possible, she'd have torn out her own tongue for giving away that little bit of information. Catheryn knew she'd have to guard her words more closely in the future. But in this, her error was complete. "Yes. Since my mother's murder a year ago."

"Murder?" A frown creased the stranger's brows. "I was told of no murder. Only of a grieving woman whose desire to join her husband led her down the wrong path."

Suicide? Is that what rumor had been let out about her mother's death? Every muscle, every bone in Catheryn's body stiffened. She clenched and unclenched her jaw. "That is untrue." Then, unwilling to permit the line of conversation to continue any further with this invader, she tightened her grasp on her coverlet and asked, "What do you want of me and Brezden?"

The stranger shook his head. "I want nothing of you. I already have Brezden."

൞

The woman lifted her chin higher. Aqua eyes, while still wary, were rapidly changing to a darker green. Gerard could only assume the color foretold a coming anger.

"Nothing? Then go. This is my chamber. My keep." She motioned toward the door. "Leave."

Gerard shook his head again. Aye, he'd been right. But along with the anger, there was arrogance and a willfulness uncommon in most females he met. Leaning down so that they were eye to eye, he spoke slowly and deliberately. "You must not have heard me. I have taken this keep. If it belongs to anyone save King Stephen, it belongs to Earl William. And I will hold it for him until his arrival." Gerard waited until he was certain the simple fact had taken hold in her mind. "Now, you can either help me control the defeated people of Brezden and assist me in finding any remaining traitors, or you can relegate yourself to a tower cell."

The lady paled but said nothing.

Gerard backed away and stared. While she called herself the lady of the keep, she'd been very ill-treated. The purplish imprint of fingers marred her throat, and drops of blood, recently drawn, had dried upon her skin. And there were marks that looked older. Her time here had not been pleasant.

Rage, unbidden and nearly uncontrolled, boiled forth. His stomach churned as his eyes again found her bruised neck. He'd seen marks like this on a woman before, and she'd lived barely long enough to name one attacker. He'd never heard the other's name —until today. He had little doubt that the man who'd marked this lady also maimed and killed Edyth.

To hold back his wrath, he clenched his hands into fists and considered the situation. Had the Lady of Brezden been left alive for a reason? If so, what? If not, and if her attacker was not already dead, would he be back to finish what he'd started?

Earl William had intended to help her, she'd said. He would not be pleased to lose her. Regardless, Gerard would protect this woman from the same type of death Edyth faced. Even if she refused his help.

Lightly touching her cheek, he promised, "He will pay for this."

The lady jerked away, but with a trembling voice, she asked, "*Will* pay?" Her pleading gaze almost made Gerard's heart cease beating. "But you saw to his death, did you not?"

A familiarity overcame him, and he was momentarily taken aback. Had hers been the piercing gaze he'd felt just before he'd attacked Brezden? He shrugged off the notion and admitted, "No." While he'd taken care of the one man Edyth described, he'd seen none that fit her description of *Satan*. He amended his answer, "In truth, I am not certain."

Silence filled the room.

As much as he'd wanted to tell her that her tormentor had been dispatched, Gerard could not lie. "My lady, it is obvious whoever did this deserves to pay for his crimes. I am more than willing to find the knave."

A cold, bitter look of resignation replaced the hope that crossed her face. Tears welled in her eyes, and she turned her head away. "Nay. If he is not already dead, then my hopes that he'd perished during the battle shown in my dream were false."

Dream? Of what was she speaking?

"Can you not see that I am willing to try to help you?"

The man ran a hand through his hair, and Catheryn

resisted the need to laugh. He offered help? Dragging her coverlet with her, she rose from the bed. Her movements were stiff. It took all of her rapidly draining control not to flinch with each step. "Help me? How? For what reason? Ah. So that I and Brezden may fill the king's coffers with sorely needed gold."

She shook her head. The yarrow's promise had been naught but a lie. And now, if Pike was truly dead, King Stephen would likely sell her to the highest bidder. All knew how badly he'd drained his treasury by this unending war with Empress Matilda. As far as Catheryn was concerned, it didn't matter who sat on the throne. Either one, Stephen with his meek, undecided niceness, or Matilda, with her cold, hateful disposition against anything English or Norman, would be as bad as the other.

Suddenly, the quiet caught her attention. The storm had passed, and hardly any sound came from inside the keep or through the window from the courtyard below. There were no shouts from men-at-arms or grumbles from overworked servants. A sick dread oozed into her limbs as a breeze blew the oiled sheepskin covering slightly free. The acrid scent of smoke, burnt wood, and straw drifted in.

Catheryn felt the blood drain from her face. Clutching her stomach tightly with one arm, she bolted to the window. Before pulling back the stretched hide, she whispered, "Dear Lord, be merciful."

The predawn sky provided enough light for her to clearly see the destruction below. Tears ran unchecked down her face as her gaze rested briefly on each dead or dying body. Among the bodies of Pike's guards were servants and freemen foolish enough to get in the way of the invaders. She should have sent them to safety with her soldiers. But she thought they would have hidden themselves away.

Instead, they had obviously tried to protect their homes, their families, and perhaps even Brezden along with its undeserving lady.

Beyond the curtain wall, Catheryn could see that the outer bailey had fared badly. Huts, storage sheds, and sections of the wall were completely destroyed by fire. The thatched roofs of a few cottages were damaged beyond repair. Livestock were wandering aimlessly or lying dead in the trampled, bloody dirt. Worse, women and children knelt alongside the lifeless bodies of their husbands, fathers, or sons.

Part of the nightmare had come true. And she'd not stopped it from being played out against the innocent. This man had indeed brought death and destruction to Brezden.

Catheryn did not attempt to hide from her misery. She had only wanted a dream of true love, the balm of an imagined fine, happy future. She'd trusted in the ancient lore of the yarrow, believing in superstition and ignoring the teachings of the church. For that, her people had paid. The shame and guilt she bore would never diminish.

Her feet carried her back across the room, and Catheryn beat her fists on the black mail-covered chest of the stranger. "What have you done?"

"Lady, I did nothing but my duty."

"Duty!" Looping her fingers into one of the ties of his hauberk, Catheryn pulled the unresisting man to the window. "It was your duty to murder innocent people? You have killed animals we needed for food. The vegetable and herb gardens have been trampled. How will I feed those dependent upon me? Where will I lodge those without homes?" She stuck her arm out the window and pointed at a woman lying prostrate over a body. "How do I offer to replace what she has lost?"

The stranger stood silent during her tirade. Hands braced on either side of the window, he looked out over the courtyard and bailey. "Buildings will be rebuilt. Livestock can be purchased. It is just the beginning of spring, so gardens can be replanted." He glanced at the floor. "And all people die."

The answer was so simple, spoken with such a lack of concern that made Catheryn lose all reason. Lifting her open hand, she swung it at the stranger's face.

Gerard caught the woman's arm before her palm made contact. Pinning her arms to her side, he leaned her against the wall.

"No harm was done to this keep that cannot be fixed. I am sorry for any who died without reason, but I can do nothing for them."

Why was he explaining anything to her? Hers was an enemy keep. Its lord, Pike, installed by King Stephen with Earl William's full backing, had turned traitor. Gerard owed her nothing. Yet, the lady's flushed face and full lips deserved more than just explanations. He felt a sudden, intense urge to gather her into his arms and promise that all would be well. His hands itched to stroke her hair—

"This is insanity!" What was wrong with him? There was no room in his heart for another woman and he'd not fulfill his desires with one who wasn't his wife. Lifting her in his arms, he carried her across the room and placed her on the bed. "Stay there."

He walked to the door and shouted for his captain then grabbed a gown off the floor to take to her. Guilt assailed him when he caught sight of her trembling lips and misty eyes, but she'd brought this on herself. Wearily handing her the gown, he ordered, "Put this on. Quickly." He tried to make his voice gentle.

"Sir? My lord?"

Gerard turned and motioned Walter inside. "I want all of this lady's things moved into the lord's chamber. Now." He ignored her outraged gasp. Whether she wanted his protection or not, she was going to get it. "Get a few of Brezden's servants to help you."

Walter scratched his head. "I meant to mention that, my lord. A *few* is all we can find, and those are all old men, women or children. There are few able bodies around."

That made little sense. Where had they all gone? She had seemed to mourn the unarmored men she'd seen dead in the bailey. While the men on the walls had been armed and fought with some semblance of experience, he'd thought the ones in the bailey were badly trained, soldiers caught so swiftly off guard that they'd had no time to arm themselves. A sinking thought turned his stomach sour.

Gerard swung back to face the lady of Brezden. Her eyes were closed, and her lips moved in what appeared to be a silent prayer, so he dismissed Walter with a wave of his hand. He waited until the captain quit the chamber before continuing.

"You had better be praying for divine intervention, my lady, for I am bone-weary of sparring with you." He knelt on the bed and grasped her shoulders, only to release her when she winced. "Damn you, look at me!"

Had she not been so bruised and battered he would have shaken the glare off her face. Shame filled him at the thought. She'd had enough torment, he needn't add more. Where had all of the keep's soldiers gone? Why had they not been present to protect their lady—if not from the evil lodged within, then why not from the evil that threatened from without?

Tipping his head to one side, he realized the answer. "You

hid Brezden's guards. The men in the bailey were the keep's servants."

She didn't answer, but her gaze skittered away.

"Somehow you knew we were coming."

She bit the unswollen side of her bottom lip.

He looked at her through narrowed eyes. He didn't really expect an answer. But he had to ask, "How did you know Brezden was going to be attacked?"

A steady, unflinching gaze met his. One side of her mouth curved into a sad, half smile, and Gerard had to lean closer to hear her odd, whispered reply. "Because I called you here. You had no choice but to answer the yarrow's call."

Chapter Three

"I had no other choice?" The stranger smirked and crossed his arms. "Do I look clay-brained to you? No one has ever thought me half-witted…until now."

Catheryn couldn't imagine they would. The last thing she'd expect from someone as well-formed as this would be for him to be a halfwit. She had to admit that she'd expected the sachet's dream offering to possess above-average looks and strength, but she'd never expected the yarrow to call forth one so—

She forced her wayward mind to cease its rambling. What difference did his appearance make? Did it change what he was, or what he intended? Did she have any better reason to trust him because of it?

Reaching beneath her pillow, she tossed the yarrow sachet to the floor at his feet. "This is what called you to Brezden."

Gerard retrieved the herb-filled bag from the floor and shook his head. When his sister was young, she'd kept charms close to her person also, but that had been years ago. "Are you not a little old to still believe in childhood tales?"

"Tales?" The woman's eyes narrowed. "You are here, are you not?"

"Coincidence and nothing more."

"I think not."

"Dreams and wishes are for little girls."

Shaking her head, she stated, "You are only half right. Wishes *are* for children. But dreams can sometimes come true."

"Lady…" He paused a moment, swallowing his impatience. "What might I call you?"

"Lady is fine."

Gerard raised his hands in mock surrender. "I have tarried overlong in your chamber. There is work to be done outside." Ignoring her frown, he added, "Get dressed. The sooner the dead are identified and buried, the sooner your people will be able to move on."

"Move on? It is that simple, is it? Cover them with dirt, turn around, and move on."

Her soft laugh grated on his nerves. "There is nothing else anyone can do. I cannot bring them back." He tore the remains of her shredded gown from her body without looking down, took the new one from her hands and pulled it over her head. "Would you rather have Pike attending to them?"

He regretted the words the moment they left his lips. As he should. She jerked away and finished dressing. "Leave me be."

"As much as that would please me, I cannot. Your presence will be required."

"To speak with the survivors."

"Yes, and to identify the dead."

A looked of pained defeat filled her eyes. "There is only one dead body I wish to view, and you have already said Sir Raymond de Brye is not dead."

For reasons he could not name, he wanted to take the

hunted look from her face. "By my hand, no, I do not believe so. But who is to say he did not fall to another man's sword?" More than anything else, he wanted to give her hope.

Sadly, the lady stared down at her fingers. "No. In the dream—"

"Cease!" His shout stopped her explanation, though he could not explain his vehemence. "This is no dream, no flight of fancy. I am no dream. I am real. All of this is real." Taking one of her hands, he slipped it under the edge of the coif he'd pushed back earlier and pressed her palm against the pulse in his neck, surprising himself. "I am flesh and blood. I am no one's dream."

His pulse pounded beneath her palm. Strong. Steady. Lifting her head, she gazed into his eyes, and he could see she was reassured. He was equally reassured, but he could not say why.

Nodding toward the corridor, he said, "Come, enough time has been wasted."

ℭ⅊

Catheryn stared at the chaos before her. A little more than half of the keep's original number of serfs and freemen were gathered among the wrecked tables that filled Brezden's great hall. What few able-bodied men who weren't lying dead outside stood next to their wives or mothers. Women clutched their children protectively. Men too old to be of any threat stood at the front of the group wringing their hands and muttering softly, while the young lads grouped together at one side of the gathering, their occasional mutinous glares making her fear for their safety. The others—the guards loyal to Catheryn—hadn't been found.

She kept her smile of triumph to herself. When the time was right, she would call them back. Until then, she could do little but pray for their well-being.

"My lady?"

The conquering lord's prompting drew her away from her worries. Before identifying the dead, he'd ordered her here to request her people's cooperation. The thought galled her. Would history repeat itself? Would she hand her people's safety, their very lives, over to what could be an unjust and cruel master? *Could* she? Her mother, the previous Lady of Brezden, had done as much when Pike had first arrived. She had spoken her piece as if the words were torn from her lips. Too naive then to comprehend her mother's hesitancy, Catheryn fully understood it now.

A gentle nudge at her shoulder drove the point home— her choices were slim. The man had taken the keep, he would remain here, in full control, until his overlord ordered otherwise.

Swallowing the bile in her throat, Catheryn slowly looked from one frightened face to the next. Her heart breaking, she sought the dearest face known to her. Agnes's pale gray gaze brought a sigh of pent-up relief. The woman appeared unharmed.

Not taking her attention from the soft, wrinkled face of her onetime nursemaid, Catheryn sought words to ease her people's fears. Stepping forward, she motioned them to do the same. Touching one familiar face then another, she reassured herself, and them, that for this moment all was well. There was no guarantee the invader was anything like Pike or de Brye. To be fair, many indicators suggested he wasn't.

"Hush, cry no more." She brushed the tears from one man's cheeks and felt her own eyes begin to well at the ancient knight's stuttering attempt to apologize for not fighting to defend the keep.

"How old?"

Catheryn nearly jumped out of her skin. She knew the owner of that deep whisper, but she'd not realized he was so close behind. Turning her head, hoping to shield her answer from Sir Ephraim, she whispered back, "He has seen over sixty summers."

The invader stepped around her and placed his hand on Ephraim's trembling shoulder, and she wondered if she would swoon from shock. The previous lord had shown not one whit of concern for any of Brezden's people. "Sir Ephraim, you have protected your lady many times over, I am sure. She cannot fault you for this one lapse."

His words seemed…kind. She felt his stare upon her and quickly followed his lead. "No. Of course not. Never." She took the old knight's cold, bony hand in hers. "Oh, Ephraim, you know how I value your wisdom. I have always appreciated your loyalty. Surely you can't think I'd doubt it now." Her gaze swept the entire assembly. "These last few years have been hard for everyone, and even though I have had little chance to say so, I want you to know that I value all of you, for you are dear to me as family. I am heartsore for any pain or torment you have endured of late, and I wish there was something I could do to make it up to you."

She paused, taking time to restrain her emotions and bolster her courage before continuing. "The fighting is over. We must all work together to rebuild our homes and our lives. I am certain you will join me in securing the continued blessing of our new protector." She turned and directed her stare at Brezden's conqueror.

Gerard refused to flinch under the scrutiny of the crowd. He was well pleased with the lady of Brezden's compliance and waited only to see if her people believed her words. He sincerely hoped, for their sake, that they would follow her lead.

It didn't take long before Sir Ephraim sought to kneel, and as that ancient knight stumbled into a steady position the others followed suit. Gerard looked back at Brezden's lady. She too had dropped to one knee, and she was motioning a few of the now giggling children to do likewise.

Assisting Ephraim to his feet, Gerard thanked him and the others for their loyalty to the king, and to the Earl of York in whose name he had claimed the stronghold. Then he turned and held out his hand. "My lady?"

As she came slowly to her feet, her eyes widened and her face paled. Gerard followed the line of her shocked stare and cursed himself. Pike's body lay in the middle of the hall. Gerard vaguely remembered ordering his men to deposit the corpse where all could see.

Finding the nearest man, he shouted, "Get that out of here!" He felt a small jerk of guilt tighten in his chest. Compelled to defend himself, he began to explain. "Lady, death was Pike's choice. He—"

She cut him off with a wave of one hand. "I care not about Pike. The devil take him with my blessing." She frantically grasped his arms, each word softer than the one before. "Please, please. I must know. Where are the rest of the fallen?"

He knew what—or rather, who—she sought. Motioning for Walter to join them, Gerard gently grasped the lady's elbow and led her toward the door. What if this Sir de Brye was dead? What if he wasn't? Gerard wondered about her reaction either way.

A lady's maid. The woman would want one. When Gerard stopped abruptly and turned to call for one, he bumped into a servant who had been following too close. The older woman caught her balance and glared up at him.

"Where are you taking Lady Catheryn?"

Catheryn. Ah, was that her name? Ignoring the wench, he quickly glanced around the hall and shouted, "Where is her maid?"

"I am Catheryn's woman."

Surprised, he looked down at the old woman now plucking on his sleeve. She looked too old to be a lady's maid, but she certainly had no shortage of possessiveness. The woman put her hands on her hips and repeated her question. "Where are you taking Lady Catheryn? If you harm one hair on her head, you will answer to me." Almost as an afterthought, she added, "My lord."

If her insolent manner wasn't bad enough, her whining voice set his teeth on edge. Still, he was in no mood to argue with her. With a low growl, Gerard turned and said, "Well, Lady Catheryn, shall we?"

Holding her back straighter, Lady Catheryn nodded.

With Walter's assistance, Gerard led the two women out into the bailey. Picking their way between the bodies of men and animals, they walked slowly from one end of the yard to the other. Gerard waited patiently for Lady Catheryn to say they were through.

If she had to look at one more face frozen in the agony of death, Catheryn knew she would go mad. She also knew that until she gazed upon the slack features of her hated enemy she would keep looking.

She paused briefly to watch as Mistress Margaret placed the last stitch in John Smithy's leg. The blacksmith seemed not to notice the pain—he was more intent on staring longingly at the midwife. The man had been in love with Margaret for as long as Catheryn could remember. Unfortunately, his feelings were not returned.

This day, his unrequited love did not matter. The midwife would have her hands full taking care of the wounded and doing what she could to make the dying as comfortable as possible. Catheryn too went back to work, resuming her search, knowing she would see these bodies, these faces in her nightmares for months to come. Some of those who died were no more than boys—boys whose souls had already been tainted by Pike and de Brye's evil. Some were less culpable. Catheryn silently pleaded with God to forgive them all their sins and to accept them with His loving grace. No more could be done. No more than wonder how this vile scene affected the man who had wrought its destruction. Was Brezden's conqueror no better than the men he replaced? He surely seemed as willing to kill.

Stopping beside the body of young Daniel, an orphan Pike had forced into his service, Catheryn knelt down and brushed a lock of hair from his face. "He was but eleven, my lord."

"Then he had no business playing a man's game."

Catheryn bit back tears. She'd be damned if she'd allow this war-hardened beast to know how badly this hurt. Taking a deep breath, she gazed up at him. "Think you he had a choice?"

The man didn't answer. Nor did he even look down at her.

"He was but a babe with no home, no mother, no food except for the scraps Pike tossed him each evening." Detesting the break in her voice, Catheryn turned her gaze back to the body of the boy. "He barely had a life, let alone a choice."

She was unprepared for the hands that grabbed the front of her gown and hauled her to her feet. She was even less prepared for the hard, angry visage before her, or for the harsh words that seemed torn from his clenched jaw.

"A life? What care had Pike or his henchmen for life

when they tortured, raped and killed their innocent victims?" As if suddenly burned, Brezden's conqueror released her. "You dare speak to me of this? What do you know of it?"

A look of agony briefly washed the man's features before he stepped away. Filled with a sudden need to offer comfort, Catheryn reached out, but he held up a hand to ward her off.

"No. Do not."

She winced at the harsh rasp of his voice, and it was as if everything else in the world stopped. For the space of a heartbeat—or a lifetime—she could do nothing but stare at the constantly changing man before her. His emotions flitted from anger to hatred to pain. What might cause one so seemingly strong to show such vulnerability? Catheryn knew not. But she did know that things as changeable as the wind were dangerous. Taking a long breath, she sought to control the rapid beating of her heart. The acrid scent of smoke briefly assailed her, but her next breath brought the cleansing smell of spring rain. Not the previous storm resembling God's wrath, but a gentle, steady shower. She tipped her head back and stared up at the gathering clouds. A good downpour would help wash away some of the terrors wrought at Brezden this day.

"Have you seen enough?"

She looked again at the man before her. His face had lost its anger, and his voice was nearly as flat as his expression. Catheryn nodded. Raymond de Brye was not here. "Aye. Yes, I have."

"Then why don't we—?"

His words were cut off by a loud shriek of terror, and Catheryn's heart jumped at the sound. A moment later she and the others were rushing toward the source.

They found it easily. A woman was screaming, staring and pointing. A wooden pike had been purposely stuck in the ground near the postern gate. Catheryn felt the dirt beneath her feet shift and sway as she saw what topped it. The horror made the rest of the death and destruction at Brezden seem tame.

Someone else screamed. Catheryn covered her ears to drown out the sound, but it wouldn't stop. Over and over the scream blasted in her ears. She closed her eyes but still saw the defiled remains of Martin, her most trusted archer, his severed head perched atop the gruesome pole. Nothing would ever wipe that sight from her mind. What had he been doing here? Why hadn't he waited with the others? Who would do something so despicable? She knew of only one man so utterly ungodly—de Brye, but he was nowhere to be seen. Why couldn't someone stop the screaming?

"Catheryn! Catheryn, stop." She heard a loud curse then strong arms closed tightly around her. "Lady Catheryn, *hush.*"

Twisting and turning, she tried to break free of the flesh and blood prison that held her, but her struggles were of no avail. As if through a tunnel, she heard her name called once more, and finally a solid object made contact with her chin. Within a heartbeat, the screams had ceased, and Catheryn felt a dark, cold fog settle over her.

Chapter Four

Reddish-hued rays from the setting sun cast a pale glow across the room, but Catheryn watched the shadows lengthen and overtake the pink evening light. A fire crackled in a nearby hearth. Subdued sounds from the bailey drifted up and through the four windows. While the noise was not at its usual boisterous level, its mere existence let her know that life in the keep resumed. Brezden would survive.

Catheryn pressed unsteady hands against her throbbing temples. Why was she abed, in what she recognized by the many windows as the lord's chamber, at this time of day? Thoughts swirled wildly back and forth, but the effort to sort them out proved too much. As soon as one image appeared in her mind, another rushed to take its place. Each was more gruesome than the next. And more confusing.

Her keep had been taken. That much she remembered clearly. There had been screams and blood. Whose? She also had some vague memory of Agnes coercing her to drink a foul-tasting wine. Why?

Certain she'd find no answers in bed, Catheryn tried to get up. Each time she struggled to rise, though, the room swam before her.

"My lady? You are awake."

Catheryn watched her maid approach. The woman's brisk movements nauseated her.

"Agnes, please walk slower." But Catheryn's mouth would not form the words correctly. She sounded like a tavern drunk. "I feel like a boat being tossed about on a stormy sea."

"Do not fret, child, the dizziness will pass."

A blur of gray hair appeared before her, and Catheryn willed herself to focus on Agnes's ready smile. Groaning, she asked, "When?"

"Soon. And right now, you should move about some. Come below and eat." Agnes pulled back the covers, permitting cool air to rush across Catheryn's skin. "You have consumed a large quantity of wine laced with a sleeping draught. Maybe in one more night, you will again feel fully yourself."

During her sleep, fur had found its way into her mouth. Shivering, Catheryn scraped her teeth across her tongue. She hoped the scraping would remove the irritation. "Wine? Agnes, I do not know how old that wine was, but I would prefer…" She paused. Squinting to better see, she asked, "One *more* night? How long have I been in this bed?"

The maid's smile faded. Her mumbled response was lost to Catheryn as she walked to the other side of the room and pulled gowns out of the wooden chest placed against the wall.

Catheryn sat up in bed only to fall back down as the room spun with the swiftness of a child's wooden top. "Agnes!"

Immediately, the maid dropped the gown back into the chest and returned. She took Catheryn's hand. "My lady, you were distraught. After the episode with Martin—" The maid's voice caught, but she quickly regained her composure. "You spoke nonsense about finding and killing de Brye yourself. How would you do that? Where would you start? Who would help you?"

Martin. All of the memories that had swirled through her mind before now took full and comprehensive form. Catheryn closed her eyes against the images, but that did not help. What de Brye had done to her archer was unforgivable. It could only have been de Brye, no one else was that vile, sick-minded, or heartless. He would pay. Raymond de Brye would suffer the agonies of hell one day. One day soon.

Prying her hand from the maid's grasp, she pressed it back to her temple. "You know I never would have acted upon those words," she muttered. But looking at the downcast face of the maid, she wasn't entirely sure. She asked again, "How long have I been abed?"

"You have slept through two sunrises." The maid quickly added, "I did not know the drink would have this effect on you. Catheryn, child, you know I would not intentionally harm you."

Smiling weakly, Catheryn touched the woman's arm. "The last few days have been unsettling to all of us. Just promise you will give me no more witch's brew." Catheryn's heart lurched at the thought. "It was your brew, wasn't it?"

Agnes's laugh filled the chamber. "Oh, yes, my lady. I did not obtain any concoction from Mistress Margaret."

"That is a relief to hear. But no more of that drink, Agnes."

"Nay, Lady Catheryn. His lordship already bade me withhold it from you. He has been most worried, not to mention angry with me."

"His lordship?" Catheryn frowned, trying to remember. "Of which lord do you speak?"

"Baron Gerard."

Her frown deepened. "Gerard?"

"My lady, you do remember that Brezden was…that Lord Pike is no longer the master here?"

Catheryn huffed. "I am dizzy, Agnes, not addled."

"Then how can you not remember Baron Gerard?"

Catheryn took a deep, steadying breath. "Are you telling me that our tall, dark conqueror's name is Gerard?"

"Aye." Agnes looked confused. "How did you not know that?"

"Simple," Catheryn said. "We were never introduced." She had not wanted to know his name, truth be told, so she'd not asked.

"But you were alone in your chamber with him. After Sir de Brye…"

Catheryn sprang upright. Fighting to ignore the spinning room, she yelled, "What? After he *what*?" She was certain that she hadn't been raped. Was there something she didn't know? Revulsion and fear overwhelmed her.

Agnes waved her hands in the air as if trying to wipe away any misconstrued intent. "Nothing, my lady. I know not all that happened there, since I'd been ordered from the chamber and those bruises… Well, I saw your bruises, so I know he'd beaten you, of course, but other than that I pray nothing. I don't know when Lord Gerard arrived, but I simply assumed that when you saw him, a strange man in your chamber, you might have asked his name."

Catheryn sneered, trying not to think of de Brye anymore. Instead, she focused her anger on Brezden's new keeper. "Oh, and you would probably also assume that if I asked this stranger his name that he would tell me? It would require manners and breeding to extend that much courtesy."

The maid glanced nervously at the door. "Lady Catheryn, you should not speak badly about Baron Reveur. He has treated your people well."

Catheryn's shout of laughter sent a blinding stab of pain through her head. "Reveur?" What kind of cruel jest had fate played to bring her a dream knight whose very name meant dreamer?

Agnes's eyes widened before narrowing into an unforgiving squint. Firmly planting her hands on her hips, she scolded, "I don't know what you find so amusing about the man's name. I swear to you, Lady Catheryn, that he has brought good to our people. Baron Reveur has been helping to repair what was damaged."

Catheryn waved off her maid's fervent defense of the man's honor. "I am sure he has done all he could to set Brezden to rights." After all, it was now under his command, so why wouldn't he see to it?

She shook her head. Regardless of what he was or was not doing, the first thing she needed to do was to destroy the cursed charm that had brought him here to begin with. Not that it would change anything, but it was obviously too powerful a charm to let fall into the wrong hands. "Is Mistress Margaret's dream charm still in my chamber?"

"No." Agnes pointed at her pillow. "I moved it in here with you."

Catheryn reached under her pillow, patting around until she located the yarrow bag. The last thing she wanted were any more dreams. She held the charm in her hand, wondering where to store it until she could see to its demise.

"I put it beneath your pillow so Lord Gerard would not find it during his visits."

"Visits?"

"Lady Catheryn, he has come regularly to see how you fare."

Her shock quickly building to outrage, Catheryn asked, "How dare you allow him into my chamber? What has come over you? Did you see what he did to Brezden?"

Agnes was unrepentant. "He did what any knight would do. He followed his lord's orders, and also the order of the king. You cannot fault him for that."

"Agnes, what are you thinking to defend him so?" What would he demand of her? What would the king or Earl William demand of her? What was the future of Brezden? She had wished for someone to rid them of Pike, but now that it had happened, she was afraid of what came next.

"I am thinking that this may not be such a terrible thing. We should be grateful." The maid shook her finger under Catheryn's nose. "Even *you* must admit that Pike's demise is not a bad thing. Catheryn, I tell you true, Baron Gerard has already more than made amends for his deeds. Already he has shown more concern for Brezden than Pike ever did."

Catheryn's stomach rebelled at the exchange. The hammering in her head threatened to overwhelm her. "Agnes, I can argue with you no longer this day, but even you must be aware that anyone would care more for Brezden than Pike. And regarding gratitude for his conquest…it is a job half finished. Pike may be dead and can harm me no further, but de Brye still lives and he is the worse threat. You saw what he did to Martin right under the noses of your Lord Gerard's men."

The maid relented enough to rub Catheryn's forehead. "I am sorry, my lady. I know how poorly you feel. But if you allow, I am certain good can still come of this. I am sure Baron Reveur will assist you in dealing with Sir de Brye."

Catheryn cringed, imagining a discussion where she admitted exactly how cruel the man had been. One way or another, she would think of a plan to take care of the man herself. "I refuse to discuss it further."

"Child, you are in no condition to discuss anything

rationally at this moment," Agnes agreed. "Come, get out of that bed and I will help you dress. They will be glad in the hall to see you up and about."

The simple act of sitting on the edge of the bed drained Catheryn of what little strength she possessed. She didn't feel equal to the task of dressing or descending the stairs. She did not want anyone's company. All she required was time alone. Some quiet moments to think and decide what to do next.

"Please," she begged, "just have something brought up."

Agnes's stiff movements and furious arm gestures made her agitation apparent as she headed for the door. "He is going to be quite angry if he finds out you are awake and refuse to come below." After pausing to turn and frown at Catheryn, the maid's expression softened. "I suppose I could make an excuse and bring you something to eat."

What difference did it make if Lord Gerard, Baron Reveur, was angry or not? Catheryn wanted to scream. Instead, she nodded. "Thank you."

Agnes left the room, and Catheryn slipped the charm back beneath the pillow, grabbed a cover from the bed, wrapped it around her, and moved to a bench by the fire. The dizziness she felt was less important than her plan. What was she to do about this tender attachment her maid had already formed? She would admit this Baron Reveur was better than Pike, but a *goat* would be a better master than Pike. That didn't mean there would be cause to celebrate if a goat conquered Brezden.

Catheryn rested her elbows on her knees and leaned her chin into her hands. The heat from the fire felt good on her face, but she knew the warmth would soon lull her back to sleep. She rose and began to pace the room, holding the blanket securely. The fabric softly swept the floor behind her, leaving a trail in the rushes.

Glancing out a window, she was pleased to see that repairs had indeed been started on Brezden. Not only was refortifying the keep important, this would keep the people too busy to worry about everything else.

She walked back across the room. What was going to happen to her? Talking to the air, she asked, "If they considered Pike a traitor, what will Earl William and the king consider Pike's ward?" Catheryn sighed and turned. The answer was clear. "I am nothing but a woman. They consider me not at all."

"You are mistaken. They consider you quite often."

Catheryn jumped at the deep-voiced answer. Looking over her shoulder, she gasped when she saw it was the man named Gerard.

She'd been so lost in thought that she hadn't heard the door open. "What are you doing here?"

Twisting around to face him, Lady Catheryn caught her blanket on the bottom corner of a nearby chest, and Gerard enjoyed watching her struggle. Her fight to free her blanket provided a glimpse of a long, shapely leg. Her creamy, unblemished skin was like a feast to his eyes, and by the time his intense perusal finished with the trim ankle, shapely calf and slender thigh, his body screamed that it was time to eat.

Gerard gritted his teeth and fought his desire. He was not a saint, but neither was he a man who saw women as the spoils of victory. Clearing his throat, he said, "I only came to see if your maid was correct in her belief that you are still too ill to leave this chamber."

She caught his focus and gasped. He almost laughed at the shocked expression on her face when she realized he was staring at her leg. Freeing the cover, she jerked it tighter about her body. "I demand you leave my chamber immediately!"

Gerard ignored her order, standing in front of a window he pretended to survey the sights outside. "Do you not think you have left your people unsupervised long enough?"

"Are you going to stand there and tell me that you have left them unsupervised?"

True, he had seen to all within his power, but he was not the lord here. These were not his people. He was here only until William released him from this duty and assigned him his next task. He longed for the day this battle for the throne ended and he could return to Reveur in Normandy. But he imagined that many of the men under King Stephen's command wished the same thing.

Gerard brought his attention back to Lady Catheryn. "It isn't quite the same. They need to see you. After all, are you not their lady?" Turning, he asked, "Are you not the one responsible for them and their welfare?"

Her voice rose slightly. "Do not dare to tell me of my responsibilities. I know them well. You are the one who killed their kin and destroyed their homes."

Crossing the room, Gerard grabbed her hands, which were still clutching her blanket. "I killed no one but the traitor and those who defended him. I destroyed nothing that cannot be repaired, and that includes the homes of hardworking peasants and serfs. I am not the one who has left them to their own devices for the last two days."

She tried unsuccessfully to break free of his grasp. Angry eyes flashed up at him. "Get your hands off me! Leave me alone!"

"You have been left alone long enough."

Dragging her behind him, Gerard walked to an open clothing chest. Stopping abruptly, he pulled her close. Her expression changed from anger to fear and back. Struggling to free her wrists from his hold, she stamped her foot and yelled, "Filthy monster, get out of here. Agnes!"

She'd not be free of him that easily. He'd thought about this woman night and day since he'd taken the keep, considered the perfect flesh she'd bared which he'd eventually helped her cover. "Your maid has orders not to enter this room under any circumstances. My man guards the stairs to ensure those orders are carried out, but you will not be harmed. At least, not by me."

He stared with appreciation at the fury he held. Wrapping an arm about her, he released her wrists and grasped her chin with his other hand. She tried to push free, but even if her arms had not been securely pinned between their bodies, she had not the strength to force him away. Still, Gerard marveled at her fighting spirit.

Holding her in his arms, his entire being sprang to life. Staring down into that arresting pair of aqua eyes, a stormy sea of color, he found himself drawn into their dangerous depths. His blood pounded tempestuously in his veins. His mind heard those parted lips cry out to be tasted, and for a moment he saw his own desire reflected in her eyes. Was it possible? A kiss. Just a kiss. The need to answer that cry was urgent.

Bending his head, he asked softly, "Spitfire, do you not realize your danger?"

His lips claimed hers, and Gerard felt Catheryn stiffen for an instant before she relaxed against him. But flames singed his lips as she returned his kiss. Flames of want and need.

Jerking back, Gerard watched desire, humiliation, and anger flicker across Catheryn's face, He frowned at the magnitude of his rising passion, knowing it would become harder and harder to control. He released her, and sharply ordered, "Get dressed, and if you are not quick about it, I will return to see that it is done by my own hand."

There was no chance she could mistake the hungry look he raked over her body. Mastering himself, he stalked out of the chamber, slamming the door behind him. Gerard leaned against the wall outside and lifted a shaky hand to his brow. He had come up here intentionally to goad her into throwing a fit. He'd hoped to prove she was healthy enough to rise, that was all. So why was he the one whose emotions now ran wild? It made no sense. He possessed much more control than he showed around this woman. At least he thought he did.

How many times in the last two days had he caught himself worrying when Lady Catheryn would not wake up? The odd concern plagued him. Gerard knew it would be unwise to care about someone who might prove as traitorous as Pike or de Brye. He had nothing to go by except her hatred of those two men and the injuries she'd suffered at—

"Oh! Of all the arrogant, rude, insufferable filthy monsters!"

His hand froze in mid-air at her screech.

Monster? She thought him a monster? For all she'd suffered, this lady had no idea what a true monster was.

Gerard flung the door open so violently that it slammed against the wall. Closing the distance between him and Catheryn in three long strides, he ended her hasty retreat. "That is not the first time you have called me a monster. But it will be the last."

She stared mutinously up at him.

He glared down when she opened her mouth, daring her to speak. Drawing her tightly against his chest, he asked, "What do you think a filthy monster would do with you now?" He laughed at her fear-widened eyes, hating himself for making her fear him but angry that she had driven him to it. "Aye, Lady Catheryn, you would do well to remember your place."

Certain she understood the unspoken threat, Gerard released her and left the chamber.

He shook his head at the sound of a solid object bouncing off the door just as it closed behind him. Not turning back to once again confront her, he continued on to the stairs, realizing that in a way, he was heartened to know her spirit had not been beaten by Pike or de Byre. Nor had it been diminished by what he had wrought on Brezden.

Mindless of the broken objects lying about, Catheryn raced across the floor. "Dreams? Bah." Grabbing the yarrow sachet, she tossed it into a corner of the hearth. "True love? Ha!" Tiny sparks flew. "Mistress Margaret can keep her spells."

She watched as a corner of the bag caught fire. Smoke rose from the smoldering herbs.

"Help? I ask for help and love and this is what I receive? What sort of help is he?" An image of Gerard's smirk flitted before her. "I'd get more help from a pig." Catheryn turned away from the fire. "A dog would provide more love than that demon." But her lips tingled with the memory of his kiss.

"Blast!" Spinning around, Catheryn snatched the yarrow bag from its ultimate destruction. She cursed again then smacked the sachet against the stone wall. Clumps of scorched yarrow fell to the floor, but she was soon certain the bag would burn no more. She tucked it back amongst the bedclothes.

"What am I going to do?" There had to be a way to turn all that had happened into some advantage for Brezden and herself. Not that she wasn't beginning to see some of the advantages already offered. Agnes had been correct, little as Catheryn wanted to admit it. The last exchange had proved it. Pike was gone, and Baron Reveur was not as wicked or uncaring as he had been. No one could be. No one—except Raymond de Brye.

Remembering Lord Gerard's orders, and his threat to come back, Catheryn quickly dressed. All the while, her mind raced. De Brye. He was a much bigger threat to her happiness and health. She did not doubt that he would return for revenge when he had gathered the appropriate forces. Until then she could only wonder and worry about what he was doing. "Where are you hiding, de Brye?"

"I do not hide. I am right here."

Catheryn froze. Surely, she was dreaming.

"Sweeting, I had no idea you'd desire me again so soon. True, we were interrupted before I could truly make you mine."

Her heart resumed beating with a heavy thud. *Interrupted...?* The hairs on the back of her neck rose, and slowly she turned to face the owner of that voice. The sight was nearly her undoing. Sir de Brye stood in the alcove, the panel open that led into the tunnel behind him, and he wasn't alone. Before the vile cur stood one of her men, de Brye holding a knife to his throat. Rolfe had a gag in his mouth, and was trussed like a hog, a thick rope securing him so that escape was impossible.

She knew how de Brye had just gained entrance to the lord's chamber—through the tunnel that connected this room to the lady's chamber—but how had he known she'd been moved? She also now knew exactly how he had avoided capture. He'd used one of the many tunnels her father built into the keep. But since her sire had created a veritable maze of tunnels, connecting passageways, and disorienting dead ends, it was impossible for her to know exactly which path had led de Brye to safety.

If she had to guess, she would assume that he'd taken refuge securely in a tunnel that led to the stables in the outer bailey until the sounds of battle had quieted. Then while she and the others were gathered either in the great hall or outside searching among the dead, de Brye had somehow taken Martin by surprise. While the knave was vile and brutal to those weaker than he, he was a coward when it came to facing a stronger man alone. Like a wolf, he performed best with a pack. Which meant he'd likely had help from inside Brezden's walls. Help that had enabled him to know how to find her, help that had permitted him to capture her men. Catheryn fought desperately not to cry out. Had she sent Brezden's faithful few to certain death?

Without thought, she took a step forward. Raymond de Brye smiled wickedly. Too late, she realized her mistake and tried to back away instead.

"No, my lady. It would be wise to stay there and not scream." De Brye twisted his blade against Rolfe's throat. A small trickle of blood appeared.

Catheryn swallowed hard and prayed that her voice would not give away her fear and anger. "What do you seek here? Brezden is lost."

"Lost? You give up far too easily. Brezden still stands. It's even being improved." De Brye's smile widened to a maniacal grin. "And I live to fight again."

"Again?" She couldn't help pointing out the obvious. "Instead of defending this keep you ran."

"They had the element of surprise and superior numbers. Why should I fight like that? Instead of face to face, it is far easier to attack from within."

She swallowed a bitter taste and sneered, "You are but one man."

"Nay, sweeting, you are wrong. Not all of my men were

within Brezden when it fell."

Catheryn tried to remember how many bodies she had seen in the bailey. No matter what, de Brye could have no more than a few left. She continued sneering at him. "Unless you have an army at your command, I do not see how you hope to regain possession of the keep."

His laugh filled the room with ice. "I have enough. Certainly, more than enough to do my bidding and still guard your six remaining men. Your archer was a fool to have left the safety of his little group holed up by the river. He thought to aid you but instead found only his own death. But not before I forced him to tell me all he knew. It was precious little, but enough so I could take the others unawares, fools that they are. My plan remains unimpeded."

Razor-sharp terror cut past her flesh and heart. But while de Brye was evil incarnate, he was at heart a coward. A lying coward. Never had the man chosen anyone bigger or stronger than himself as a victim. "You will lead your force to attack Brezden?"

"Beloved, you misunderstand." De Brye reverted to the oily voice Catheryn had come to despise and fear. "I said nothing about attacking the keep myself."

"Then who? I can think of no one here who would help you."

De Brye's expression settled into a mask of pure evil. "You."

"Me?" A surprised gasp burst from her lips. "There is nothing in the world that could convince me to do anything for you."

"You are wrong," de Brye promised. Then he ran his knife down Rolfe's arm, the blade easily cutting through the thin fabric of the guard's tunic. Blood gushed from a long wound that laid open both flesh and muscle, but it was the look in Rolfe's eyes that Catheryn would never forget. Beneath the pain and the hatred for de Brye, she saw a desperate plea for help. A plea she could in no way answer. At least not now.

De Brye pointed his blood-drenched knife in her direction. "I will not hesitate to maim and kill every one of your men, Catheryn." He motioned toward the opening behind him. "You will find them there, one by one."

"But—"

Flourishing his grisly weapon, he cut her off. "And when I am finished with them, I will move on to those you think safe at home." He picked up the length of rope attached to Rolfe and gave it a tug.

Tied to the other end were two small children from the village. Tumbling through the doorway came Sarah, an eight-year-old blonde who had a smile for all and spent most of her time helping Mistress Margaret gather herbs, and her younger brother Matthew who could usually be found tagging behind his father at the blacksmith's where he worked.

The children were trussed to each other with the rope. Their hands were bound before them, and gags prevented them from making more than muted cries. She didn't need to fully hear their cries of fear, not when she could see it so plainly in their red, tear-filled eyes. They were terrified and confused that an adult would treat them in such a cruel manner.

Catheryn fell to her knees. She would rather suffer de Brye's sick attention herself than let these children be harmed. They were innocent of anything and completely defenseless. "Let them go, please, return them to their parents. I beg you, take me instead."

"You beg so prettily." He laughed at her plea before

slapping his weapon against his leg. "A tempting offer. But it does you no good. Their parents are no longer here. And I'll not release them until Brezden, and you are mine, and for that to happen I need you here."

He'd killed the children's parents? Catheryn's heart constricted knowing he'd not hesitate to slaughter the orphans. She would do nothing to risk their precious lives.

Lifting one eyebrow, he stared down at her. "And before you decide to spend any more time alone with Gerard, Baron Reveur, you might want to consider one thing."

Her mind leapt. She hadn't spoken Gerard's name, so how did de Brye come to know his enemy—by his given name, no less?

"Ah, yes, sweeting, I see your mind working. I'll answer your questions for you. Reveur and I are old friends. We've, ah, shared a few things in this life, so you might want to keep that in mind." His voice lowered, and with a raspy near-growl he added, "I'll not share you."

Gerard and de Brye were friends? Catheryn couldn't imagine that. Acquaintances? Perhaps. But de Brye was a cheat, a coward, and a liar. He thought nothing of bending the truth to suit his needs. What exactly had the two shared?

Her attention was diverted as de Brye pushed the children back toward the escape passage while dragging a near unconscious Rolfe with him. "You will tell no one of this visit. Do not think for a heartbeat, Catheryn, that I do not have people loyal to me inside these walls, some newly arrived at Brezden but sure to fit in. Gold and pain speak loudly when offered in the correct manner. I will know every move you make." He paused to place his knife against Rolfe's throat. Looking at her intently, he added, "Soon I will return, and you will do as you are told."

Catheryn remained still until the panel slid back into

place. Only after she heard the footsteps from the other side fade away did she rise and stumble to a bench. Her limbs shook from anger and fear. De Brye was a monster. Hopelessness washed over her, and its intensity took her breath away. Who could help her?

Her men had foolishly fallen into de Brye's clutches, he had two of Brezden's children, and she wasn't yet sure how much she could trust Lord Gerard. With de Brye's hint that one or more of Gerard's men might be a spy, she'd be a fool to speak to Baron Reveur. What was she to do?

Forcing air between her clenched teeth, she willed herself not to cry. Not to give up. Somehow, some way, she'd defeat de Brye—or die trying. Her men, the children and her people were her first concerns.

Outside, in the courtyard, a man laughed. A loud, strong laugh. The sound floated up through a window and brushed against her ears, beckoning her to the opening. On shaking legs, she followed it then leaned against the wall for support, gazed down into the courtyard, and found herself marveling.

He could laugh. He could joke with other men. He was not just the demon knight she'd seen in her dream. But she supposed even the devil could laugh.

As if sensing her presence, he looked up. His smile disappeared. In its place came an expression she could not decipher. While it was not anger, she doubted that emotion lay far beneath the surface.

Catheryn straightened her shoulders and held his stare until he nodded, indicating she should come down to him. She stepped away from the window in agreement. It was time. Time to join him in the hall. Time to discover his intent here at Brezden.

Most of all, it was time to take control of her destiny and her people. It was long past time to stop trusting in childish dreams.

Chapter Five

"And then the harlot…"

Gerard ignored the bawdy jesting of his men. He didn't care what the harlot said to the king, or what the king did about it. Nor, at this moment, did he care about fraternizing with the men gathered around him. His attention was focused on the woman who'd just turned away from the window.

"My lord! Baron Reveur!"

It was all Gerard could do to tear his gaze from where Catheryn vanished. Even though he couldn't see her face, he knew something was wrong. Maybe by her curt nod of acknowledgment when he first spotted her in the window, or maybe by the rigid way she held herself. He couldn't place his finger on it, but he knew. And simply knowing she was upset bothered him more than any words could describe.

"Baron Reveur?"

Impatient to see Catheryn, Gerard glared at his squire. "What?"

The small gathering of men ceased talking and backed slightly away. It amused Gerard that these grown soldiers could be intimidated with just a look yet his squire did not flinch or cower. Gerard quickly recognized his lad's excitement and bade him continue.

"My lord, Earl William approaches."

Gerard's curiosity about Catheryn evaporated. "Of all the snook-backed luck." He headed for the main gate. "What in the name of God brings William so quickly?"

He'd fully expected the Earl to arrive. After all, he had taken on this mission in William's name. Brezden did owe fealty to the Earl of York. But he hadn't expected William to leave the comfort of his castle quite so suddenly.

"Were there any front riders? Any messengers?" he asked the breathless squire following along behind him.

"No, my lord."

Gerard stopped, turned, and stared. "Then how can you be certain it's William?"

Impossibly, the squire's already red face darkened further. He shuffled his feet in the dirt. "Well, um, my lord…" The lad paused and looked up at the sky. "The, um… He is, um…" Stopping to take a deep breath, the flustered boy finished in a rush. "There is no mistaking him, my lord. It is without a doubt Earl William. No one else could be as—"

Gerard cut him off with a laugh. "Enough." He didn't need the boy to explain further. No one else was as big as William, if not in height, in width. The Earl had earned the nickname 'le Gros' for more than one reason. Not only was he large, at times, William could be brutally cruel.

Mounting a nearby ladder and climbing to the top of wall, Gerard grimaced at the sight. William was one of the few who traveled with at least fifty men on horseback and just as many on foot. Judging by the line of wagons trailing behind, the oncoming visitors were planning to stay more than a few days. He wondered how the people of Brezden would react to this sudden arrival, and he prayed they would be up to the rather daunting task of offering the appropriate respect and comfort.

Motioning the men on the walls to lower the drawbridge and raise the portcullis, he descended to the bailey. Soon Earl William entered, and Gerard realized his earlier fears were needless. The men of Brezden paused at their work, doffed their caps and bowed. While the women and children scrambled for a glimpse of the newcomers.

Gerard himself simply stood with his arms crossed and shook his head as William dismounted. It took two men to assist the Earl in that task, and Gerard couldn't help but wonder how long it would be before he was unable to ride a horse, let alone mount and dismount one.

William turned to glare at Gerard. "This is how you welcome your overlord to your castle?"

Gerard laughed at William's glare, knowing from those twitching lips that the man only feigned anger, then found himself suddenly clasped in a bruising embrace. Trying to extricate himself from the bear hug, he mentally noted not to underestimate the man. Despite his size, the Earl could still move quickly and there was no doubting his strength.

Once free, Gerard tapped William on the shoulder with one fist. "No, this is how I bid a friend welcome to his own keep."

"That remains to be seen."

Gerard's humor left him. "Pardon me?"

"Come." William motioned toward the keep. "Let us speak inside."

ॐ

Catheryn descended the stairs with trepidation, and when the fresh scents of lavender and spice floated across her nose her anxiety increased. After her mother died, she'd become used to the filth Pike permitted to accumulate in Brezden's great hall. The few times she'd tried to remedy the situation she'd tasted his brand of discipline. She'd quickly decided that sweet smells and a clean hall weren't worth the taste of her own blood.

She paused, and another scent caught her attention. Whitewash. Newly applied. The strength of the aroma brought tears to her eyes. The memory of the last time the walls were brightened in this manner brought tears to her heart. They had regularly been refreshed in her mother's day, but Pike had never seen fit to wipe away the filth and soot.

It took no amount of thought to determine who was responsible for this change. But one question did plague her—why had he done so? How long did Baron Reveur plan to remain at Brezden? Would he be around long enough for her to determine his trustworthiness? Should she, as Agnes prodded, seek help from Gerard?

No. If she sought help from Baron Reveur, de Brye would learn and carry out his threats. She would not risk her men's or the children's lives in such a manner.

"My lady!"

She glanced at her obviously flustered maid before descending the remaining few stairs. "Yes, Agnes, what is it?"

"Earl William has arrived."

If it were possible, Catheryn knew that her heart would now be lying on the floor amongst the clean, sweet-smelling rushes. What was the Earl of York doing at Brezden? He'd not bothered to make an appearance when either of her parents died. Nor had he bothered himself with the daughters of those loyal to him. Instead, he'd seen fit to support King Stephen's decision to appoint Pike as guardian. Had it not been for her mother's intervention in sending her sisters away, all of them would have been left to Pike's "kind" ministrations. Then instead of coming himself, he'd sent Reveur to dispatch the traitorous Pike.

No, she had no interest in meeting this overlord of Brezden. As far as she was concerned, he could go straight to the devil, and spend time with Pike.

Biting her tongue, she tried hard to force a smile to her lips but realized that she failed miserably. "When can we expect his lordship's presence, Agnes?"

"Now."

The answer came from two places at once—Agnes, who was backing away as rapidly as possible. And Gerard.

Looking over at him, she bit back a gasp. She had heard that William le Gros lived up to his name, but she'd never imagined just how massive he was. Even though Gerard was taller, the man standing beside Gerard dwarfed him. She also knew that the Earl was around forty years old, nearly twice as old as Gerard must be, but William held his years well, he did not give the appearance of someone who would soon be regarded as elderly. Instead, he looked like the commanding warrior who had led the Battle of Standard against King David and his barbarians only four years earlier. A titled warrior who would not suffer disrespect lightly. Ignoring the swimming of her head, and the pounding of her heart, she approached the pair. Regardless of whether she wanted to meet the overlord of Brezden, he was here. She had little choice but to greet him appropriately.

Catheryn drew in a breath and knelt low, silently praying that Earl William would not suddenly decide she should share Pike's fate for treason. "Welcome to Brezden, my lord. I hope everything has met with your satisfaction thus far." She had the strange sensation that Gerard breathed a sigh of relief at her words, but she was too afraid of the Earl to chance a glance to be sure.

"My, my. What have we here?" William asked, as he

reached down, grasped her hand and assisted Catheryn from the floor. "I knew Brezden still housed one of the daughters, but never did I guess how fine a woman she had become."

The Earl's voice was as smooth as cream. Catheryn felt like a horse on the auction block, being turned around so he could look at her, but she forced her humiliation and terror down to meekly reply, "Thank you, my lord." The words tasted bitter as they left her lips.

"Yes, yes, fine indeed."

"My lord, is there anything I can get for you? Have you eaten? Would you like to rest a while? Might I have a bath brought for you?" Catheryn tried not to ramble, but words just kept coming. Anything to make him stop staring at her.

"Nay, nothing at this moment," the Earl replied. "I would like to sit and just visit for a while." Catheryn glanced at Gerard. He did nothing but shrug as he motioned toward the fire.

The Earl was soon comfortably situated in the only high-back chair. Catheryn took a seat on a stool while Gerard leaned against the wall. Without any formalities, the Earl bluntly asked, "You are still a maiden?"

Catheryn felt the heat of embarrassment and anger rise. How dare he ask such a crude question of her? But making an issue of the Earl's appalling lack of manners would probably not be wise.

Aware he was still waiting, she answered, "Yes, my lord."

"How is it you have remained unclaimed so long? Was there no betrothal?"

Catheryn's heart missed a beat. Was this question a trick? Did he truly not know that Pike had repeatedly tried to gain the king's permission for de Brye to wed her? "Not that I am aware of, my lord."

"We need to take care of that immediately." The Earl

must have seen the blood leave her face, because he leaned forward and patted her hand while adding, "Now, now, not to worry. As your overlord, I will make sure you are taken care of properly."

His hot and sweaty hand made her feel ill. Uncertain how to respond without letting him know how ungrateful and disgusted she felt, Catheryn remained silent. It would not be wise to anger this man. He held her life—and the fate of Brezden—in his hands.

"Surely you see the need?" William asked, with a firmer tone. "I must have a strong arm in this part of the shire. You cannot hold Brezden from all of King Stephen's enemies."

Steeling herself, she looked at the Earl and nodded. "Oh, I see it now. Forgive me, my lord, for being so silly. Yes, of course, you will see to it all. I know I may trust you to do what is best."

She wanted to gag on her own words, but Catheryn was rewarded by a big smile from William—a smile that never reached his eyes. Forcing herself to give him a bland look of resignation, Catheryn willed her rapid breathing to slow. But when the Earl reached out to smooth a braid that hung over her breast, she stiffened with fear and renewed anger.

A shiver ran up her spine. Catheryn felt as though she'd just been threatened. But what could she do other than try to remain calm and hope the man drank himself into a stupor tonight? Or maybe he would be so tired from traveling that he would seek his bed early.

The Earl leaned back in his chair and called for wine before he dismissed the men and servants from the hall. Catheryn's gaze quickly sought Gerard's.

Once again, he was her best chance at protection.

Gerard met Catheryn's pointed regard. She was looking to him for help? Inwardly, he sighed. Who else was there?

He noted her white face and pale eyes and wondered what William was truly up to this time. If the Earl was looking to Catheryn as the vessel for his third bastard, he could look elsewhere.

Gerard moved away from the wall. "So, tell me, Lord William, how was your journey?" He flashed a small smile at Catheryn and watched some color return to her face.

"Fine. Thankfully, we encountered no delays."

Thankfully? Having known the Earl for his entire life, Gerard knew better. William liked nothing more than a good battle. If there were no delays, then the Earl was in all likelihood bored. "How did you find the king and his family?" He took the stool Walter brought him and positioned himself between William and Catheryn.

"They are as well as can be expected. Stephen is now physically in possession of the crown with the church's blessing." William shrugged. "But he is mentally still recovering from his long ordeal."

"He was not injured?"

"No. Matilda's men may have captured and held Stephen, but they did not dare harm him."

"How is the queen?"

William raised his hands, palms up, and laughed. "Maud is…Maud. What else can I tell you? She is in control and mothering everyone, especially her husband." After shouting for one of his squires, the Earl asked, "How have you found Brezden, Gerard? Has all been well?"

"Fine."

Gerard hesitated while forming a further answer, and the Earl sorted through a packet his squire handed him.

"There have been no difficulties of note." Gerard glanced down and added, "Nothing I could not handle."

"I see." William smirked. "Ah, here it is." Pulling a rolled parchment from his packet, the Earl held it out.

"What is this?"

"It's from Stephen."

Gerard barely noted the wax seal that held the cords wrapped around the letter. Flicking both to the floor, he unrolled the parchment. A moment later he was crushing the document in his hand, turning on William to ask, "How long did the two of you conspire before you agreed upon this?"

"Not long. It made sense."

Clearly unsure what was happening, Catheryn spoke up. "What? What is amiss?"

Gerard's tightly reined ire exploded. He threw the crumpled letter at her, and shouted at William, "This is absurd. You have both lost all powers of reason!"

The Earl laughed again, and in the background, Catheryn retrieved the balled-up parchment from the floor. Smoothing out the wrinkles, she scanned the cause of Gerard's outburst. "No." She dropped the note to the floor. "Oh, no," she repeated hoarsely.

Gerard spoke with a snarl. "I see the lady agrees with me."

Tears of laughter formed in William's eyes as he rose. Slapping Gerard on the shoulder, he said, "Come, Gerard, you deserve something for your work here."

Gerard jerked away. The wound of his previous grief was still too raw. "You know why I accepted this mission, and you think to repay me with a new wife?" He glared at Catheryn. "A wife I do not need or want?"

Catheryn stepped back. "Do not look at me. It was none of my doing."

Wiping the tears from his face, William asked, "Was there something else you expected?"

"No. Nothing. I wanted only Pike's head. I wanted

revenge for what was done to Edyth."

Edyth? Catheryn could not help but wonder who Edyth was and what had happened to her. Who was she to Gerard? His wife, she'd guess, given his reaction. And since the Earl was now offering her hand to Gerard in marriage, the woman must have died. At Pike's hands or at de Brye's? It mattered little. Either way, the death would not have been pleasant. And now Gerard was being offered her as a replacement he obviously did not want.

Catheryn shuddered and watched Gerard's fingers curl around the grip of his sword. Looking at William, who was no longer laughing, then back to Gerard, she had one question. Turning to the Earl, she asked, "Why me?"

William answered matter-of-factly. "I need this keep. Stephen needs this keep. With the River Humber so close, it must remain in trusted hands. The danger of an enemy sailing in from the North Sea is too great to risk. We know of no one better suited to holding it than Gerard." He sighed then admitted, "To be honest, the idea was Maud's."

"Maud's idea?" Catheryn watched Gerard wipe one hand across his face. "Who did you say wears the crown?"

"Mind your tongue, Reveur. Because you are like family, I ignore your belligerence, but even you will not disrespect the queen."

That was an interesting piece of information, and Catheryn wondered how long the two men had known each other.

Gerard took a step back and bowed his head. "Forgive me. I meant no disrespect." He raised his head. "But why do the two of you think this is a good idea?"

"I don't have to explain anything to you." William waved at the decree that had fallen from Catheryn's hand. "That says it all."

70

"William…my lord…"

With a heavy sigh, the Earl finally asked, "Do the three of us not pose a strong, powerful force in Normandy and France?"

Gerard shrugged. "How could we not, when Reveur lies directly between Aumale in Normandy and the queen's lands in Boulogne?"

"Why would not want the same here in England?"

"But…"

"Your mother, sister, and vassals are more than capable of overseeing Reveur in your absence. And you know that both Maud and I would send in reinforcements if they were needed."

Gerard conceded the point. "Yes, Reveur is in capable hands for now. I am loyal to King Stephen, so I would remain in England to lend support without being given property that I would only have to care for. And to care for it well—"

William stared at him as if he were daft. "Many men have holdings in both England and Normandy. You have the money and the men to be able to manage two properties." He cocked his head. "I love you, Gerard, you know that. But if you refuse the king you will look rebellious. During times like these…"

Catheryn eyed Gerard. The more she thought about it, the more he seemed the best candidate the Earl might offer. Interrupting the two men, she said, "Marrying me would not be pleasant for you I am certain, Baron Reveur, but you would gain a strong keep and its wealth. No man can—"

Gerard whipped around. "Get out!" he growled through clenched teeth. "What do you know of me or what I can do?"

She wasn't going to argue. By the tone of his voice, she'd

not win. But as she turned toward the stairs William thundered, "No! The girl stays. This concerns her."

Oh, Lord, what to do now? If she stayed, Gerard would flay her. If she left, William would.

Gerard solved her dilemma by lightly touching her shoulder. "Stay," he said. His voice was surprisingly kind. Perhaps even a bit regretful.

They all sat back down, and the Earl let out an exaggerated sigh. "Good, that is better. Gerard, you have done an excellent job here. I cannot find a more appropriate way to thank you." He looked at Catheryn. "You cannot defend this keep yourself. As much as you may dislike the idea, you must have a strong man at your side, and Brezden's people already know Baron Reveur."

Gerard came to the edge of the stool. "William." He paused to eye Catheryn briefly before continuing. "There is another option no one has taken into consideration."

Catheryn did not like the sound of this. The gleam in Gerard's eye looked more unholy than good.

"Yes, Gerard? You will not rest until you tell me, I am sure. What else can we do?"

"This keep is yours. Why give it up? You could add to your coffers by keeping Brezden entirely and offering the lady's hand in exchange for gold."

William intently studied him. "To the highest bidder?" He looked from Gerard to Catheryn and began to nod. "She would bring a tidy sum. It would have to be a loyal vassal, and yet…"

Catheryn was speechless. A cold sweat broke out on her face. Somehow, some devious way, de Brye would win the bid. He would find some underhanded method to convince William of his honor just like Pike did with King Stephen before, and that was too much. She leapt from her stool crying out, "No, my lord, no!" Oblivious to the cold, hard, rush-strewn floor, Catheryn fell to her knees and grasped the Earl's leg with a trembling hand. Forcing herself, she raised her head to meet his startled gaze. "Please, my lord. Earl William, I will do whatever you ask of me. *Just do not do this.*"

Gerard was instantly at her side, his hand on her arm. "Sweet Jesu, Catheryn, what are you doing?"

William's keen stare held her frozen. "What are you afraid of, lady? What are you not saying?"

Catheryn's eyes darted here and there. She did not trust the Earl to be sympathetic, but perhaps she could push him back to his original plan. Anything was better than finding herself married to de Brye. "Sire, I wish to marry no one, but I am not foolish enough to think I will be allowed that freedom. Since that is the case, I—"

Her chin was caught by a large, strong hand. The Earl's eyes pinned her in place. "Keep your secrets, woman. I will not force them from you." As he lifted her head higher, Catheryn felt a moment of panic. Was he going to snap her neck? He did not, but his next words were almost as terrifying. "Anything I ask of you?"

Catheryn heard Gerard hiss. She stiffened her spine, and drawing a quick breath, she whispered, "Yes."

The Earl held on to her chin for a few agonizing heartbeats. His bruising grip brought tears of pain to her eyes, and a slow smile spread across his face. "You will agree to this marriage? To Baron Reveur?"

"Yes."

"With no further arguments?"

"Yes."

The Earl's hand fell from her chin to her arm, and he helped her to her feet. Catheryn hung her head as she rose, too afraid to discover what else he might ask of her. But the

Earl said nothing, and it was Gerard who frightened her. She bumped him as she turned around, and the look on his stark, white face was one of pure anger.

Her insides quaked, but she stood still and met his glare without flinching. His brows formed one thick line over his fiery eyes, and that square jaw was clenched so tight Catheryn wondered if his teeth would break.

A half step brought him tight against her, and Catheryn was sure he could feel her shake. "Get up to your chamber, woman, and stay there until I tell you to come down. It seems the Earl and I must discuss a wedding."

Without hesitation, Catheryn lifted her skirts and ran for the stairs. She heard Earl William's booming laughter follow her all the way up to the safety of her room.

Chapter Six

Gerard turned, livid. "What has taken hold of your mind, William? We have been friends for a long time. You have never done anything this high-handed before."

Still laughing, William answered. "Look at you, Gerard. I have known you all twenty-one summers of your life and you are not getting any younger. Your wife is dead and a year later you still remain alone."

"What does Edyth's death have to do with my marrying *Catheryn*?" Half of him itched to grab his sword and finish the job William's many enemies could not. "And since when did my state of marriage become your concern?"

"Since the queen commanded it of me. Now, Gerard, be still." Pushing him down on his stool, William poured wine the servants had brought earlier into a goblet, and then shoved the vessel into Gerard's hand, asking, "What is wrong with marrying her?"

There were many answers to that question, but Gerard chose a simple one. "The girl is not for me."

"Girl? Granted, *I* may think she is young, but in truth, she is nearly the same age as you. Still, telling me she 'is not for you' isn't enough of an answer. What is wrong with her?"

Running a hand through his hair, Gerard shrugged. "She

is not capable of running a keep." He knew that he was being unfair. The condition of Brezden had nothing to do with Catheryn. Nonetheless, it was an easy answer.

The Earl scanned the hall. "Everything looks in order."

"No thanks to her. If you had seen the filth that used to cover this keep…"

William studied his fingernails. "I understand that your interactions with the Lady have been at times, ah, somewhat heated."

There was only one possible way William could have known that. Gerard searched the hall and quickly located his captain. Walter stood in the far corner, trying desperately to disappear into the wall.

"Do not flay your man with your hot looks. He escorted me into this keep and only answered my most direct questions."

Gerard groaned. "What else did you glean from my man?" He could just imagine. An excellent captain of the guard, Walter was not equipped to play the other games William liked so well, such as those of diplomacy and intrigue.

"I know that there is a part of you that would be eager to have this girl as wife."

"A whore could satisfy that part of me. I do not need a wife for that."

"Oh, aye, now *there* is an excellent argument to not wed her."

William's flippancy angered Gerard even more. "She has no respect for authority. I could never be certain she was following orders."

He was not prepared for the Earl's laughing reply. "*You* speak to me of respect for authority? *You?* Orders? We are discussing a wife, a woman, not a steward for one of your keeps!"

"I would expect a wife to do as she was told."

William shook his head. "I do not see where you would have much difficulty convincing anyone to follow an order. Still, how could you expect this girl to meekly do as you bid? Were you not the one who killed her men, damaged her keep, and from what I understand burst in on her naked? True, I ordered the attack, and you did not seduce nor abuse her, but Gerard, if you were my son, I would beat you black and blue for your current stupidity."

"Stupidity?" Gerard threw his drinking vessel to the floor and rose. He'd had enough of William's nonsense. "You're the one who thinks it wise to marry into a nest of vipers. It is wise to marry one raised by those who—?"

The vivid memories of what he'd witnessed the day of Edyth's death closed his throat. Gerard could not speak of the atrocities done to his wife and child. Not even to save himself from this unwanted marriage could he voice his nightmares. But that didn't stop the horrors from filling his mind. He swayed on his feet, unsteady from the force of his visions.

Walter quickly crossed the hall. "My lord, do not."

Gerard knew he looked and sounded crazed. He heard the concern in his captain's voice but waved the man away. He'd told no one of the horrors of that day, and he'd sworn Walter to silence. No one but he and Walter had seen the destruction and the atrocities committed in his keep. He'd permitted no other hands to tend to the dying Edyth. No one else had been allowed to touch the already dead babe she'd clutched to her chest. Pike had been dispatched. He had to find the other man responsible.

His breath, ragged and painful, tore from Gerard's chest. He gritted his teeth, forcing the rapid pounding of his heart and head to slow. Other than Catheryn and Walter, no one else knew about de Brye. But Gerard kept the devil a secret from William for a reason.

Vengeance would be his and his alone.

Grabbing a slender thread of control, Gerard stared at the Earl and admitted the truth. "Yes, I do desire the lady, but I cannot take her. I would never know if the act were out of desire or…something darker. I cannot marry her. I am not ready. Whose face would I see? Catheryn's lovely, living countenance, or Edyth's mask of death? Find someone else to marry her."

The Earl slowly rose. Gone was Gerard's trusted friend and confidant. In his place was William, Count of Aumale, Earl of York, Lord of Holderness. The man's many titles enveloped him like a cloak, and one look at his reddening, angry face made Gerard aware that nothing he said would change the man's mind. He had lost this argument.

"Enough. You fostered at Aumale, paged for my father, squired for me. King Stephen may have knighted you on the field of battle and given you your title, but I gave you your training, your spurs, horse, and armor. I am your overlord. I am truly sorry for your loss. But it is over and done, you cannot change what happened at Reveur. You are here. You are free. You have a title. You have the money and men with you that it will take to hold this keep. Even more, *your king and queen have ordered it.* You have no acceptable reason to refuse. You are going to marry Lady Catheryn of Brezden if I have to beat you into it. I will do whatever it takes to ensure Stephen's order is followed." William paused. "Do you understand?"

Gerard tasted bile in his throat. Refusing to marry her would cost him everything. Agreeing would cost nothing but his soul.

"Yes."

Gripping Gerard's shoulder, the Earl sighed. "Do you seriously think Lady Catheryn had any responsibility in Edyth's unfortunate end? Even you know better than that. Have you not quenched your thirst for revenge yet, Gerard? Must you destroy yourself for something that was not your fault?"

"Not my fault? Are you mad? I should have been there."

"Just as I should have been at his side when Stephen was taken at Lincoln. I cannot undo what has already happened, and neither can you."

Gerard was silent as he stared down at the floor. Life with Edyth had been calm and steady. Life with Catheryn looked to be anything but. He didn't want a life of unending fighting and arguing. He just wanted to be left alone. But his fate was sealed.

"When?" he asked.

"On the morrow." William pulled him into an embrace of friendship. "There are no impediments. The banns have been waived. Any monetary or property disputes can be settled later. Come, it will not be as bad as you think."

Gerard pulled himself free. Saying nothing, he bowed, then turned on his heel and left the hall.

∞

Catheryn sighed. Ever since she'd heard the heavy door to the hall open and close hours ago, she'd been going over the men's conversation. She wondered if either realized the fragments she'd overheard. And if she'd heard, de Brye might have also. Or one of his minions.

Shivering, she pushed the thought of de Brye from her mind and instead focused on what she'd heard. Even with the missing pieces, Catheryn garnered that Gerard's wife was dead and somehow Pike and de Brye were likely involved.

By the dismal tone of Gerard's voice, she had the impression she really didn't want to know what had happened.

How could Earl William or King Stephen expect Gerard to take her as his wife? She could think of no way to spare him, or herself, from that fate. He was not going to be an easy husband for anyone, and if her inklings were correct, she was the worst possible choice for him. And to think she'd called him here to Brezden. It was little wonder he'd torn through this keep like a storm gone wild. In fact, it was amazing that he'd not meted out more punishment in his rage and grief.

Marriage. Rolling over onto her side, she closed her eyes and tried to think. How could she have agreed to it so easily? Yet, how could she not? She had no choice. And though she sympathized greatly with Gerard's plight, Catheryn could not help fearing more for herself.

Familiar, heavy footsteps stopped outside her door. Catheryn knew it was Gerard. Why was he here now?

She opened her eyes and her stomach tightened. At the same time, she heard the distinct click of the hidden panel in the bedroom alcove. De Brye. Dear Lord, she hoped her men and the children were still safe. She prayed that little Sarah and Matthew hadn't witnessed their parents' demise. She would do nothing to provoke a rash act that would threaten any of their lives further. As easy as it would be for her to call for help and see him killed, she could not. Not yet.

Gerard's footsteps did not move away from her chamber door. From the alcove, the panel hissed slowly open. De Brye was entering.

Bolting from the bed, Catheryn moved toward the alcove. *"Go. Get away from here."* She knew that if anyone heard her whispered warning it would look as if she were protecting her enemy, but that couldn't be helped. Again, she whispered urgently at the slightly open panel, "Get out!"

The door to her chamber banged suddenly open. Gerard barged in. "What is wrong?"

A vile oath issued from behind the hidden panel, one meant for her ears alone, and she hoped the sound carried no further. Spinning around, she approached Gerard while asking loudly, "What are you doing in here?" With luck, her voice would cover any noise of the panel door sliding closed.

"Someone was in here. I heard you. Is all well?"

Gerard's concerned gaze shot from one corner of the chamber to another, and Catheryn's heart tripped over itself. She had to remind herself that this was not the time to go soft. "There's no one in here. See for yourself, my Lord."

He made a quick search then stood before her, unconvinced. The smell of ale on his breath indicated what he'd been doing while she contemplated their future—or lack of a future. "I was not hearing things."

"Are you sure?" Catheryn shrugged and glanced around. "I see no one here but you and me." He frowned but made no comment.

Her sigh of relief caught in her throat when she looked up at him. He looked tired and sad. The image of a child, lost and unsure of what to do next, flitted briefly across her mind, and Catheryn fought the urge to brush away the dark lock of hair that had fallen across his face. Then her perusal dropped to his shoulders and chest, erasing the image of a child, and she took a step back.

"What are you doing in here?" she repeated.

He closed the distance between them. "I heard you tell someone to go away."

Heat emanated from him. It curled around her, inviting. To keep herself from placing her hands on his chest,

Catheryn clasped them behind her. "Before that, you were outside my door. What did you want?"

"To talk. To explain."

He brushed a strand of errant hair from her face, and Catheryn took another step back. She nearly groaned when he moved with her. "There's nothing to explain. You made it quite clear what you thought about marriage." She tried to sound angry, tried to keep her breathless voice under control. She knew she failed miserably.

"My thoughts matter little. We have no choice."

"So, what is there to talk about then?"

His fingers lingered behind her ear. Tiny shivers running down her neck made it harder and harder to think. "That it would be easier if we could find some common ground."

Catheryn gasped as his touch trailed down her neck. She closed her eyes against the sensations his gentle caress inflamed. "There is nothing we have in common, my Lord. Nothing we share."

Gerard had spent the evening and part of the night arguing with himself, railing against the injustice of William's order, but above all else, one thought kept coming back to him—none of this was Catheryn's fault. Therefore, he had to make some sort of peace with her before the morrow. He'd not take an unwilling and hate-filled woman as a wife.

At the moment, Gerard wanted nothing more than to hold her. To bury his face in her hair. To breathe in the scent of her. He knew half of his wants were caused by the ale he'd been guzzling, but it was more than just the drink. He'd felt something between them from the beginning.

"There is nothing we share? Then we shall have to find something," he said. Then he pulled her into his arms.

Within the space of a breath, Gerard felt her relax against him. Her breasts pressed against his chest and their hearts beat in unison. He sent a fast message, a powerful order to his suddenly errant mind—he would not take her to bed this night. He would *not*.

Strands of her hair tickled his nose. He smoothed the silken mass and let his hand come to rest on the side of her neck. Searching for words, he absently brushed her soft skin with his thumb. "I will not make a good husband for you."

"I know that."

He breathed in the scent of flowers, light and fragrant, and he bent his head to rest his lips just below her ear. "But I will not beat you. I will not harm you. I will care for your keep and your people."

She moved slightly against him. A soft moan floated to his ears. The low, gentle sound ran warmly the length of his body, pausing to ignite small fires in his heart and groin. "That is good to know, my Lord."

He slowly moved his hand along her shoulder and back up the side of her neck. Just the sound of her voice, soft and breathless, threatened to make him forget   his resolve. His thumb gently brushed her soft flesh and a shiver rippled through her. He found it interesting that such slight contact could give this lady a reaction that no amount of contact had brought Edyth. Interesting and—to be honest with himself—rather pleasing.

Catheryn made a sound deep in her throat and then gasped. "What are you doing to me?"

Drawing her forward, he rested his forehead against hers. Was she truly so innocent? "Catheryn, it is called desire. It is fleeting and brief. Do not let it rule your head." His words were for himself as much as her.

She tried to pull away. He would not let her go but held on tightly. He was not ready for them to be separated.

"I feel as if this wave will carry me away." Placing one

hand on his chest, she asked, "Are you affected in the same manner?"

It had been so long since he'd permitted any emotion to rule him besides anger. He mastered himself, and said, "It used to when I was a boy and desire was new. But when I grew up, I learned that things like desire, passion, and love have no place in a man's life."

Catheryn felt as if some demon imp had invaded her heart and soul, tearing her in half. She wanted nothing more than to prove Gerard's words false. One side of her mind said that he would think her a whore. A cheap strumpet. The stronger side laughed and told her it didn't matter, they'd be married on the morrow, so what difference would it make?

She slid one hand around his neck. With the other she stroked his cheek, coaxing his lips to meet hers. Having only his hard, demanding kiss for experience, she imitated that.

Instead of thrusting her aside in disgust, Gerard gave in. His lips parted easily under hers, but his tongue quickly gentled her intensity. She found what came next, a more soothing give and take, far more enjoyable. She pressed her body tighter against his and melted against the hard planes of his chest.

Gerard wrapped his arms around her and with a groan moved both of them to the bed. Lying by her side, he slipped one leg between hers and ran a hand down her, stroking her from breast to thigh. Slowly. Thoroughly. She felt her heart speed up. Steady and strong, her pulse pounded in her head, her throat, her chest, and her stomach. It thumped with an impatient ache between her parted legs. No matter how she moved, Catheryn couldn't get close enough to him to ease the throbbing.

Breaking away, Gerard gave a hoarse laugh. "Catheryn, has no one ever told you not to play with fire?"

She heard the smugness in his voice, but at that moment it mattered little. She'd never felt so swept away by an emotion, not even fear or anger. She was dizzy with it. Drawing his mouth back to hers, she whispered, "No, they haven't. Show me why not."

With a low moan, he covered her lips with his own and rolled atop her. Holding her head between his hands, he kissed her eyes, her nose, her lips, and her neck. As if with a will of its own, her body rose up against him. His breath burned like fire against her ear.

"Shh, Catheryn, not tonight. But I admit I was wrong. Perhaps overwhelming passion does have a place in a man's life. It would be damned easy to forget myself with you."

Catheryn felt a sudden embarrassment and shame. She tightly closed her eyes and bit her lower lip.

Still nuzzling her ear and neck, Gerard whispered, "No, none of that. I issued a challenge you couldn't refuse."

His words did not ease her shame, especially as her pulse steadied. "I apologize. I acted like a...like a..."

He stopped her by placing a finger over her lips. "Catheryn, look at me."

She warily met his gaze. Relief flooded her when she did not see disgust.

He removed his hand and lowered it to her breast, and even through the layers of fabric, she could feel him circling her nipple with his thumb. He kneaded and teased, sending new and unfamiliar pangs through her. Like small bolts of lightning they streaked from her breasts to her toes, and when her nipple hardened beneath his caress she gasped. Straining toward his hand, she closed her eyes against the sensation.

He stopped and once again said, "Look at me."

She found the courage to do as he bid, and only then did

he resume his movements.

Staring into his eyes, Catheryn couldn't decide which burned more, her body or her face. A smile curved his lips. He brushed a kiss across her forehead and remarked, "Catheryn, no strumpet would ever be as embarrassed as you are now."

He trailed his tongue along her lower lip, and Catheryn grasped his shoulders. Unable to bear any more she cried out, "Stop, Gerard, please."

He did so, and she felt bereft of his touch when he stopped his teasing torment and rolled onto his side.

After what seemed a lifetime, her breathing returned to normal. Her heart slowed. But the feel of his touch lingered on her breast. The taste of his kisses remained on her lips.

Gerard cupped her cheek and turned her head toward his. "So, I was wrong. Again."

She wanted to laugh but had not the strength. "It is not a normal occurrence, is it?"

"Oh, it has happened once or twice." His smile lit the now darkening room and Catheryn wondered if he knew how devastating the expression truly was.

"My Lord," she replied, "I must agree you were wrong. I would say that, if nothing else, we do have one thing in common between us. Desire."

He agreed but asked, "Do you think it is strong enough to carry us through a lifetime of marriage? What about faithfulness and trust?"

A serious discussion was the last thing she wanted. She would always be faithful to her vows and hoped he would too. But she didn't want to discuss trust with him, at least not right now—not when several moments ago she'd lied to him about talking to anyone. Catheryn knew that once they wed, she would have no choice but to start trusting him.

Only then—after they were truly wed and she knew that while he might become angry, he wouldn't leave her to fend for herself—would she explain about de Brye, her men, and the children. So instead of discussing the qualities in a marriage, she asked, "Is desire not a place to start?"

"I think the Holy Church would disagree about desire having any place in a marriage, let alone it being a place to start. Marriage is a duty, a way to provide heirs for the future, not a pleasure."

Turning away, Catheryn growled. "Think you I care what they say? These supposedly holy men refused to bury my mother in sacred ground next to the man who loved her. I do not believe God would condone such a thing."

Gerard groaned raggedly, as if unwilling to debate her opinion. "Then I guess it will have to be a place to start."

A soft, almost soundless click took Catheryn's breath away, and panic assailed her. She'd foolishly forgotten about de Brye. The madman could have killed them both! Had Gerard heard? She glanced at him. He was lying on his back with his hands behind his head. His eyes were closed, and he didn't appear ready to protect himself.

"Are you hungry? Have you eaten?" she asked, eager to bring him back to his senses. De Brye was a coward and would never attack while he was alert. She knew that soon she would confide in Gerard, but not now. Not yet.

Gerard stretched and sat up. "No, I am not hungry, but I need to seek my bed."

Catheryn's heart fluttered. Beads of sweat covered her face and back. She didn't want to be alone in this room tonight. There was little doubt that de Brye would let pass what he'd surely heard and seen this day without seeking her out, so she patted the warm spot he'd just left. "Why don't you stay? There's no need for you to leave. If we're to be married…"

He did not speak right away, and her heart plummeted, but she said nothing, waiting for him to work out whatever was running through his mind. Finally, he leaned over and ran a hand down her cheek. "You are afraid of something."

It wasn't a question, so she didn't answer. She still was not ready to confide.

"Catheryn, you might be permitted to keep your secrets from William, but someday you will have to share them with me."

She bit her lip. Her heart screamed, *Now. Tell him now.* But her mind cautioned her to wait.

"Please, Gerard. Just stay."

She nearly cried with relief and gratitude when he grabbed a coverlet and a pillow and placed both on the floor. "All right. I will not sleep in your bed this night, my lady, but I will not leave you." He put his weapon alongside the makeshift bed, saying, "And this sword will protect you from any who dare threaten."

The room fell silent while he arranged himself, his cover and the pillow. Catheryn climbed beneath her covers, comforted, certain that de Brye would be deterred from entering. Not tonight. Not with Gerard on guard so nearby.

From the floor, in the darkness, a voice whispered, "Regardless of what has gone before or what you think, I will always keep you safe, Catheryn. As your husband, it will be my duty, my obligation. One I accept willingly. Trust that I will not fail you in this."

Chapter Seven

"Are you ready?"

Agnes's voice broke into her sleep, and Catheryn stretched. The cool morning air convinced her to open her eyes, at least long enough to find the covers the maid had removed. She retrieved them from the foot of the bed then curled beneath them.

"Wake up, Lady Catheryn. It is your wedding day and we have to get you ready."

"The sun has barely risen. Go away."

Her wedding day? Catheryn sat up, instantly awake. What the maid said sifted through the fog of sleep.

A man rose from the floor alongside her. Both women turned their heads, and Gerard leaned across the bed and placed a quick, chaste kiss on Catheryn's brow.

"What is the meaning of this?" Agnes's voice reached the level of a near shriek. The sound tore at Catheryn's ears.

"It means nothing. But I've other tasks to attend." Gerard cast a guilty glance toward Catheryn before making a quick exit.

Leaving the explanations to her.

"Thank you, my Lord." The comment tossed at his retreating back did not pause his steps.

"Lady Catheryn?"

Coughing to cover her laugh at Gerard's hasty escape, Catheryn gained a moment to think. "Truly, it was nothing." She pulled the sheets from the bed. "Would there not be evidence if anything happened?"

Agnes's thorough inspection of the bedcovers seemed to satisfy her fears. But not her questions. "Then what was his lordship doing in here? And why was he sleeping on the floor?"

Catheryn reasoned that a half-truth would work better than a lie. "He was sick with drink. I was frightened by a noise. The idea seemed rational at the time."

Agnes did no more than scowl. Pulling Catheryn from the bed, she began a furious whirl of undressing, dressing and primping her—to which Catheryn paid little attention. Her gaze kept straying to the hidden panel. The door seemed well sealed at the moment, and she hoped de Brye was not sitting on the other side. Not that he would miss the chance provided him right now. With only her maid for protection, they were easy targets.

Now that Gerard had left the chamber, her thoughts whirled round and round. Should she tell him the truth? Should she try to thwart de Brye on her own? Should she confide in Earl William? Should she keep her fears and plans to herself? She had no good answers. Only more questions.

"Agnes." Catheryn ran her fingers over the third, and hopefully last, gown the maid had slipped over her head. "Why am I doing this?"

"Do you not want to look presentable for your own wedding?" Deftly lacing one side of the gown, the maid moved to the opposite side. "You are the lady of this keep. It would not be proper for you to appear unworthy of your position." Her hand moved down to smooth out the long skirt. Sighing, she shook her head sadly. "If only your dear mother could be here."

Catheryn yanked the skirt of the gown from Agnes's preening fingers. The sudden urge to scream was overwhelming. "Quit blathering. You know I wasn't referring to the clothes." But the older woman's slumped shoulders and downcast face made her turn away. "I'm sorry, Agnes. I did not mean to snap at you. It must be thoughts of what will happen this day."

Her guilt was relieved a little when the maid patted her arm. "I know, sweeting. That is only natural."

"Why me?" Catheryn asked again, softer this time, looking at the ceiling. "Why must I marry him?" Just because he'd grown on her didn't mean that she wanted to be wed to him.

"Why not you?" The frown on Agnes's face warned Catheryn that she wasn't going to like the rest. "Why should you have a choice in your marriage partner? Even if your parents were alive the choice would not be yours. And you know what decision Pike would have made. You know this, child. You can do nothing to change your fate."

"And he will be *my brave, true love*," she half-sneered. She found it impossible to believe it might be true, even if things had changed a bit last night.

Agnes snorted. "You are in no position to dwell on dreams of love." The maid smoothed Catheryn's hair, trying to ease her chiding words. "For right now, what you need to face is that you and Brezden were taken by this man. It seems to me that your only choice is to marry, or join your father and his men in their graves. Is that what you want?"

"No," Catheryn mumbled.

Agnes grasped Catheryn's shoulders. "Will it be so terrible? At the very least can you not be happy that you are not being given to someone as evil or repulsive as Raymond de Brye?"

That much was true. Gerard was young and far from repulsive, as she'd experienced last night. Lifting her head, she said, "You are right, Agnes."

"Catheryn, do not be so certain that love will always be denied to you. Baron Gerard is not a bad man. He may come to be what you are seeking. Remember the dream."

She did, but she wondered if love would ever come of this union. Still, Catheryn kept her thoughts to herself and sat silently while Agnes finished.

Gerard once again entered the chamber, asking, "Are you ready?"

Rising, Catheryn brushed imaginary wrinkles from her gown before replying. "Yes, my Lord."

Glancing up, Catheryn found herself feeling a little sorry for Gerard. The look on his face had shifted to one of sadness. No one should be forced to marry against their will. This was his life, not William's. While she agreed, she didn't know what they could do about it.

She watched Gerard force a smile onto his face.

"Come," he said. "William will be waiting."

The couple walked downstairs. There, Gerard relinquished Catheryn to the Earl, saying, "I will await you at the village's church."

Catheryn watched him leave then turned to the Earl. "My lord William, is there no other way?"

"Nay, child." Sighing deeply, he tried to reassure her, though his arrow missed the mark. "Do not worry about him. He will come around."

❧

Gerard walked slowly toward the church. Even though it was a fine spring day, his heart was as heavy as the plodding

92

footsteps that carried him to his fate. He reached into the *aumoniere* hanging from his belt. Besides a few coins, the pouch held three rings. One was the plain gold band he had once given to Edyth.

His fingers closed over the smooth green stones of the other two. The rings were cold from the many years they had spent in his pouch. His mother had given him the two emerald rings, right after his father died. Except for size, they were identical. One had been his father's. The other had been his mother's. She had made him swear to bestow the smaller ring only on his true love when he found her.

Exactly what was true love? He should have asked her when she'd given him the rings. He'd once thought it was some gentle, comforting emotion that two people easily found once they wed, some mutual bond they would share. Some unseen attachment between them that would keep them transfixed, needing only what the other person could provide. Now he was no longer certain that his idea of true love even existed.

He'd cared greatly for Edyth. She'd had a gentle, calming way about her that had always made him feel at ease. He'd respected her and trusted her completely, as did all who knew her. She'd been a good and faithful lady for his keep and people. But still, something he couldn't name or identify had been missing. Some longing buried need, deep inside, had gone unfulfilled.

At times, in the dark of night, he would watch her sleep and wonder what she felt about him. Did this reserved, quiet woman ever think about him? Did she miss him when he was away? Were there ever any moments during the day when she wanted to lean against his chest and be held in his embrace simply for the joy it might provide?

He didn't doubt that Edyth cared for him, but after their

child was born, he would see the way she gazed upon the babe and selfishly wished that just once she would turn that look of pure love and reverence on him. Then, of course, he would feel like a self-centered fool for wanting more, when he knew that, all in all, his life had been good.

Clenching the rings briefly, he wondered why he had never given Edyth his mother's ring? Releasing the small emerald one, he pulled out the plain band. No, he doubted if he would ever know what true love was, let alone find it one day.

Now he was to be cursed with a wife he didn't want, a woman who kept too many secrets for his comfort. A woman who lied to his face. Did she think him a dolt? Only a dead man would have missed the soft click of a latch being slid back into place last night when he entered her chamber, and then she had been afraid for him to leave. What was she hiding?

If she refused to confide in him soon, he would have that chamber dismantled piece by piece. He would find that hidden door.

ℭℜ

Catheryn followed the Earl outside to the bailey. She squinted against the brightness of the day. Even though she only owned three presentable gowns, it had taken so long to get dressed to Agnes' satisfaction that the sun was already at its zenith.

Taking her hand, William led her across the bailey to the village church where the wedding would be held. They had decided not to do it in the keep's small private chapel but down where Brezden's people could see and participate.

"Lady, I am sorry that your wedding must be so hasty, but I cannot linger. There will be no betrothal ceremony, and the feasting will not be large or long. I fear you may look back on this and find it lacking."

Lacking? She'd expected nothing for this wedding, no public ceremony, no feasting at all, so how could she find what William had put together lacking in any manner? "How kind you are to concern yourself."

William looked at her in question, clearly unaware of what she'd suffered over the past few years. Catheryn smiled wryly and continued, not wanting to go into the past. She would focus on the good.

"Lord William, how many ladies of my standing can say that not only did the Earl of York attend her wedding but escorted her to the church door? I thank you for this. I am truly grateful." She was also grateful that she could no longer be wed to de Brye. The more she considered, the more Gerard seemed an escape. Yes, she would focus on that whenever she felt forced into this wedding.

The Earl smiled. "Do not thank me yet. If I remember correctly, you vowed to do something. Anything I asked."

Catheryn shuddered. All gratitude left her, replaced by cold fear.

William chuckled, reading her face with a sigh. "Young woman, as much as I would surely enjoy myself, I do not want you in my bed." He snorted when she loosed the breath she had been holding. "Lady Catheryn, you are marrying a man dear to me both as a friend and an ally. The fire I see in his eyes whenever you are around cannot be ignored. I would not let him escape from you no matter how desperately he wanted, even if the king and queen had not ordered this."

She shook her head. "I do not understand."

"I know, and I am sorry there is no time for lengthy explanation." William stopped. "Suffice it to say the Gerard you know is not the same man I know. The only emotions your Gerard knows are anger and indifference. He has become cold and remote. He no longer looks at women and—"

Catheryn raised her hand. She wasn't sure they were talking about the same man, not after last night, but the Earl didn't need to finish his description.

William stopped talking. A moment later he grinned. "Walter tells me that you are the first person to fire Gerard's blood since Edyth died."

Catheryn felt herself blush. She wasn't certain how to reply, but William did not require a response.

"Gerard is of no use to me, to Stephen, or to his lands and people if he cares about nothing except a thirst for blood. It is of grave import that he be useful, especially now when the kingdom is—"

Yes, yes, Gerard and the kingdom. But Catheryn could stem her impatience no longer. "You still have not told me what it is you expect from me."

"What I 'expect from you' will make you think me daft. But, trust me, I am not. Do you think I fail to see Gerard's sadness? Do you think I fail to see him seeking self-destruction in a quest for revenge, *a quest that will never end*? He captured this castle and killed Pike and yet still he is not happy. Catheryn, I do see all of this and more, but his Edyth is never coming back."

Catheryn was confused. Where was the Earl headed with this? And if he recognized such pain in a man he called friend, why had he done nothing to help Gerard? She had lost both of her parents but had Agnes to help her wake each painful morning. Gerard had lost a wife and child. Who had helped him to face each day? Anyone?

The Earl took a slow breath before finishing his thoughts. "It is time Gerard faced a new life, whatever that life might bring. If all I can give him is someone to fight and argue with, that is what I will do. I want you to promise me that, regardless of your feelings for Gerard, you will not go soft on him. Never permit love to smooth the edges of your temper or tongue."

She swallowed her surprised laugh. "Love him? *Gerard?* Lord William, I think you have little to fear in that."

William shook his head. "You misunderstand. I care not if you love him, I care only that you keep his fires burning if you come to do so."

Keep his fires burning? Catheryn shook her head. The Earl meant that she was to *provoke* Gerard? He was looking for an escape from the pain he felt. Looking for vengeance. Would not provocation and anger add to his suffering?

"My lady, I know the idea must seem cruel to you, but trust me, Gerard was raised by my sire and I know him well. The only way to direct his anger away from this foolish fixation on revenge is to bring it on yourself." When she didn't respond to that ludicrous suggestion, William added, "He will never harm you, Lady Catheryn. Never. He will simply make it his mission to bend you to his will."

All comfort had left her, all sense that this marriage might be an escape disappeared. "And how will this bending not hurt?"

The Earl's smile was fraught. "Trust me, it will not hurt. Gerard will find…means other than violence to convince you his ways are best. Kinder means, and yet persuasive."

Catheryn felt her face burn hot remembering the previous night. "Oh."

The Earl laughed. "Good. I see you do not mistake my meaning. Gerard has never harmed a woman in his life."

Catheryn wanted this conversation to stop—now before it went any further. Turning away from the Earl, she said, "I will try, William."

"That is all I ask."

As they resumed their walk, Catheryn noticed that the yard in front of the church was filled with people. Standing close to Gerard was Walter, and the guard had his arm around a crying Agnes.

Then the almost-forgotten sound of Pike's cruel laughter filled her ears. Catheryn stumbled slightly, and her feet slowed of their own accord.

William's hold on her hand tightened. "Lady Catheryn?" His voice had reverted back to that of a lord, cold and questioning. But that laugh. Pike's laugh. Had it been her imagination, or had Pike's ghost been warning her not to go through with this marriage?

What was she doing? *Escape.* The thought ripped through her mind. But quickly looking left and right, Catheryn knew she'd not get through the line of men that stretched across both sides of the path. It was too late. There would be no escape. She knew that. She'd known that since yesterday.

Squaring her shoulders, she took a deep breath. "I am fine, William. I simply tripped."

His look of disbelief was brief, but the Earl made no further comment as he led her forward.

When they reached the steps, the fat little priest next to Gerard asked, "What can I do for you, my children?"

The Earl stepped forward. "Father, we come for your benediction. This couple seeks your blessing on their vows of marriage. *Willingly.*" He stressed the last word.

Looking at Gerard, the priest asked, "Is this true?"

Gerard answered in a strong, steady voice, "Aye, Father."

"Are there any reasons this couple should not be joined?" the priest called out.

"Nay," William answered loudly.

"Who gives this woman?"

"I, William Albemarle, Count of Aumale, Lord of Holderness and Earl of York," came the Earl's booming reply. Placing Catheryn's hand on Gerard's arm, William smiled at her before stepping back. None could question his approval of the union.

Turning toward her, Gerard tipped her chin up with one finger. "I, Gerard, Count of Reveur, dower you with the manor, farms, and fields of Keene's Gate in Reveur."

William gasped. "Gerard, it is not necessary—"

Gerard's steady gaze never left her. "I would not dishonor myself, or Catheryn, by offering any less." Smiling slightly, he added, "And they are mine to give."

Slipping a heavy, plain gold band on her finger, Gerard continued. "From this moment on I take you as my wife, and I offer this ring as a token of my pledge." He hesitated. "Do you accept me as your lawful husband, Catheryn of Brezden?"

Catheryn wanted to laugh. Accept? She could see no other choice, not with William and all of his men surrounding her.

Taking a quick breath, she forced herself to reply. "Yes, Baron Reveur. I, Catheryn of Brezden, do accept you as my lawful husband from this moment on." She wasn't sure, but she thought she heard a sigh of relief. Had it come from William, Walter, or Agnes?

Gerard turned back to the priest, whom they all followed into the church.

It was crowded, and they all stood shoulder to shoulder. As mass was said, Catheryn gazed around the small wooden building. It was dark. The slits for the windows were up high, and they were too small to allow much light to pass through. Plain timber pillars formed support for the roof.

The service almost at an end, the priest called for the

marrying couple to come up front. Holding her hand, Gerard pulled Catheryn down to kneel with him before the altar. She did so reluctantly, thinking again of her mother's death and burial. They were covered with a white linen cloth, and the priest chanted a blessing. When he finished, they rose, turned, and left the church.

She had not paid any attention on her walk to the ceremony, being preoccupied as she was, but now Catheryn could not help but notice how much Brezden had been put back to rights. Gone were the remains of charred buildings. New patches had been overturned for vegetable plots. Those waving and shouting their blessings did not have the appearance of a beaten people, they looked and sounded happy.

Gerard was quiet as he led her back to the keep. Catheryn wished there was a way to lift the clouds from him. She didn't like how unhappy he looked. If nothing else, he had unknowingly saved her from many worse fates. She was indeed grateful for that.

"Catheryn? Where are you now?"

"I am sorry, Gerard, what?" She had worried that he would be quick-tempered and moody this day and hoped to spare him any unnecessary frustrations.

"It was nothing," he said, leading her up the stairs and into Brezden's overcrowded Great Hall.

"Please, Gerard, what did you say?"

"I simply wonder what kind of entertainment the Earl has planned for us."

"What do you mean?"

"Well, he will do *something.*"

"The Earl hasn't been here long enough to plan anything. He said that there would be little—"

"Did you see the size of the baggage train he arrived

with?" Gerard pointed at tables already set up and laden with food then directed her attention to the musicians milling around in one corner. "No, there was never a choice for either of us. Our marriage, this meal, and this evening's amusements were taken care of long before William crossed your borders."

Catheryn said nothing. How little control she had over her fate.

Her husband paused and shook his head. "The rest of this day and evening should prove interesting." He glanced down at her. "What did our crafty Earl request of you? I saw you speaking with him on the way from the keep."

Catheryn sucked in a breath. What could she tell him? "Nothing."

His eyes widened in apparent disbelief before he took her arm and dragged her into a private alcove off to the side of the hall. "What did William ask of you?" he repeated.

"Gerard, I, he…" She wasn't sure how much to reveal. Then she realized that if she remained silent, she would be the target of Gerard's ire, just as William requested. And she'd promised to try what the Earl asked. "Nothing that should concern you."

At first, she was afraid that he would be angry, that he would strike her, but nothing was farther from the truth. As predicted, Gerard's face grew confident. He backed her into a corner, against the wall and smiled. "I will find out eventually. You know that. So why not just tell me now?"

Yes, why not? "Gerard, he cares about you. He truly does."

"Oh, yes, that is obvious." He ran his finger along her jaw and up behind her ear. Cupping the side of her head, he leaned forward and whispered, "What else did he say?"

He was going to seduce the answer from her? Even

though the Earl had warned her of this, it was a surprising tactic. Gerard teased the side of her neck with his lips, and Catheryn's heart thudded.

"This is not fair, my Lord." She placed her hands on his chest to steady herself.

He trailed his lips up to her mouth. "Nothing is fair." He kissed her once. "Life is not fair," he whispered before kissing her again. His tongue coaxed a quick and eager response from her, and his lips lingered briefly on hers before moving to her ear. His voice was soft and low. Its deep timbre sent little shivers of pleasure down her back. "Tell me, Catheryn."

Her resolve was weakening, along with her knees. "He explained what I had to do for him."

Gerard froze. "And what, pray tell, could that be?"

She leaned forward, running her hands up his chest, trying to draw him back, but he stepped out of reach.

"What does the lout want from you?"

She looked up at him and promised, "He wants nothing for himself."

Gerard laughed harshly. "William always wants something for himself. He does nothing from the goodness of his heart, my Lady."

She narrowed her eyes. "Surely you do not believe that he requested anything immoral of me?"

"I would believe anything of William."

Catheryn's passion turned instantly to anger. "And you would believe anything of me, apparently, if you think I would do something immoral just because he asked. I appreciate your trust, my lord."

"Trust?" Gerard snapped. "What have you done to prove yourself trustworthy?"

She had listened to more than enough. Scooting away

from the wall, Catheryn stepped out from the shadows. "Stand here and snarl at yourself, my Lord. I have other things to attend."

Gerard pulled her back. "I can imagine."

He ignored her gasp of outrage. Leaning down, he locked his mouth over hers, and she felt herself respond despite her anger.

She felt him laugh silently when she wrapped her arms around his neck to hold him to her. And this time he didn't break away.

No, she was sure, he was just as caught in a crashing wave of desire as she.

Chapter Eight

A shuffle of feet broke them apart.

"My pardon, Lord Gerard."

"What?" Gerard growled, and Catheryn almost laughed. Her husband looked truly incensed.

The young page held his ground. "My Lord, the Earl sent me to find you."

Catheryn spoke up. "Tell him we will be there directly."

Gerard's lips were damp against her forehead as the page disappeared. "We will continue this later."

"If that is a promise, I look forward to it."

He hadn't moved yet, except to take her face in his hands. "Catheryn, I will not calmly stand by while another man touches you. Not even if that man is my friend and liege lord."

"You have no cause for worry."

"Make certain that does not change."

Stunned, Catheryn realized that her husband was deadly serious. A sarcastic retort about ownership and possession sprang to her lips, but she held it at bay. Instead, she merely nodded and stepped out of the alcove when he released her.

Surveying the hall, she noted that someone had shown a deft hand in arranging this banquet. Sideboards were laden with pork, fish, and redressed peacocks. Snowy linen cloths covered each long table.

As they walked across the hall to the main table, men from both Brezden and Reveur cheered. Catheryn was pleased to find more proof that Gerard had gained the allegiance of her people. Reaching the table, her husband waited until she sat down before he took the chair next to her. She wondered if Gerard was as angry with William as he acted. She truly hoped the men's friendship would not be strained to the breaking point by this match, nor by William's maneuvering.

The Earl was standing nearby. "Welcome to the Lord and Lady of Reveur and Brezden," he said, and then he sat down. "I hope you do not mind, but I took the liberty of ordering entertainment."

"So, I see," Gerard replied.

Catheryn tried to soften her husband's bitter words. "Gerard, what is a celebration without a fine meal and a little entertainment?"

"What indeed?" asked Gerard, nodding toward the overladen tables. "And this celebration is an amazing feat for a man so briefly in our keep."

Catheryn watched the beating pulse at her husband's temple and wished the Earl had been a little less generous. It was the Lenten season, after all. But William waved away Gerard's comment.

"I do not think any present will gainsay my largesse."

Gerard's low laugh rang a warning in her ears. "My Lord William, is there any in York or even all of England who would gainsay you on anything?"

"Other than you? No."

"Gerard, please," Catheryn begged. The Earl had not yet risen to the bait, and she did not wish a fight to ruin everyone's enjoyment of the feast. Brezden's people had been through much these last few years and deserved a time of merriment, even if she agreed fully with Gerard's displeasure.

Gerard glared at William, saying nothing. Then, glancing at Catheryn, he bowed his head. "I shall let it pass."

"Yes. Do," the Earl said. "For the night at least a truce, and to seal that truce I will pray God forgive all those present for obeying my desires."

Clapping his hands, the man ordered the meal begin. As she guiltily picked up a knife, Catheryn could not help but look forward to savoring it. Course after course found its way to their table. The pork had been cooked over a spit and was basted with a garlic sauce. A rich, thick wine- and -raisin sauce was spooned over the peacock. Gerard placed select bits of meat and vegetables in their shared trencher, cut up several pieces, and pushed them over to her side.

The Earl and Gerard discussed a hunting party planned for the morrow. It seemed the Earl wanted to take out a new falcon he had brought along, and Gerard wanted to test the skill of Brezden's hounds. Having eaten her fill, Catheryn excused herself from the discussion and with little notice made a hasty exit. The overcrowded hall was stifling. She needed air. Air and a moment or two alone. She had just the place in mind.

Retrieving a cloak from her chamber, she raced up the keep's curving tower stairs. It had been many months since she'd been permitted this escape. Pike had mistakenly thought she'd be desperate enough to throw herself from these high walls. More likely she'd have tossed him over the edge.

Thankfully, the door was no longer locked, and she stepped out onto the battlements. Dusk slowly overtook the land, casting lengthening shadows. She'd always liked this time of day when the hustle and bustle below slowed to near silence. The settling quiet let her think, and there was still enough light to see without the benefit of a torch.

Springtime air, brisk and fresh, whipped her cloak around her. The quick chill was a welcome respite from the stuffiness of the hall, and Catheryn leaned against a crenellation. To hold this moment forever would be a blessing indeed.

"Are you satisfied, Lady Catheryn?"

Her stomach churned. How stupid had she been to come up here? "Satisfied?" She spun around and inched away from the wall.

"I was to be your husband, and well you know it." He was barely visible in the deepening shadows, but de Brye's harsh voice rang clear.

She needed to distract him, had to get him away from the door and her only escape. "What choice had I? When has any woman ever had a choice?"

"You could have declared a prior betrothal."

"That would not have been true." And the hounds of hell would have had to be at her heels. "Besides, such a ploy would have been useless. Earl William already carried writs from the king."

"You could have said you were not virgin. Your strong and handsome lord would not have accepted sullied goods." His voice was bitter. He was moving away from the door, toward her.

"Would not that have been easy to disprove?"

"Or easy *to* prove."

Catheryn gasped. "What are you saying?"

"Ah, my beauty, you break my heart." He moved closer. "How can you not remember what we did?"

No. Certainly, she would know if he'd completed his dastardly act. "You did nothing that night except knock me senseless."

"Are you sure?" His mouth slanted into a smirk. "How, Lady Catheryn, in your limited experience, can you be so certain?"

Her head spun, but she'd be damned before letting him know exactly how uncertain she had been until she'd realized that he hadn't raped her. "I would know."

"Would you now?"

She kept her concentration locked on him. "Of course."

He snickered, then asked, "How is that, my lady?"

Catheryn shrugged. "There would be signs."

She kept moving away from him, but de Brye inched along the wall in pursuit, shaking his head. "What kind of signs? How can you be sure I wasn't gentle and loving? Perhaps I took the utmost care of your tender, unused flesh."

She remained silent, grateful that the falling night hid her burning cheeks.

A cold, mirthless laugh filled the air, and then de Brye backed her against the wall. "Or are you perhaps thinking of blood? Wipe that notion from your mind, sweeting. Not all virgins bleed."

Catheryn knew she was near to panic, which no doubt was his intention. She had to remain in control, though. She *had* to. Her life probably depended on it. De Brye was a madman who would not brook being thwarted. What revenge would he now seek?

"However, if you would like your blood spilled this time, I can make it possible. There are ways."

At first, she didn't understand. Slowly, his vile meaning dawned on her. He grasped her arms before she had time to flee.

"Ah, yes, my beauty, there is plenty of time. Time to warm my cock in your blood, if that is your wish. Time to let the whole world know who first tasted your innocence and who will enjoy you again. Now. Here."

No. Struggling, she tried to reason with him. "No, we cannot. Not here. Not like this."

His grip tightened, and Catheryn knew she'd be bruised. Briefly, she wondered what Gerard would say when he saw the marks, but then she realized how silly that was. She had greater fears to attend.

"Here and now is the perfect place," de Brye growled. "No one will hear your screams, nor my groans of pleasure. Not with the celebration below."

His mouth came down over hers, hard. The stench of stale wine and ale attacked her nostrils, and she could do nothing to stop from gagging.

In the space of one day she'd been ordered to marry by one man, yelled at by another, and now a third sought to assault her. Catheryn's mind screamed, "Enough! No more!" Had she not been the one who'd said it was time to take charge of her life? That time was now.

When de Brye pulled her forward and pressed his groin against her belly, she felt his hard erection. Cocking back her leg, she rammed her knee forward with all the force she could summon. Thankfully, it was enough. His hold released and he toppled to the floor. Not pausing to see his reaction, Catheryn ran in through the door and down the steps.

Holding her hand over her mouth to keep in the bile, she avoided her chamber and kept running for the stairs leading down to the hall. Skirting the great hall, she ran for the kitchens.

There would be people there. People meant safety. Safety,

and perhaps a chamber pot.

She was right on both counts. And the servants had enough sense not to ask the lady of the keep why she was vomiting.

All but one.

"My Lady?"

"Oh, please," Catheryn groaned. "Agnes, go away. Leave me be."

"Lord Gerard sent me to find you."

Catheryn wanted to laugh as she stood upright. The last thing she needed at this moment was Gerard.

The maid unfastened the brooch on Catheryn's cloak and handed the garment to another servant. "Lady Catheryn, what has happened?" She passed a cool, wet rag over Catheryn's face and neck. "Come, child, sit down."

Catheryn didn't have the strength to argue. Allowing Agnes to lead her to a stool in a more private corner, she wondered how to calm herself enough to return to the festivities.

Agnes knelt in front of her. Brushing the stray hairs from Catheryn's damp forehead, she shook her head. "Your lip is bleeding." Wiping the blood away, she stared into Catheryn's eyes. "I know that look of fright well, child. What has happened?"

"Nothing. It is nothing." Catheryn wanted nothing more than to throw herself into Agnes's arms and cry, but the time for tears was past.

The maid plucked at Catheryn's gown, smoothing and straightening. When she brushed a hand down the sleeve, Catheryn flinched without thought.

Agnes paused. Then she laid a finger on Catheryn's upper arm and pressed.

Catheryn jerked away, gasping. "Oh, please. Don't,

Agnes. Don't touch me." She bit her now swelling lip, fighting tears.

Throwing her arms around Catheryn's waist, Agnes cried out, "He is here! Oh, Lord, he is back."

Catheryn patted the maid's head. Keeping her voice to a whisper, she did not deny it. "Yes. He never left, Agnes."

"You must tell Lord Gerard or the Earl."

"No. I cannot. I cannot even explain to you. I have said too much already." She tugged at Agnes's arms, reluctantly pulling out of the woman's embrace. "Please, swear to me you'll tell no one. Agnes, my life—no, all our lives depend on secrecy."

"My Lady, your husband will see your bruises. Only someone blind will not notice your lip. How will you explain?"

Catheryn shrugged. "Gerard will know nothing for a fact unless I tell him. He will rail, he will demand answers, but he will get none."

"But—"

She looked at her maid and smiled sadly. "Agnes, what is the worst he might do? Kill me? Beat me? Somehow, I do not think either within Baron Reveur's nature. And I can live with his anger." A bitter laugh escaped her. "Have I lived with anything better since my mother died?"

"I do not agree, Catheryn. I think your safety depends on confiding in your husband. He will help you."

"I cannot."

Rising and shaking her head, Agnes patted Catheryn's leg. "You will see in time that I am right, but this is your choice to make. Is there anything I can do for you now?"

Catheryn ran a hand over her disheveled hair "Without going to my chamber, can you make me presentable?"

"Of course."

Agnes was as good as her word. In very little time Catheryn was ready to rejoin the men. She took several deep breaths on her way back to the hall, and it required every single one to regain her composure. Holding her head high, she at last convinced herself that all would be well. She'd worry about her lip when or if anyone questioned her. She'd worry about her other bruises… later.

"Ah, here she is. Please, Lady Reveur, join us." William patted the bench next to him. "If you are finished eating, we can have this cleared away and then begin the entertainment."

Another course after what just happened? Catheryn's stomach rolled at the thought. "I am done. Please, have it cleared away. What do you have planned for us?"

"Nothing grand. Not on such short notice." But the Earl signaled for the tables to be moved.

Catheryn snatched a large cushion to recline on and placed it between Gerard and William. She had no desire to be alone with her husband just yet. It was all she could do to avoid his searching glances. Agnes had arranged her hair so that it fell in ripples over her face, and Catheryn took full advantage of that makeshift curtain to hide her lip.

Wine and ale flowed freely as musicians and jugglers performed for them, and Catheryn soon realized that whenever her goblet of sweet, warm wine ran low, Gerard had it refilled. He was trying to get her drunk. Catheryn also noticed he was successfully chasing a like condition himself.

Unused to heavy drinking, she soon began to feel a little woozy and declined another refill. "No, Gerard, please. No more."

"You may want to allow your husband to decide your limit," William suggested, presenting her with a smug, indulgent smile.

Did he consider her nothing more than a poor, witless dolt? Was she not capable of deciding for herself what or how much to drink? After a quick glance at two sets of narrowed eyes and one arched brow, she knew that both men were certain they knew so much more. But since it was too little of a thing to argue, she allowed Gerard to pour more wine.

"Wise choice, my dear wife."

Even though the beverage helped numb her fears, it grated that she was always treated as a child or a possession. She found herself muttering, "Yes, it is what every woman needs. Plenty of men to tell her what to do and how or when to do it."

"Plenty of men? How many others have had the pleasure of ordering you about?" Gerard did not sound amused.

The impulse to laugh nearly overwhelmed her. If the wine had been meant to help her relax, it had succeeded beyond anything Gerard could have hoped. "First my father. Then Pike. Now you, William and…"

"And *who*? Who else has ordered you about, Catheryn?"

She'd spoken without thinking and almost said de Brye's name aloud. Now she wished she could cut out her own tongue. Catheryn shook her head. "No one. I was going to add that I was tired of it."

He didn't look at all as if he believed her. She felt Gerard's stare and knew she'd not be able to avoid him, so shifting slightly away from the firelight Catheryn swung her hair over her face and met his stare for a moment. How was she going to guard her wayward tongue when she could barely feel it? She glanced down into her goblet. The deep red liquid bore a remarkable resemblance to blood. But whose blood? Hadn't she just been foolish enough to nearly mention de Brye? The blood would be her own. Her heart beat furiously.

Closing her eyes, Catheryn fervently prayed for a miracle. Opening them, she was shocked to find Gerard leaning on her cushion. Keeping her head down, she eyed him over the rim of her goblet. His piercing gaze locked on her. With all of the other commotion in the great hall, his half-lidded stare remained focused solely on her. The thought that this handsome, strong man was more interested in watching her instead of the jugglers or musicians made her forget her previous fears.

She lowered her gaze to his mouth, and when his lips curved into a slight smile, she could not believe the wanton desire that overtook her. It required every ounce of willpower she possessed not to reach out and touch him. Her pulse pounded madly in every part of her body. She wanted to feel Gerard's skin beneath her hands, wanted to be consumed by his heat. Wanted to learn everything she had yet to learn about being a woman.

What was wrong with her? How could just a look, just a smile make her so desperately crave the touch of a man? Maybe she was little more than a whore. These feelings couldn't be natural.

Her head spun, and she was at a loss for a remedy. But if the wine had brought about these unholy desires, maybe a little more would take them away. Tipping the goblet for another swallow, she was startled when Gerard stayed her hand.

"No more."

He cupped the back of her head and leaned in to kiss her, and Catheryn forgot her retort. His lips tasted of wine, cinnamon, and honey. The heady scent of him was more intoxicating than any drink or perfume. She wanted to spend an eternity with his lips on hers.

But his kiss was brief, ending the instant his tongue swept

114

over her lip. "What is this?"

"What?" Looking away, she tried to decide what to tell him, but her mind was clouded with drink. With lingering desire. With guilt.

His hold on the back of her head tightened. He forced her to look at him. Brushing her hair from her face, Gerard demanded, "Catheryn, answer me. Now."

She couldn't think. Frightened by the pronounced tick in his cheek and rigid jaw, she answered with the only thing her muddled brain could quickly offer. "I—I wasn't watching where I was going and ran into a wall."

She tried to pull away, but he wouldn't permit it. His stare went cold and hard. A vein running from his eye to his hairline was prominent and pulsing. His disbelief was obvious, and Catheryn wanted to run away and hide. This was going to be a nightmare, yet she could think of no way to avoid it.

Releasing her, Gerard ordered, "You have but a few moments to get yourself situated in my chamber." Signaling for Agnes, he added, "I will have the truth this night, Catheryn. Do not doubt it."

She suddenly wanted to postpone the bedding for as long as possible as a cold knot of fear grew in her stomach. "Gerard, can this not wait? It is still early."

"No." His tone left no opening for an argument. Yet he didn't look like a man eager to get at his wedding bed. "Come, my Lady." Agnes tugged gently at Catheryn's sleeve. "Your clothes have already been moved."

Following like a compliant lamb, Catheryn wanted to scream. This was not how she had envisioned her wedding night. She had never dreamed the bridegroom would come to their bed in anger.

Agnes opened the door to Gerard's chamber, and even

though she'd not been in this chamber in years, Catheryn vaguely noticed the elegance of the room. Her parents had reserved its use solely for infrequently visiting royalty. It was all she could do to force a sense of calmness to her quaking limbs as she undressed with Agnes's help then quickly climbed into the big, curtained bed.

Agnes sat down alongside her and touched the bruises on Catheryn's arms. "My lady, I know not how to ask this, but I must."

"No, Agnes. De Brye did no further damage than what you see."

The maid's audible sigh of relief would have been laughable about any other question. "There is still some hope then. If you can keep Baron Reveur from seeing these marks until you are well and truly wed, you may yet avert any questions."

"*Some hope?*" Catheryn repeated. "What you mean is *a very tiny thread* of hope. How will I manage to keep them hidden?" She held out her arms, and candlelight flickered over the red and purple fingerprints already evident on her pale flesh. "It has always been my curse to bruise easily. Never could I hide a fall from a tree or a dunk in the stone-bed creek. I'll not be lucky tonight either."

"Now think just a moment, Catheryn. We are not speaking about an anxious parent closely observing their child. We are talking about a man coming to his marriage bed. If you think he will be looking at your arms, we need to have a quick discussion about men. With some artful covering up—"

"I can't very well wear a gown."

"No. But we have your hair. And we have a bed with plenty of covers." Agnes looked about the room. "And we have far too much kindling for the fire. And too many candles."

The maid scurried about the chamber. She snatched more than half of the tallow candles from the wall and floor sconces, extinguished them and tossed them out the window, leaving the light in the room little more than a faint glow. Almost all of the extra kindling followed. There would be a need for a great many covers this night.

"There. That should help."

Catheryn hugged her. "You are a treasure."

They heard the sound of footsteps approaching.

"Quick, get into bed," Agnes ordered. "Roll over on one side and use your hair for the other arm."

Catheryn did as she was bid. "Oh, Agnes, if this does not work, he will kill me."

Agnes smiled. "Oh, Lady, do not be afraid. I believe you are right that he is not that sort of man."

"You don't understand!" She'd not told Agnes about her near slip of the tongue, nor about the other fears revolving around de Brye. Now that her wedding night was at hand, she worried. What if de Brye hadn't lied about raping her? She'd been so certain she'd know if she'd been violated because of his usual brutality. But he'd claimed he might have been gentle, and the sudden unknowing would drive her mad.

Quickly grasping her maid's hand, she asked, "How does a man tell if his wife is a virgin? How does he know if she is pure?"

Agnes's eyes grew round. She leaned close. "What are you saying, Catheryn? I thought—"

Before she could explain, they were interrupted by the boisterous sounds of men at the door, and Catheryn bit back a nervous laugh as they heard the priest perform a useless ritual to bless the marriage bed. She had little faith that her maid's sly tricks would work. Even if they did, what would Gerard do if he discovered his wife was not innocent? What would she do or say to explain?

Half carrying and half dragging Gerard into the room, Walter and William quickly stripped him. He stood straight and wandered over to the bed, drawing back some of the covers that shielded her from his gaze. Then Gerard nodded.

"Yes, William, you were right. She is a fine-looking woman."

Catheryn longed to yank the covers out of his hand. Fine-looking? He sounded like he was appraising a horse or a side of beef.

Her displeasure actually overwhelmed her fear.

"Enough, Gerard." William pushed her husband into bed. "We will see you on the morrow. Maybe."

Chapter Nine

Gerard watched Agnes and the others leave. He then turned to the woman lying at his side.

Catheryn. The woman who was now—or soon would be—his second wife. *Wife.* The word tripped oddly across his mind. A thick, uneasy silence had descended after the closing of the door, and a suffocating stillness filled the room, making it hard to breathe and harder to think. He'd told Catheryn that this would be the night for answers. But it was also a night for passion. Which did he require more? Rubbing his temples, Gerard knew which choice could wait.

"Catheryn…it would go easier between us if you would just tell me what frightens you."

She turned her head away, and he barely heard her mumbled response. "I cannot."

Why did she have to be so stubborn, so infernally contradictory? How could a woman be so afraid of something Gerard couldn't see, yet stand so strongly against him? His first impulse was to shake her until her teeth rattled, but he'd learned long ago to ignore such impulses. You didn't gain willing partners by beating them into cooperation.

Leaning close, he ran his finger along her lip. "Does it

hurt?"

"A little."

Gently and ever so slowly, he smoothed his tongue over the swelling. He stopped at the rough ridges of a broken gash. He knew Catheryn had the odd habit of chewing on her own lip when she concentrated, but she would never bite herself that hard. Cupping her cheek, he turned her head toward the light. Using as little pressure as possible, he drew her lip down with his thumb. Then he fought back frustration. There were no marks on the inside of her mouth. He had a gangly sister who, on occasion in her youth, had found walls with her face. Each time she had, there was more damage caused by her own teeth than the stone.

"You did not run into a wall."

The fear glimmering in her eyes was almost more than he could bear. Gerard released her, unable to stop memories assailing him. Beaten and dying women had that same look in their eyes, and it never failed to turn his blood to ice.

"Who did this?"

She shrank away from him.

"Are you hurt anywhere else?"

She shook her head vigorously. "No."

He didn't believe her too-quick denial, and before she could stop him Gerard tore the sheet away and tossed it on the floor.

Catheryn pulled her hair around her like a curtain, but he knew she sought more than warmth. She sought to *conceal*.

It took fewer than a dozen or so curses for him to charge across the chamber, grab the tall, branched candlestick in the corner of the room and pull it over. He tore down the bed curtains and threw the heavy fabric to the floor. Then, with a challenging gaze, he dared her to stop him.

She gave in with grace. Closing her eyes, she brushed her

hair back and let her arms rest at her side.

Gerard sucked in his breath. "It's nothing? A wall?" He ran a finger around the outline of one bruise. "Tell me, wife, which wall in Brezden has hands?"

"None," she admitted.

Gerard placed his hand over the bruises. So, he'd not been imagining things last night in her chamber. He'd clearly heard her tell someone to go away. Later he'd heard the click of a latch. "These were made by a man."

She nodded.

Straddling her on the bed, he placed one hand on each side of her head. "Look at me." He waited until she complied. "Whoever was unwise enough to lay his hands on you is a dead man. I will break his neck with my bare hands, Catheryn, and you will watch."

Her eyes widened, but she made no comment.

"This will not bother you?"

"No."

"These marks were not caused by an angry lover who perhaps became a little too lusty?"

"No, Gerard. No."

He believed her. She had suffered a man's cruel touch, and after he had vowed to keep her safe. "Is the lout within these walls?"

She hesitated then shook her head. "I do not think so."

"Is it the same man who killed your archer?"

In the dim light he watched her pale. With great effort, she sought to turn away, and that reaction and her silence gave him his answer. It was de Brye. He had the sneaking suspicion that she'd been about to say his name earlier in the hall when she'd complained about men ordering her about.

He should feel outraged. Anger should be at the forefront of his emotions. Instead, he felt drained. Disgusted.

Defeated. The ghost of his worst enemy haunted him even here on his wedding night, and his wife would not tell him the truth.

He shoved himself upright and strode to the fire. "A pox on you, Catheryn. How can you protect a man so vile?"

"Because this is nothing. Nothing compared to what he is capable of doing."

Her answer was barely above a whisper, but it felt as if every word was screamed in his ear. "I know exactly what that blackguard is capable of doing."

He turned around and stared at her. "And, with or without your help, I will see to it that no other man or woman suffers his atrocities again."

She sat up. Hugging her arms around herself, she returned his look. "Gerard, I—"

He wanted no more of her half-answers, no more of her meaningless assurances. "Shut up, Catheryn. If you will not tell me where he is, just keep quiet."

Surprisingly, the woman fell silent. The woman who thought nothing of calling him a filthy monster more than once, the woman who was protecting his enemy. He laughed and shook his head.

"You find this amusing, my Lord?"

"Not at all. Nothing about this day or night has been amusing. But what else am I to do? You refuse to give me the information I seek, and I have neither the strength nor the desire to argue with you. I have never beaten a woman in my life, and I am not about to start on our marriage night, no matter how you might tempt. So, what do you suggest?"

"Nothing. Maybe you should just go."

"*Go?* And provide the Brezden with enough gossip to last a lifetime? You think that would be wise? No, Catheryn, it seems you are stuck with me this night."

"This night only?"

She sounded far too hopeful. "If you desire, that can be arranged."

"That would suit me fine."

She was infuriating. Maddening. She tossed his emotions out on a windswept sea, made him feel as confused and awkward as a boy first struggling to become a man. And she was his wife. Every deceiving, secretive, beautiful speck of her.

Poking the fire in the stone hearth, he asked over his shoulder, "Do you require anything?" This was their first night as man and wife. Not exactly how he'd envisioned spending their time together.

"No."

"Are you certain you've no other injuries, that you are whole?"

"What are you suggesting?" Her voice sounded strained.

Gerard turned away from the fire and stared. She averted her face, but even in the dim light, he could see her jaw tighten and her lips thin. "I am simply trying to determine if there are any injuries to your person that I could not see." He walked toward the bed. "What are you hiding? What do you not wish me to discover?"

"Nothing."

"Then what do you fear I was suggesting?"

The fierce look she directed toward him took Gerard aback. He'd seen her angry, flustered, and sad. None of those expressions came close to describing the look on her face now. Creases marred her forehead and uncontrolled fire flashed in her eyes. Her lips were drawn tightly together.

Raising her head higher, she spread out her arms. "Just let this be over with."

He took one step forward and stopped when she

flinched. What did she think he was going to do to her? Approaching slowly, he kept his voice low. "Catheryn? What is this about?" He frowned. Was she using this odd, misplaced bravado to hide her nervousness?

"Come, Gerard. Let us end this not-knowing. Bed me. Take me. Do whatever it is you do and let us discover whether I am a virgin or not."

He froze. "Let us *discover*? I would think you should know."

She shook her head. "Well, I do not." Lowering her arms, she wrapped them around her waist. "I do not know."

The fierceness left her expression, but the anger remained. Anger and something he couldn't put his finger on.

As her words fully registered, his own anger flared. He took a step away from her and tried to step back from the sudden pounding of his own heart. "How can you not know?"

She didn't answer, and Gerard closed his eyes against the increased throbbing in his head. This day had been too long. Too much wine, too much food, too much everything. Now this.

"It is simple, Catheryn. Either you have lain with a man or you have not."

Looking back at her, Gerard was amazed to see confusion cloud her face. Nothing made any sense to him.

"What game are you playing, Lady? If you are seeking to have this marriage annulled, be warned—you will lose all, not I."

"It is no game, *husband*." She made the word sound like a curse. "You do not trust me any more than I trust you. I thought only to get this question out in the open. Perhaps I spoke too quickly."

"Obviously." Then again, maybe she'd simply had far too much wine herself.

"I could have remained silent."

Gerard couldn't help but laugh at the truth in her statement. "And hoped I couldn't tell?"

Her brows rose. "Could you?"

Slapping one hand to his chest, Gerard staggered backward in mock horror. "You wound me. My pride is crushed."

"You make light of this? You make fun of *me*?"

His smirk faded. "No. The knowledge that my wife may or may not have lain with another man is not a joking matter. I find little humor in it." He swaggered back toward her. "But I promise you, I would know."

Catheryn turned away, unable to continue the conversation she had so rashly started and unwilling to move forward and discover the truth.

Gerard stopped her, placing his hands on her shoulders. "Catheryn, I know not what fancies flit about inside your head—"

"Fancies?" Ducking out from under his touch, she grabbed a cover from the floor and wrapped it about her shoulders. "I am not given to flights of fancy."

"If I could finish?"

"Oh, please do." She flapped a corner of the blanket at him. She suddenly wished he would do something to cover himself.

"What makes you think you *may* have bedded another man?"

"Were you not the one to find me the night you attacked Brezden?"

"Yes."

"Was I not senseless?" Catheryn watched as Gerard's

recollection brought understanding.

"So, you think this attack upon you included rape?"

She swallowed dryly. "I have reason to fear that may be so."

"And you feared I would hold that against you."

"You and…what will others say if there is no blood on the sheets in the morning?"

He came nearer. "Blood comes from many places."

"Wouldn't they know?" She was finding it extremely difficult to swallow.

"This marriage was forced upon us. I care little what others may think they know."

"But—"

He stopped her words by placing a finger over her lips. "If you were pregnant with another man's child right now and I was to say in the morn that I was well satisfied, no one—not William, the Church, nor the king—would question me."

The warmth from his skin against her mouth and chin did little to help her think. "I am not."

"Not what?"

"Not carrying another man's child." Her recent monthly flow attested to that.

He cupped her cheek and turned her face toward his. "That is good."

His breath whispered across her lips, and Catheryn leaned closer. She placed her hands against his chest for balance. "Gerar—?"

It wasn't his finger that silenced her this time, it was his kiss. His lips, so warm and gentle against her own, took away her words, her thoughts, and her breath. And when he pulled back, Catheryn rested her forehead against his shoulder.

"Who gave you this power over me?" she whispered.

"Surely I am bewitched. You touch me and I cannot think."

"This is not a night for thinking." Taking her in his arms, he slowly moved them toward the bed. "Tomorrow you may think all you like, but tonight, Catheryn, let this rest. Let everything rest."

"Let it rest? The words are easy to say, but I wonder what you will do if I am truly not your virgin bride?"

He stripped the blanket from her faster than she could blink, backed her onto the bed and loomed above her. "Listen to me, for I will say this only once. If in truth you were forced, it does not matter. *I will not forsake you.* You are mine, Catheryn, and nothing that happened before this moment means anything. Do you understand me?"

The force of his words and the seriousness of his gaze brought tears to her eyes, and she stroked his cheek. "You are an odd man, my husband."

"Perhaps." Rolling onto his side, he brought her with him. "But I am all you have been given."

An exaggerated sigh escaped her lips. "Then I suppose I will have to keep you."

He growled low and she laughed, but she stopped laughing when he brushed his thumb over one breast. Suddenly, he was the one to laugh.

"You were saying?"

Catheryn leaned forward. "*Nothing.*"

He swept his hand over her belly, across her thigh, behind her knee and back up. She closed her eyes as his ministrations continued. Were those arrows shooting through her veins tipped with ice or fire? She couldn't be certain. Maybe they were laced with both.

He nipped and kissed the sensitive skin along the side of her neck, and his lips kept the flames alive. His hands danced up to a waiting breast then finally down to tangle in the soft curls between her legs. Catheryn tipped her head back, moaning low, and offered her neck further to his attention.

Pulling her closer, he moaned deep inside his chest, and the sound vibrated against her breasts. Catheryn was swept along with his passion. Claiming her mouth with his, he kept his touch light, but that kiss left no room for any other thoughts. If she were to die this night, she would never forget the inferno of his body next to hers. Never forget the way his hard mouth softened to devour her. Never forget how she could be consumed by just one darkly seductive look.

She wanted to be enveloped by him. To breathe in the heady aromas of sandalwood and smoke that surrounded him. To feel his hands stroke fire into her blood. To taste the sweetened wine that had flowed over his lips and tongue. She wanted to look upon this beautiful warrior she had married and become lost in his returned gaze.

His hands were everywhere, quickly coaxing a response and igniting new fires each place he touched. His kiss demanded complete compliance, and she let her whole being melt to his desire.

Lights flickered behind her eyes as a calloused palm cupped a breast, lifting it to meet his descending mouth. Her legs parted as his searching hand found soft, moist warmth, and while his fingers deftly performed the dance his body would soon repeat, she felt like a tiny boat being buffeted by a stormy sea.

Gripping him tightly, Catheryn marveled at the undulating waves threatening to carry her away—and then through a murky fog, Raymond de Brye's evil face loomed before her. His hands clawed at her breasts, and she gagged on the smell of his fetid breath.

"You are mine. I will kill you before I will share you with another."

128

Catheryn froze. The warm, swelling waves crashed against a rocky coast. The fire turned to cold, fear-filled shards of ice. Fighting against de Brye, she yelled, "No! Monster, stop. He will know. Stop."

Pushing against his shoulders, she cried out with relief only when he released her. She quickly tried to escape him, but he restrained her and grasped her head between his hands.

"Catheryn, open your eyes."

Slowly she blinked away the fog and gasped in horror. "Oh, my God. Oh, Gerard, I am sorry."

Longing to wipe the look of anger and sadness from his face, she reached up to stroke his cheek. He knocked her hand away and rose. "Don't."

How could she have been so lost in terrors of her mind? How could she have let a nightmare intrude on what was such a beautiful time? Is this why de Brye had taunted her earlier? Had he been sly enough to know that terrible thoughts of him would intrude on her wedding night? "I am sorry. Forgive me, it will not happen again."

"Stop." He didn't turn around to look at her. Instead, he retrieved his clothes and hastily began to throw them on. "Don't grovel, Catheryn, it doesn't become you." He stepped into his boots. "And don't lie."

"I swear—"

Gerard came back to the bed and leaned over her. "Go to sleep."

She grasped for the right words to keep him here. "But this our wedding night."

He sighed as he pulled the covers up and over her. "Yes, it is. But I'll not share it with a third person."

"A third person?"

"Since you have called me a monster on more than one

occasion, I can only believe I am the monster you begged to stop. I have to wonder who the 'he' is that will know."

Catheryn gasped. Dear Lord, he had it backward. He thought she was pushing him away in fear of *de Brye's* discovery? "No, no, you don't understand."

"I understand enough."

"Gerard, please, I am—"

"Sorry? I know. So am I."

She knew that nothing she said right now would make him return to their bed. He was in no mood to listen and she didn't know how to force him to hear her words.

"Where will you sleep?"

Gerard shrugged. "Not here."

"What will William and the others say?"

"I care not."

"But we haven't, we didn't—"

"Consummate our marriage?"

Catheryn nodded.

Gerard's short bark of laughter rang bitter in the chill of the chamber. "And we won't." He laid his hand on her cheek and stroked his thumb over her lips. "Not until you crave me and my touch so badly that I am no longer a monster in your eyes, not until there is no room for anyone else in your mind or in your soul."

Chapter Ten

Catheryn snuggled closer to the warmth at her back.

She'd spent a long, cold, dark night cursing her fate, her life, and de Brye. Then she'd cursed her childish belief in dreams. She'd just fallen asleep, wrapped in as many covers as she could find when Gerard crawled into bed. She knew by the scent of sandalwood and spice that it was he, and she knew by the possessive yet ever-so-gentle caress that briefly stroked her hip. No one else could mimic his touch. No other hand would ever feel as welcome to her as his strong, calloused one did. No one but Gerard—

Gerard?

Instantly awake, she scooted away. "I think you must be lost, my Lord."

"Keep your voice down." He pulled her back to his chest and threw his arm over her waist. "William is on his way to bid us farewell."

"The sun has not yet risen. He cannot wait?"

The steady beating of Gerard's heart tapped against her back. His breath brushed warm across her ear, and he molded his long legs behind hers, coarse hairs tickling the back of her thighs. Squirming to escape the mild irritation, she realized they were both undressed. Her next realization chased all thoughts of William and the placement of the sun from her mind. She held her breath as the warm flesh nestled against her backside hardened and grew hot.

"Oh, my."

She quit moving about, the irritation against the back of her thighs forgotten. Her breath quickened along with the beating of her heart. She could feel Gerard's heart echo the same rhythm, and she could hear his breathing keep pace with her own.

He hooked one leg over hers and easily turned her onto her back. Dizzy with anticipation, she closed her eyes. She wanted him to touch her, to stroke her flesh. Longed for the feel of his hands on her skin. The taste of his lips on hers. The fire. The ice. She waited for the thrill of both to rush through her.

But he didn't move. His hand remained motionless on her stomach. He did not kiss her, nor did he move the leg still capturing hers.

Opening her eyes in confusion, Catheryn stared into Gerard's burning gaze. Anger? Desire? She wasn't certain. She whispered his name.

He slowly lowered his head. "I don't know where you go when your eyes are closed." His kiss was brief. "But I know I'm not there and I like it not."

Seeking to assure him that the incident of last night would never be repeated, and wanting to explain that he'd been so mistaken, she stroked his stubble-covered cheek. "Gerard, I—"

A loud, boisterous sound of men approaching their chamber stopped her words, and Gerard threaded his fingers through her hair. Quickly he whispered, "Now is the time for your lies and half-truths, Catheryn. Show William how pleased you are with your marriage."

He thought her such a well-practiced liar that she would easily be able to hide her confusion and worry while putting on a false show of happiness for the earl? Did he truly think so little of her? "Why you—"

He stopped her outrage with his lips. She pushed at his shoulders but could not budge him. His chest shook with laughter at her futile attempts to free herself, and the moist, insistent caress of his tongue sweeping over hers weakened her desire to fight. He slipped his leg firmly between hers. He pressed the hard length of his thigh against her soft mound, and Catheryn found the fire and ice she'd wanted only moments ago. Now, instead of pushing at his shoulders, she clasped him more tightly to her. The world began to slip away.

Gerard deepened their kiss, imitating the age-old dance she hoped they would soon repeat with their bodies. Releasing her head, he stroked the fiery ice into her flesh, into her blood. Her breathing quickly became ragged. Wherever his touch fell, she burned for more.

Tearing away from his kiss, she gasped, "Oh, Gerard, please." An unknown urgency filled her.

The chamber door banged against the wall, permitting William and four of his men entrance. "See, men? I told you they'd not killed each other."

At that moment Catheryn would have gladly murdered the Earl where he stood.

With a short laugh that sounded oddly unsteady, Gerard sat up, tucked the covers about her and turned to their unwelcome guests. "Why would any assume that, William?"

Motioning the others from the room, the Earl ignored Gerard and turned his attention to Catheryn. "How are you this fine morning, my Lady?"

She fought to still her jagged breath and racing heart.

"Morning?" She glanced briefly to the window opening. "I see no sun yet, Earl William. But I am fine this night."

"Gerard, your wife appears a bit grumpy before the light of day."

Her husband reached under the blankets and grasped Catheryn's fisted hand. His touch gave her a little reassurance. However, she still retained the urge to commit murder.

Answering William, Gerard said, "Aye. Seems you are right. Perhaps lack of sleep explains it, though." Catheryn unclenched her teeth. "What can we do for you, my Lord?"

Only a fractional lift of one eyebrow gave any indication that William took offense at her directness. "I came to bid you farewell and to see how married life settled on you, Lady Reveur."

Married life? Why didn't he just come right out and ask her how the bedding went? Grasping the covers, she began to sit up, but Gerard tightened his grasp on her hand. She took that as a silent warning and allowed her overwrought temper to settle.

"I find marriage…" She paused, searching for the right word. Gerard pressed his fingers into hers. "Fine. Simply fine, my Lord."

If William disbelieved her, he said nothing. Instead, he nodded and turned his attention to Gerard. "I apologize for leaving in such haste, but I've received word from York that requires my immediate attention."

Gerard released Catheryn's hand and rose from the bed. Pulling on his clothes, he asked, "When will you be ready to travel?"

"All is ready now. My departure awaits only my word. By the time the sun rises I hope to be well on my way."

Her husband's slight hesitation caught Catheryn by

surprise. She had no idea what bothered him, but she knew something did.

Gerard asked, "So you've been busy all night making plans?"

The look William directed toward her and then Gerard told Catheryn more than his words. "Yes. And I'm not the only one who's been occupied with…surprising tasks."

He knew. Catheryn felt her heart painfully skip many beats. Somehow the Earl knew that Gerard had not spent the night in his marriage bed.

Her husband, however, did not back down from William's pointed look. Instead, he shrugged. "Things normal to one person may not be considered so by another."

The Earl accepted this with a curt nod. Before quitting the chamber, he said, "I bid you farewell, Lady Catheryn, and I hope to see you again."

"Godspeed, William."

Gerard returned to the bed. "Go back to sleep, Catheryn."

Her pulse jumped when he leaned over to place a kiss on her forehead. "Will you come back here after William leaves?"

"No."

Her body cooled as quickly as if someone had thrown a bucket of ice water upon her. "Why not?"

He stood and stared down at her. "Nothing has changed."

He was wrong. His earlier reaction left little doubt in her mind that he desired her, that he wanted her. She felt she had overcome her previous fears and was ready for him to make himself her husband in all physical ways. Hadn't she demonstrated as much? Then why—?

An awful thought came to her. "This was all for William's

benefit."

"Partly, yes."

Humiliation, anger, and regret all raced to the fore. She couldn't tell which controlled her more. Fighting to master the emotions battling inside her soul, she clutched the covers tightly and sat up. "Why you… You are nothing but a…" Words escaped her.

"I am a what, Catheryn? A monster?"

Now was the time for her to soothe herself and tell him the truth. Instead, she found herself saying, "You are a jack-a-nape, Gerard."

"I beg your pardon?"

She wanted to scream, but she wasn't at all certain her anger was solely at him. A large part of it was at herself. Why, oh, why could she not control her emotions around him? They were supposed to have this conversation when they were both calm and well able to hear and understand the words being said. Not when she was so angry that she longed to shove him from the room and never look at his face again.

Unfortunately, she'd have to stand up and release the blanket. She did not feel up to being naked before him again. At least, not right this minute.

Catheryn took a deep breath and glared at him. "You, Lord Gerard, are a jack-a-nape. A fool. But you are *not* the monster from my fears."

Something flashed in his eyes. Relief? Understanding? Whatever the brief flicker had been he squelched it quickly, and asked, "Then who is?"

No. She was not having this discussion now. Catheryn knew herself well enough to know that she'd end up saying the wrong thing. Her tongue always got the best of her mind when she was emotional. Hadn't she already proven that these last couple days? How many times had she spoken only to then wish she'd kept her mouth closed?

She shook her head. "Nobody." When he turned away, she softly said, "You were supposed to have been my dream knight."

He turned back to face her. "I told you the day I arrived that I was no one's dream. I am a flesh-and-blood man, with a man's wants and desires. Something you should realize now instead of later."

"I don't disagree," she hissed. "You are no answer to any woman's dream."

His face drained of color. "Tell me, wife, where was the passion, the desire, we were to build this marriage upon? Are your promises always given so lightly?"

"I…" if she twisted the covers any tighter between her fingers, she would reduce the fabric to threads. "I am not the one who left the chamber last night."

"True. But I cried out against no one else in our bed and then refused to explain why."

She gave up trying to explain anything to him. "And I told you it would not happen again!"

"If you wish, I could open the door. Then the entire keep would be certain to hear you."

The keep? Now he cared about the inhabitants of the keep? Not even de Brye made her as angry as this. Fulfilling William's request would prove the easiest task she'd ever performed. Clenching her teeth, Catheryn ordered, "Get out."

He laughed but didn't move.

"Blast it all, you toad. Go away and leave me alone."

"I will."

"When? After you've tormented me a little more?"

When he did nothing but stand there and look at her, Catheryn sighed with resignation. Arguing with him would

137

prove her death one day. "It was all a waste of your time anyway."

"What was?"

"The show you put on for William. It was a waste. He knows."

Gerard raised an eyebrow. "Does he? How? I didn't tell him. You said nothing." He stepped away from the bed. "And your appearance when he entered the chamber should have told him otherwise."

"My appearance? What has that to do with anything? I am in bed, where any sane person would be at this time of day."

He shook his head. "I find your ignorance interesting, wife."

Catheryn longed to wipe that smug look from his face. "What are you talking about?"

"I am talking about the look of a woman in the throes of passion." He continued as he headed toward the door. "Lips swollen from kisses. Eyes glazed with longing. Fast and ragged breathing… It was obvious, Catheryn."

"Ah, I succumbed to your experienced touch so well, did I not?" Vexed beyond rational thought, Catheryn cursed. Rage coursed hotly through her veins and a loud, heavy pounding drummed in her ears.

"Yes, you did." His tone softened a bit.

"But not you, eh, Gerard? You felt nothing. Just doing your duty, husband? Covering up our lack of marriage."

Pausing, his hand on the door latch, he turned. A brief smile crossed his mouth, and she saw the gleam in his eye and wished she knew how to read the emotion that lurked there. Humor? Desire? It didn't matter, for at this moment she hated him.

He sighed. "You are not stupid, Catheryn. It is a little hard for me to disguise my desires."

"Then why humiliate me so?"

"I said I only did it *partly* for William's benefit."

"Partly? And the other part?"

The gleam in his eye brightened. "When I told you last night that I would not take you until I knew that I alone filled your mind, body, and soul, how did you think I was going to know when the moment arrived?"

She was taken aback. He was making no sense. "I gave it no thought."

He opened the door, shaking his head. "And how did you think I planned to ensconce myself, my kisses, and my touch, in your mind and soul?"

"Why would you go to so much trouble?"

"Perhaps, Catheryn, you should give both questions some serious consideration."

Speechless, she stared at the empty spot he had just vacated. Falling back down onto the bed, she wondered if he planned to torment her until she died.

ଓଃ

Torment her he did, just as she tormented herself. For a week—seven long days—Gerard invaded her thoughts. At night Catheryn lay alone in his bed and remembered the feel of his hands on her body. Her heart pounded with the memory. Her heart raced. Thinking of anything except his touch proved impossible. Everything—his lingering scent, the feel of the sheets against her skin, a soft breeze that gently lifted her hair—reminded her of their brief and interrupted time together.

If the nights were unbearable, the days were no better. A flash of his smile quickened her pulse. A brief encounter in a dark alcove brought his lips down to cover hers. At meals his fingers would brush against hers and linger when he handed her a goblet.

He'd warned her. Gerard had told her that he intended to invade her mind and soul. She'd just had little idea how effective his methods would be. How much longer did he intend to continue this attack on her senses? She was weak, powerless to stop his assault.

Catheryn swallowed a bitter laugh. Weak? Powerless? That said too little. He was like a potent herb that beckoned her near only to mock her when she answered its call. There was no escaping him. She'd toss and turn until the wee hours of the morning only to fall into a restless sleep filled with dreams. She'd awaken in the morning as tired as she'd been the night before.

Yet this morning something was different. Screams of women and shouts of men tore her from her slumber, and a thick, noxious smoke swirled into the chamber.

Grabbing her gown from the floor, Catheryn threw it over her head and raced to the window. The sight that met her worried gaze caused her knees to go weak and her stomach to roll. Angry red and orange tongues of fire engulfed the stable in the outer bailey. Men, women, and children had formed a line and moved buckets of water from a well to the fire.

"Catheryn. Lady Catheryn!"

Agnes's urgent cry spurred her into action. Running past her frantic maid, she raced down the stairs, out of the keep, and to the bailey. Hot embers and ashes pelted her. The smoke choked her, thick and cloying, stinging her eyes, nose, and throat. But the discomfort of her body was nothing compared with her fear.

Where was Gerard? She quickly scanned the line of bucket-carriers even though somehow, she knew he'd not be amongst those fighting the fire from this distance. No. He'd be closer. She darted toward the fire, fighting her way through the mad rush of men leading frightened, rearing horses to safety.

Someone grabbed her arm. "Lady, no. Stay here."

It took a few heartbeats to realize the ash-blackened man holding her was Walter, Gerard's captain. Shaking off his grasp, Catheryn ducked away. Her heart pounded against the inside of her ribcage. She'd cursed her husband's very existence a short while ago and now… "God, forgive me. I meant him no harm."

Wicked tongues of fire sought freedom from the confines of the stable. Shooting through the roof and window openings, they reached toward the sky—and toward nearby buildings. Buildings Gerard and the men had just recently rebuilt.

A crash of timbers gave the flames more height, more heat. Shielding her face, Catheryn shrank away from the living inferno. Men ran from inside. Coughing and stumbling blindly, they escaped to the safety of the bailey, but one unlucky soul exited to the sound of his own screams as fire engulfed both his head and back. His frantic motions fed the flames, giving them free rein to consume him.

Catheryn lunged forward, knocking him to the ground. At the same time, buckets of water drenched them both. She rose sputtering, but the unrecognizable body lying in the mud didn't rise. She'd acted too late. The man was gone.

Unable to stand the not knowing any longer, Catheryn screamed over the din of shouting voices, "Gerard!" She snagged the first man she turned to. "Where is he? Where is Baron Reveur?"

The man motioned toward the stable, confirming her worst fears. While the sight and smell of burnt flesh had not revolted her stomach, the thought of Gerard being inside that hell on earth brought bile to her throat. Sweat, more from fear than heat, trickled down her back and stung her eyes. Her heart raced so hard and fast she thought it would burst.

She stared at the building before her. Even though it was almost entirely engulfed, she could spot the door. Her mind shut out all other thoughts but one—she needed to get her brave but stupid husband out of that stable. Now. Whatever was left inside needed no rescuing, it could not be alive. She just hoped her husband was.

Taking a deep breath, Catheryn grasped her gown and held the hem to her face.

"No!" Walter left her no escape this time. He captured her in a bear hug that no struggle could break. She kicked at him. Twisted in his hold. Pounded her head against his chest. All to no avail.

The tears she'd been holding back since she'd seen the smoke from her chamber burst through. "Let me go to him. He needs—"

Looking up, she swallowed her words. The tears falling from her eyes were mirrored in the captain's. The world spun around her. A loud, insistent buzz throbbed in her ears. The yells and actions of those still battling the fire disappeared in a haze of pain. Her legs buckled. Had it not been for the strong arms holding her, she'd have fallen to the ground.

"Oh, God. Oh, God, no," she railed against the obvious. Then silently she begged, "Oh, please. Tell me You did not send me a dream simply so I could watch him die. You sent him to me, did You not?"

A touch, light and insubstantial, filled with promise wrapped around her heart. That slim thread of hope was all she needed. Catching Walter off guard, Catheryn broke free from his hold and rushed to the side of the stable.

Smoke poured from the doorway, and the fierce flames there were still growing, seeking to match the rest in size and strength.

But then a huge form, covered in dripping wet horse blankets, cursed and stumbled free from the building.

The odd-shaped form was Gerard and his warhorse. Catheryn grabbed one corner of the sodden mess while a shocked Walter tugged on another. The destrier's wide eyes rolled with obvious fear, but as long as Gerard kept his hand wrapped in the animal's thick mane it offered no one harm.

"Gerard." His name rushed from her lips in a breathless whisper. She quickly ran her eyes the length of him, looking for signs of injury, then shaking with relief she offered a prayer of thanks. She knew that throwing herself at him looked foolish, but she cared little.

He ran one filthy hand through her hair and clasped her to his chest briefly before pulling her away. "There is no time." She cringed at the sound of his voice, hoarse and raspy from the smoke. It had to pain him to speak.

Turning around, he pulled something from the horse's back and gently handed it to Walter. She'd been so intent on Gerard's safety that she'd paid little attention to anything else, but Catheryn gasped when the cover fell away to reveal sparse locks of thin, gray hair and a limp body.

"Ephraim!" Horrified, she barely caught the saddlebag Gerard tossed her before it hit the ground.

"Go," he ordered her and Walter.

Catheryn tugged at his arm. "Come with us. Let me—"

He pulled free and shook his head. "No. Go."

As much as she wanted to argue, she knew that now was not the time. He had little voice left and still had orders to give. And she had a trusted servant to attend. Still, before leaving Catheryn gave orders of her own. "Gerard. Be careful. If you come to harm, I...I will *kill* you."

His smile cut a line of white that flashed across his blackened face, but he just pointed toward the departing Walter.

Catheryn tossed the saddlebag over her shoulder and gave chase. A mewling whimper escaped the leather, and she found herself exclaiming, "What the devil?" Pulling the bag off her shoulder, she opened the flap. A small, dirty kitten hissed at her from the bottom of the bag.

Closing the flap, she shook her head. "Shh, hush, little one." Who but her husband would think to rescue something as small and useless as a kitten?

Entering the keep, she handed the bag to Agnes. "Clean this up a little, give it something to eat and put it in my chamber." She held back a laugh when Agnes opened the bag and peered inside. "Gerard rescued it from the stable."

"My Lady."

Agnes and the kitten were forgotten at the sound of Walter's voice. Approaching the captain where he stood beside a swiftly set up cot, Catheryn asked, "How is he?"

Walter cleared his throat and shook his head. She glanced down at Mistress Margaret, who was kneeling by Ephraim. The woman rose and, before moving on to the next person needing her care, paused to whisper, "I am sorry, my lady."

Catheryn knew without having to ask that Ephraim was neither strong enough, young enough, nor healthy enough to recover from the smoke he'd inhaled or the heat that surely had seared his throat and lungs.

She owed him much. This man had no business trying to fight a fire, but when had he ever shirked any task? Never. Catheryn dropped to her knees beside the cot. Memories of a strong, capable warrior filled her mind. Also, old as he was, Ephraim was her last connection to her father. And now...

Brushing some of the soot and ashes from his face, she fought the tears clogging her throat. Nothing would lessen the pain twisting in her chest, but she vowed not to let him see the fear on her face.

He turned his head toward her light touch and opened his eyes. "Lady Catheryn."

Her name, spoken in such a hoarse, ragged voice, nearly broke her heart. "Is there anything you want?" she asked, forcing a smile to her lips. "Anything I can get for you?"

He shook his head. The little effort brought spasms of coughing to his slight frame.

Walter handed her a cup of water and helped her lift Ephraim to a half-sitting position. The man took but a swallow or two then turned away from the remainder. He tried to speak after they lay him back down and saw to his comfort as best they could.

"My lady, I saw..." He closed his eyes tight and swallowed slowly.

Pushing a lock of hair from his face, Catheryn sought to bring him some sense of peace. "Hush, Ephraim. It matters not what you saw."

He weakly grasped her hand. "I *must.*"

Leaning closer, she lifted his hand to her lips and kissed his crooked, age-bent fingers. "I am listening." She despised the quaver in her voice but knew not how to stop it.

"Save Brezden."

Her lips trembled with her smile. "I will."

"I saw him. *Him.*"

"Who? Who did you see, Ephraim?"

"The fire..." The old man's eyes widened. She heard strangled sounds coming from his throat and knew his time was close at hand, but still, he struggled to convey his message. "The fire..." He clutched at her hand and closed

145

his eyes.

Catheryn felt tears run down her cheeks. She brushed away the droplets that slipped onto his face. Then Ephraim's pale eyes opened and met hers.

"De Brye."

His words were barely above a whisper, but she heard. And they brought a sickening chill to her veins. "Ephraim, that is not possible."

Of course, it was. While she still constantly worried about the children, she'd put de Brye out of her mind as best she could, but he clearly hadn't put her out of his.

Ephraim didn't respond. His grip went slack. She laid one hand on his chest and leaned over to place her ear against his mouth, but he breathed no longer. Her father's last trusted knight was gone.

And there was worse. De Brye had started this fire. Why? He was after her, not the peasants of Brezden. Though he had never before hesitated from harming the innocent, this showed a change in plan that was terrifying. Guilt piled in on top of all the other sins weighing heavy on her heart and soul. If she'd just done as Pike and de Brye commanded, none of this would have happened. Brezden would not have been attacked. Gerard would not have been forced to take a wife he did not want. This stable would not have burned. Ephraim would be yet alive.

She had to get away. There had to be a way to escape this assault on her heart and mind. There had to be a way to make everything right again.

Releasing Ephraim's cold hand, she stood and turned to find herself meeting her husband's icy stare.

"Gerard, I—"

His jaw tightened. His tortured gaze matched her own suffering, and Catheryn knew that he'd heard Ephraim's final words.

Her husband pointed to one of his men. "You. Take your lady and lock her in a cell. Do not let anyone in, or her out." When the soldier hesitated, Gerard shouted, "Now!"

Shock nearly swept the floor from beneath her feet. Staggering toward him, Catheryn cried out, "Why? Why are you doing this?"

Defeated and humiliated, she beat on his chest before the guard could reach her. "Damn you, answer me, Gerard!"

He closed his hands over her arms and pulled her to him. Then in a strange, confusing nightmare, she felt him quickly pass his lips across her forehead before he handed her over to the guard.

"Gerard!"

He closed his eyes for a moment, and Catheryn nearly fainted when he reopened them. Any previous evidence of pain or remorse had been replaced by the blankest and coldest look she'd ever seen.

Motioning for Walter, her husband turned and left the hall.

Chapter Eleven

The shame of it threatened to eat him alive.

Why did doing the right thing, the thing that had to be done to protect Brezden and its foolhardy lady, suddenly seem so wrong? Ignoring the guilt twisting in his gut, Gerard stared down at Catheryn. Sunlight poured through the cell's narrow window, casting a hazy glow about the sleeping woman. She looked like an angel. He knew better. For two days he'd avoided her.

Her tangled, unkempt hair flowed across her pillow and pooled on the floor. Drawn to the silken waves, he knelt beside her and lifted the curtain of hair back onto the mattress. He permitted his hand to linger, to caress the wild curls twined about his wrist and fingers. Unable to resist the urge to touch more, Gerard stroked the back of his hand across her cheek.

Her skin was soft, pliant, and warm. He brushed the pad of his thumb over her lower lip, which was relaxed in sleep. The swelling from their wedding day was gone. The only reminder of de Brye existed only now in his mind.

Catheryn opened her eyes. In the fog between sleeping and waking, she smiled at him, a soft, sensual smile that stole his breath away.

He knew the instant the fog cleared. Her smile flattened. Creases marred the smooth skin of her forehead as she frowned. Jerking away from his touch, she asked, "What do you want?"

Peace. A quiet life. A home. A family. The same things he had always wanted. Things Pike and de Brye had stolen from him. And his wife seemed set on helping that villain.

Instead of voicing his thoughts, Gerard brutally pushed them back and rose to his feet. "Ephraim's burial service is today."

"Will I be permitted to attend?"

"With me, yes."

She sat up and glared at him. "Should I feel honored?"

"Catheryn, I did not come here to argue with you. Either you attend or you do not. It is up to you."

"Of course, you didn't come to argue. Arguing is not in your nature. Not when it is easier to accuse and then walk away as you have more than once."

When she held her head at that defiant tilt and her eyes flashed with fire, she was quite charming, which was one reason he enjoyed goading her so. But Gerard gained little enjoyment from the current situation. She was referring to their wedding night and the next morning. Perhaps he should have found a way to force her into explaining her outcry when he'd first tried to make love to her, but he hadn't and now the time for demanding explanations was past. "Are you coming?"

She ran a hand over her hair and then held out her arms. "I can't go like this."

He reached out a hand to assist her to her feet. "A bath awaits you in our chamber."

"Our chamber?" Ignoring his offer of help, Catheryn stood and brushed her ruined gown into place. "You mean

149

your chamber." She waved toward the mattress. "I believe this is my room."

"Only when necessary."

"What does that mean?"

He'd hoped to avoid this conversation until later, but since it now loomed before them, he answered, "As long as you remain at my side, you can leave this cell."

"At your side?"

"I believe that's what I said."

"Like a trained hawk tethered to your wrist. Like a slave in chains who—"

"I never said that."

"Then explain yourself to me."

"It is simple, Catheryn. A good commander keeps the enemy within sight at all times."

She backed up a step. Placing a hand on her chest, she asked, "I am the enemy?" She then pointed at him. "And you are the good commander?" Before he could respond, she waved one hand in the air, closed her eyes and took a deep breath. "Let me see if I have this correct. I am so dangerous that you keep me locked up and under guard."

He sighed. "Men have died because of your lack of action."

Her head snapped back like someone had struck her, and she glared at him as if he sprouted a second head. "You cannot blame me for that fire. I would never bring harm to anyone at Brezden!"

"No? Your archer was murdered. Two more men perished in that fire. All three died because you saw fit to protect a murdering traitor. A man you still protect!" Gerard cleared the distance between them. He stood so close that he was certain she could hear the blood rushing through his veins.

Lifting her chin, she stared up without flinching. "More will die if I talk."

"Then through your association, you are also considered a murdering traitor."

Tears welled in her eyes, but they did not fall. "That is not true."

"Is it not? Good. Then it will not bother you to attend the funeral of your victims."

"You bastard."

He laughed, though he felt no mirth. "That is all you can come up with? For the last two nights, you used curses I never heard even on a field of battle. Now all you can do is defame my mother?"

Her eyes widened with surprise. "What do you mean? What did you hear?"

"Who do you think guards your cell at night? Who do you think sits outside this cell listening to your ranting and raving? My men? I would not subject them to that."

"You? You sat out there and never bothered to answer me?"

"Answer your curses? To what end? I will not argue with you anymore. It serves no purpose."

"Dear God," she breathed. The tears that she had been holding in check now fell. "Forgive me, but I hate you."

"Good," Gerard whispered, hoarsely. He reached out and grabbed her arm as she turned away, pulling her against his chest. "That just makes everything easier."

He was surprised at both how strongly her cries tore at his heart and how hard it was not to tell her that he lied, but until he had the information he so desperately needed, she'd not know that he kept her in this cell for her own safety. He could not guard her every moment of every day, and he knew not whom in Brezden he could trust. A locked cell seemed the only answer. De Brye thought little of killing innocent people. Gerard wasn't about to risk her life, no matter how angry it made her.

"Come. You need to clean up."

Catheryn shook her head and tried unsuccessfully to pull away. "Leave me alone. I do not want to go."

"You sound like a spoiled child. Have you not yet learned that we don't always get to do what we want?"

"I did not kill Ephraim!"

Her broken words caught on a sob, and the ragged sound sliced through his will, admonishing him to soothe her fears. Gathering her close, Gerard buried his face in her hair, and whispered, "I know you did not. Catheryn, can you not understand? If I cannot be at your side, I must be certain you are safe."

Realizing he'd said too much, he released her abruptly and ignored her questioning glance. Turning her toward the door, he growled, "Your bathwater is getting cold."

⚬

Catheryn stood in the middle of the chamber. Gerard's admission had surprised her. His declaration overwhelmed her anger, pushing the pain and hurt into the shadows. But while she was eager to question his motives, she was not willing to tax her emotions any further this moment.

Turning her attention to her bath, she gasped softly. When Gerard said a bath awaited her, she'd expected something simple. Not—this.

Instead of the small, round wooden tub she normally used, someone had brought up a large oval one. She'd heard of them but had never seen such a thing. What would it feel like to soak comfortably in a hot bath without having her knees drawn up to her chin? Without having to sit on an uncomfortable stool? Oversized drying cloths hung by a blazing fire. Even if the water in the bath grew cold, those cloths would be warm.

She had little fear the water would be cold. Steam curled up from the tub. The mist carried a heavenly scent, rich with an unfamiliar spicy and exotic aroma. Alongside the tub was a table set with an array of combs, a thick bar of soap and a small bejeweled decanter.

Unable to ignore the beckoning warmth and heady scent any longer, Catheryn crossed the room to dip her hand into the water. A sigh escaped her before she could swallow it, so to cover her display of pleasure, she asked, "From where did all this come? It is not mine."

No answer met her question. Turning around, she stared at Gerard. The deepest shade of red colored his face.

Embarrassed? Gerard?

He looked everywhere but at her. "It is yours. A cache of supplies arrived from my mother."

"Your…mother?" It was hard to imagine.

"Yes. My mother. The woman you so recently cursed."

Ashamed of herself, Catheryn ignored that remark and ran her fingers over the combs before picking up the decanter. She pried free the cork stopper and lifted the bottle to her nose. Its contents where what scented the water in the tub.

"Your mother has wonderful taste."

Afraid she'd drop what had to be expensive perfume, she carefully set the bottle back on the table. "I could understand her sending food, clothing, or household goods. But Gerard, a tub?"

"It is one of the simple pleasures she most enjoys."

"How odd."

"Yes, well, she does have odd notions at times."

Casting her attention back to him, Catheryn wondered

153

what he was so embarrassed about. Again, a dull flush had crept up his neck and covered his face, before he motioned toward the cooling bath. "They are awaiting our arrival, Catheryn."

She glanced around the room. "Where is Agnes?"

"Your maid has been retired from duty for a time. I will have to suffice."

"What?" She was not taking a bath with him standing there.

"You heard me. Now get into the tub."

Her heart tripped inside her chest. Her throat constricted, making breathing difficult. "By what right do you dismiss my maid?"

He crossed his arms. "By right of lordship."

She noticed the bulge in his arms as he flexed his muscles and wondered if she'd lost her ability to reason. Was it wise to argue with someone who could snap you in two? What if William had been wrong in his assumption? What if Gerard had lied too? What if someday he lost the temper he so rigidly held in check? She pulled at her bottom lip with her teeth. Where Pike and de Brye had always been cruel, neither man was as powerful as her husband. With little effort, he could—

"Stop."

She tore her attention from his chest and arms to warily look at his frowning countenance.

"Your emotions run plainly across your face." He approached her, and deftly untied the laces on her gown before she realized what he was doing. "You have given me more than enough reason to beat you, were I to believe in such treatment. I do not."

She tried to move away, but he snatched the skirt of her gown, effectively thwarting her escape.

"From the first day I found you in your chamber, I had every right to do with you as I saw fit. You are headstrong and possess a tongue that would make an asp kneel with admiration. But for all your bravado, you are still smaller and weaker than I." He lifted one hand before her face and spread his fingers wide. "I could crush you with one grip." He curled his hand into a fist. "Or kill you with one stroke."

Gasping, she leaned her head away. From another man, his words might sound like a threat, or outrageous bragging. Gerard spoke only the truth.

He uncurled his fingers and gently cupped her cheek. "Ah, Catheryn, did I not say I would never act in such a vile manner?" He shook his head and half-smiled. "Who would torment my days if I was ever so foolish?"

She forced breath into her air-starved lungs and willed her legs not to fold beneath her, but she could not will herself to speak.

"You should know by now that I will not raise my hand against you in anger."

She believed him. The palm resting so warmly against her cheek spoke not of a harsh, cruel man, the demon she feared lay deeper. She could grow to love this man she professed to hate. It was not his hands nor his fists that brought her fear. Once she allowed him into her heart, into her soul, he would not have to use any physical force to bring her harm. It would take no more than a word or an absentminded gesture, for then her defenses would be down. That, she feared, would be more deadly than any horror caused by Pike or de Brye.

"I swear, Catheryn, I will never harm you," Gerard repeated.

He did not speak of the pain she feared, yet his oath meant much. She looked up, and he appeared so serious, so intent on making her believe his words, that she couldn't ignore him any longer.

"I know you will not strike me." She rested a hand against his chest. "But, Gerard, sometimes words have more power than a fist."

He nodded in agreement. "Yes. But we might already have a place where even words hold no power."

She was confused. "Where might that be?"

He glanced about. "Does this room hold any entrances other than that?" He pointed to the main door.

"None that I am aware of."

"Then why not declare this a room of truce?"

"Your chamber?"

He rested his forehead against hers. "Our chamber."

She was still confused. "How can words have no power in here?"

"If we do not fight, if we do not argue, if we do not bring spite into this room, then the words we speak here will have no power. At least, no power that will cause the other pain."

As strange as the idea sounded, it held interest for her. "Always leave our ire at the door? Sometimes it will be hard."

He brushed his lips across hers. "Do you hate me?"

She hesitated a moment, then decided to be truthful. "Sometimes I think I do."

Threading his fingers through her hair, he tilted her head and slanted his lips over hers. It was a glorious kiss, one that reminded her of all the happiness that had come before. Happiness that had never yet failed to be ruined. And yet, she could not think of that.

About the time she thought her knees would buckle, he lifted his head. "What about now? Do you hate me now?"

"Oh, heavens, how do I know?" Breathless, she grasped the front of his tunic for support. "I cannot think."

Sweeping her into his arms, he laughed. "That, my dear wife, is how we will leave the ire at the door."

She found herself laughing. "Perhaps I will need to anger you daily."

He was laughing too. "I am certain it will not require much effort."

This strange, yet marvelous, idea of his might indeed be a flash of brilliance. Then again, would it would be wise to agree to something that would, with an absolute certainty, chip away at her resolve not to care too much for him?

"Catheryn?"

Startled, she focused on her husband as he lowered his hand to her gown. "Yes?"

"Is this worth saving?"

"Not unless you can perform miracles." The gown was torn, stained with soot from the fire of a few days past, and beyond repair.

A smile lifted his lips, a glow of mischief lit his eyes, and before she realized what he suddenly found so amusing, Gerard grasped the hem of her gown with both hands and tore the fabric up past her breasts.

She spun away. "What are you doing?"

Taking up the slack of the gown, hand over hand he pulled her back to him. "Something I've always longed for."

She tried not to laugh at the devilish look on his face and slapped at his hands. "What might that be?"

"Strip a gown off a woman's back." He yanked the fabric between his hands and succeeded in tearing it all the way through the neckline. Running a finger around the top edge of her undergown, he looked at her and lifted one eyebrow in silent question.

She cocked her head. "If you destroy that, you will have to replace it."

"I will replace it with two."

Catheryn closed her eyes and tried to ignore the sound of more fabric tearing. The cool air rushed against her heated flesh, causing her nipples to pucker and a shiver to run the length of her body, but Gerard chased away the cold with his hands and body. Slipping his fingers under the shoulders of both ruined gowns, he slid them halfway down her arms. His mouth was warm against her neck. Embers of fire trailed along her shoulder and back up to the sensitive flesh below her ear.

"Open your eyes, Catheryn. Know it's me."

Lord, how could she think it was anyone else? Still, she did as he asked. Through eyes glazed with desire, she looked at him.

Here stood the man who'd tormented her day and night. He'd seated himself so firmly in her mind that she could think of no one but him. Here stood the man she wished she could hate. He wore such an expression of want that, at this moment, she'd gladly give him all he desired. Here stood the man who'd had her locked in a cell because of de Brye's cruel act. His touch was so tender, she longed for nothing more than to feel his hands upon her flesh. Here stood the man who'd attacked her keep. His kisses easily made her forget the destruction he'd wrought.

She'd needed him. She had called him here, and without realizing it he had answered her call. But he wanted answers to questions that would bring nothing but death to Brezden and Brezden's people. If she were to be a good lady, what was she to do?

She bit her lip to keep from crying. She hated him. She wanted him. She needed his help. She could not help him. If this was how it felt to go mad, she would rather die.

He brushed the tears from her cheek and drew her face

against his chest. "Oh, Catheryn, what am I to do with you? Your body claims that you desire me as much as I do you. Your eyes tell me something different."

Slipping her tattered dress off her arms, he tossed it to the floor. She wrapped her arms around him and held him close. The well-worn cloth of his tunic rested softly against her face, but no words came to her lips.

"At this moment I would like nothing more than to shake all of your fears and doubts from your mind." He stroked her back then rested his hands on her shoulders. "Such a tactic would be useless, however. You would hold your tongue until I'd shaken all the teeth from your head, and then you'd look silly, and I'd not know what to feed you!"

He purposely sought to chase away her concerns with nonsensical words, and she tried desperately to hold in her laughter. But one giggle escaped. "Gerard, you have lost your mind."

"I know." He brushed his lips over hers. "Since the moment I saw you, I have been a senseless dolt."

She did not want him to go, but he slowly moved away from the circle of her arms and glanced toward the tub. "I would imagine they are growing anxious for our arrival. I will leave you to your bath."

"Stay." As much as she longed to sink into the scented water, she did not want this moment to slip away.

The flush that had covered his face earlier returned. "You do know why that tub is so big?"

"Because your mother liked to soak her entire body in comfort?"

"No." Gerard's hoarse laugh rang out. "She enjoyed sharing it with my father."

Catheryn's breath caught in her throat. The bath did appear big enough to hold two people, and the subsequent visions springing to her mind caused her cheeks to heat. Visions that did not appear as distasteful as one might imagine.

Keeping her focus on Gerard, she narrowed her eyes and walked backward toward the tub. "This will fit two people?"

He backed toward the door. "Yes. Easily."

"When was the last time you had a bath?"

Gerard did not answer, just closed the distance between them in a few, quick, long strides. Lifting her in his arms, he hungrily claimed her lips in a kiss that sent the world spinning away. She clung to his shoulders, frustrated that his tunic separated her skin from his, and when he moved his lips to her breast, she sank her fingers into his hair, seeking to hold him closer.

He slipped one arm beneath her knees and cradled her close for a heartbeat before lowering her into the bath. The now-lukewarm water served to snap her haze of desire.

"Gerard!"

He placed one last slow kiss on her lips. "We have not the time, but do not for a moment think I will forget the invitation, Catheryn." Reaching for the soap, he tossed it to her. "I would like nothing better than to wash every speck of your body." He breathed an exaggerated sigh. "In fact, I might enjoy the task more than you."

Just the thought of his soapy hands running over her caused the cool water to be forgotten, but he rose and headed toward the door. Flashing her a quick smile, he laughed. "Pull your mind away from those thoughts, my Lady, and finish your bath."

CR

Gerard closed the door to the chamber and stopped. What had just happened? He wasn't certain, but he did know that his conversation with Catheryn had not worked out as

160

planned. He looked back at the chamber door. Had he told her that until de Brye was captured or killed she'd have no freedom? Searching his mind, he only remembered hinting at it. Now that he thought about it, there were many things he'd not said.

He turned back to the door then paused. The simple thought of her in the bath fired his blood with lust. *No.* The things he'd not spoken could wait, at least until he was better able to control his feeble mind.

What happened to him when he was in her presence? Instead of focusing on the safety of Brezden and those who depended on the keep's well-being, he found his attention drifting to her mouth. Or her eyes. Or the way her breasts rose and fell with each breath.

He was supposed to be angry with her. He *had* been…for about a dozen heartbeats. He was supposed to have laid down the law. His law. Her tears had reduced that intention to rubble.

If he wasn't more careful, if he didn't maintain a tighter grip on his wandering thoughts, he would lose this keep. If he could not find his usual sense of control, it would be an easy thing for de Brye to destroy all, including both Gerard and the woman who was driving him mad.

Motioning to the guards waiting further down the corridor, Gerard ordered, "If anyone tries to enter this chamber, I expect your shouts to be heard in the bailey. No one enters or leaves without me at their side. Understood? No one."

Chapter Twelve

Catheryn stared down at her father's grave. Would she ever be able to visit the site without experiencing the twist of heartache?

Five days ago, at Ephraim's burial service, she'd been surprised by the swelling of her heart. Emotions—grief, loneliness, anger over her parents' deaths—had rushed to the fore with all the intensity of a raging river. She'd wanted to visit her mother and father's graves that day, but Gerard had insisted they wait. Ephraim's daughter had invited those from the village to join her at the cottage she shared with her father, and he wished to be among those making the additional final farewell.

At first, the people at the cottage had been shocked by the appearance of the Lord and Lady of Brezden, but Gerard's easy way with the men vanquished their edginess. Catheryn was glad they attended. She hadn't had much contact with many of those outside the keep for years and was grateful for the chance to renew old acquaintances. But it had taken another five days before Gerard brought her back to her parents' grave sites. True, he'd been busy rebuilding the stables, but she could have come alone.

She swallowed a laugh. Alone? She'd not been alone in

five days now. If she wasn't at Gerard's side, she had Walter as a shadow.

Of course, being watched by either man was better than sitting in a cell.

She'd finally had to shame her husband into bringing her to the cemetery. Now, his dark looks made it clear that he'd not liked her tactics one bit. Would she ever understand Gerard's moods? Maybe in a dozen lifetimes.

A beam of sunlight danced off the etched metal adorning the cross marking her father's grave, but dead vines and weeds from the last two years of growth twined about the cross and covered the ground. She'd not been permitted to care for this small, sacred plot of ground, Pike had forbidden it. The jagged scar on her arm burned with the memory. Any who saw the ill-healed wound would assume it had been obtained from a childhood accident, they would not think the bite of a lash had caused the disfigurement. She'd only sought to protect her mother, who in turn had been seeking to protect her headstrong daughter. Neither had come away unscathed.

Catheryn's gaze wandered to another cross just outside the wooden fence protecting the consecrated graves from rooting animals. "Oh, mother, what am I to do?"

No answer was forthcoming. None had been expected.

"Do about what, Catheryn?"

Having forgotten her unwanted company, she gave Gerard a cursory glance before centering her attention on the mountaintops far beyond Brezden. "Nothing, my Lord."

How she longed to be a bird—a falcon, with the ability to spread her wings and soar into the clouds hanging low over those distant peaks. The freedom to come and go at will. The power and the right to live a life without constraints. She tried to shake off the strange longings coursing through her, but they only grew stronger. Of course, the responsibilities and limitations of her life remained like a thick, heavy mantle about her shoulders. She was a woman. When had she ever been free? Had the decisions to come and go, to stay or leave, even to eat or to sleep, ever been hers to make?

Gerard stepped into her line of vision. No, never. She would never be permitted such freedom. And suddenly the coming days stretched out long before her. Each day would blend into the next, and before she knew it, she would be lying in the cold dirt like her parents. She would die never having known freedom. Never having tasted true love. They would cover her with the earth, and all would be lost. But what could she do? Nothing.

Catheryn closed her eyes against the useless moisture building behind her eyelids. Her breath caught in her chest, and she fought to swallow beyond the pain thickening in her throat.

Suddenly Gerard gripped her shoulders. Unshed tears blurred her vision and cast a misty glow around him. "Catheryn. Talk to me." Gesturing toward the graves, he tilted his head. "Tell me of your parents. Talk to me."

Confusion swirled through her mind. "Why would you wish to know of the dead?"

He shrugged. "I ask nothing more than for you to tell me of yourself and your family."

Catheryn was incensed. This was not important to him, so why did he insist upon knowing? "There is not a great deal to tell."

"Were your parents kind to you?"

"Yes."

"You had no brothers or sisters?"

"Two sisters."

164

"Where are they?"

"France, with distant relatives."

"How long have they been there?"

"A few years now."

"You learned to read and write?"

"Yes."

"Mathematics? Religion?"

"Yes."

Making himself comfortable on the grass, Gerard pulled her down beside him. "One-word answers are not *talking*."

To quell her sudden nervousness, she pulled out some of the weeds covering her father's grave. "I find it odd that now you wish to talk about meaningless things."

"You are my wife. Is it not natural for me to be curious?"

"I would not know, my Lord."

"Gerard."

She looked at him blankly.

"My name is Gerard."

"Oh." What was this man seeking? He appeared serious. No trace of amusement, not even a smile, crossed his face. "I would not know what is or is not natural for a husband or wife, Gerard."

He plucked a weed from her hair. "What was it like growing up at Brezden?"

"The same as it was anywhere, I imagine." Her childhood seemed so far away. It was hard to remember, harder still to find words. She pulled another vine from the ground and tossed it aside. "People here used to laugh. Even after a hard day of work, there were things to talk and smile about. It was a happy place."

Gerard glanced toward the keep. "And someday it will be again."

"I find that hard to imagine." She shook her head. "No.

The comfort was beaten out of Brezden a long time ago. It would take a miracle to bring it back."

"Not so much as a miracle, Catheryn. Trust would bring happiness back to these people."

For a reason she could not name, his assumption grated on her. "You presume much for a new lord."

He chewed a blade of grass for a few moments before answering. His eyes seemed to flicker. Finally, he said, "I think you are wrong."

"What do you mean?"

He ignored her question and posed one of his own. "Who beat the life from Brezden?"

The hairs on the back of her neck rose. Catheryn saw the dangerous ground he was headed toward and liked it not. "I'm certain you know the answer to that."

"Humor me."

"Pike."

"And his man de Brye?"

"Not until later."

Gerard moved to the other side of Catheryn's father's grave and began to yank at the weeds. The look he shot her was not one of patience. "Do not force me to drag every sentence, every word from you."

Tossing a handful of vines aside, she fought to keep a snarl from her voice. "Why do you want to know this ancient history?"

"Brezden is my home too."

"And you want the people to like you."

His laugh caught her off guard. "*Like* me? What has liking to do with anything?"

"Would it not make things easier?"

"How long ago did your father die?"

"A little over four years ago. Why?"

166

"So, you were a child of what? Thirteen? Fourteen?"

"Fourteen." Catheryn tossed her hair over her shoulder. "But I was not a child."

Gerard's eyes rolled briefly to the sky. "Actions and experience make one an adult, not intelligence or age. I would wager at fourteen you were a child."

Comparing what she knew about life now and what she'd known then, she conceded. "Go on."

"You probably believed everyone liked your father."

"They did."

"Why do you think that?"

"Everyone laughed and joked with him. From his knights, to the craftsmen in the village."

Gerard lifted his eyebrows in obvious disbelief. "Everyone?"

She could think of a few who disliked him, but not many. "Almost everyone."

Her husband shrugged. "Then your father was probably a weak, ineffective leader."

She was tempted to throw the clump of weeds and dirt she held in her hand at his head. "My father was a strong commander! No one ever thought to naysay his orders. Never do I remember an argument about any decision he made."

"The freemen who followed his orders, do you think they enjoyed having someone tell them what to do? Do you think they did not chafe from time to time?"

She huffed. "Whether they chafed or not, they did as they were told."

"Because they liked your sire? Because he could tell a good joke? Because he knew how to laugh? Or did he threaten them from time to time?"

"No. They did it because he was their lord and they…"

She glared at Gerard and cursed silently. "You've made your point, my Lord. They trusted him."

Instead of gloating, her husband merely nodded. "And I need them to trust me. Do you understand that? I care not if they *like* me. Trust is what makes a strong and happy community."

"Yes," she murmured. "I understand."

"Do you also understand that I need them to follow my orders without question or hesitation? I cannot have them concerned about what you might think or do to contradict me."

"These are my people."

"That may be true. However, I am responsible for their safety now, not you."

Regardless of the shining sun, Catheryn grew cold. "What are you saying, my lord? Do you wish to take all away from me? All responsibility, all decisions are to be yours? Are you seeking to cut me off from my people? Will you succeed in finishing what Pike started? Do you think I will stand by idly while another lord treads on Brezden, grinding it into the dirt to satisfy—?"

A clump of earth landed in her lap. "Give over, Catheryn. Had I sought to grind Brezden under a heel, the deed would have been accomplished long ago."

Exasperation tinged his words. She searched his face for signs of anger but found only a tired countenance staring steadily back at her. Still, she needed to understand what Gerard was truly after.

"Am I not your wife? Is not Brezden as much my responsibility as it is yours?"

"Yes, in most instances it is, but you are not going to lead men into battle. You are not going to meet de Brye on the field. You are not going to take up arms at the gates."

"Will you not be leading your own men into whatever battle may arise?"

He stared at her. "I plan to send many home to Reveur in order to keep it safe. So how many men do you think I should keep here? There seem to be very few of the right age to draft into service from the townsfolk. If only you'd had men who were loyal to you instead of Pike. It doesn't seem impossible, seeing as he was a cruel and unkind leader."

"Mine are—" Catheryn stopped herself. What was she about to tell him?

"They are mysteriously absent from the keep if you have any. Seemingly nowhere to be found."

Catheryn averted her face. "You've looked?"

"Of course."

"And you found no one?"

"Not a soul."

Her heart fell. Even though de Brye told her that her loyal men-at-arms were held under his guard, she'd hoped a few might somehow escape. That hope died with Gerard's declaration.

He reached across the grave, and with the crook of his thumb turned her chin so she again faced him. "You expected me to find them?"

"No. I…"

"Do you know where some are?"

Unable to meet his searching look, she jerked away.

"Catheryn, did you send them out of the castle?"

She studied the vine twined around the cross grave-marker. "Yes."

"Did they make it to safety?"

"N—" Her throat burned. Her heart ached with the knowledge of what she had done. Hoping to steady her voice, she took a deep breath. "No. They did not."

She half expected him to rail at her, but his silence piqued her curiosity. Warily she glanced up. The frown on his face made her wish she'd not looked.

After a few more silent moments, he sighed and shook his head. Directing his focus to her, he went back to the beginning of their odd conversation. "Tell me of yourself, of your childhood."

She shrugged. "My childhood? Do you wish to know of Brezden or of me?"

A half smile lifted one corner of his mouth. "Both, if you please."

Not seeing any harm in his request, she told him about her lessons in writing, learning to ride a horse, the horrendous chore of learning to sew. He listened attentively, which made it easy to continue. He laughed when she recounted tales about learning to fight with the stable boys and again when she confided in him about the squire who'd tried to teach her how to kiss. She explained what she knew about the changes her father made at Brezden upon his return from a journey abroad that he had made as one of King Henry's men-at-arms. He had declared the upper chambers of the keep better suited for his family as they afforded a small measure of privacy. He'd also brought back household furnishings to make their dwelling much more comfortable.

Then came Pike. Catheryn shivered with revulsion when she told Gerard about the man's introduction to Brezden. He had come seeking refuge with his 'long-lost cousin by marriage'—at least, that's what Pike had called her father. The Lord of Brezden had no reason to doubt Pike's claims and had welcomed him with open arms. Within a short time, Pike started carrying on about holding a tourney at Brezden. Soon everyone was looking forward to the event, and her father had little choice but to bow to the fervent pleas of his soldiers.

"This is where your father was killed?" Gerard prompted when she fell silent.

"Yes. Somehow a sharpened, reinforced lance replaced the blunted one Pike was to use, and my father's shield switched for one of inferior quality. Before all in attendance, Pike delivered an instantly fatal blow to my father."

A look of confusion fell upon Gerard's face. "No one questioned how it occurred?"

"Pike interrogated the squire responsible for his weapons. The boy was branded a murdering knave and slain immediately thereafter."

"King Stephen was your father's overlord, why was he not involved?"

"The king was preoccupied with planning the battle at Clitheroe against the Scots."

Gerard nodded. "How did Pike come to remain at Brezden?"

"He didn't remain. At first he left, which provided my mother great relief. She didn't trust Pike from the first moment she met him. But my father could not be made to see anything wrong with the man. After his death, my mother received missives from our families in Normandy and France that confirmed her worries about Pike. It seems he was considered a liar, a thief, and not to be trusted."

"Yet your mother permitted him to return?"

"No. He petitioned King Stephen and the newly titled Earl of York to be named Brezden's guardian." Catheryn's laugh tasted bitter as it rolled off her tongue. "As soon as my mother learned of the petition, she sent my sisters away."

"But not you?"

Catheryn shook her head. "I was not about to leave my

mother alone. She was still mourning the loss of my father, and I knew she disliked Pike. I could not leave her."

"Your mother did not issue a plea to King Stephen or William?"

"Yes, of course, she did. The king was convinced that she was too distraught to know what she was talking about. And William…" Catheryn paused, uncertain she should speak badly about the Earl.

He finished her sentence for her. "And William was too occupied with his new position to be concerned about the affairs at Brezden." Gerard shook his head. "Still, I cannot fathom Stephen blindly accepting Pike's words."

"So, you doubt it happened? Was Pike not here when you attacked Brezden?"

"Yes, he was, but that still does not explain how his petition was granted so easily."

"You did not know Pike. He was clever. He could play upon your emotions so effectively that you would be uncertain what you thought, or felt. In that moment of uncertainty, he always found a way to force his will over your own."

"And de Brye?"

"He arrived much later—and it soon became obvious that if Pike was clever, Raymond de Brye was his master. And they meant Brezden's people ill."

"If your lady mother knew from the beginning how dangerous de Brye was, why did she not send another plea to Earl William?"

"By the time she had proof that his outward acts of kindness were a ploy, it was too late."

"Too late? How?"

With her fingers, Catheryn viciously attacked the vines twined about the grave-marker, wishing that instead of weeds it was de Brye's face beneath her claws. "He was kind, even pleasant to us at first. Whenever Pike would fly into a rage, de Brye would soothe him and protect us from harm."

"Your mother appreciated his efforts?"

Breaking a nail, Catheryn winced and shook her head. "No. From the first day, my mother said he was too nice, too kind. She trusted him not but went along with his act always waiting for his darker side to come forth."

"What about you?" Gerard stayed Catheryn's now-bleeding fingers with his hand. "What did you think?"

Guilt, humiliation, and anger fed the force of her admission. "I thought he was sent from God."

"Catheryn, you were too young to know any better." Releasing her hands, Gerard moved to sit behind her. "The honest, trustworthy man who'd always protected you was gone. Who could fault you for thinking de Brye a welcome reprieve from Pike, especially if he came under the guise of kindness?"

Catheryn stiffened when his arms came around her, but she didn't pull away. "My father had been gone nearly two years. I was not so young. I was old enough to be married and have children running about my own keep. Instead of listening to my mother when she tried to talk to me of marriage, I made our lives a hell on earth."

"How so?"

His question fell softly on the nape of her neck. She longed to lean back against Gerard's broad chest, but a lingering wariness teasing at the back of her mind kept Catheryn upright. "He treated me like a favored child when I wished to be seen as a woman. His warm glances, honeyed words, and lingering touches were reserved for a woman who had little use for any of his attention."

"Your mother."

173

She couldn't bring herself to say the words, yet that did not stop them from ripping her heart to shreds. Yes, her own mother—the woman who had given her life, who had seen to her care and happiness. The woman who had protected and comforted her had become her enemy. To this day Catheryn did not understand her actions. Did not understand them, nor could she forgive herself.

Strong arms tightened around her as Gerard pulled her against his chest. His heart tapped a steady beat against her back. His fingers were warm against her cheek. He softly stroked and gently coaxed her wary body to relax against him, overcoming her resolve to keep some distance between them. Temporarily safe in his protective embrace, she drew in a shaky breath.

A breeze ruffled her hair and Gerard smoothed the windswept tresses back into place. The aroma of sweet woodruff tempered by the spiced scent of sandalwood filled Catheryn's senses with a modicum of peace.

"How did he react to your mother's rejection?"

"No. No more." She struggled to twist free from his hold. "Please, Gerard, let me go. Ask me no more."

His hold fell away, but before she realized what was happening, she found herself seated across his lap. He gently pulled her close. Engulfed by his sweet, warm caress, she clung to the safety he offered. Safe. Protected. These were things she'd never thought to feel again. Then, before she could protest, her lips were covered by his.

Catheryn wanted to scream with outrage. She also wanted to melt against him. She wanted his kisses to stop— tomorrow. Knowing that he would not cease this calculated seduction until he'd learned all made her want to sob. Nonetheless, she surrendered.

Too soon Gerard broke their kiss. The cold, sharp pang

of abandonment swept over her, but the warmth of his touch against her cheek banished the chill.

"Catheryn, my shoulders are large and well able to bear any weight you see fit to place upon them. I am your husband, and as long as I walk this earth there is no burden you need carry alone."

The tears she wanted to shed earlier slipped past her closed eyes and down her cheek. Oh, how she longed to believe him. To know she was not alone. To have someone she could trust without doubts would be a dream realized. But dreams were for children and never came true. Never. Or they came true as nightmares.

And yet…The image of a dark knight thundering toward her raced through her mind. An oft-repeated verse rang in her ears.

Thou pretty herb of Venus's tree, thy true name is yarrow.

One of her tears cascaded over Gerard's fingers. Leaning forward, he kissed it from his hand and then others from her lashes. He rested his forehead against hers and whispered, "Ah, Catheryn, you will rip the heart from my body with these tears of yours."

Trust. It was a small word. So much rested on so few letters.

She opened her eyes and looked into the shimmering gaze so close to her. His regard was steady. No anger, no mockery, no disgust. Reaching up, she brushed her fingertips across his cheek before threading them through his hair. *Oh, dream knight of mine, what is our fate to truly be?*

Not wanting to watch his expression change when she told him of her mother's death, she lowered her head and rested the side of her face against Gerard's shoulder. "De Brye pursued my mother. When she rejected de him, he turned mean. Crueler than Pike had ever been."

Gerard said nothing. He tilted his head and rested his cheek against the top of her head. He ran his hand over her hair, letting it come to rest for a moment at the nape of her neck. The heat of his body radiated through his tunic, warming her. The steady drumming of his heart calmed her racing pulse. Seeking solace from the memories, she burrowed into his embrace and forced herself to continue.

"It was then that I realized my mother had been correct. Raymond de Brye was scum. But by then it was too late. He had already seen my childish jealousy and sought to use it against us."

She paused, searching for words to describe those last few days with her mother. How could she explain the guilt she bore and the terror she'd felt? How could he understand?

Gerard's deep voice broke into her thoughts. "Catheryn. Do not think about what to say. Just say the words as they come."

"I had…I was…" Taking a slow deep breath, she fought to gain a measure of control. "I nearly hated my mother at the time, and she acted only out of love and concern. She sought to protect me. I was unworthy of her love and she knew it."

Gerard shook his head. "That is nonsense. You will never convince me that your mother ever, not even for one heartbeat, thought you unworthy of her love."

Catheryn couldn't stop the harsh laugh from escaping. "She said as much."

"What exactly did she say?"

"I was too busy sobbing onto her lap to listen to her words."

Gerard's chest shook. She didn't need to look to know he was chuckling, and she hissed, "You find that humorous?"

"No, Catheryn, not at all. But somehow, I find the picture

of you sobbing on her lap very easy to imagine. I still cannot believe she thought you unworthy of her love."

Ignoring him, Catheryn continued. "She made me vow not to leave my chamber that night. She also made me promise to always look after Brezden. The keep was my responsibility, and so were those inside. Our family owes them much."

"We will, Catheryn," Gerard vowed. "I promise you, we will always look after Brezden."

"No!" she nearly growled. "Don't you see? She made *me* swear. Me, Gerard, just me. I have failed her, Brezden, and its people."

"You failed no one. This is far from over."

Unable to bear his comforting words, she pulled away and stood. She glanced at her mother's grave and then back. "You do not know just how badly I did fail."

Gerard leaned back on his elbows and looked up at her. "Then tell me. Convince me that your miserable childish mistakes were true sins."

"She died that night." Wrapping her arms about herself, Catheryn gripped her waist tightly. "I hid in my chamber while she screamed." Bile rose to her throat, nearly choking back her words. "While de Brye shouted and raged, I cowered in a corner with a cover pulled over me."

"Catheryn."

Gerard rose. His voice was sharp but held a modicum of kindness. When he sought to touch her, she moved beyond his reach.

"Their fight moved from her chamber to the hallway outside my door. I could hear his slaps through the door as they landed. Every word they shouted at each other reached me with ease." Catheryn shook with the memory. Even though she'd not seen the horror with her own eyes, her mind had readily supplied the vision. "When de Brye said he'd take me as his wife instead of her, my mother told him it would be only over her dead body. He responded by saying that did not pose too great a problem. The next thing I heard was her scream. I later learned that she tumbled down the stairs." Catheryn covered her mouth to hold back the sobs. "Then there was silence. Nothing but deathly silence."

Gerard reached out. Catheryn backed away, half seeing him. Fog swept across her vision. Suddenly, de Brye stood before her, and the blood dripping from his hands belonged to her mother.

"No! Stay away."

Before she could evade the demon coming toward her, he grabbed her arms and pulled her against him. Praying for help, she struggled against that hold of iron. When kicking and twisting did not gain her freedom, she pummeled his sides and back with her fists.

"Catheryn, I am sorry. Forgive me."

She paused at his words. Forgive him? Why would de Brye ask forgiveness? *Oh.* The stench of stale wine or ale did not assault her nostrils, and the arms around her were not de Brye's. When she looked up at the man holding her, the mist that temporarily clouded time cleared from her vision.

What had she done? Drained of emotion and of the strength to stand, she sagged against him. "Gerard, I am sorry."

"You have no reason."

"But—"

He cut off her words with a brief kiss. "Hush."

Lifting her in his arms, he walked over to a tree and sat down against it. After settling her on his lap, he rested the back of his head against the bark and closed his eyes. Catheryn nestled into the cocoon made by his chest and arms. The steady rise and fall of his chest and the warmth of his embrace lulled her into an easy peace that bordered on slumber. She would have been content to stay like that forever, never having to worry about another thing, but far too soon the clamor of horses cruelly drew her from her wishful thoughts.

Gerard sighed wearily and opened his eyes. "What now?" He glanced toward the road and cursed at the armed party filing in through their gates.

Catheryn felt his heart leap. "Who is it?"

"Earl William. He is back."

Chapter Thirteen

Each step Catheryn took back into Brezden filled her heart with dread, and the urge to turn and run nearly overwhelmed her. It wasn't the twenty or so strange men milling about the bailey that threatened her composure. It was their manner of dress. Their armor and weapons did not suggest a social call.

Quelling her trepidation with a hard swallow, she followed Gerard toward the keep. Countless questions formed in her mind, questions that made her lose concentration on the uneven ground beneath her feet. She stumbled, and Gerard turned around at her soft curse.

"Lady Catheryn." He clasped her hand and shook his head slightly, speaking low so that none of the soldiers might hear. "Pay them no heed."

Her gaze traveled from him to William's men and back. "But—"

Gerard draped an arm across her shoulders, pulling her to his side. "You don't wish them to think we've any cause for worry." He smiled and nodded at the Earl's men before resuming their walk toward the keep.

Catheryn fought to paste a haphazard smile on her face before whispering, "We *don't* have cause for any worry." At least, none that she could think of.

"I know that."

He drew his thumb along the side of her neck. Her cheeks warmed and her pulse quickened. Would she ever grow accustomed to his touch? Somehow, she doubted it.

Quickly, before she forgot the matter at hand, she asked, "Why do you suppose the Earl is here?"

"I've not the slightest idea. Perhaps he missed our company."

Catheryn shot Gerard a look of irritation and tried to move away. He simply tightened his hold to keep her by his side.

Before walking into Brezden's Great Hall, Gerard ducked into an alcove, pulling her along. She could tell he meant to comfort her, so she wrapped her arms around him and rested her cheek against his chest. She was more than willing, at this moment, to take whatever strength he could offer.

He placed a kiss on the top of her head and brushed his cheek across her hair. "Catheryn, there is no need for fear. All will be well."

"I am not afraid."

His chest shook with subdued laughter. "No?"

She shook her head. The lie fed her a measure of bravery.

"Good." He placed his hands on her shoulders as if to move her away. "Then maybe we should join William in the hall."

At the last second, she tightened her clasp about his waist. "No. Not yet."

"Baron Reveur!"

The shout shook the keep and took away the option of waiting any longer. Catheryn frowned. Something was not right. On his last visit, Earl William had never used Gerard's title, and he had never shouted with such vehemence. She stiffened against her husband for a moment before releasing

181

her hold and audibly drew in a breath before squaring her shoulders. Then, pointedly staring at him, she said, "It does not sound as if all is well, Gerard."

He nodded in agreement then offered his arm. "Shall we?"

The hand she placed upon his forearm shook slightly. Reaching across his body, he covered her hand with his and squeezed it gently. "We are not feeding lions, Catheryn."

Shrugging, she replied, "I wouldn't be so certain of that."

Walter approached from the doorway. "My lord, should I summon your guard?"

Gerard shook his head. "No. We'll wait and see what William is about."

Catheryn was thankful that Walter stayed close at hand. It had already become obvious to her that it would require a small army to remove Gerard's captain from his side when danger threatened.

As they stepped into the hall, one glance at the Earl of York's expression told Catheryn more than she wished to know. Then, before she or Gerard could issue a greeting, William pointed at her, nodded toward his men and ordered, "Seize her."

Her breathing ceased for one or two painful heartbeats. It was as if time came to a standstill and a curse froze on her lips but not on her husband's. His oath echoed in the hall. All in the same movement, Gerard grabbed the sword hanging at Walter's side, yanked her behind his back and brandished the weapon before him.

William's men stopped their advance.

"What is this meaning of this, William?"

Catheryn wanted nothing more than to hide her face in the fabric covering Gerard's back, but the need to stand up for herself forced the cowardly thoughts aside. She stepped away from her husband's protection…only to find her wrist caught in a near bone-crushing grip. The gentle, caring man of earlier was gone. The warring knight had returned.

The Earl pushed his men aside as he crossed the hall. The anger that had been evident a moment ago grew into rage. He didn't stop his approach until the point of Gerard's sword rested against his chest. "You would protect a traitor against your king?"

Gerard lowered his weapon as Catheryn gasped and stepped back. "Of whom do you speak?"

William's already red face darkened more. He raised his arm and pointed a meaty finger. "That murderous bitch cowering behind you."

Catheryn flinched against Gerard's back. She sank her fingers into his tunic with a hold that would quickly tear the linen to shreds. *Traitor? Murderous?* She closed her eyes. Surely the world had gone mad. There was no other explanation for the Earl's accusations.

Gerard tensed beneath her touch. Opening her eyes, Catheryn watched in horror as he leveled his sword and twisted the tip against William's chest, easily tearing through the tunic to come to a stop against a chainmail hauberk.

Friends or not, Gerard owed William fealty. Had he suddenly lost his mind? His action would put not only himself, but all of Brezden in danger. William Le Gros had a reputation of cruelty to those who incurred his wrath.

Everyone present gasped at Gerard's audacity. The sound echoed in the otherwise silent hall, and the Earl's men took a step closer. Walter motioned to several of Gerard's men who had gathered behind him. Instantly obeying their captain, the men advanced. One handed Walter a weapon.

"My Lord Earl…" Gerard paused. His hesitation told Catheryn that he was carefully choosing his words. "Surely someone has told you a falsehood. My wife has not been out of my sight since our marriage."

William smacked the sword tip away from his chest. "Coming from a man who spent his wedding night in the stables, that lie is almost laughable, Baron Reveur."

Ignoring Gerard's tightening hold, Catheryn stepped out from behind him. She glared at William. "How dare you presume to know what took place that night? You know nothing!"

If the Earl's stare had been harsh before, it grew even more fearsome. His eyes widened and then narrowed to mere slits. A tick, strong and steady, pulsed rapidly in his clenched cheek. He tightened a grasp on his sword hilt.

It was all Catheryn could do not to take back her words and retreat to safety. But where did safety lie? Behind her husband? At what cost? His life? The lives of his men? No. She stiffened her spine. She'd see this struggle through to the end, regardless of what it cost her. Gerard should not pay for whatever had stirred up this hornets' nest.

Mentally beating back her fear, she stepped closer to the Earl. Gerard released his hold on her wrist and followed. Walter took up the position on her other side. Both men used their swords to shield her from any assault.

Blinking at the sight of the two weapons crossed before her, Catheryn raised her gaze to William. "I may be guilty of many things, my Lord, but treason is not among them."

"You think not?" William looked from one sword point to the other. "I am an envoy of King Stephen." He nodded toward the weapons. "Is this not an act of treason, committed for your benefit?"

The hairs on the back of her neck rose, for he spoke the truth. "They seek only to protect me."

"Protect you?" His features twisted into a mask of

disbelief. "If you are innocent, as you claim, why would you require any protection?"

Gerard spoke up before she could answer. "When I was coerced into this marriage, did I not swear an oath to protect her from any threat? Including you, William."

"You also swore an oath of service to me." A wicked smile crossed the Earl's face. "And to your king."

"I have always served faithfully."

William grunted. "Until now. It seems that not only have you forgotten your sworn duty, but you have forgotten how to follow orders."

Catheryn felt the exasperation she heard in Gerard's ragged sigh.

"What proof do you offer for your accusations?" her husband asked.

The Earl motioned to a band of men standing at the back of the hall. With no further prompting, the group carried a bundle forward and dropped it at the Earl's feet, obviously containing a concealed body. Whose? Part of her wished to know the identity and part of her dreaded the knowing.

Pointing, Earl William ordered, "Lady Catheryn, the honors are yours."

She glanced at Gerard. He lowered the tip of his sword as if to flip the covers back, but the Earl kicked away the blade. "Nay. I want her to see what she has wrought. Then I want her to offer proof and a denial."

Catheryn held her breath, slowly knelt, and pulled the coarse covering away from the man's face. She paused for a moment, overcome.

"All the way, Lady Catheryn."

She gagged as the stench of rotting flesh seared her nostrils. She couldn't do this. But Gerard nudged her with his knee. "Breathe. The smell will lessen with each breath."

Bile rose to her throat. Unable to bear the smell any longer, she quickly pulled the covers free and stood. Gasping for fresh air, she turned her face away from the body before she saw who it was.

"Those are Brezden's colors!"

William laughed at Gerard's shocked statement before demanding, "Explain this, Lady Catheryn."

She passed her gaze over the corpse's green and gold tunic before turning to Gerard. "I...I cannot explain," she said. Placing a hand upon her husband's chest, she added to William, "I did not kill him."

"Maybe not by your own hand." The Earl held out a missive. "This might interest you, Gerard." Her husband took and unrolled the parchment. "Where did you obtain this?"

"It was concealed on the dead man's body. I returned directly to Brezden, seeking to right the wrong I did by giving you this...this woman as wife."

"The contents are so important that you rode directly back to Brezden?" Gerard sounded surprised. He narrowed his eyes for a moment before dropping his attention back to the letter.

Catheryn leaned forward. "What does it say?"

The expression on his face changed as he read. Like a serpent uncoiling in her belly, fear grew. Cold and strong, it seeped into her veins, chilling her to the bone.

She bent to retrieve the document as it fell from Gerard's suddenly lax fingers. He stopped her by forcefully pinning the note to the floor with his sword.

"Damn you, Catheryn."

His voice was hoarse and hard, his hold on her arms brutal as he dragged her upright. She sought to pull away, but he jerked her back.

"Gerard, please, you are hurting me."

"Shut up. At least you are alive."

William added, "For now."

The floor beneath her tilted. The penalty for treason was death by hanging.

She clutched at Gerard's tunic. "I did nothing. I swear to you. Nothing."

His pained look tore at her heart. He closed his eyes as if the agony were too much to bear, and Catheryn knew in that instant she'd do anything to take it away. *Anything.* The knowledge surprised her. She'd not realized the depth of her feelings for this man. When had she grown to care? How had he slipped unseen into her heart?

When he opened his eyes, he presented her with an ice-filled stare. She'd expected it, so was not surprised. She relaxed in his still brutal grasp, and asked, "Gerard, what did it say?"

William answered. "It was a list of supplies to be delivered to the Empress, along with a short missive about the gold and men you would be sending her soon."

Not breaking eye contact with Gerard, Catheryn shook her head. "I did not write that, my Lord. And I do not know that dead man."

The Earl's bark of laughter held no trace of amusement. "Are you going to tell me that Brezden Keep is filled with people who can write? How many others here know what available supplies, wealth or men Brezden possesses? Who else besides you would have that accounting at hand? Please, Lady Catheryn, do not think me dim."

"I did not write that, my Lord."

William stepped closer. "Then who did?"

Gerard searched her face. Catheryn remained still and prayed he would find the truth he sought, or at least some trust.

His hold weakened, and he answered William's question, "Raymond de Brye."

Catheryn nearly fainted with relief. Yet, she knew there would be more questions, questions that this time she'd have little choice but to answer. Answers that would ensure her men's death. She gasped softly. And along with their deaths would be the murders of two innocent children.

"Who is Raymond de Brye?"

She turned her head and stared at the Earl. "My Lord?" Was this some type of sick humor?

"This Raymond de Brye. Why have I not heard his name before this moment?"

William had directed his question to Gerard, who answered, "But you have. Many times."

Catheryn pulled out of his hold before her husband could respond, or stop her. "My mother wrote to you of de Brye. She begged you to intercede on our behalf."

William shrugged. "I remember no missive from your mother. No plea ever reached my hands." He squinted at her in disbelief. "What are you seeking to do, Lady Catheryn? Is it so easy for you to concoct tales to cover your traitorous deeds?"

Dismissing her with a shake of his head, the Earl turned his attention back to Gerard. "Has she bewitched you? Are you so besotted by a lovely face that you have lost all ability to reason? There is no Raymond de Brye. He is naught but a cover for her duplicity."

Gerard stared quietly at her, so Catheryn gasped and backed away. The pain throbbing in her temples was nothing compared with the ache in her chest. "You think me capable of that much deceit?"

His gaze moved briefly to the ceiling before coming back

to rest on her. She wanted to scream, to rage at him, to force him to defend her. By his smug expression, he knew it, so Catheryn bit her lower lip. If nothing else, the action would keep her from saying anything foolish.

He flashed her a look she could not decipher before he turned to William. "You are mistaken, my liege. There is indeed a Raymond de Brye." Handing the sword back to Walter, he waved the captain away, but this was exactly what two of the Earl's men awaited. They grabbed Catheryn's arms. Held securely between them, she could not break free.

"Wait. I want to hear this." William raised his hand. His men relaxed their hold but did not release her. "So, tell me, Gerard, who is this de Brye?"

Without waiting for an answer, William strode toward the hall's main table and sat down. Gerard followed. So did Catheryn, but not of her own volition. Her jailers marched her to stand alongside the table as the Earl offered Gerard a goblet of wine.

"Well?"

Gerard waved away the drink. "De Brye has been a pox on Brezden for years. I have yet to capture the murdering knave."

William seemed shocked. "Who is this villain? From whence does he come?"

"No one seems to know. He just appeared."

William motioned toward Catheryn with his goblet. "This is true?"

"Yes, my Lord. We tried to—"

He cut her off with a wave. "Cease. Other than yes or no, your comments are unwanted."

"But I only—"

This time Gerard stopped her. Without taking his attention from the Earl, he reached out and placed two

189

fingers over her lips. "Do not."

Under any other circumstance she'd verbally lash out at the high-handed action, but common sense rushed to the fore. This was not another circumstance. This was still possibly treason.

She swallowed her outrage but couldn't stop the imp who coaxed her to kiss the fingers covering her lips. Gerard's eyes widened, but it wasn't until the men still holding her snickered that he removed his fingers.

William leaned across the table. "Are you two finished?"

Her cheeks flamed hot. What had she been thinking? Obviously, she wasn't. This was neither the time nor the place to suddenly act the brazen whore.

Gerard shook his head and visibly swallowed. "I know of Raymond de Brye. I believe he was with Pike when they attacked Reveur Keep."

"When he killed your wife and son?" the Earl said. Catheryn choked on a hushed gasp.

"From Edyth's description, I would say de Brye did the act, though Pike may have issued the orders."

Gerard's unemotional tone sent a shiver down Catheryn's spine. From the snippets of the men's long-ago conversation, she'd gathered that Gerard's wife had meant a great deal to him. Was his pain so great that he still felt the need to cover it with the appearance of indifference? Or was there something else going on?

William frowned. "So why is he not dead? How did you not kill him when you attacked this keep?"

Catheryn wished there was a spell that could make her disappear. She had no urge to be present when Gerard told William of Brezden's secret tunnels, tunnels she still had not shown him though she was certain he knew. Treason indeed—against her husband, not Earl William or King

Stephen.

"Either he was not here, or he escaped before we arrived."

This time she did not manage to choke back her gasp. William looked from her to Gerard and growled, "I do not believe either one of you. Baron Reveur, you have until I count to ten to tell me what is taking place here, or else." He pulled out a dagger, and after admiring the shining blade, grasped the front of Catheryn's gown, pulled her down, and held the weapon to her neck. "One…."

Gerard paled but did not attempt to stay William's hand. "Two."

Keeping her focus locked on the Earl, Catheryn gripped the edge of table for support. She would need it when he learned her secret.

Gerard pounded the oak table with his fist. "He was here when I attacked Brezden. Instead of facing his attackers, he chose to beat and attempt to rape another woman."

William lifted a brow. He glanced at Catheryn, who managed a slight nod of agreement.

"Three," the Earl pronounced.

"He escaped. I do not know how, William." Gerard ran a hand down his face. "But there are many ways he could have made a bid for freedom."

"Ah, but he has been back, has he not?" Both Catheryn and Gerard looked up in surprise. William shook his head. "Please, do not think for a heartbeat that I lack wits. You never left my side during your marriage feast, Gerard. Yet your wife somehow gained a broken lip."

Catheryn was glad she'd held on to the table, otherwise she'd have fallen forward onto the Earl's knife. But there were more dangerous questions yet to come.

"Four."

Gerard sighed, then admitted, "Yes, he has been back. He recently returned to start a fire in the stables."

"The stables? Then he must have help from inside." William pulled Catheryn closer. "Are you certain it is not your wife?"

Leaning across the table, Gerard laid a hand on top of the Earl's. She wasn't certain if she wanted to laugh or cry at the vision of the two men holding a knife to her throat.

"Five."

"I am positive my wife is not assisting de Brye...of her own accord."

Earl William looked furious. "What does that mean?"

"I think he has threatened her, or her people. I think she seeks to protect those dear to her and has unwittingly played into his hands. She will not confide in me, so I am not certain."

Catheryn closed her eyes. Her husband had not looked at her, but his voice was condemning. Perceptive was not quite the right word. It was not close to strong enough to define how well her husband seemed to know her thoughts, her secrets, her mistakes.

"You are unable to get this woman to tell you what she does without your permission? Do you require help in locating a backbone, Baron Reveur?"

"My backbone is located right where it belongs, my Lord."

To Catheryn's relief, William sheathed his dagger. A rush of gratitude weakened her knees, had the two guards not reclaimed their hold on her arms, she'd have fallen across the table.

"So." William rose. "What we seem to have here is a hindrance which blocks you from accomplishing your mission. A hindrance that is easily removed."

Catheryn's relief fled. Nausea twisted her stomach, and Gerard stood with such haste that he toppled the bench to the floor.

"She is not a traitor."

"I am not certain I believe that. There is, however, a way to prove it true or false."

Catheryn wasn't sure she wanted to hear his explanation, but Gerard urged him to elaborate.

"It's simple. I will hold Lady Catheryn hostage at Scarborough as a surety that you will find and dispatch the traitor."

"Scarborough?"

"Aye. You heard me correctly. The Earl of Richmond will be in attendance for a tourney, so there will be plenty of people to keep a watchful eye on your lady."

Gerard's expression grew hard. His eyes blazed with anger. "There is no need for that."

The Earl shook his head. "I say there is. Would you care to fight me on this, Baron Reveur?"

All breathing ceased. Not a sound rippled through the hall. Catheryn watched in dismay as her husband's hand wavered over his dagger.

Unwilling to witness what could become a frightening tableau, she whispered, "I will go." When neither man appeared to hear her, she raised her voice and said again, "Gerard, I will go."

He turned his head toward her. "It is not your decision to make."

This time, William's laugh was not one of amusement. It sounded like more of a growl. "The only decision to be made is whether she hangs here and now, or comes as hostage with me."

Catheryn released the breath she'd been holding as

Gerard's shoulders slumped. He was not happy with the outcome, but what did he think he could do against the Earl of York? She would not have had him doom himself for her.

Reaching out, Gerard cupped her chin, lifting her head so that their gazes met. Her heart ceased beating as he stroked his thumb over the lips he'd tried to silence earlier. "When do you leave?"

What emotion lurked behind his eyes? Worry? Fear? She wasn't certain, and it frightened her.

"How touching." Earl William mocked Gerard's display. "We leave with first light. But do not think you have this night to devise any plan between you."

Gerard lowered his arm and turned. "What does that mean?"

"You may have full run of your keep, Gerard. But she will be under constant guard in her old chamber."

"No!"

Both she and Gerard had shouted the word, and the Earl slammed his fist on the table. The cracking of wood echoed through the hall. "No? You tell me no? I am your overlord, and you will do as I say."

Catheryn's blood ran cold. Who would kill her first, Earl William or Raymond de Brye? Would she live long enough to make the journey to York, or would she meet her fate this very night?

William motioned to his men. Without hesitation, they tightened their grasp and led her toward the stairs.

Ahead of Catheryn, Walter gathered Gerard's men into a group and led them from the hall. He was most likely doing the wisest thing. By getting the men out of the keep he might prevent his master from doing anything rash. Any attempt to rescue her from her fate would be useless. Had she only confided in Gerard as Agnes urged, she'd not be in this

194

position. She did not wish for Gerard to suffer any more for her foolishness.

She heard her husband's already angry voice rise. "You are insane, William."

"And you, Baron Reveur, have reached the very end of my patience." The Earl's outraged response made her want to weep.

Chapter Fourteen

Gerard walked around the two bound and gagged guards in his chamber. "What do you think, Walter? Do they not look like a fine pair of trussed hogs?"

"Oh, aye, my lord, that they do."

Lifting one guard's head, Gerard peeled back the man's closed eyelid. "Mistress Margaret said they would be dead to the world for the entire night. I just hope her brew doesn't leave them dead to the world forever."

Walter's eyes grew round. "Don't say that even in jest."

Heading toward the window, Gerard laughed. "It will be fine." He grabbed the rope his captain had used to gain entrance to the chamber and tossed one end back outside.

"My lord? Would it not be easier to just use the door? Now that the guards are drugged?"

Gerard paused with one leg hanging out the tight window opening and flashed his captain a grin. "Ah, but nowhere near as fun. It is but a short drop to the ground. And since our men still guard the outer walls, they will look the other way. Besides, this will give me a chance to finally inspect that infernal tunnel."

While Walter seemed no more pleased by the entire scheme, he offered no argument. "Just be careful. I would hate to have to kill Earl William because of a…a senseless prank."

"Thwarting that man is not a prank and far from senseless. Just see to your duties. As long as everyone follows orders, all will be more than well." Gerard offered his captain a quick salute, hauled himself over the window ledge and out into the dark night.

He'd been right—it was just a short drop to the ground. However, it had been ages since he'd climbed a rope. At least the descent was easier than the climb up must have been for Walter.

Waiting until his captain pulled the rope back into the chamber, Gerard scanned the darkened bailey. Not many figures wandered about. He hurried across the open space and entered the kitchens, where the cook barely noted his presence, giving no more than a quick nod before turning away and mumbling something nonsensical about a busy night. Gerard grabbed a lit torch and slipped through the door that led down to the storage rooms.

Two of his men already waited there, but they were not alone.

"Agnes?"

What was Catheryn's maid doing here? Before he could ask, the flustered woman answered. "I only wanted to see Lady Catheryn, my Lord. I meant no harm."

He waved away her worry. "You know about this tunnel?"

"Yes. I see you do, too."

Gerard frowned. "Maybe I have been seeking answers from the wrong person. Does everyone else know about Brezden's tunnels?"

"No, my Lord, not everyone. And tunnels? I know only of this one. I used it to reach the kitchens quickly when my charge was but a babe."

Gerard nodded. "That makes sense. But you will not be using it this night."

Agnes opened and closed her mouth. "But I…" Wringing her hands in obvious agitation, the maid tried again. "But, my Lord, I must—"

He cut her off by grasping her hands gently in his. "I promise that you will see Catheryn before she leaves in the morning. You have my word."

The maid's sigh of relief was audible. "Thank you, Lord Gerard."

"Now go. Seek your bed and sleep well."

The maid left, and Gerard turned to his men. "Ready?"

At their nod, he led the way.

"Then let the night begin."

❦

Catheryn lay across her bed, staring out the window while absently stroking the purring kitten at her side. Jewel—she'd named the kitten for its bright emerald eyes—had proven to be a good companion in her hours of solitude, especially now that the sun had set and night had fallen, capping an already dark day with even more gloom.

Turmoil raged wildly within her. There was no honor, no wisdom in fear. Yet she could not assuage the abject terror running rampant in her heart and soul.

After William's men escorted her to her chamber, she'd tried to be brave, going so far as to open the door and try to exit. The moment of bravery was cut short when the guards forcefully pushed her back into the room and threatened to guard her from the inside if she so much as poked her nose out the doorway again. Their demeanor was not the sort she'd welcome in her chamber. They seemed near as brutal as de Brye.

She turned to look at the door. If the guards had left the locking bar, she would have dropped it across to protect herself from them. Of course, then how would she fend off the danger possibly lurking within? Her focus drifted to the alcove.

This could not go on forever. This fear of de Brye and what he would, or would not, do had to end. Why had she not confided in Gerard when she'd had the chance? Surely, he would be willing and able to concoct a plan to overcome de Brye.

Jewel sprang to her feet. Until now, the fluffy ball of reddish-blond fur was content to lie still at her side on the bed. Suddenly the beast's fur stood on end, and the normally gentle animal hissed and jumped from the bed. A low growl rumbled from her throat as she entered the alcove, and Catheryn's heart froze in her throat. What had the animal heard?

Frantically searching for a weapon, Catheryn cursed. The chamber had been stripped of any item she could use in her defense. Should she summon the Earl's men for help?

Before she could decide, Jewel pawed at the hidden door. Her fur smoothed out and the hissing ceased. In the short time she'd known the animal, Catheryn had learned one thing—Jewel did not take kindly to strangers. Whoever was behind the panel was someone the kitten knew. The pounding of her heart slowed to normal. It had to be Agnes. Her maid was the only other person besides de Brye who knew the passage. Happiness filled her. It would be good to see and touch a friendly face.

The panel slowly slid back. The well-oiled hinges made no sound in the quiet room, and candlelight danced off the tip of a sword as it preceded a shadowy figure through the doorway. Not Agnes. Catheryn gasped and swung away from the door. But before she could call out for William's men a hand covered her mouth.

Sweet Mary, she'd expected de Brye to come this night. How had she let down her guard so swiftly? Closing her eyes, she prayed for a swift and painless end. *Dear Lord, forgive me, but I am truly a coward.*

The hand over her mouth did not tighten in a cruel or threatening manner. Instead, another hand fell on her shoulder and spun her around. At the same time, she heard the secret panel slide back into place.

The aroma of sandalwood drifted across her senses. She opened her eyes just in time to see Gerard bend his head to hers. He gently coaxed a kiss from her lips.

Anger from the fright he'd caused prompted her to kick him, and he instantly released her.

"That is a fine welcome, wife."

She ignored his sarcasm. "How long have you known about this tunnel?"

A heart-stopping smile spread across Gerard's face. "Ephraim told me when we were in the stable. He was afraid de—"

Catheryn cut off his explanation with a wave and glanced toward the chamber door. Keeping her voice just above a whisper, she warned, "We are not alone. William's men guard the door."

"Do they?" Her husband's continued smile sent shivers to her toes.

"Yes. And if you don't stop smirking at me, I'll kick you again."

Holding her hand, he tugged her toward the chamber door. Pausing before it, he tapped twice with the hilt of his sword and then stood back.

Walter opened the door and tipped his head in a salute.

200

"All is well here, my Lord. Are the others in place?" Gerard responded, "They are."

The others? Had they lost their minds? "What are you two doing?" She peered both ways down the corridor, and William's men were nowhere in sight. "Are you trying to get us killed?"

Gerard pulled her inside and closed the door. "No. I am seeking a night with my wife."

The look on his face said as much, if not more than his words. A thrill of anticipation rushed through Catheryn but worry and logic quickly pushed that aside. "Where are William's men?"

Gerard stroked her cheek with the back of his hand. "In my chamber. They are bound and gagged but unharmed. Your Mistress Margaret has more concoctions at hand than an apothecary."

She leaned into his touch. "What will they think when they awake?"

He cupped her chin and stroked her lower lip with the pad of his thumb. "They will know for a certainty that they were fools."

"How will they explain it to their lord?" Parting her lips, Catheryn teased Gerard's thumb with her teeth and tongue.

Dropping his sword, her husband pulled her into his embrace. "They will not. They will never admit their stupidity to William."

The floor swayed beneath her, and Catheryn held on to Gerard's shoulders for support. "Why are you here?"

"To banish ghosts." He threaded his fingers through her hair. "To fulfill a promise." Lowering his lips to hers, he finished on a whisper. "And to finally claim my wife as my own."

His statements sent her world spinning, and his kiss left

201

her breathless. She longed to make this moment last an eternity because when the morning came, she might never see or touch him again.

A strangled sob tore at her throat, and he broke their kiss and held her head steady so he could stare into her eyes. The candlelight glittered like a multitude of stars in his irises. A frown marred the smoothness of his forehead, though, and he lifted her in his arms and crossed the room. He settled into the chair placed before the window opening and held her on his lap. Moonbeams poured in through the uncovered window and spread a soft, gentle light across them.

Catheryn rested her cheek against Gerard's shoulder, content to be held in his arms. Jewel landed in her lap for a moment before sniffing the two of them and then heading off to the comfort of her makeshift bed in the corner of the room.

"Are you going to cry?"

His question startled her. She swallowed back the tears that threatened and shook her head.

"If you are, do so now."

The invitation was hard to resist, but she succeeded. "No. I am fine."

"Good. I'd not have you shed tears for something that will never occur."

Looking up, she asked, "William will not take me in the morning?"

"You know he will."

Catheryn lowered her gaze. She bit her trembling lip. "Oh."

"No. Look at me."

Complying with his order, she was amazed to discover his features blurred by the tears gathering in her eyes.

"Catheryn, I know you are afraid. I swear to you, though,

William will not harm you. This is naught but a well-devised ploy to gain my cooperation in finding Brezden's traitor."

"Why then did he not just ask?"

"Every now and then he feels compelled to prove to me who is in charge. And he also knows that if word gets out about the traitor before I find him, King Stephen will want an explanation as to why such activity is taking place on William's lands. The Earl would rather threaten me into completing my task quickly than have even a tiny grain of doubt cast in his direction."

Her voice shook. "What if you fail again?"

"He will rage. He will shout. He will swear to strike you dead, but he will not. Trust me on this, he will never harm you." He brushed the hair from her face. "And I will not fail this time."

"It could take a while to find de Brye." He could be hiding anywhere. Along the river. In the forest.

He nodded in agreement. "If he is not still waiting in the area, that is true. So, we need to make enough memories this night to last."

The thought of being away from Brezden, away from her people, away from Gerard for any length of time made Catheryn ill. "Oh, God, I cannot bear the thought." Why hadn't she told him earlier of de Brye's plans and intentions? She had meant to save her people but now the sacrifice seemed so great.

His arms tightened around her. "You will bear what you must."

That was not the answer she wanted to hear, and Catheryn turned her head away. "You are cruel."

"I am honest."

"I am frightened, yet you tell me I might not return home for weeks or months?"

"You think so little of me?"

She swung back to face him. "Think so little of you?"

"I am hunting but one man."

"He is not a man," she spat. "He is Satan."

Gerard's features hardened but his voice remained steady. "So, I have been told."

Catheryn was confused. "By someone else? Who besides me has told you about de Brye?"

"My first wife." The steadiness of his voice grew as cold and hard as his expression. "Right before she died in my arms."

"I am sorry," Catheryn whispered.

"Why? Did you give the orders to sack Reveur?"

Catheryn shrank from the bitterness in his tone. "No."

"Did you beat Edyth to an unrecognizable pulp before raping her and then killing our new-born son?"

"No." The bitter taste in her throat choked Catheryn. "I am sorry because I have done nothing to help you find the man who took so much from you."

His expression softened. "You can still change that, Catheryn."

"But how? How can I tell you what you need to know without the loss of more lives? The only thing I know is that he has my men, the few loyal—" She cut herself off, horrified by the thought of Sarah and Matthew still in de Brye's grasp.

Gerard's deep sigh filled the room. "Do you not think your men are willing to give their lives for yours? Have you so little faith in their loyalty? Is that not the duty of a vassal?"

"No." The thought appalled her. Her stomach churned at the idea. "I cannot permit them to die for me."

"You cannot permit it? Who gave you the power of all life and death?"

204

"They are Brezden's men. They are my men."

"No. They are not your men." He stared at her. "Brezden is not yours."

She moved to stand up, but Gerard wrapped his arms tightly around her. "You are going nowhere, Lady Reveur." Hearing him call her that shocked her enough to keep her from fighting. Grasping her face between his palms, he forced her to again look at him. "What will it take to make you realize that you are not alone? Catheryn, you are not capable of rescuing our men from de Brye. I am."

She pushed at his chest and cried, "He will kill the men and…and the children."

"Children? He is holding children captive?" A mask of anger dropped over Gerard's face. He tightened his hold more and pulled her closer. "My God, woman, why did you not tell me sooner? Do you think this man will hold to his promise simply because you do not speak? He will kill them in the end anyway."

The words stopped her heart. "No. He said—"

"Cease. Do not be a fool. Listen to me. He will kill them all."

She couldn't break his hold. They were nose to nose. He held her so close that she could feel the heat of his breath. "No. No, he woul—"

She stopped mid-sentence. *Yes, he would.* Raymond de Brye wouldn't hesitate to perform any foul act and murdering his hostages would ensure no one lived to give evidence against him, assuming any petition was ever brought to King Stephen. What had she done? Was it too late?

She stared at the face so close to hers. "*Our* men?"

Gerard nodded.

"You are willing to help me?"

The hands still holding her face shook. She saw the barely perceptible tick in Gerard's cheek jump to life, and the silence in the room became nearly unbearable. Finally, through gritted teeth, he answered, "First and foremost, I came to Brezden for Pike's and de Brye's blood. That has never changed."

For some unexplainable reason, Catheryn's heart fell. Still, lowering her gaze, she said, "Brezden owes you much."

His hands slid from her cheeks to the back of her head, and Gerard covered her lips with his own. After a brief, albeit all-consuming kiss, he rested his lips close to her ear. "You are my family, Catheryn, my future. I will do anything to protect you…but I need your help."

She was his future? A thrill rippled through her. His words flowed warm through her veins, and quickly, before she lost her nerve and fear of de Brye settled back in place, Catheryn gave him the information he sought. "The entrance to more tunnels is behind the one in my alcove. He threatened to kill my men, along with little Sarah and her brother Matthew, if I told anyone. He has already murdered the children's parents and he's been sneaking back into the keep to cause mayhem and destruction—like at the stables. He said he had agents and spies in the castle, ones who recently arrived, so I thought perhaps they could be some of your men. I thought I could eventually trick him, outthink him, cause him to—"

Gerard leaned back and shook his head. "Clever. A secret door behind a hidden panel."

She shrugged, taken aback by his offhand forgiveness. Or was he just postponing his anger? "Yes, well, my father thought it safer to conceal the true entrance to the bolt holes."

"What is behind the tunnel to and from the kitchen—"

"*Tunnels.* There's more than one. If you had turned around and felt the wall behind the door into the alcove, you would have found another sliding panel. Behind that is two sets of stairs leading down into more passageways. The one to the left will take you below Brezden, under the postern gate and out to the river."

"And to the right?"

Catheryn shuddered. "To the stables."

"I know that the entrance into this chamber from the kitchens was for the nursemaid. Is there another one on this floor?"

"Yes. There is also one in the lord's chamber, as I'm sure you've guessed."

"And Pike and de Brye somehow found them."

"Yes. But I was not aware of their knowledge until after you attacked the castle. I don't know where it leads to, or if there is more than one entrance."

Gerard sighed. "Are there any more?"

"If there are, I am not aware of them." He raised one eyebrow, so Catheryn lifted her right hand and added, "Upon my honor. I know of no other tunnels."

He held her close for a moment. "I am surprised they did not kill you long ago. They could have done anything they wished to you, Catheryn. You could easily have suffered a fate as gruesome as Edyth's."

His look, when it came to rest on her, was not filled with anger or blame. Marveling at the warmth his expression conveyed, she stroked his cheek. "I am truly sorry for your loss, Gerard."

He kissed her fingers as she ran them across his lips. "Why? What reason have you to be sorry?"

"Because you must love and miss her. Was that not your whole reason for attacking Brezden?"

"Love?" He frowned before shaking his head. "It was vengeance that drove me, the vengeance Edyth was due."

Gerard's admission settled heavy on her heart and confused her. Should she be happy that he'd not loved his first wife? Wouldn't that leave room for her? Could she teach him of love herself? But what did she know of love?

Directing her thoughts back to her husband, she asked, "Do you not miss her?"

"I used to. She filled my mind night and day." A slight half grin crossed his face. "Lately I find myself occupied with thoughts of another."

A warm flush heated her face. She paused, her fingers resting on his lips. Uncertain how to reply, she said nothing, and her confusion mounted when he grasped one of her fingertips with his teeth. She gasped as he slid his mouth down to cover her finger. The moist, silken warmth of his tongue sent flame-tipped arrows to start a fire between her legs.

Catheryn's heart slammed against the inside of her chest. Catching her breath, she asked, "What are you doing?"

He released her finger and moved his lips to her neck. "Banishing ghosts. Fulfilling promises."

The feel of his mouth, the heat of his breath caused the fires to spread. She arched her neck beneath his touch. "I don't understand."

"Who asked you to understand?"

As much as she enjoyed his attention, it made no sense to her. She forced the words from her mouth. "How can you talk of Edyth in one breath and seduce me with the next?"

"I can do nothing about things that happened before this moment." He deftly untied the laces at the back of her gown, and the cool night air rushed against her exposed shoulder. "I can do nothing about things that might happen after this moment." He grazed the tender flesh between her neck and shoulder with his teeth. "I can only act upon what is happening right now."

Her breath came fast and hard. Talking was an effort, thinking even harder. "Gerard, I do not think this is—"

The words died in her throat as he brushed his thumb across her breast. "Save all thoughts for tomorrow, Catheryn." Lifting his head, he smiled down at her. "Right now, all I care about is what you feel."

She sighed. "I feel as if I've died and gone to Heaven."

His laugh was soft. "Not yet you haven't." His touch was like fire. "But you will."

The promise curled her toes with delight. Eager to feel more, to be closer, she pressed her body against his. Soon, though, even that closeness was not enough to satisfy the longing that pulsed in her veins.

"I don't know what to do."

Keeping her in his arms, he stood and lowered her to her feet. "Just trust me, Catheryn. Do not be afraid. I will not harm you." He lifted her chin with the crook of his finger and thumb. "Open your eyes."

She looked up at him, enthralled. "No one else invades my thoughts," she promised, thinking back to their wedding night.

"Good. Then maybe the ghosts are banished."

Yes, the ghosts were de Brye and Edyth. And tonight, perhaps they might be exorcized forever if only Gerard would work the same magic on her flesh that... Embarrassment drew the flames racing through her nether regions to her face.

Her husband smiled. "I see you agree."

Catheryn tried to turn her face away, unsure, but he brought his hand to her chin and held her in place. He repeated his words of their wedding night. "I will not take you, I will not make you my wife until you crave me and my touch so badly that there is no room for anyone else in your mind or in your soul."

Without thinking, she moaned.

"Are you afraid?"

"No." Fear had nothing to do with the emotion sweeping through her.

"Do you trust me?"

"Yes." The breathlessness of her voice caught her off guard.

"Then turn around." He released her chin and stepped away.

Doing as he bade, she trembled as he finished untying the laces of her gown. Every place his fingers brushed, tingled. A shiver mixing pleasure and anticipation rippled down her spine as he slid the gown slowly down her body.

The shiver grew to a tremor when her thin chemise followed. He found that soft spot on her neck with his lips. Tipping her head to permit him free rein, she gave herself up to the sensations running the length of her. She leaned back against his chest for support. He trailed his hands along her belly, up her rib cage, and cupped her breasts. Hot and cold. Fire and ice. All collided at her core.

Seeking to ease the drumming there, she pressed her thighs together. Shifting behind her, Gerard slid his leg between hers. He teased and tormented her with his hands and mouth. Easily, he coaxed a response wherever he touched, from the tips of her breasts to the now insistent throbbing between her thighs. The heady scent of sandalwood invaded her being. It screamed his name in her mind. Even without seeing him, she had no doubt who drove her wild.

His touch alternated between teasing and demanding. From light to hard. From fast to slow. The combination fanned the fires to an inferno. His warm breath, as ragged as her own, rang loud in her ears. It echoed in her mind, through her body. The pounding of his heart against her back tapped a strong, steady rhythm into her soul. Time froze. No moment other than this one mattered. There was no yesterday, no tomorrow. No other people but the two of them existed.

He nudged her legs apart with his own. She readily complied. Closing her eyes against the sudden spinning of the room, she gasped when he slid a finger along the warm, wet cleft leading to her core.

He whispered against her ear. She felt the heat of his breath, heard the tone of his voice, but not the words. Turning her head toward the sound, she caught his lips with her own. Whatever words he'd whispered into her ear held no meaning. She cared little about them, was caught in a haze of need, of desire.

Slowly, he broke their kiss. Her heart pounded. The throbbing in her body intensified. She dug her fingers into the tunic covering his body. She groaned with need, desire, longing—for what? Resting her forehead against his chest, she gasped, "Gerard, please."

"Please *what?*"

His voice was ragged but demanded an answer. He wanted her to ask for release. She leaned into him, and desperate need wiped out any thought of pride. "Take me. End this torture."

He stripped off his clothes and laid her on the bed before the pulsing, or the longing could lessen, but he avoided the arms she held out to him. Instead, he slid his body down the length of hers. His breath was warm as it brushed over her breasts and stomach. Yet he trailed his lips and tongue lower.

The inferno raged out of control when he graced her with a too-intimate kiss. Catheryn stiffened. When she tried to rise, he captured her with his hands, one on a breast, the other resting flat over her stomach. Then he caught her gaze.

"Trust me."

Shock left her speechless. What was he—?

The next touch of his mouth drove all coherent thought from her mind. His lips, his tongue, and hands were everywhere. He touched her in ways that stole her breath, steadying her with one strong hand and answering her needs with the other.

The bed beneath her fell away. She dropped into a whirlpool. Her heart raced. Her flesh quivered. Burying her hands in his hair, she called out Gerard's name as she burst around the madness that was stroking and coaxing her to heaven.

Floating slowly back to her body, Catheryn opened her eyes to find Gerard looming above her. His smile, so tender, brought tears to her eyes. Tears he kissed away. Resting the palm of her hand against his cheek, she whispered, "I didn't know."

He chuckled. "You still don't."

The unsteadiness of his voice reached her through the haze, but her question died on her lips as her vision cleared enough for her to focus on his features. Perspiration beaded on his forehead. A bright sheen glittered in his eyes. His chiseled jaw tensed with what appeared to her as pain.

Placing her hand against his chest, she felt the hard, erratic pounding of his heart. The beat matched the heaviness of his breathing. Catheryn shifted her gaze back to his face while sliding her hand along the hard planes of his stomach, and his eyelids fluttered closed. The smooth flesh

212

quivered beneath her touch.

She stopped. "Gerard? Is something wrong?"

Ignoring her question, he moved to settle his erection against the pulsing entrance to her womb. He pressed into her, but her body tensed at the tightness. Something was…not quite as she'd expected. She braced her hands against his shoulders.

"Ah." He rested his lips against her ear. "Catheryn, you were not raped. And love, your body is more than ready for me. Are you?" His ragged breath burned hot against her ear, and she forced her trembling limbs to still. She could do no more. "Catheryn, help me. Open for me. Do not make me do this alone."

He'd taken her to the heavens and back. He'd already fulfilled two of his promises for this night, he'd banished ghosts, and he'd easily coaxed her into wanting him with every fiber of her being. It was time for the fulfillment of his last promise. At this moment, there was nothing she wouldn't do for him.

Slipping her arms about his neck, she threaded her fingers through his hair. "Kiss me." She wrapped her legs around his thighs and whispered against his lips, "Claim your wife as your own."

He filled her. The instant he did, he came to a stop. Catheryn froze for an uneven heartbeat before greedy desire beat off a short-lived flash of pain. Digging her fingernails into his shoulders, she sought to lose herself in Gerard's kiss. It was not hard to do.

He shook as he began to slowly move, gently sliding out and back into her. There was no pain. Only a deep yearning for him to continue. She shivered with the thought of the pleasure. There was so much more to come. At least, there was tonight.

Threading her fingers through his hair, she broke their kiss. "Love me, Gerard. If this night is all we are to share, love me well."

He gripped her face between his hands. "You are wrong. This is not our *only* night. It is only our *first*."

His touch gave her the vow of memories that would last a lifetime. He moved against her, bringing a sigh of pure delight to her lips, and his eyes glistened with the promise of all their tomorrows. She returned his offerings by giving him her body, her heart, and her very soul.

Chapter Fifteen

Propped on one elbow, Gerard gazed down at the woman dozing next to him, his wife in more than name. He cursed the time they'd wasted. They could have had many nights of such ecstasy had he not permitted his pride and temper to get in the way. He could have had the information about de Brye weeks ago had he thought to use a measure of kindness instead of anger.

He cursed his failings as his father's voice ran through his mind. How many times had his sire encouraged him to utilize patience and logic when dealing with his headstrong sister? Countless. It had been many years since he'd had contact with a stubborn female, however. His father's lessons had fallen to the wayside. Edyth had seemed the perfect wife—meek and mild. The thought to raise her voice against him never entered her mind. Somehow, he doubted if this wife would be the same. She would never be content if ignored for long periods of time as he fulfilled his service to the king.

Ignored? Gerard shook his head. How could one ignore someone who invaded your thoughts night and day?

Candlelight played across her hair, shimmering off the fine threads of gold woven among the light brown. Then a frown creased her forehead and her hand sought him.

The frown vanished when she rested her fingers against his stomach. Her lips turned up in a brief but satisfied smile, and the sight of her lips and the memories of the night fanned the heat of Gerard's desire. He groaned with the need to bury himself in her. To feel her hot, wet flesh tighten around him.

Concern overruled his baser needs. She had a two-day ride ahead. He did not want that journey's discomforts to poison their night of passion. For that reason, he'd joined their bodies but once. The rest of night had been spent learning other ways to reach satisfaction. Desire could be flamed with nothing but a look or a touch. Fulfillment could be found many ways. Even he had learned something.

Of course, as erotic and thrilling as her lips and hands on his flesh felt, he would rather bury himself in her, feel her hot, wet flesh tighten around him. Gerard laughed in desperation. So much for controlling his thoughts.

Time grew short. As much as he'd like to stay here and watch her sleep, little time was left. There were things he wished to tell her. Things about William and the Earl's wife Cecily that she needed to know.

He stroked her cheek. The skin reminded him of velvet, soft and pliant.

Catheryn's eyes fluttered open. A gentle smile curved her lips. "Good morning." She moved closer and placed a hand against his chest.

"Not yet it isn't, but we must talk."

"We will have many days to talk. Can you think of nothing else to fill the remainder of the night?"

"You are leaving when the sun rises. That has not changed."

"But I told you what you need to know. There is no reason for me to leave Brezden. You and William can—"

"Until de Brye is dealt with I want you gone from here."

"But—"

"Cease, Catheryn." He took a deep breath, forcing his impatience aside. "Do not argue with me. I cannot devote all my attention to capturing de Brye if I must worry about your safety at the same time. And I do not wish to tell William everything until after his tourney with the Earl of Richmond."

"Why not?"

Gerard knew his reasons, but he also knew they would sound misguided when put it into words. And yet, "There is nothing William enjoys more than a good fight. That's how he became an earl to begin with, but a moment's hesitation was nearly his downfall. He, too, left the field of battle at Lincoln, permitting the king to be captured. If I tell him everything now, he will cancel the tourney that's already set with Richmond and order all of his men here. He will still send you to Scarborough for your safety—and to torment me no doubt."

"Why does he torment you on purpose?"

"I have been trying to understand why, myself, and the only reason I can think of, other than some need to show me who is in charge, is that his pride has not yet recovered from what happened at Lincoln." Somehow the risk of Stephen discovering a traitor loose at Brezden had brought back all the guilt and remorse William experienced after that disgrace. Lincoln had been the only other time, in Gerard's memory, when the Earl had been so unreasonable, agitated and distrusting of all. He shrugged. "Like a wounded animal, William is striking out at those within his reach." Which meant him and Catheryn.

Catheryn frowned. "But Earl William was not the only noble to flee the battlefield, leaving the king alone to be captured."

"True, but that changes nothing in William's eyes." He dragged a hand through his hair before coming back to the difficulty at hand. "If William were to pull his troops from Scarborough to Brezden while you were at his castle, it would leave you unprotected. What if de Brye does have spies within our walls and he found out where you were?"

She gasped in answer to that question.

"Catheryn, I can't have that. I *will* not. Besides, if William cancels the tourney now, the Earl of Richmond will ask questions. It will not matter if William explains to him or not, either way, Richmond will go to King Stephen."

She finished his thought. "And once again the Earl will feel as if he's failed the king."

Gerard nodded. "Yes. Can you imagine how unreasonable William would become?"

She raised a brow at him. "Husband, I say you worry far too much about your earl."

Curling a lock of her hair around his finger, he explained. "He is not just my liege lord. He is my friend—nay, he is more like a brother."

"If I had not guessed that before, I know it now." She placed a palm on his chest. "Then why not speak to him as a friend? Are you not able to allay his worries?"

"You think I haven't tried?" He covered her hand with his own. "It is nearly impossible to dislodge a notion once William has it set in his head. No, the best thing to do right now is be as good a vassal as I can and wait for him to realize all is well truly between he and Stephen." Although suddenly becoming meek and obedient would make William wonder what was wrong. No, it would be best if, while doing his duty, he didn't treat William any differently than usual.

"I fear you may care too much about a man who could

destroy us. But while I can't imagine him being more difficult than he already is, even I know it would be unwise to enrage him. So, to save us any more of William's wrath and prove yet again that you are still his loyal man, you are going to see to de Brye yourself. Yes?"

"Yes."

She bit her lip. "Gerard, I cannot bear the thought of—"

"No." He cut her off before she could voice her fear. "I will not fail, Catheryn. My men and I will be successful."

"You had better be." She sighed. "Even though I gave you what you wanted, I am still to be the Earl's prisoner?"

"Yes. So, to speak." Surely, she saw that this was the only way for her to stay completely safe.

She stared into his eyes. "Will you always use gentle touches and soft words to gain what you want?"

A fist to his gut would not have caught him as off guard. "Is that what you think?" When she tried to roll away, Gerard grasped her arm. "Answer me. Is that what you think last night was about? That I was trying to get information?"

"I don't know." Her words were clipped.

He released her arm and moved to leave the bed. If she was seeking to goad him into a fight, she was close to succeeding. He would not let her. Why did she seek to argue, to tussle, to—

"I have never been away from Brezden."

The slight tremor in her softly spoken admission filled him with shame. Catheryn wasn't seeking a fight. She was afraid.

He turned and looked at her. Terror had fallen across her face, and he hated it. If there was a way he could wipe that expression from her face forever, he would. He could think of nothing that would convince her the fear was unnecessary. He could only help her to live with it. And only

219

for the time they'd be apart.

Pulling her into his arms, he lay back down and cradled her atop his chest. "Catheryn, all will be well."

She shook her head. "Not until I am back here in your bed."

"That will happen soon."

"Not soon enough, Gerard. I can hardly bear the thought."

Neither could he, but this was the best option. Especially if de Brye had spies or agents within the castle. "Then don't. Do not think about it."

Crossing her hands on his chest, she propped her chin on top of them. "How do you propose I do forget?"

He thought for a minute. Maybe she could use the same trick he'd learned, the trick that allowed him some respite right after the death of his wife and son along with the sacking of his castle. "What things bring you pleasure?"

Amazed, he watched a blush color her cheeks before she answered, "You."

He smiled. "Things you can think about in public, Catheryn."

"Oh." Her brow furrowed and she shrugged. "A walk in the sunshine. To breathe spring air. A warm blazing fire in winter. The scent of baking bread. A quiet room. A day with no shouting. A night sky filled with stars."

Jewel landed on the covers next to them with a small squeak. Gerard scratched the kitten's head and was rewarded with a throaty purr.

Catheryn continued. "This ball of fur." She scooted forward and placed her lips on Gerard's. "And you."

"That is all?"

"It is enough."

She'd added none of the things his sister would have

listed. No gems, no rich fabrics or furs, no chests of gold, not even a simple piece of jewelry. Of all the things she mentioned, there was not one item he could give her to keep as a reminder of Brezden and him. Except perhaps the cat.

Gerard glanced out the window, searching for another tack. The fading stars still twinkled in the semi-dark sky. He turned his attention back to her.

"Close your eyes." When she did his bidding, he slowly and gently circled her back and shoulders with his hands. "Picture the night sky filled with stars." He kneaded her shoulders. "Can you see them?"

"Yes." Her answer came in a hushed, steady whisper.

"Every time you are afraid, whenever you feel alone, close your eyes. Think of this moment." She opened her eyes. He purposely ignored the sheen of gathering tears and set her aside. Rising from the comfort of the bed, he pulled her from the rumpled nest and led her to the window. "Look at the stars, Catheryn." Standing behind her, with his arms wrapped about her waist, Gerard rested his chin on the top of her head and pulled her close. "Every night before you seek your bed, find the stars and search for the moon."

"And you?"

"I will do the same and remember this night."

She took a deep breath. "How long will such a memory be enough?"

He paused. "What are you asking?"

"In the days since we have been married, we have shared a bed only one of those nights."

Ah. Gerard knew now where her thoughts strayed, but he wanted them voiced. Here and now. "And?"

She inhaled loudly before asking in a rush, "How many of those nights have you sought your bed alone?"

If he laughed, she would never forgive him. If he raged,

she would think him guilty. As her master and lord of their household, what she thought should not matter to him, but oddly enough it did. Even though he'd known her less than a month, her thoughts did matter to him. A great deal.

Turning her around in his arms, he grasped her wrist and placed her hand against his chest. "As long as my heart beats, I will be true to you. I swore a vow that I have not yet broken and will not break as long as I live." He held her startled gaze and lifted her palm to his lips for a kiss. "The vow is sealed." He closed her fingers over her palm. "Hold this sealed vow in your hand for as long as your heart desires. Always remember that no matter what your eyes may show you or what your ears may hear, that what I have told you and shown you in this chamber tonight is the truth."

"I will hold it longer than forever. I will not forget. Every night I am not at your side I will find the stars and I will search for the moon."

He didn't want to mention the possibility, but he knew William. More than that, Gerard knew Cecily. "What if you are in a room with no windows?"

Catheryn gasped, but her voice did not falter. "I will close my eyes and seek them in my mind."

Gerard nodded. Folding her into his embrace, he held her close. "Catheryn, do nothing to anger William's wife."

Catheryn stiffened. "She is cruel?"

"No, not intentionally. Yet she will be jealous of your youth, of your looks, and she holds a grudge against me that might cause her to be mean-spirited."

"A grudge against you? Why?"

He did not want to poison her against Cecily, but Catheryn needed to know the reason for any seemingly unwarranted unkindness. "She wanted…" He paused, wondering if this was something he should tell his wife.

Worry that she might learn of it from another forced him to continue. "I refused to share her bed."

"Ah." Catheryn shook her head and made a face. "She is married to the most powerful man in this part of England. She lives in a castle fit for royalty. I mean not to slight or offend you, but for her to seek out the company of one stationed below her husband seems...odd."

"No offense taken." Gerard laughed. "She is married to a man who knows not how to honor their bed. I think she meant to repay him in kind." His laughter died. "It is not likely, but if William should seek you out—"

Catheryn pushed against him, breaking their embrace. Her eyes blazed. "I will run a knife through his black heart."

Gerard smiled wryly, imagining his wife could do just that. "Fair enough. Just promise me that you will bite your tongue and do as Cecily asks." He knew it was a difficult task, but in the end, it would serve Catheryn better to swallow her pride and let the spoiled woman have her way.

"I promise." Catheryn turned her head and glanced out the window at the waning night. "The day is arriving."

Brushing a curl from her cheek Gerard answered, "Far too quickly."

Grasping his hand, his wife tugged him toward the bed and pushed him down on the mattress. He didn't resist. He too wished to steal another kiss, another touch. But too quickly another kiss, another touch led to soaring desire, and with a ragged curse, he rolled away.

She swept her fingertips down the length of his arm. "Gerard?"

Unable to form complete thoughts, he ground out, "No, Catheryn. The ride...You will not—"

She lifted his hand to her lips and kissed his palm. "For every pain I feel on the coming journey, I want a beautiful

223

memory of how it occurred."

Groaning, Gerard closed his eyes and tried to think of anything but the warm, soft woman beside him. But she would not be dismissed so lightly. She gently grazed his chest with her fingernails, and he could not stop the shooting desire her actions caused.

"Gerard, I have waited for you a lifetime. My dreams foretold of your coming. I did not believe them. Now I do. Love me. Forget all but this moment and love me."

His will to argue dissolved. He gave himself up to the moment, carrying her with him.

☙

Catheryn stood alone in the hall and fought her urge to rail against the unfairness of life. She had already bid farewell to Agnes. The leave-taking had not been easy, but then she'd not expected it to be. Since the day she was born, she had counted on Agnes's presence. Her nursemaid, her friend, her confidante had always been readily available.

Never had Catheryn been further than the demesne lands surrounding Brezden. She'd always dreaded the thought of marrying someone who would take her away, and it had been yet another reason she'd fought so hard against going to France with her sisters.

Regardless of her fears, she was leaving now. Her chests had been packed and loaded onto a cart that was already headed toward Yorkshire. Who knew when she would return?

She spun as William and Gerard entered the hall. The Earl looked angry. Her husband looked smug. Was it possible he had somehow changed the Earl's mind?

William addressed her. "Lady Catheryn, your husband and I have discussed the details of your visit to Scarborough."

"Visit? My Lord Earl, you make it sound like I am going on holiday."

The Earl glared at Gerard. "Yes, well, I know you're going as a hostage, but your treatment will be one of a guest."

Gerard added, "A cherished guest."

Catheryn graced her husband with a soft smile of gratitude. He nodded in acceptance.

William looked from her to Gerard and then back. His perceptive gaze drifted from her head to her feet, and red suffused his face. He clenched his hands into fists and swung around to Gerard. "It is not possible."

Surprise crossed Gerard's face for an instant before he draped a bland look of question over his features. "What isn't?"

"There were guards posted outside her chamber door and at the foot of the stairs. And you were guarded too."

"Yes. And?"

"You have…you have—"

Gerard spoke over William's spluttering. "What? Sullied your prize? Destroyed your plans?" He pulled Catheryn to his side. "You thought I would be foolish enough to hand my virgin wife over to your care?"

William grasped the hilt of his sword. "You were supposed to rid Brezden of traitors."

Gerard answered by grasping his own weapon. "So, now we finally come to the meat of this matter. I had hoped better from a friend than—"

"You disobeyed orders."

"I did not. I captured Brezden and dispatched Pike to his maker."

"You permitted the other traitor to escape. By your own admission another man lives who defied King Stephen, and he—"

"You think to punish me by taking my wife hostage? If you truly believe de Brye exists, how is she the only possible writer of that letter to the Empress? You would part me from my wife unfairly. What do you have planned for her?"

William had the nerve to look affronted, but he stayed silent. Catheryn ground her teeth.

Gerard did not stop his assault. "Do you have another betrothal already arranged, then? Have you found someone more advantageous to reward than myself, your loyal servant and the king's? Has the pope issued his consent for the annulment of her existing marriage?"

The Earl shook his head. "No. Neither."

"Then what were you going to do? Kill her? But then, why would you care if she is virgin?" Gerard released his sword.

William eyed Catheryn with a look that chilled her blood. "By all accounts she is a traitor." He directed his stare toward Gerard. "And you are a lovesick fool."

"Lovesick? Because I made certain that you cannot so easily hand my wife over to another?"

The smug laughter that sprang from Gerard's lips froze the blood in Catheryn's veins. Her heart ceased to beat. Had she been wrong? Did he not care? Had Gerard only used her for his own shallow ends? She swallowed against the pain ripping through her chest as William gave his reply.

"Maybe if you're not panting after the wench like a rutting stag, you'll be able to find this clever traitor de Brye!"

"And maybe I won't. What then?"

"Then King Stephen will know that you are another traitor despite my many reassurances to the contrary. He will come in with an army and tear this keep to the ground. And Heaven knows what he will do to me."

Spoken with such utter certainty, the Earl's bald

226

statement should have angered or frightened Catheryn, but she was numb. Her emotions, non-existent. Catheryn didn't care what they did with her or Brezden if Gerard did not truly care about her. She just wanted to leave this place. Now. Quickly. Before her wounded heart fell from the open gouge in her chest.

The anger on Gerard's face eased slightly. "King Stephen will do nothing to you. This you have to know, William."

"I know nothing of the sort."

Her husband closed his eyes and shook his head before staring at the Earl to ask, "You have informed the king of all of this?"

"No. I wanted to give you the chance to prove your loyalty—and Brezden's."

"A chance to prove my loyalty? Rubbish. You are well aware of my loyalty to you, and to Stephen. You are reminding me who is in charge."

William nodded, and perhaps his eyes looked a little sad. "Yes. We are not in Normandy. This is England. When it comes to Brezden, you will take your orders from me—as you swore to do when you accepted the castle."

Gerard growled, "I will follow your orders concerning Brezden, as I have always done, but my wife is no traitor."

"Your wife is Brezden. She will remain in my hands until this matter is over."

"You harm one hair on her head, and I call upon God to make all the days of your life hell. Your sheep will die. Your vineyards will burn. Your dikes and canals will fall into disrepair."

William's eyes widened. "That is a little much for a woman you profess not to love."

"I will protect and defend my wife with a vengeance."

The Earl remained silent for the space of a few

heartbeats. "Regardless of what you do, Gerard, someday this woman will die, too."

Gerard shrugged. "Not at your hands. Not before her time. No man will do that to me again."

Catheryn gasped. She had been caught up in Gerard's impassioned defense, but now she was again wondering his motive for protecting her.

The Earl's face hardened. Turning to her, he ordered, "Bid your husband adieu and let us be on our way."

As if in a dream, a nightmare with no end, Catheryn turned to Gerard. William strode toward the door, giving them time for a brief farewell, and her husband pulled her into his embrace and held her close. She kept her arms at her side.

"What is this, Catheryn?" Gerard spoke softly, so only she could hear.

It took a few deep breaths for her to gather her courage and get past the hurt constricting her throat. Before she left, though, she had to know. From his lips to her ears, she wanted to hear his answer. "Do you care for me at all? Was last night nothing more than a game and a pissing contest?"

She caught a brief, fleeting glimpse of confusion cross his face as Gerard released her, and then stepped back. "Already you have forgotten." It was not a question, and he did not wait for an answer. He grimaced and muttered, "Think what you will. I care not. I have much to accomplish."

The words he'd spoken in front of the window earlier floated back, but before she could stop him, he turned and walked away.

"Gerard!" Her call did not make him cease his hasty exit. He walked by William without pause and disappeared through the door of the keep.

"Lady Catheryn," William called.

With the burden of guilt and shame resting heavily on her shoulders, she slowly joined the Earl at the door. Surprisingly, the look he gave her was full of pity. She hoped he would let the incident pass without words, but he did not. He shook his head and said, "That was not the way to encourage him to be quick about finding de Brye."

Catheryn bit sharply on her bottom lip. Did the Earl truly believe de Brye existed? If so, why play these games? And even if Gerard did find and kill de Brye, what difference would it make? He'd not want her back. She'd likely poisoned their relationship by once again distrusting and accusing him.

William lifted her chin with the side of his hand. "Lady Catheryn, do you not wish to return home to Brezden quickly?"

Home? She gazed about the hall. This had not truly been home since her father's death. It was a prison, little more than a large cell with occasional friends in attendance. Well, until Gerard arrived. He'd brought a measure of life back to Brezden, a measure of happiness. And she'd just spurned all he'd done. "No, my Lord. It might be better if I never returned."

The Earl dropped his hand and grunted. "A day from now you will regret having spoken those words."

Motioning toward the door, he led her out into the bailey. Men, women, and children lined the path leading to her saddled and waiting horse, but Catheryn looked beyond them, searching for the one person she desperately wanted to find. But Gerard was absent. He did not stand in the crowd. She could not locate him along the path, nor by her horse.

She slowed her steps, unwilling to leave until she could set things right—or at least until she could gaze upon the chiseled face that had become so dear to her. William nudged her shoulder, interrupting her search. Frowning in irritation, she transferred her attention to him. He pointed through the crowd, toward the gates, and she shifted her gaze in that direction to find Walter standing before the wall. When Gerard's captain met her look, he hiked a thumb, pointing up.

There, leaning over the wall, stood Gerard. His back was to her, but he was there and that mattered greatly. Her heart fluttered with hope that he might yet bid her farewell.

Her hope died as she mounted her horse and followed the Earl and his men out of the bailey. Gerard did not wave, he did not make any signal at all. Clear of the gatehouse she turned in her saddle and craned her neck, still seeking her husband, hoping he might make some gesture. Tears blurred her vision, but she easily picked him out of the men lining the wall. He stoically met her frantic gaze.

It was all upon her. Despite her fear that he had used her last night, she must show him that she cared. She must risk her heart and trust him.

Lifting her arm to wave farewell, she paused and then held her hand high in the air and curled her fingers into a fist. She would hold his sealed vow tightly until the day she died. It took only one breathless moment for Gerard to return her gesture.

Chapter Sixteen

Scarborough Castle, Yorkshire, England

For the second day since her arrival, Catheryn watched hordes of people pour into William's castle.

When he'd said there was to be a tournament, she'd thought that meant fifty or so men. More than that had already set up accommodations. As far as her vision could travel there were tents of every size, shape, and color, and still more people entered Scarborough's gates. It was a blessing, she supposed. While she desperately missed Brezden, Agnes, and Gerard, at least she could fill her time by watching the soon-to-be participants of the tourney. Men practiced everywhere they could, the inner and outer yards, the grass outside the castle walls, even in the barren fields.

Of course, no amount of entertainment could dilute the fact that William's lady detested her. From the moment Catheryn entered the castle, Cecily saw fit to mock and degrade her at every turn. It became a welcome respite to seek the solitude of the tiny chamber she'd been given. Here, even guarded as she was, away from the noise and bustle of the crowd, she felt a semblance of peace.

The room itself was fine. From the soft, overstuffed

mattress on the bed to the floral tapestries hanging on the walls, the chamber had the ability to soothe and to quiet a worried heart.

"Lady Catheryn?"

She jumped away from the window at the Earl's question. She'd not heard the door open. "My Lord?"

"Is there anything you require? Anything you want?"

Taken aback, she frowned. "No, not that I can think of. May I ask why?"

William fidgeted. He looked around the room. He put his hands behind his back only to fold them before him again. He gave the appearance of a child who'd been caught in the act of mischief.

She shook her head to clear the picture from her mind. "Earl William? Is something wrong?"

"No." He paused. "Well, Lady Catheryn, we seem to have a bit of difficulty."

Her heart skipped a beat. What had happened? Had Gerard failed? He'd only had four days, not nearly enough time to locate, capture and kill de Brye. Was King Stephen pressing to raze Brezden and execute her and—

William took one look at her face and quickly cleared the distance between them. "Oh, no. No, my Lady, it has nothing to do with your situation. I am sorry for worrying you." He grasped one of her trembling hands. "It is King Stephen. He and his queen are due to arrive at any moment."

"Queen Maud and King Stephen are coming?" Catheryn's heart skipped again. She was awed to be in the presence of royalty. The chance to be presented to a king and queen did not happen to everyone, and apparently, she had nothing to fear from them. Not yet.

"Aye. Don't you see? There lies the problem."

Problem? Oh. This was about her. About his belief that

she was a traitor. "I understand, my lord. It would not be seemly to have one as lowly as I in your hall and—"

The Earl shook his head. "My God, woman, do not seek to put words in my mouth. You don't understand at all." He lifted her chin with his thumb. "Lady Catheryn, you are far from lowly. Was your sire not a baron? Did he not once fight at the king's side? I cannot find words to tell you how sorry I am about failing to come to yours and your mother's aid when you so desperately needed me."

She was shocked. The man truly seemed remorseful, which went against his every action to this point. "It was not your fault, my Lord. You did not receive the missives." She was not sure what else to say.

"Regardless, I should have come to see for myself how the baron's family fared." William laughed softly, wryly, *apologetically*? "Now I hold his eldest daughter hostage. Don't you see? That's where the problem lies."

"Because I am a hostage?" It still made little sense.

"Because I never wished for Stephen to discover that fact. He knows nothing of any of this. I wanted...I expected no crisis to arise from this situation."

Ah, Gerard had been right. The last thing the Earl wanted was for Stephen to know what was happening for fear it would be seen as yet another failure. She offered what she considered the best solution to his dilemma. "Release me and all will be forgotten. Your problem would then be solved."

He dropped his hand. "If only it were that simple. Your husband must understand who rules. Here in York I give the orders, not Gerard. I cannot have my men running about doing as they please, when they please. I cannot let them have wives who tell them half-truths, cannot let them settle in when there are traitors yet to be caught and hanged."

Catheryn's annoyance overrode her shame. "And I am the tool you use to teach him?"

The look he shot her spoke volumes, reminding her of her guilt. "Aye."

Gerard had been correct in this assumption, also. "So, what do you propose?" She guessed at what he was going to say, but she wanted to hear it.

"This chamber is far from where the King and Queen will reside for the few days they are here. I cannot, will not, allow you to leave this room."

Catheryn breathed a sigh of relief. "Gladly will I remain within these walls." When he looked at her like she'd gone mad, she explained, "I thought you were going to lock me in a cell."

"Do not speak too soon, Catheryn. This will be a cell of sorts. I cannot leave the men posted outside the door. It would draw attention."

She stepped back. "You would leave me alone and unguarded? Would not I become a target—?"

William cut her off. "No. Gerard would kill me. I would kill me." He paused, frowning as if lost in thought. Finally, he suggested, "I could leave the guards here, and if they were noticed, I could say you were an honored guest."

He hadn't thought this through. "Why would an honored guest not be presented to the King and Queen?" Catheryn added as an afterthought, "Unless perhaps I'd become ill."

"No!" William shook his head. "Queen Maud would insist on seeing to your health and well-being."

"The other choice would be to lie about who I am. Earl William, I cannot trust myself to keep up that sort of pretense."

"Then I see no other option." He pulled a large ring of keys from his belt. "I will have to lock you inside."

Catheryn sighed. "How long will King Stephen be here?"

"A few days at the most. It will not be long."

She took a moment to consider and then decided that she had no real choice. Besides, had she not endured worse at the hands of Pike and de Brye? She nodded, giving the Earl permission to do whatever was necessary to maintain his honor and Gerard's safety. She did not want any question of her husband's loyalty.

Confusion filled her as William opened the door of the chamber and permitted a man carrying lumber, hammer, and nails to enter. "What are you doing?"

"A woman leaning out this window will give the lie away." The Earl then waved the carpenter to his task.

It took little time before thick boards choked off most of the breeze and light that entered the chamber. Only a small slit between the boards remained, and Catheryn shuddered while imagining the next few days. Still, she'd suffered worse, and with luck this would be the end to her suffering. Gerard would soon capture de Brye, and then all would be well. She would believe that.

William dismissed the carpenter and peered out the narrow opening. "You can still catch a glimpse of the comings and goings from time to time if you so desire."

"Thank you," Catheryn muttered, not knowing what else to say to the man who'd just cut off her link to the outside. Quickly then she tried to think of anything else she might require in the next few days. "What about food, drink and," she felt her face flush, "the other necessities?"

William scratched his head and furrowed his brow. "I will find a servant I trust to keep their mouth shut…or the Earl of York will be your personal maid for a time."

Catheryn wanted to laugh at the look on his face, but he'd brought this on himself. "As long as you don't forget, my

Lord. I get angry when not fed. I could probably kick down this door if I had to. Just ask my husband."

William laughed and headed for the door. "I promise. I won't forget."

She watched the door close behind him. As she listened to him turn the key in the lock, her heart lurched. She was now, in essence, completely a prisoner.

Catheryn forced her breathing to remain even. This situation was only for a few days. Anyway, what would she have to say to the lords and ladies present? What could she discuss with them? She doubted if they'd relish hearing about Pike or de Brye. For a certainty they would laugh at her mooning about a husband she'd known for less than a month. It was better this way. Truly it was, and—

Her rationale fell aside. She'd failed miserably at convincing herself of the logic of this decision. Silently she raged. This wasn't fair. It was yet another example of men forcing their will upon her with no thought to her happiness.

The blast of a horn called her to the window. Leaning her head against the wood, she peered through the narrow opening between the slats. The slot was not sufficient to gain a broad view, but she scanned the instant formation of men in the bailey. Sweeping her eyes over the perfect lines of men standing at attention, she glanced at the procession riding past. There was no doubt that royalty had entered Scarborough. From the many pennants fluttering in the breeze to the men guarding the procession, it was a show that screamed "The King has arrived!"

This far up in the corner tower, she was unable to discern individual faces, only the many bright colors of clothing, horse trappings, and standards. Her gaze drifted from those now entering the yard to the groups still outside. As it did, her heart tripped. Green and gold? *Brezden?* Surely, she was mistaken.

Squinting to see better, she gasped. Green and gold standards indeed fluttered in the breeze. Silken tabards that she herself had once helped sew covered the chests and shoulders of men in a small party toward the rear of the line.

She tore her gaze from the approaching men and raced to the door. He'd tricked her. Gerard was here. That was the true reason the Earl was hiding her. The next time she saw William, she'd burn his ears with curses. "Damn you!" She beat on the wood with the palm of her hand. "Rot in hell, William!"

Rushing back to the window, she tried to scream through the slats. The wood effectively swallowed her voice, though, because not one head, not one set of eyes so much as glanced up.

She tugged uselessly at the boards, but they were held securely over the window, the only damage she caused was to her own fingers. She'd soon torn her nails into jagged, broken ends, and Catheryn fought the urge to throw herself on the bed and scream in rage. It would gain her nothing. Resting her head against the barrier once more, she consoled herself by watching her husband approach.

◌

Gerard closely watched the people lining the road that led into Scarborough. Hundreds of faces, and not one of them his wife, waved and cheered the procession entering the castle yard.

Riding through the gates, he sought another face. That one he found easily.

Dismounting and handing the reins of his horse to his squire, Gerard approached William. The Earl looked shocked to find him here, but Gerard knew better. King Stephen had sent messengers to all his vassals requesting—

237

nay, demanding—their presence at this tourney. Gerard just hoped it was not for some precipitous reason.

Clasping the Earl's shoulder in greeting, Gerard leaned close. "Where is she?"

"Safe from you."

Gerard smiled and nodded at several other lords passing by. "In a cell?"

"Not exactly."

"Shall I ask Stephen, or perhaps Maud, for assistance?"

The Earl smiled. "It is a fine day for a hanging."

Gerard swallowed his anger. "I *will* find her. Why do you feel it necessary to hide her when I visit? What is *wrong* with you, William? You are so worried about what King Stephen may or may not say, think, or do, that you are near crazed. Why? Has something happened to my wife that I should know about?"

"Not yet."

Throwing caution to the wind, Gerard asked, "Again, what is wrong with you of late, William? Other than your own self-torture have you suffered any vile consequence because of Stephen's capture at Lincoln? Has he sought revenge against any of his noble vassals?"

William ignored his questions. Instead, he warned, "If she comes up missing, I'll send an army to take her back."

"You do that, William. You do that." Gerard bowed, more to mock the man whom he'd used to call friend than for anything else.

Then he entered the castle.

Inside, he glanced up the main spiral staircase. Where would that blackguard William keep his wife? If not in a cell, then where? The Earl was being ridiculous. Not that the ruse would be effective, Gerard vowed. He'd find Catheryn if it took all night, even if he had to dismantle the Earl's entire keep. He'd had recent experience at dismantling keeps, or at least breaking down their hiding places. There probably wasn't one wall left in Brezden untouched. It had taken no more than a few hours after Catheryn left to discover that there were more tunnels than those she knew about. One way or another he'd find every one. And he wound find de Brye. Or he'd die trying. Nothing could have drawn him from Brezden except the King's command. It was all he could do to walk away from Brezden leaving only half his force behind to guard the keep and people.

Before he could begin his search, King Stephen called for an immediate gathering. At its end, Gerard knew three things.

One—William would not be holding his tourney. Too many men could be injured, and Stephen needed them all whole and able to fight.

Two—They would be leaving for Northampton in the morning. He'd decided it was time to gather and attack Empress Matilda.

Three—Gerard had but a few hours to find Catheryn.

A fresh breeze might stir his mind. Gerard left the hall seeking air, and as he walked about the bailey he stared up at the castle. At first, he paid no attention, his mind on other things, but at last something drew his gaze. Almost every window on this side of the castle glittered with candlelight as was natural in the early evening. All but two.

Gerard stared harder at those two windows. A large figure—a man, perhaps—stood in one. The other appeared empty. No…a tiny slit of light peeped through. The opening was covered, and that made him frown. On a night like this, with its mild breeze, one would think the occupant would want to take advantage of the air.

Heading for the stables, he sought Walter. "Where is

Catheryn's gift? And find me something to pick a lock with."
It had been years since he'd picked a lock. He'd learned from
Count Stephen of Aumale—William's father—when he was
little more than a boy. The Count found it a useful way to
engage and distract the lads just arriving at Aumale to foster.
If nothing else, the competitions that arose from the learning
kept the Count and his household from having to suffer the
angst of homesick boys.

If the room he'd seen with the covered window was
where Catheryn was held, he'd never be able to scale the wall.
Still, he couldn't be sure. There had to be a way to find out
who was inside.

His captain handed him a medium-sized wooden box.
"Here. She's getting riled at her confinement."

Gerard caught the reddish-blond bundle as it tried to
jump out of the box. Putting the cat back, he closed the lid.
"Come, Jewel. I have a task for you."

"Will this work?" Walter handed him a length of long thin
metal. "Found it by the smithy's forge."

"Thank you, that should suffice." And as he turned away,
Gerard told his captain, "If anything untoward should
happen, and I am not in attendance in the morning, gather
all my men and head for Reveur."

"But my Lord—"

Gerard waved off Walter's words. "I have no time for
questions. Just do as I say." He left the man speechless and
headed back to the castle.

He was nothing more than another figure walking about.
No one took any notice of him. Slipping in past
Scarborough's crowded Great Hall was easy. He took the
steps of the spiral staircase two at a time to the third floor
and was amazed that William had posted no guards
anywhere. The man was mighty sure of himself to think no

one would snoop about these chambers.

Suddenly, heavy footsteps approached. Gerard ducked into a shadowed doorway and held his breath, praying that Jewel would make no sound. The guard kept on walking, but this put a crimp in his plan. How often did this guard make his rounds? Would there be enough time to locate the correct door and break the lock? It had been a long time since he'd tricked a lock into opening. He hoped he still remembered how.

As still as death, Gerard stayed in the doorway and counted. The guard didn't reappear again until he reached one hundred. That was little time, but it would have to be enough.

As soon as the guard vanished, Gerard pulled the cat from the box and walked to the door he prayed was Catheryn's. Placing the cat on the floor, he waited. And counted.

At first Jewel walked away, but a noise soon drifted through the door and the cat turned back and sniffed. It took but a moment before the animal started pawing at the wooden portal like she knew who was inside. *Catheryn.*

Gerard grabbed the beast, muffled its mewls and raced back to his hiding spot, waiting again until the guard was out of range. Then, pulling the slim metal from his belt, he stuck it in keyhole and tried to turn the lock. For a moment he panicked, certain he'd reach one hundred before tripping the lock and opening the door. At the count of ninety, however, his heart slowed as he finally unlocked it.

Bolting inside, he handed a stunned Catheryn the cat's box before softly closing the door and lifting a finger to his lips. He added another fifty to his count, to be certain the guard was far enough away not to hear, and then used the tool to lock the door from the inside, ensuring that should anyone check the door nothing would seem amiss.

"You do enjoy thwarting death, don't you, my Lord?"

Her words lacked the bite he'd half expected, and he could hear the tears before he saw them. Turning around, he opened his arms. "You left before I could bid you farewell."

She was in his embrace before he could smile. He carried her to the narrow bed and laid her upon it, but his conscience forced him to admit, "Your keep is a mess."

Catheryn touched his face. She kissed his chin, his lips. "I care not."

Adjusting her on the soft mattress, he covered her with the length of his body. She felt so good. So soft. So inviting. It was hard to believe that in four days' time he could miss anyone so much. His heart ached with an unfamiliar longing.

"I will set Brezden to rights before you return," he vowed.

"I am certain you will." She ran her tongue down his neck. "It matters not. Since I am still here at Scarborough, I assume you have not yet found de Brye?"

"Not yet. But we have been searching for him without end." He tasted her eyelids, her cheek before seeking to meet her lips. He was lost. Lost in a kiss that promised all. That promise took his breath away and called to his heart in a way that was frightening. For a moment he feared that she'd been in league with de Brye all along, but he pushed the thought away. He was being foolish because this intense emotion was so new.

Jewel jumped up on the bed. Her purr, loud and insistent, roared in his ears. The kitten had not seen her mistress in days, and it was obvious she was not going to give up until she got some attention. For that reason, Gerard broke away with a groan. Tracing a finger down Catheryn's heated face he whispered, "If there were time, I would make love to you all night."

The animal squeaked when Catheryn hugged it close to her chest. "I would be happy with once."

"We cannot chance being caught. We are not at Brezden."

Holding the kitten with one hand, Catheryn sat up and ran the other down his chest. "Who would know? What could they do? We are husband and wife!"

He grabbed her hand and placed a kiss on her palm. "You are a hostage. William still threatens to see you hang."

Catheryn slipped her robe off her shoulders.

Gerard pulled the garment back into place, slowly and with great regret. "No. Now, how have you been treated?"

Running her cheek across Jewel's back, his wife shrugged. "I am not harmed. Cecily is unkind, but I survive by staying in this room."

"Damn him! This was not our agreement." He looked around at the boarded-up window and his blood boiled. No one could treat his wife in this manner and not pay. Not even a onetime friend.

Catheryn rested a hand on his arm. "It will be fine, Gerard."

He growled. "It is fine to keep you in a locked room with one small candle for light?" His rage grew with every word. "No open window for air? If you can choose this, what was the other option?"

"No. You misunderstand. The boarding up of the window happened just today. I was told it was so the King would not see me, and I believed that until I spied through the cracks and saw Brezden's green and gold colors ride through the gates. It was done so you would not find me."

She stretched up to place a quick kiss on his chin. "I am delighted a little thing like boards did not prevent you from

243

finding me. I usually have free run of the keep but I choose to stay up here because I'm away from Cecily's sharp tongue. At times, this room has been a solace."

Gerard winced. "Has she been terrible toward you?"

"Not really. Terrible would be Pike or de Brye. Cecily has taken her pleasure from provoking me, as if she's begging me to lose all common sense and give her a tongue lashing that could get me hanged."

"I am truly sorry for all of this."

"It isn't your fault." Catheryn shook her head. "It is mine for not telling you what you needed to know immediately. I could have averted all this."

Gerard caught his breath. He'd never expected to hear that admission from her, and it softened his heart. "No, Catheryn. I think we must both shoulder the blame."

"How so?"

He scratched Jewel's head. Then, pulling his wife onto his lap, he threaded his fingers through Catheryn's hair. "That first night when I attacked Brezden I should have forced you to speak the truth."

Her laugh was small, but it was music to his ears. "You think you could have?"

Using his forehead to tip her head back, he lowered his lips to her neck and nipped the tender flesh. "I *know* I could have."

"Prove it, my lord."

She squirmed in his lap, and he doubted the movement was an accident. Even if it was, the effect would have been the same. His blood surged to his groin, and he knew she could feel his erection. Then her low, throaty moan gave away her intentions.

"Behave, Catheryn."

"Go to—"

He swallowed her curse with his lips. Then, despite his will, despite his intention to not spend too much time in her chamber, he found both of them naked within a few breathless heartbeats.

As his heart swelled with emotion, he heard his own hoarse voice as if through a fog. "God, I have missed you."

❧

Catheryn jerked awake when the door to her chamber opened. William, Cecily, and the carpenter entered. Swallowing a smile, she bid good morning to the trio. Had last night been a dream? No. She knew by her tired, sluggish body that Gerard had definitely been there.

"What brings you here this morn, my Lord?"

The carpenter removed the boards from the window, and William answered her query. "We are setting off to join King Stephen."

"Join him? What about the tourney?"

"That has been called off. Instead, we ride to battle."

"The King has already left?"

"Aye. With the first morning light. Your confinement is at an end, Lady Catheryn."

Her heart lurched, knowing Gerard would soon be leaving, but there was truly little else he could do. He'd brought her Jewel for a visit, though he'd taken the cat away again after. He'd made sweet desperate love to her. He'd bid her farewell, properly this time.

"You will be leaving, too?" she asked the Earl.

"Yes. Cecily will see to your welfare."

She wanted to laugh aloud. If Cecily didn't have her strung up from the closest tree by nightfall, things would be going better than she expected.

As if reading her thoughts, William promised, "You will come to no harm." He looked at his wife. "Upon my word as the Earl of York, you will come to no harm."

Catheryn wasn't too certain that would help, but his word was better than nothing. "Thank you, my Lord. Have a safe journey and wish my husband well."

"Oh, speaking of your husband." William ducked back out into the hall and returned with a wooden box. "He left this for you."

She had to choke back tears as she opened Jewel's cage and pulled the kitten to her chest.

Cecily's screech surely resounded over all of England. "That animal will not reside within these walls!"

William sighed. "Please, wife, let her and her cat be."

The woman turned away in a huff that did not bode well for Catheryn, especially since William then left the two women alone.

Catheryn wrapped her robe about her and walked to the window. Standing next to Cecily, she stared out at the assemblage below.

The men were mounted and clearly waited only for William's orders to leave.

The Earl joined the group a few minutes later. Both women watched in silence as the procession then headed out the gates. All but one lone rider. Smiling, Catheryn leaned out onto the window ledge and thrust her arm outside, and holding it high, she closed her hand into a fist. The rider, still motionless in the yard, mimicked her odd wave before joining those now leaving Scarborough.

"Who do you shake your fist at, Catheryn?" the Countess asked.

Burying her face in Jewel's fur, Catheryn hid her smile and answered, "No one."

Chapter Seventeen

"I want that cat out of here." Cecily sneezed again. "If you refuse to do it yourself, I'll have it taken away and seen to."

Catheryn stared at William's wife before turning to go back up to her chamber. She'd listened to the woman's raving for little over two months now and was sick to death of it. How much longer before the men returned, and Gerard could resume his search for de Brye? How much longer would she be held hostage by a man with a shrew for a wife?

"Where do you think you are going?"

Catheryn paused. "To my chamber."

"No. First of all, it is not *your* chamber. And we have some arrangements to discuss."

Closing her eyes, Catheryn counted to ten before returning. As she sat back down on a stool near Cecily's chair on the raised dais in the great hall, she asked, "What arrangements are those, my lady?"

Tilting her head, the Countess looked down her nose in a supercilious fashion. "I am having a party at the hunting lodge in three days, and you will attend."

"A party? Your husband is gone, and you hold a party?" Catheryn rose from her seat. "I hope your gathering is a success, my Lady, but I will not be attending."

She made it as far as the stairs this time before Cecily's snide tone stopped her. "Either you attend, or I will inform William of your husband's visit the night before they left."

Catheryn caught her breath. "I know not of what you speak."

"And I am certain you do. I have already questioned a stable boy who overheard your husband and his captain talking. I am quite certain that William promised to turn you over to King Stephen as a traitor if Gerard so much as *looked* for you."

"He must have been mistaken." Wishing she had the stable boy's neck between her fingers, Catheryn resumed her climb toward her chamber. "It wasn't my husband he overheard."

"No?" When that didn't stop Catheryn's flight, Cecily followed her to the bottom of the steps. "How do you think you'll look in a noose? The boy described the men dressed in green and gold tunics with enough detail for me to know the men's identity."

Turning, Catheryn came back down the steps. "I still say the boy was mistaken."

"Say what you will. I believe the lad, and so will William."

Nodding, Catheryn accepted defeat. "What am I required to do?"

A cruel smile crossed Cecily's face. "Serve."

"Serve?" Catheryn swallowed.

"Yes. You think yourself too high and mighty to serve food and drink at a party?"

"I am the wife of a Baron, the daughter of another, and a Lady in my own right."

"And Baron Reveur swore fealty to my husband." Leaning close so that they were nose to nose, Cecily added, "It's that or hang."

248

"Fine, my Lady," Catheryn said. "I will serve at this party of yours."

A loud commotion in the bailey drew both women outside, and Catheryn breathed a brief sigh of relief. William and his men rode through the gates! Heart racing, she quickly searched the returning party, but Gerard was not among them.

Rushing to the Earl's side, his wife threw her arms about his leg. "Oh, you are home at long last!"

Catheryn wanted to throw up. The woman had not mentioned her husband in a kind or wifely way from the moment he left.

William gazed down at his wife with a besotted look. In an aggravating sort of way, his devotion amused Catheryn. She found it hard to believe that the man who'd accused Gerard of being a lovesick fool was wrapped around his own wife's calculating, conniving finger. This man was the terror of York? This man was instrumental in defeating the Scots at the Battle of Standard?

"Yes, I am." He glanced up and saw Catheryn. "And how have the two of you been faring?"

Catheryn remained silent. Cecily, however, did not. She waved at Catheryn as if dismissing a servant. "Oh, you can go now."

Lifting her eyebrow, Catheryn remained where she stood.

"I said you can go now. Get you gone from my sight."

"Go to hell, Cecily."

William freed his leg from his wife's embrace and got down off his horse. "Enough!" He ushered both women back inside the keep, and the moment they entered the hall, he turned toward Catheryn and pointed a meaty finger at her. "You will give my wife the respect due her." Then he loomed over his much smaller mate. "If this has been happening during my absence, it will stop now. You will cease treating Lady Catheryn like a common serf."

"Then, dear husband, lock her up like the prisoner she is supposed to be."

"Hostage, Cecily. She is a hostage, not a prisoner."

A familiar argument. When she'd first arrived at Scarborough William and Cecily had discussed it more than once. Oddly enough, it was an argument that William never won.

She rolled her eyes as Cecily batted her lashes and gazed adoringly up at her husband. "Yes, William. A hostage. I do forget." The woman fluttered her hands as if seeking words from the air. "It is so hard to remember when she is so…so…" She peered around the Earl at Catheryn. "When she is such a common and plain sort of wench."

"This common and plain woman you speak of is my friend's wife as well. Forget that not, Cecily."

"Ah, yes. She is. Whatever possessed a healthy, strong, enticing man like Gerard to take on a wife like her?"

"I did." William's words sounded forced. As if they issued from between clenched teeth.

"Oh, silly me. That's right." Cecily stroked his arm. "Tell me, beloved, why could you not find someone like Edyth? At least she knew how to be a good wife."

Catheryn fled without asking leave. She knew that if she didn't get away from Cecily quickly, she'd strangle the woman, so she escaped to the only secluded spot she'd found other than her chamber.

The tower facing the water gave her a wide vista. Catheryn stared at the waves crashing against rocky mounds between the castle wall and the sea. Huge, white-crested mountains of water roared toward the walls and upon contact with the immovable stone shattered into countless, broken droplets.

A servant. A personal maid to the Lady of York, that's what Cecily wanted to make her. And she had little choice. It wasn't that she minded the work. When allowed, she'd performed physical labor at Brezden. But Cecily was seeking to humble her. The Lady of York had many servants that could easily be ordered to work at this coming party. Why her?

She leaned against the damp stone wall and her gaze roamed the ocean waves. "What is taking him so long?"

"If you will remember, he has been with the King."

She almost fell over the tower wall into the water far below at the unexpected answer. Catching her breath, she stared at William. "I know that. But you are here now, so where is Gerard?"

"He has been at Brezden for over four weeks now."

"And?"

William extracted a missive from the inside of his fur-lined cloak. "And Brezden, my Lady, provides a refuge for a traitor and possibly his smuggling activities."

Her already low spirits sank even further. Smuggling at Brezden? How much worse could this get?

William waved the scroll in front of her face before securing it again in his cloak. "Before you ask, I'll tell you. No, he has not yet found and removed de Brye." Turning to leave he added over his shoulder, "He did mention something about your men though."

Catheryn watched the Earl's retreating back for a moment before his words sank in. Spurred to action, she ran to catch up. "William! My Lord, please."

She grabbed the tail of his cloak before the door at the base of the tower closed, and without turning, the man said, "Is there something you want? Something I can do for you?"

"What else did Gerard say? About my men. What about my men?"

When he did turn, the look on his face made her wish he hadn't. It was obvious by his furrowed brow, red face and the tick in his cheek that he was in a fine rage. "Tell me, Lady Catheryn, why were your men not in Brezden the night Gerard attacked?"

She needed to remember who this was. Regardless of what she thought of the man, or what she thought of the way he handled his wife, this was the Earl of York. Her life rested solely in his good graces, and a lie would serve no one. "Because I sent them to safety."

"How?"

She paused. "There is a tunnel which leads out of Brezden."

"And how did you know they needed to seek safety?"

"Because I dreamt of Gerard's coming."

William's eyes widened before he snorted, and then turned back around to leave.

"No, wait. It is the truth, my Lord. I had the village midwife make me a magical sachet so I could dream of my true love." The words sounded ludicrous even to her own ears. "It was an act of desperation, of childishness. Have not you seen children make such charms?"

"Children, yes," the Earl said. "Grown women, no."

Catheryn tried unsuccessfully to keep the despair from her voice. "It was all I had left."

William faced her. "All you had left? What does that mean?"

"Pike and de Brye made my life a living hell. Fanciful dreams were all I had left. But instead of dreams, I had nightmares of the destruction to come. I had dreams of Gerard as a killer, destroying all in front of him and—"

"And you believed these night terrors to be true?"

"Weren't they?"

William nodded. "In this case yes. But do you trust all your dreams as if they are real?"

"No." She shook her head. "There was a difference with this one. It came night after night and would not leave me alone. It told me of true love and Gerard. It…it…" She could not bring herself to finish.

William studied her for a moment, then he pulled the previous missive he'd shown her from under his cloak. "What will you give me for this?"

"I have no gold."

"You possess more than gold, my Lady."

Gasping in shock, she took his meaning. She placed both hands over her heart and whispered, "You promised Gerard you would not harm me."

"We are not speaking of harm."

It took all the strength she possessed to back away and not simply tear the page he held from his hand. "I will not lie with you."

His intent perusal slowly drifted from her head to her feet. "The thought hadn't crossed my mind, but it might be an entertaining notion to be sure." He laughed at her outraged hiss before adding, "I am not interested in Gerard's leavings."

If he was trying to goad her to anger, it was working. "Then what do you want, my Lord?"

"Me? Nothing." He teased her with Gerard's note by holding it out then snatching it away. "However, Cecily requires your presence at her next gathering."

"Lady Cecily has already spoken to me of this." Catheryn shuddered to think of what else the woman had told William. "I have already agreed to attend. But I still don't understand what is so special about this party."

The Earl smiled, and she knew the answer would not be to her liking. "She is holding an…intimate party at the main hunting lodge."

Was the Earl suggesting what she thought? "And what will she be hunting?"

"Knowing my wife," William shrugged, "anything she can catch."

"And you, my Lord, what will you hunt?"

At her question, he laughed. "I? Nothing. I do not attend Cecily's private parties, and she does not inquire as to how I amuse myself those nights."

Despite his obsession with his wife, perhaps the Earl truly did cheat on her as Gerard suggested, but clearly the agreement was mutual. That idea of such a marriage sickened her. "How quaint. You are a church-going man, do you not fear the fires of hell?"

He stepped so close that Catheryn had to tip her head back to meet his irate glare. "And you? Do you not fear the thought of hanging, or burning at the stake?"

"I fear many things." She backed up several steps. "But your implied threats are not among them."

He shook his head, clearly amused. "You can be quite bold at times, Lady Catheryn. Do you have enough bravado to attend one of Cecily's gatherings?"

He kept saying attend, not serve, and Catheryn believed that to be significant. The Lady of York unquestionably kept secrets from her husband. "I will not be intimate with any of her guests. I would rather be confined to one of your dark cells."

"No one will force you. But if you should find one or two guests to your liking, no one will stop you from enjoying their attention."

The nervousness his strange grin inspired dissipated with the return of Catheryn's ire. "I would never dishonor my husband so!"

"He would never know."

"It matters not. *I* would know."

William waved Gerard's missive under her nose. "Will you attend, or not?"

She didn't understand why her presence at this event was so important, but she longed to touch something from Gerard's hand. She had to see the words he had written, wanted to know all that happened at Brezden. Closing her eyes, she nodded. "Yes. I will."

William placed the letter in her hand. "The gathering is in three days."

She did not open her eyes until she heard the door close. Holding Gerard's note close to her heart, she looked up at the darkening sky. As she had done every night without fail since leaving Brezden, Catheryn sought the moon and found the twinkling stars.

⌘

She stood in the dark. Lost and alone, Catheryn sought escape from the terror hunting her. The pounding of her heart echoed into the murky blackness and returned louder and stronger than before. Her fear was a living, breathing monster. It sucked at her strength and at her very will to live.

There came the wild crashing of men moving closer and closer. Shouts. The sounds drowned out her throbbing heart. Laughing, jeering wickedly, the men reached out for her. Grasping her arms, they dragged her to the ground. Her cries of fear ceased. Her voice fell to a hushed whisper of a prayer. The useless plea for mercy and a quick end to the horror floated from her lips to the darkened sky.

Men, their faces covered with bawdy masks, stripped off their clothes. Drunk with only thoughts of lust and blood, they fell upon her. Her scream split the night.

"Gerard!"

"Catheryn!" His answering shout ripped him from the clutches of his nightmare. Sweat drenched his body. His heart drummed loud in his ears. Gerard drew in great breaths of air, willing his heart to slow, his blood to cool, his fear to abate. He released the crumpled sheets in his hands.

A small, square bundle of cloth fell from his fingers. Retrieving it from the bed, he turned it over in his hands. One edge was scorched as if it had been tossed into a fire and quickly rescued from certain destruction. Where had he seen this before?

"You had no choice but to answer the yarrow's call."

The words—Catheryn's words from the night he'd attacked Brezden—floated into his memory. This was her dream charm. The sachet had been beneath the pillows on her bed, the very same bed he'd slept in every night since he'd returned. So, were the legends true? Could a person dream of their true love by simply sleeping with this sachet?

Gerard laughed weakly at his sudden fancy. No. It was nothing more than lack of sleep and the long hours spent on horseback and on foot combing through the fields, woods, countless caves, and other hidey-holes along the river searching for de Brye that set him on edge.

Swinging his legs over the side of the bed, he rose and walked to the window. The night air was cool on his naked flesh, but he beat his fist on the wall anyway. He missed her. They'd been apart just over two months and already it felt like a lifetime.

Stephen's march to capture Empress Matilda had come to an abrupt halt in Northampton, where the King had fallen ill. The campaign was postponed, and relieved of duty, Gerard rode straight back to Brezden to resume his manhunt. He had located de Brye's camp and a few of his men, but the villainous knight and those he held prisoner were absent. That may have made sense if one considered the missive William had found on the body of the dead man he'd dragged back to Brezden. If Raymond de Brye was in league with the empress, he was likely at her side. He'd return now that the conflict was postponed, however, and when he did Gerard would be waiting.

In the meantime, Gerard searched the other tunnels and caves. He'd been seeking Brezden's missing men and the two children. Instead he found enough evidence to hang his wife. There was no doubt in his mind that de Brye had planted maps of the tunnels and forged missives to the empress, but had anyone else found these items, Gerard knew they'd come to only one conclusion—Catheryn was a traitor. He had to capture de Brye before any more incriminating evidence surfaced.

Gerard turned away from the window and donned the clothing he had earlier draped over the bench. He tucked the discarded sachet into his belt and leaving the chamber he climbed the steps that led to Brezden's tower. There a chill wind buffeted him. The cold air helped to dispel the lingering remains of his nightmare.

"My Lord."

"Walter." He did not need to turn to recognize the voice. Had he known the captain was here, Gerard would have looked for solitude elsewhere.

"The men have stowed the documents in your chamber."

"Good. An inventory was taken of the items promised in the missives?" He wanted to make certain none of Brezden's supplies had made their way to the Empress.

"Yes, the clerk will have the list for you in the morning."

His captain's words caused Gerard's guts to twist, and he

leaned on the ledge of the wall. How many times had de Brye entered the keep without anyone knowing? Any one of the people residing inside the keep could have been killed, murdered while the lord of the keep was doing other things. Raymond de Brye had been within reach from the beginning of their marriage and Catheryn had kept the knowledge to herself. And he had let her. He had permitted the woman to get too far under his skin. She had slipped into his blood, into his heart too easily, and doom lay in caring too much. He knew that.

Things would be different. They had to be. Once this task was complete, once de Brye was dead and Catheryn returned to Brezden, things would be different. No more would he plead with her. No more would he permit her tears to weaken his will. No more would he seek to allay her fears when so much might rest on information she withheld. No. When she returned, she would find a husband she could not deceive. A man she could not bend. She would become the obedient wife she always should have been.

It all sounded right to his mind, but his heart snickered at the thoughts. His gaze drifted to the night sky. *"Gerard!"*

The hair on the back of his neck stood on end. He shook the strangeness from him and leaned backward on the ledge. Quickly searching the keep walls, he could see no one but Walter.

"Gerard!"

His blood raced ice-cold through his veins. When he touched the dream charm on his belt, the bag pulsed with life. Heat suffused his fingertips. A fog misted his vision. She stood in the dark. Lost and alone, Catheryn sought escape from the terror hunting her. The same dream as before. Gerard's heart swelled, then stopped with fear.

In his mind, shouts and the wild crashing of men coming

closer and closer drowned out the sound of her throbbing heart. Laughing, jeering wickedly, they reached out to her. Grasping her arms and dragging her to the ground. Now his heart crashed against the inside of his chest in a wild, frantic pace. Her scream split the night. One word tore from her lips.

"Gerard!"

Closing his eyes, he could see her. The scent of her terror seared his nostrils. The fear evident on her face pierced his soul.

He pounded the wall before ordering, "Walter, gather the men. Arm them well."

"My Lord?"

Turning to face his confused captain, Gerard forced himself to keep his voice steady. "We ride to bring the Lady of Brezden home. Tonight."

Walter blinked once before answering. "It is about time, my Lord."

"There is never a time for committing treason. Things shall be different soon."

"We could ride for Reveur after regaining Catheryn. The men would not begrudge a return home."

"A coward's escape? Walter, I never thought to hear you suggest the easy way out."

"Not cowardly, my Lord. Expedient."

Gerard choked on his laughter. "Expedient? You mean it is what my lady mother would wish."

His captain had the grace to look confused. "My Lord?"

"My lady mother." He pinned Walter with a knowing stare. "Surely you did not think I was that ignorant?"

His captain said nothing, but his gaze darted everywhere else.

"Since my father's death you have served my mother, my

captain or not. Tell me she issued no orders in reference to my welfare."

"You are her only son." The man's reply was a mumble.

"Yes, but her son has outlived the need for a nursemaid." Walter's complexion darkened. "Has it been that obvious?"

"Obvious? Lord, man, you have walked in my shadow since Edyth's death. If danger came from anywhere, it came from breaking my neck as I tripped over you."

"But—"

Gerard raised his hand, cutting off his captain's explanation. "I am not chastising you. I am trying to tell you that I am finally whole. The crazed grief is gone, Walter. You need not watch my every move."

His captain nodded but said nothing.

Gerard clasped the man's shoulder. "I would have no other guarding my back."

"Thank you, my Lord." Walter's smile eased Gerard's guilt for making the man uncomfortable. "I will be certain to inform your mother of your well-being."

"Good." Gerard turned to look back out over Brezden's lands and the darkened forest below. He contemplated for a moment then added, "Walter, be certain to tell the men what we go to do. Give them the choice to come, or to remain here. I will not force them to take up arms against the Earl. I may break my vow of fealty, but I do not demand they do the same."

"I will, my Lord." The captain paused. "Think you it wise to prepare all the men for a swift ride out of England? Your mother's will or not, it is the wise choice."

Stiffening his shoulders against the weight of the crime he was about to commit, Gerard nodded in agreement. "Yes."

The captain opened the door to the stairway, but instead of leaving he added softly, "Do not lie to yourself, Gerard. You are not yet whole. A piece of you resides at Scarborough."

Gerard sighed wearily. "I know."

Waiting until the door closed behind his captain, Gerard gazed up at the dark sky. As he had done every night without fail since Catheryn left Brezden, he sought the moon and found the twinkling stars.

Chapter Eighteen

"William." The Earl did not lift his head from the accounts on the table, so Gerard took another step into the lord's private chamber. "My Lord Earl."

Still not looking up, William responded. "What do you want, Gerard? Why are you here?"

"I am taking my wife home."

Slamming the ledger closed, William stood. "By whose orders?"

"My own."

"And de Brye?"

"He is not at Brezden. I have captured some of his men, though. They will testify that he exists. I just await his return…and ensnarement."

"So, he is not yet captured?"

"No." A detail that nagged at Gerard constantly.

"You are dressed for battle. I can assume your men await your return from a safe and strategic place?"

"How astute, William. Yes, they do."

The Earl's jaw clenched. "Has Brezden made you as unruly as your wife?"

Gerard half smiled. "Has she been a burden?"

"I am amazed Pike or de Brye did not kill her for it."

Gerard bit his tongue, tried not to think of that. "They tried."

"And you. Why do you permit her to continue?"

Gerard could not mask his impatience any longer. "Because I find it a refreshing change from the bland females at court. Where is my wife?"

"You think it that simple? You walk in here dressed in mail, helm and spurs, draw your sword and demand her release?"

"No. I don't think it simple." Gerard hesitated. How much could he tell William without seeming insane? "My wife is in danger and I intend to remove her from harm's way."

"Danger?" The Earl's expression revealed surprise. "She is in no physical danger here. No one can harm one hair on her head without my direct order."

Gerard sighed. "William, I cannot explain other than to say that I know with all my fighting senses that death stalks her even here."

The Earl frowned. "I have never found cause to fault your judgment in battle. But this is no battle, Gerard. Perhaps lust for this woman has set your normally keen senses askew."

"Lust has nothing to do with it." Desire maybe, but not lust. That was a distinction he would never before have made. "Where is my wife, William?"

The Earl's face hardened. "Again, I will ask you. Did you think to walk in here, demand her return and then simply walk out?"

Gerard shook his head. "No. I had planned on attacking your castle. I'd resigned myself, and my men, to committing treason to take back my wife, God be my witness." He paused to gather his thoughts a moment before admitting,

"But as I rode up to your walls, I remembered that once we were friends."

Hand on his sword, Gerard continued. "I recalled that our lands border each other in Normandy and that your father and mother reared me as much as my own parents. I thought about all the times our people shared the work of harvesting, and I remembered that once your mother and mine were close companions."

The Earl ran a hand down his face. "I knew giving you Brezden would never suit. How am I to remain the Terror of York with you around?"

Biting off a smile before it reached his lips, Gerard offered, "I could leave. I could return to Reveur."

"Stephen would have both of our heads. This rebellion with the Empress requires all the men and gold he can lay his hands on. To let you return to Normandy—"

"King Stephen already knows my desire. My *plan*."

"And?"

"The missive was only just sent two days past. There has been no time for a reply."

William sat on the edge of the table and toyed with his writing quill. "What did you tell him, Gerard?"

"Never fear. I told him nothing that will bring his wrath down on *your* head."

Both men shook their heads. Stephen was indeed wrathful, sometimes to his detriment.

William grimaced. "So, he knows nothing of me holding Lady Catheryn hostage? Nothing of your ulterior motive for attacking Brezden? Nothing of de Brye's escape and subsequent smuggling operation, since we believe that de Brye is the one responsible for all that?"

"No, nothing. Not unless you told him. He knows only that I wish to remove my wife from England, that after doing so and seeing to her safety I will return. That was my promise."

"You think he will agree to your absence with such a flimsy reason?"

Gerard smiled. "I sent the missive to Maud."

"To the queen?" The shock in William's voice was evident.

"Of course. Why not? It was worded as a matter of love, and therefore Queen Maud will bend over backwards to see that Stephen permits my humble request."

"How you gained that woman's good graces when I could not is baffling."

"I can't answer that. What I do know is that Maud reminded me of my mother, and I treated her with the same respect. You, on the other hand, ignored her."

William's face registered disbelief. "I never ignored Maud."

"William, please, you ignore any woman you know you can't bed. It would not kill you to at least be kind."

"You have listened to far too many troubadours."

"Have I? Tell me, William, who has the queen's ear and who does not? Who do the other men trust around their wives and daughters, and who do they not?" Resting his palms on the table, Gerard leaned across the expanse of oak and spoke clearly. "Where is my wife?"

Lost in apparent thought, William answered, "At one of Cecily's parties."

Jerking from what felt like a blow to his stomach, Gerard bolted upright. "What?"

"She is at a gathering."

"Catheryn, my wife, is at one of Cecily's *gatherings*?"

William stood and glared at Gerard. "You heard me correctly. She is attending a party. She was given the choice, and freely accepted."

Gerard twisted to the side and slapped his gloves on the table. "I want answers. Now." He'd known William too long to believe any claptrap about choices. He could imagine what Catheryn's choices had been. He would never have imagined that his onetime friend would send her there, though.

"It is useless to argue. She is there."

Blood rushed to Gerard's head, causing his temples to throb and his vision to blur. He blinked to clear the red haze. "How long has this…*party* been going on?"

"A while."

"All day?"

"No. Actually, it should…" The Earl glanced out the narrow window. "Well, since the moon is just now moving into view, the gathering should be starting about now. Are you worried, Gerard?"

"About my wife's fidelity? No. About her level of disgust? Yes."

"You are now referring to *my* wife."

"Your wife? William, we are speaking of a woman who lives to love. And do not play innocent with me. We both know who taught her those ways. That is the only reason you do not run a sword through her. She was once—"

"Stop before you go too far, Baron Reveur."

Gerard shook his head. "Are you going to tell me that my wife and yours have become such good companions that they even enjoy spending time together?"

"Well, they do get along," William suggested.

"Get along?" Gerard almost laughed. "Like fire and oil."

"I give up." William raised his hands in mock surrender. "Our wives hate each other. However, Cecily recently admitted that she found Edyth charming."

At that, Gerard did laugh. "Well, it was hardly mutual.

266

Edyth was horrified by Cecily's actions at our wedding. It isn't every day a guest tries to seduce the groom."

"She meant nothing by it." William's red face belied his calm voice.

Gerard shrugged. This line of conversation was headed nowhere, and he would no longer spar with William about ancient history. "My wife. Where is this party being held? I will collect her."

William scanned the room as if looking for a place to hide. He said nothing, and Gerard's heart thumped in his chest.

"William, is it here within the castle?"

"Not precisely."

It was obvious that William was not going to volunteer any information on the topic. "Where?"

"Near Caitune."

An urge to fling himself across the narrow space between them and beat the Earl to a mewling mass nearly overwhelmed Gerard. Instead, he grasped the hilt of his sword and mastered his temper. "Play no more games with me."

William backed away and sat on a bench by the fire. Lifting his hands dismissively, he said, "She is doing nothing wrong, simply attending one of Cecily's gatherings."

"Where?" Gerard repeated. But dread rushed alongside his anger.

"The south hunting lodge."

"My God, man, a *bathing* party?"

William nodded.

Memories of the first party he had attended at that lodge assaulted Gerard, nearly knocking him from his feet. While the party was…educational, he certainly didn't want his wife there. He retrieved his gloves, turned on his heel and headed toward the door, stopping only when his onetime friend called out his name.

"Gerard!"

Gerard stopped without turning. "I must go. Whatever you have to say will have to wait until I return to England."

William sighed, and the noise was full of regret. "You need not leave the country. I will not come for you, or your wife. But you *must* find a way to capture de Brye. Quickly, before the King hears rumors of treason. He will surely burn Brezden and everything in it to the ground, then come for me."

Gerard was positive William was wrong on that last part and was worrying for naught. King Stephen could not afford to cast off one as rich and powerful as the Earl of York. But after allowing this much time to pass without saying anything to the king, it was certain someone would pay for withholding information about a traitor. It was likely that someone would be the Lord of Brezden.

He nodded. "Thank you. And fear not, William, I will find de Brye."

❦

Catheryn stared at the sight before her. No amount of blinking cleared her vision. No amount of wishing stopped what she heard. How had she let Cecily coerce her into coming here?

Easily, she reminded herself. Earl William had ordered her to attend this disgusting party with his wife. The pair had insisted that it was an honor to be chosen to act as a servant here…but Catheryn stared at the revolting tableau before her and wondered where the honor lay. Surely not here.

She'd had little choice, though, it was this or take up residence in a cell. While she didn't believe William would toss her into one, she couldn't be certain about his lady.

Unlike her husband, Cecily was no friend of Gerard's. And Catheryn had seen Scarborough's cells. If Cecily tossed her into one, Catheryn knew she'd not last a day. Enclosed in one of those dark, tiny rooms tucked so far beneath the keep…if the dark didn't drive her mad, the rats scurrying across the dirt floors would have. Still, she wondered if she'd made the right choice.

From the many kettles of water kept warm on fires outside, to the numerous huge tubs filling every room of the lodge, there was an overabundance of everything—laughter, food, drink, baths. And far too much exposed flesh. The sight of such wantonness repulsed her. She did not find the crude display exciting. Not only did it embarrass her, she found that any respect she might have had for those in attendance died a quick and easy death. They displayed themselves as if walking about naked in mixed company with veritable strangers were an everyday occurrence. Had they no shame? No pride?

Simple decency demanded they cover themselves, but the only thing covered on the bodies inside the lodge were faces. Every guest wore some type of mask or hood, some adorned with feathers and some nothing more than scraps of decorated fabric tied around the wearer's head. Their secrecy bothered Catheryn more than their nakedness, truth be told. Other than being well able to determine male from female, she knew not who she served.

A wide slat of wood balanced across the middle of each double-sized tub. There she was to place food and drink. Her hands shook while she carried trays of wine goblets. There had been one other serving girl helping inside with the food and drink, but she'd easily been coaxed to join the bawdy fray.

Catheryn twisted and turned to avoid grasping hands as

she walked between the tubs, and her wits nearly left her when it became obvious that not all of the seeking hands belonged to men. They were drunk, these women. Or they were under the spell of some herb. Incense burned in every corner of the lodge, and fear that the sweet, strong smell was to blame for the women's behavior kept her well away from the thin columns of smoke.

Her face burned. She tried to avert her gaze, but everywhere she looked couples were seeking pleasure in a variety of ways, both in the tubs and on the pallets Cecily so thoughtfully provided. As she had done every night since she'd been away from her husband, she whispered, "Oh, Gerard, hurry."

Needing air, Catheryn stood by a window and breathed in the cool night breeze. She leaned against the wall and stared up at the dark sky. Wisps of clouds partially covered the moon, but she could see the twinkling stars against the inky blackness. Closing her eyes for a moment, Catheryn decided she'd had enough of this senseless entertainment. It was time to brave whatever punishment would come.

Just as she decided to tell Cecily she was done serving, someone shouted at her, "Wench, more wine."

Catheryn swallowed a deep breath of air and steeled her resolve. Maybe, just maybe, if she kept her thoughts on serving wine and pretended this was all nothing but a bad dream she could somehow get through the night.

"Wench!"

Grabbing a pitcher of wine, she approached the shouting guest. His wayward hand snaked out, and she backed away— right into another seeking palm. When she slapped at that man's hand, she found her wrist captured in a hard grasp that she couldn't break.

The first man snaked his hand up inside the hem of her

gown. Fear, shock, and disbelief held her momentarily still. He stroked and caressed her ankle, calf, and moved his fingers up toward her thigh.

Jerking her leg free, Catheryn gritted her teeth and nearly growled, "Earl William said I did not have to entertain. Get your hands off me."

The second man, the one holding her wrist, laughed. "William is not here, is he?"

"Oh, Catheryn, relax." A woman waved from the next tub and Catheryn recognized the Earl's wife despite her mask. "Enjoy yourself." Cecily's eyes were glassy and red-rimmed.

Catheryn fought to keep her wits intact. "My Lady, your husband said—"

"Nothing. He said nothing." Cecily's brittle laugh boded ill-will. There'd be no help coming from that quarter. Not that Catheryn had expected any.

The first man continued to paw at her leg. The second man cupped her bottom and squeezed.

Catheryn brought her wine jug down on the first man's head. She then thrust the broken jug toward the second. Just as she was about to thrash him with the jagged pottery, someone else grabbed her arm.

Her outraged gaze raked the new intruder. He towered at least a head over her. His face was concealed in an elaborate hood adorned with black feathers and jewels worthy of a king's ransom, but his gaze burned through her. Something felt familiar about his eyes. They seemed to pierce her.

Catheryn's heart raced. Her breathing quickened with fear as the stranger reached out and slapped away the other man's hold, pulling her toward him. Then he moved her toward the stairs leading to the upper floor of the lodge, his touch gentle but his hand around the back of her neck held her securely.

"Release me. Now." She struggled against him but was no match for his strength. Catheryn's breathing ceased. She'd not willingly mount those stairs. She'd not willingly commit adultery. She'd rather die.

When they reached the steps leading up to the private chambers, she stiffened her legs. The disguised man bent to lift her in his arms, so Catheryn swung around and slipped from his hold. Running to the door of the lodge, she sighed a breath of relief when her hand fell on the door. Her relief had come too quickly.

He grabbed her from behind, opened the door and pushed her out into the night, and only then did she recognize him. His laugh froze her blood as she recognized de Brye's bitter tone. Her stomach churned. The scream building in her throat could not fight its way past the bile choking her.

"Ah, sweeting, I have waited far too long for this. You will not escape me now—or ever again."

❧

Gerard was grateful to not have to ask for directions. Having attended one of Cecily's gatherings at the lodge, he remembered the way.

He led his men swiftly across William's land, south along the coast, past fields and the town of Osgodby, then slightly west into the forest near Caitune. His heart drummed along with the horses' hooves. Steady and strong, that pounding rhythm underlined the only goal in his mind and soul. Find Catheryn. Save Catheryn. Before the terrors of his nightmare became a reality.

It was impossible to believe that Catheryn had willingly gone to this party. What trick had the Earl and his Lady used as coercion? Catheryn would be like a fish tossed upon the shore, out of her element and helpless. She was nearly an innocent in the ways of lovemaking. Their few nights of shared passion could not prepare her for what she would witness at that lodge. He himself had been shaken, and he'd not been a green boy in the arts of seduction. The unending sight of entwined flesh had left him speechless. From one partner to another, the guests took their pleasure. He'd found it embarrassing to witness at first. But, with the help of two lusty bawds, his youthful embarrassment had swiftly dissolved and his education was broadened.

But he did not want his wife exposed to such acts. Not without him. Not outside the privacy of their own chamber. Not with *others*.

Her presence at this party had no purpose other than to humiliate her, and to anger him. It was a shameful and a dishonorable way to ensure his outrage.

Outrage? Amazed at the strength of his conviction, Gerard shook his head. Was he getting old? When had the wicked, randy follies of youth become something shameful? Immediately, however, he found the answer—since he'd left youth behind and become a man. Since he'd married and discovered someone who depended on his honor and needed his protection.

His *protection*. Now there was a horrific thought. How well had he protected Edyth and their infant son? Not at all. He'd not be guilty of another wife's death.

The fires burning outside William's hunting lodge drew his attention to the problem at hand, getting Catheryn away from Cecily, away from William and back safely to Brezden. He and his men thundered into the clearing before the lodge, drawing their swords as they came. Frightened servants scurried out of the way as cauldrons of water were knocked from their fires. Guests, copulating under the stars, paused in their acts to stare blankly at the intruders. And Gerard's worst fears were confirmed by their unfocused gazes. Reddened and glazed, their eyes spoke of Cecily's incense of lust. When lit, the opium-laced herbs emitted a sickly-sweet aroma that beckoned all into a world of uninhibited passion.

If his wife had been exposed to that drugged herb, he reminded himself, she'd not be responsible for her actions. But still he'd kill any man who'd touched her.

Ignoring the masked guests outside who were too lost in lust to be of any harm, Gerard rode toward the lodge. Kicking the front door open with his foot, he guided Bastard inside, the horse shying away from the smoke permeating the air.

"Catheryn!" Gerard shouted, only to be greeted by amused chuckles from those few guests who bothered to pay attention.

Walter slid past him in the doorway, having dismounted and now squeezed past the destrier with great care. "My Lord, I do not think—"

Gerard glared down at him. "Good. Don't. Find my lady and let us be gone."

Walter nodded. Then, after displaying a brief expression of horror, he warily ventured further into the lodge and toward the stairs.

Gerard guided his horse around unconscious bodies, not caring if they were passed out from an overabundance of wine and sex, or dead from an overabundance of the cloying smoke. What had Catheryn thought when she'd witnessed this vile orgy? Had she been shocked? Had she been angry? Had it captured her interest? No. That thought was unfair. While another woman might find the sights and notions here irresistible, Catheryn would not. Gerard again steeled himself against the knowledge that he might very well find her entwined in another man's arms against her will. It would take all the strength he had not to kill the foolish scum.

No. He drove the thought away. She would not be in another man's arms. He would not find her entwined with anyone else. She was not here. He would find her somewhere dark and dank, punished by Cecily for not participating.

A curse built in his chest and raged from his lips. He started backing his horse out of the lodge, and he shouted for his captain. If he could not locate Catheryn, maybe he could find Cecily.

Walter appeared almost instantly, dragging a naked, angry Lady Cecily with him. Apparently, his captain had the same thought.

"What is the meaning of this, Gerard?" the Countess asked. The woman who used her wealth and power to force other women into acts that they would not otherwise perform. The sound of his name from her mouth nauseated him.

Gerard stared down at her. "Whore, let my name not cross your lips again. Where is my wife?"

"Whore?" she screeched at him like a fishwife. "Who are you to call me whore?" Waving her hand about, she asked, "Is my mind suddenly ailing? Do I not remember you, Baron Reveur, enjoying the pleasures of this lodge?"

He ignored that. "Where is my wife?"

The Countess refused to answer, so Walter shook her.

"She left. With a man, Baron Reveur. A big, strong, capable man. One who terrified her with his laugh and with no more than a word or two had her running screaming from this lodge. Does that answer your question, Gerard?"

De Brye. It could be no other.

Gerard's hand convulsed over the rounded pommel of his sword, but he mastered himself. William would be angry if he found his wife dead, even if he'd soon replace her with

275

another. Instead, Gerard ground out another oath, then wheeled his horse around, knocking one staggering man to the floor, and fled the lodge before he did something he'd regret.

Circling the clearing, he fought to control his raging emotions. Fear was something he'd not often felt, and it clouded his thoughts. Never in battle had he felt any such weakness, this horrible pounding of his heart, or the cold sweat that now coursed down his neck.

Never before had he been unable to form coherent thoughts or devise a plan that would bring victory to him and his men. The forest was vast. There were many places Catheryn could have been taken. Where would he find her? More important, would he get to her in time?

Stopping his mount, he took a deep breath and gazed up at the sky, seeking the moon and finding the stars. He closed his eyes and prayed.

Where are you, Catheryn? Where are you?

Chapter Nineteen

Catheryn opened her eyes to stare into nothingness. No light broke the cold dark surrounding her, enveloping her in a thick cloak of dread.

Her back rested against icy, damp stone. Stiff from being in this slumped position for God knew how long, she groaned with the effort to move. A chain rattled across the hard floor as she tried to cross her legs before her, and reaching out, she felt metal links firmly circling one ankle. She was chained in the dark like an animal.

Her heart raced. Sweat covered her body. Something like fear—but worse—shot through her limbs. Terror. Horror. Disoriented, she could discern nothing. Was she alone? Were there others about? Was de Brye sitting somewhere within reach? Barely able to breathe, she gasped, forcing her lungs to fill with air.

Panic overwhelmed her. She would die without ever seeing Gerard's face again. Without ever touching him or kissing his lips, she would be killed. And he would never know how much she loved him.

It was irrational to love a man she'd only known a few months. Insane to love a man who'd attacked her keep and locked her in a cell. Unreasonable to be consumed by a man with whom she'd only spent a few nights. Irrational, insane, unreasonable…but real.

There was no one else she'd rather share her life with. No one but Gerard could make her knees go weak with just a smile. Or set her pulse racing with a look. Or send her heart soaring with a kiss. No one but Gerard would listen to ramblings about her parents, her childhood, would show a hard exterior, but be gentle inside. No other man had ever bothered to ask. No other man had pretended to care. And what knight but Gerard would give her poetry as consolation, telling her to find the stars and seek the moon to know that all was well? Burying her face in her hands, Catheryn willed herself not to cry. If any tears fell now, they'd never stop.

The pain from clenching her teeth was almost her undoing. Agony shot through her jaw like an arrow. He had hit her. Outside the hunting lodge, de Brye had slugged her and she remembered little else. Vaguely she recalled being slung over the back of a horse like a sack. A bitter taste in her mouth brought a blurred memory of someone forcing a vile liquid down her throat every time she'd started to stir, but that was all she could force from her groggy mind.

Gingerly moving her jaw back and forth, she felt her stomach rebel against the pain but was relieved to find no bones broken. They were only bruised. And sore. What would de Brye do with her? Kill her? That was likely the least of what he planned. The tortures he would inflict before her death were frightening beyond words.

Choking back a sob, Catheryn swallowed hard. *I will not cry. I will not show that vile slime my fear.* To do so would only inflame his desire to build upon her terror.

She ran her hands down her body, poking and prodding. For right now she was whole. She could detect no damage, no pain except for that in her jaw. That meant whatever de Brye planned was being saved until she woke. She slumped back against the wall, hoping he would think she was still unconscious. Maybe she could gain enough time to gather her strength and her courage. Both would be needed—along with her wits.

"It will not work."

Catheryn froze. He was here and probably had been the entire time. She remained silent. Refusing to respond might make him think he was mistaken, that she still slept.

His approach was silent, his footsteps unheard over the sound of her breathing and the pounding of her heart. She nearly fainted when a hand grazed her shoulder. Gagging at the smell of his rancid breath, she fought the urge to scream.

De Brye drew one finger up the side of her neck, across her cheek and down her chin before closing his fingers around her throat. "You will die, sweeting."

His grip tightened, cutting off her air. She refused to struggle, and simply closed her eyes. In the semi-dark chambers of her mind she could see his evil grin. She could see the mad light shoot from his eyes.

His grip relaxed. "But not before you beg me to end your life."

She flinched when his other hand closed around her thigh. His fingers dug into the tender flesh and gritting her teeth did little to diminish the pain.

De Brye nibbled at her chin, caught it between his teeth and bit hard enough to draw a gasp of pain. He released her chin then moved his lips closer to her ear. "Fear not, my love, you will scream for me. I have ached to hear the sweet melody for far too long." He moved his hand higher on her leg.

Would he kill her outright if she fought him, or would he

only beat her until she could no longer move? Until she could no longer fight. Until she no longer cared.

When his hand came to rest between her thighs, she lost control of her will and could not remain still beneath his squeezing fingers. Surging wildly against his vile touch, she threw him off balance. A loud oath echoed in the darkness.

"You will pay for that, sweeting."

Catheryn twisted and came up on her hands and knees. She could only hope that if she kept moving, he would not be able to find her. Of course, she'd not taken the chain into consideration. Instead of seeking her in the dark, de Brye found the length of chain. Slowly, steadily, he dragged her back.

She clawed at the wet, smooth floor, praying that her fingers would find something, anything, to latch on to, but she could find no purchase. Fire burned at her fingertips as they dug at the rock floor, breaking her nails and gouging her flesh. The stone scraped her knees as she was pulled kicking and screaming to de Brye. She'd not give up. Not without a fight. But nothing she did could slow his pull.

He latched a hand on her ankle and finished pulling her to him. Finding her head, he grabbed a handful of hair. "It is truly too bad that I have no time for this now." His was tone of awful sick regret. "I would so enjoy giving you a small taste of what is to come."

"Go to hell."

The words had barely left her mouth before a hand cracked against the side of her face, sending her forcefully back to the floor. Her head bounced against the stone. Slipping slowly into unconsciousness, Catheryn closed her fingers into a tight fist and whispered, "Gerard."

⚬⚬

Raymond de Brye waited for one of his men to bring a lit

torch, then sent the soldier back out of the chamber. He chuckled to himself. The caves beneath and behind Brezden had proven useful once again. Who would hear the lady's screams from this, the farthest recess at the rear of the farthest cave? No one but he.

Grasping his crotch, he briefly rubbed the throbbing hardness. But, no, he would not waste himself. He would wait until she awoke, wait until he had more time to savor this conquest. The thought of her cries as he buried himself inside her flesh nearly drove him wild with desire, so he kicked her in the side to alleviate his pain. The lady remained unconscious, oblivious of what would come.

Baron Reveur and Earl William had forced his hand by taking this woman—*his woman*—to Scarborough. He hadn't planned on acting so quickly, not until he was ready to leave Brezden for good, but Reveur had gone to collect her from there and surely intended to take his bride back to Normandy.

For a while he'd been afraid that she had slipped through his fingers, but luck—no, fate—had intervened. Joining Lady Cecily's bathing party had been easily accomplished. The whore welcomed any and all who wished to participate. And when he'd seen Catheryn at the hunting lodge, Raymond knew that the angels had smiled on him. The time had finally come. Now there was no need for rushing the task he'd so long envisioned, and if the taste of success would have been sweet before, it was even sweeter now. Now he would destroy two instead of one. In one stroke he could kill the Lady of Brezden and send the soul of Reveur to the fires of hell.

He felt a brief moment of sorrow for Catheryn but shook it off. His actions were justified. Had not the angels told him repeatedly that he was within his rights? Had not the first

Lady of Brezden sworn he could have her daughter? True, she had promised that daughter over her own dead body, but now the Lady was dead at his hands. He quivered in pleasure at the memory of sending her tumbling down the steep stairs of the keep. He'd stared down at that broken body knowing that her daughter, Catheryn, now rightfully belonged to him and no other.

Unfortunately, he'd not been able to claim his rights immediately. Baron Pike had panicked and demanded that they leave Brezden for a time, going to Normandy. He'd said that Raymond acted rashly and foolishly. But, had he? Even leaving Brezden for that time had been fortuitous. Had they not happened upon Baron Reveur's keep?

A divine blessing, that. Baron Reveur's keep. Baron Reveur, the man who decapitated John de Brye, the only other person Raymond ever cared for. His brother. His brother who had died on a bloody field of battle. It was then, holding his brother's lifeless body, that the angels had spoken to Raymond for the first time. They told him over and over that revenge would right the wrongs done to him and John. And so, he'd sought revenge. From that day forward, he'd lived only for two things. The second was to make Reveur pay.

It had been an easy thing to force that cleric to write the missive to call Baron Reveur away from his keep and slitting the cleric's throat ensured that none would be the wiser. The babe, however, had been far too easy to kill. What sport was a newborn? Of course, Lady Reveur had fought like a wildcat. Of that he'd enjoyed every moment. He'd made her suffer in ways he'd not even dreamt until that day.

De Brye glanced down at Catheryn and thought of his first reason for living. That was to find a woman to become his wife. His plaything. His slave. But the woman he'd so carefully chosen had married his enemy. She belonged to Raymond—her own mother had said so—yet she'd become the new Lady Reveur. Raymond's rage knew no bounds. Catheryn would pay for her treachery by an agonizingly slow death…and by killing her, he would make Reveur pay once again.

He kicked Catheryn one last time. Again, she did not move. Bending down, Raymond brushed a stray lock of hair from her face and said, "That's all right, sweeting. Sleep. Rest well. You will need all the strength you can muster."

∽

"Gerard!"

It was a silent cry, one none of his men could hear, and one that brought him again and again back to this very spot. He had followed the sound in his head back here from Scarborough, to near Brezden, abandoning the idea that his wife was dragged off to be dealt with in the woods near the lodge. His men had said nothing, not even Walter. He prayed he was right. Perhaps there was still time. His dreams promised there was still time. He'd been clutching Catheryn's dream sachet and praying the dreams were right.

"They have to be in there," he muttered to himself.

After tucking the dream bag safely into his pouch, Gerard crossed his hands over the edge of his tall saddle, leaned forward, and stared down the river's steep bank. He had little fear of being seen. A thick line of brush and trees concealed him and Walter, but there appeared no need for secrecy. No standing guards were evident. Now and then a man would leave the cave, patrol the river for a short distance and then return. Either de Brye was a fool, or he was so confident of himself that he felt no need for guards.

Or he was not there. But Gerard would not allow himself to think that. He would believe in magic and dreams. He

283

would believe in finding his wife.

"Do you have a plan of attack?"

Glancing at his captain, Gerard noted the man's haggard appearance. In the last four days neither of them had slept more than a couple hours at a time. It had been a day and a half to Scarborough and another day and half back to Brezden. Then they'd combed the caves and riverbank. He prayed again to any God who would listen that this hunch, this odd feeling, this magic sureness about her location, was not wrong.

"My Lord?"

"Other than getting a look inside that cave and removing Catheryn if she is there? No. I have no other set plan. But we shall succeed."

"Gerard."

He jumped. Turning in his saddle, he stared in amazement at William.

"Baron Reveur," the Earl added.

"Go away, William. I have no time for your games." Directing his attention back to the river, he searched the bank to find again the cavern mouth of de Brye's hideout. A bush there moved. Waving the soldiers behind him back, Gerard moved out of sight himself. "Or has your wife complained about my treatment of her guests?"

"That is not why I am here." William kept his voice barely over a hushed hiss.

Not taking his intent stare from the river, Gerard gritted his teeth. "If you came to take Catheryn back, we will first have to find her." He turned and leveled a steady glare at the man. "And then you'll have to kill me."

Gerard meant it. He'd not permit William or anyone else to ever take his wife from him again. The mistake should never have occurred the first time.

He waited for a thundering reply, but what he saw stunned him. William's shoulders fell. The man seemed to age before his eyes. "I came to help you find your lady—and to, in some way, make up for the wrong I have done."

If William's appearance had startled him, the man's words left him speechless. Gerard simply stared.

"Cecily was angry with you for disturbing her party and told me all." William glanced to the cloudless sky for a heartbeat. "I assume the man who took your wife was de Brye. I will deal with my wife later. This is my fault, and I offer you my assistance."

A great weight fell from Gerard's shoulders. Perhaps they were still friends. "Thank you, William. I welcome your help."

The Earl fumbled with something behind his saddle that Gerard could not see, but the instant William pulled the box around he knew what it held. At the same moment, William said, "Lady Catheryn left this behind. I thought she might want it. Not that here and now is the appropriate time."

Pitiful cries echoed from inside the box, cries that echoed the ones he fought to hold inside himself. Gerard took the box, opened the lid and lifted the kitten in his hand. Tossing his helm to Walter, he pushed back his coif and rubbed his cheek against the beast's fur just as he'd seen Catheryn do so many times. Soon Jewel's cries turned to throaty rumbles. The cat put her paws on his cheeks and nuzzled his chin. He remembered laughing at Catheryn for teaching the silly animal to hug like that, but it didn't seem quite so humorous now. He was grateful to William for having made this gesture.

Gerard motioned to one of his men, swallowing hard. Putting the cat back, he handed over the box to him. They weren't that far from Brezden Keep. The man could ride there and back in very little time. "Keep this safe and see that it gets into Agnes's hands immediately."

The man saluted sharply and rode away

"So, have you located de Brye?" William asked.

"We have searched all the tunnels that I am aware of and closed off the tunnel entrances into the keep so de Brye cannot get back into Brezden easily. I think they are holed up in that cave just over there."

"Ah. What do you plan?"

"I need to get inside that cave."

William laughed, then looked from Gerard to Walter. "That sounds logical. But you should do nothing until darkness falls. Sleep. Both of you. That is what must be done."

"No," Gerard said. "Not until I can share a bed with my wife."

William sighed. "You will do Catheryn no good if you are so exhausted that you cannot hold your sword. Would you risk her life by moving too weak to be victorious?"

A wave of blood rushed through his veins and Gerard smiled. With the speed of a diving falcon he unsheathed his sword, and before William could reach for his own weapon, Gerard rested the sharp tip against the Earl's neck. "Too weak to defend my wife? Never."

At that moment, three men entered the clearing and brought the exchange to an abrupt end. Two of the men were Gerard's. The other was obviously a prisoner, and by the way he was held not a well-liked individual.

Stopping before Gerard, one guard cuffed the struggling captive. "Be still! We are not yet finished with you." He turned to Gerard. "Lady Catheryn is indeed held in one of the caverns below us. And this lout here," he hitched one thumb at the captive, "does not think his master has had enough time to do much harm to her."

A fog pulsed hot through his veins. Red. A blood red haze poured into Gerard's being, sizzled in his ears, colored everything around him. He seethed with rage, but slowly he dismounted. "Who are you?" His words were thick, heavy. The metallic taste of blood not yet shed coated his tongue.

The prisoner shrank back, stuttering. "I-I am n-no one."

Edyth's dying cry pierced Gerard's haze. He stepped toward the man, clenching his fists at his side. He would never be free from guilt until de Brye's lifeless body lay at his feet. He would start with this soldier and end with—

"Gerard!" The sound of Catheryn calling his name ripped through his mind. Tore at his heart. He was the knight of her dreams. Magic had led him to her, both the first time and now, and already he'd let her down. What was he doing?

He grasped the front of the prisoner's tunic with a force that tore the cowering knave from the hold of his captors. "What harm has already befallen my wife?" he growled. "Tell me now or I will have my men cut you into tiny little pieces."

The captive turned a pleading gaze to William, but the Earl turned away with a laugh and dismounted to stand beside Gerard.

Gerard shook the prisoner. "What harm has already befallen my wife?"

Shaking his head, the man stumbled over his tongue, seeking to save his life. "She is still alive. I heard her cries not long ago."

Still alive, but that's all the prisoner could tell him? De Brye's demise would be slow. Not until he howled for death would Gerard permit the devil his wish. He took a deep breath before asking, "Then what harm has he caused?"

The captive paled visibly in the waning light of day. Raising his hands, he pleaded, "Do not kill me."

Gerard smiled. "You are already dead. But if you wish the chance to save your miserable soul, you need to confess. Now."

His statement terrified the man, to what level was noticeable to all by the sound of water hitting the forest floor at the prisoner's feet. Raising his amused gaze back to the captive's ashen face, Gerard asked, "Are all of de Brye's minions as cowardly as you? Is that how he keeps you in service?"

He waited for a moment for the man to answer. When no words were forthcoming, he released the prisoner. "He is useless. Kill him."

As he'd expected, the man's tongue suddenly loosened. "She is battered a little and was drugged a few times. There is a gash on her forehead from when she was taken…but he has not tortured her as of yet. They leave for France tonight."

That admission brought both Gerard and William to attention. "France?"

The man shook his head. "Aye. They go there to start their lives as husband and—"

"Over my dead body." Gerard's gritted reply cut off the rest of the prisoner's words.

Wife? De Brye thought to make Catheryn his wife? Did he think running to France would keep him safe?

De Brye would not be safe if he ran to the ends of the earth.

William stepped closer to the man. "How do they leave?"

The prisoner sank to his knees. "By ship. A ferry will conceal them until they reach the coast, where they'll transfer to the ship."

"Ship?" William frowned. "I've no reports of a new arrival at the docks."

288

"The ship is not docked in Yorkshire, it awaits them on the other side of the river off Grimsby, my Lord."

Gerard ignored William's growl at learning the ship was outside of his lands and asked the prisoner, "When do they leave?"

"Tonight. After all is dark. The ferry was already sighted downstream."

De Brye had chosen well the night for his escape. There would be no moon to reveal his movements. None would be the wiser. Or so he thought.

"Does he suspect he is being watched?" Gerard asked.

"No. He believes you are looking for him near Caitune. There is a great deal of activity in the area there."

Gerard lifted his eyebrows, and turned a questioning gaze to William.

The Earl smiled. "My men are combing the woods around the hunting lodge and north to Scarborough. They are led by a man of your coloring and size. He wears the green and gold tabard you so thoughtfully left at the castle."

Gerard frowned. "I left no clothing at Scarborough."

"No? Oh, that's true. Then I guess one of Brezden's men-at-arms visited your wife in her chamber."

Gerard felt heat flush his face, but he tamped it down with a curse. It wasn't as if he'd sneaked into a strange woman's chamber.

He'd sought a night with his wife. That was all. It was William who'd acted the villain and locked her away.

Sensing his discomfiture, the Earl dogged the subject, a tactic at which he excelled. "I wonder who it could have been? Why did she let him in? How do you think the man gained entrance to your lady's locked chamber, anyway?"

Walter coughed and turned away, but William ignored him.

"I know it could not have been you, Gerard." The Earl scratched his head in false confusion. "There is a distinct memory of my ordering you to stay away."

"Cease, William," Gerard growled. "This is not the time."

The Earl cuffed him on the shoulder. "It is the perfect time. I suppose I am saying I know what you did and forgive you—as I hope you've forgiven me."

Gerard ignored him. There truly was no time. "So, what do we have? We know Catheryn is in that cave. We know they leave tonight." He paced the clearing, ticking off the facts on his fingers. "We know she has been battered but not beaten or tortured. Yet." He glared at the man now kneeling in his own urine. "But you said she'd been drugged. Is she capable of moving?"

The prisoner lifted his head. "Yes, but she is in chains."

Snapping the man's neck might have been Gerard's response had William not stepped in. "He might yet prove useful. Let him live a while longer."

The prisoner spoke up before Gerard could address the Earl's ludicrous idea. "I could help. Truly! If you would spare my life, and assist me in escaping the devil I serve, I could help."

"How?" Gerard towered over the man. "What could you do? Had you been willing to do the right thing, you would have done so already."

Lifting his head, the prisoner gazed directly at Gerard. "I can enter that cave without anyone giving me a second glance. I can obtain the key that will unlock the fetters about her ankle. I can…"

William snorted. "What? Lead her out of the cave? Walk her by de Brye without notice?"

"No." Shaking his head, the man admitted, "That I cannot do. It would only serve to bring my death and hers."

What the captive said held a note of truth. He could enter the cave without causing a stir. He might indeed be able to lay his hands on the key, and he might possibly have an opportunity to unlock her chains before de Brye sought to move her to the ferry. Gerard contemplated the idea further before turning his frown upon the man.

"Why would you do that? Why should I believe for one heartbeat that you will not rush straight to de Brye and warn him of us? What would stop you from telling all? What would stop you from being as despicable as the very man you have served all this time?"

He watched in amazement as the captive's chin began to tremble. Tears gathered in the man's eyes as he visibly fought to control his emotions. "I have not seen my wife, or youngest daughter, in two years. I serve de Brye only to keep them safe."

"Safe from what?"

Tears slipped down the man's cheeks. "Safe from sharing the fate of my oldest daughter." He sucked in a deep breath before continuing. "She was only eleven when de Brye forced himself upon her. I came too late to save her from that—and from death. But I was able to save my wife and other child by offering myself as slave to him. He is the devil's servant."

Walter's strangled gasp could be heard by all. William made a clicking noise with his tongue but otherwise remained silent.

Gerard bit the inside of his lip to keep from asking any more questions about his captive's family.

"You say you are a slave," he growled finally. "How many slaves are as free as you? You appear to come and go as you please. You are not in chains. You do not appear beaten. How do I know that—?"

291

Denise Lynn

Lifting his arms, the man slipped his coarse tunic over his head. Scars, old and new, crisscrossed his chest, and when Gerard walked around the prisoner, he saw the same lacerations on the man's back. His stomach tightened at the sickening sight, and at thought of what de Brye might to do Catheryn should he be given any more time with her.

"Put your tunic back on," he ordered the captive. "This is how de Brye controls his men? By keeping their wives and children under threat of rape and death? And with a whip?"

"It was not a whip."

William gasped. "A *blade*? The man is that good with a blade?"

Their prisoner nodded. "Aye. He has a thin-bladed dagger that he loves like a daughter—and that he treats better than ours."

"And none of you fight him? Not one of you stands up to this demon and skewers him where he stands?" William sounded appalled and confused.

"I am but one man. And there are those that assist de Brye willingly." Pausing, the prisoner glanced at the ground. His brows furrowed in thought before he eyed the Earl. "Are you married, my Lord? Do you have a mother, or a sister?"

Ignoring the man's insolence, William waited for him to finish. So did Gerard.

"How far would you go to protect the women in your family?"

How far would he go to protect Catheryn? Gerard had heard enough. "Get up."

Slowly the man rose. Bowing his head, he appeared to await death. But this day, he was lucky. Gerard had seen the horrors de Brye inflicted on women and children. He knew what the demon was capable of doing, and he knew what ordinary men would do to save those they loved. He himself

292

would walk into the bowels of Hell to pull his wife from the man's clutches.

"If you can unlock my lady's chains," he promised the captive, "I will grant you freedom."

The prisoner lifted his head. A look of hope so powerful, so grateful, fell across his face, it strengthened Gerard's certainty that the man could be trusted. And yet, he had to make clear his position.

"But if you prove a liar, I will make de Brye's brand of torture appear mild. I will come for my wife tonight. See to it that she is free from her chains after the sun has set."

"Aye, my lord." The man fell back to his knees and wrapped his arms about Gerard's ankles. A moment later he was up, and disappeared into the forest.

Both William and Walter looked at Gerard as if he'd lost all ability to reason. William grunted, "Are you certain that was wise, Gerard? To put your wife's safety in the hands of that blackguard?"

"I am certain of only two things at this moment." Gerard closed his eyes and fought off the nightmarish vision that would not leave him. "De Brye will die this night, and Catheryn will come home."

Lightning cracked across the sky and thunder rumbled loudly in the distance. The sound reverberated through him, lending him strength, but as Gerard stared out at the approaching storm, he found himself wondering. One had roared around him the night he captured Brezden. This time, would nature's fury prove an omen of good or evil?

Chapter Twenty

The ground beneath Catheryn shook with the force of the thunder echoing through the caverns. The rage of this storm matched the one in her heart. The walls trembled. Holding her hands to her ears, Catheryn sought to shut out the sound.

De Brye thought to kill her? He thought to make her beg for her own death? She grabbed the rock beside her and held it tightly in her hand. It would be a poor weapon, but it was the only one she could find. While using it to end a human life bothered her, this man was almost inhuman. Indeed, he was a devil.

The sound of approaching footsteps rang out between the crashes of thunder. She gripped the rock until its jagged edges tore into her palm. Bravery was not a trait she came by easily. Over the last few years Pike and de Brye had sought to beat the strength of spirit from her. Gerard had given her some back. She was sick unto death of being afraid. No more. No more tears would fall from her eyes. No screams would be torn from her lips.

More than one person approached. How would she protect herself? Her heart raced for a painful moment before she willed it to slow. The light from the torch blinded her. She held the rock behind her back, waiting for the lead figure to come closer. Catheryn knew she'd have to hit de Brye hard enough the first time. There'd not be a second chance.

When the footsteps stopped it was not de Brye's voice that floated down to her ears. "Lady Catheryn. Please, make no sound."

Her eyes adjusted to the light. The sight of Rolfe was like a feast for her soul, replenishing hope. She'd thought him dead. After the way de Brye cut him the night Brezden fell, she'd been certain the man bled to death. Apparently de Brye's blade had had only severed the flesh and nothing that lay beneath. Rolfe knelt and twisted a key into the manacle around her ankle.

"How do you come to be here?" Grasping the front of Rolfe's tunic, Catheryn whispered very softly. "Have I gone mad? Are you a ghost?"

Rolfe shook his head. "No. I was left for dead." He nodded to his companion. "This man saw to it that I lived."

"Then why did you not return to Brezden and to me? Why did you come here to——"

"We are at Brezden, my lady. Or near enough."

Catheryn shook her head. "That cannot be."

"My lady, it is true. The river is just outside this cave. Brezden is but a short distance."

So, de Brye had brought her home, and he'd stayed hidden underground like the snake he truly was.

"I did not return to the keep because I have only been on my feet two days," Rolfe continued. "I have not the strength to fight my way out. I am given freedom to wander these caves but nowhere else. But you, you can now escape."

She feared asking but couldn't bear not knowing any longer. "The children, where are Sarah and Matthew?"

"We moved them first while de Brye's men were going through supplies to be loaded onto the ferry. It was easy enough for the two of us to coax the children into sacks and then haul the precious bundles into the woods. No one paid any attention to two men moving sacks that small. With the help of Lord Gerard's men, Sarah and Matthew should already be under Agnes's protection." Rolfe patted her arm. "My lady, forgive me, but if this goes wrong, de Brye would not hesitate to use those two babes to bend you to his will. Now, two sacks filled with plant bits, leaves, roots, and stones lie on makeshift pallets in another cave."

Catheryn breathed a sigh of relief. "No, you did well, Rolfe. There is nothing to forgive."

As she tried to stand, the second man leaned down. "Do not leave just yet, Lady Catheryn. De Brye is close at hand."

She gave a soft cry, and Rolfe covered her mouth with his hand. He shook his head. "Take heart, my Lady. Soon this will be…" His voice broke, proving his weakened condition. He removed his hand from her lips. "Soon this will all be over. Soon we will be back at Brezden."

Rolfe's companion knelt close to Catheryn. "I know this will be hard. But you must wait here until I signal to you."

"A signal?" Catheryn shook her head. "A signal for what? I don't understand."

"Your husband is nearby."

"No. He will charge in and—"

The man soothed her fears, cutting her off. "He and his men were spotted, and I was sent to scout the area. Since de Brye holds my family as hostage he thinks he can trust me."

Catheryn's heart jumped. Could this man be trusted? So much hung in the balance.

"Yes, my Lady, your thoughts are plain on your face. You have little reason to trust me, but I told de Brye your husband's group was nothing more than a hunting party."

"And he believed you?" She found it hard to credit his

words. "Why?"

The man shrugged. "As I said, he holds my family—my wife and daughter—as surety for my obedience. Do you think many serve him willingly?"

Catheryn was shocked. "You risk your family's lives for mine?"

"Are you not the Lady of Brezden? Is it not my duty to give my life for that of my Lord or Lady?"

Catheryn shook her head. "I do not know you. You are not from Brezden."

A hopeful smile crossed the man's face. "At the moment I serve the Lord of Brezden, and if all goes well, maybe then I will be permitted to serve you also. Brezden may yet become my home, and I can right the wrongs of the past. Other lives I should have protected." His smile faded. "De Brye already murdered my oldest daughter. He must do no more evil."

His daughter? Catheryn almost wept for the man. Was there no limit to the crimes de Brye would commit against others? "My lady?" the man prompted. "You will wait for the signal?"

"Why must I wait?" If Gerard was nearby, why could she not simply rush from the cavern? Even if de Brye took chase, her husband would protect her.

The man stared at her. "I am sure Lord Gerard is a capable leader. While he would rush in to save you, he does not know the layout of these caves. There are numerous caverns, ones that connect and some that are dead ends. Lord Gerard and his men could search for days only to lose you. Down here, de Brye has the upper hand."

"But you—"

"My Lady, I know only the way from the mouth of the cave to the nearest connecting caverns and into this cave.

Beyond that, nothing. He will not come until nightfall. And there is no guarantee you won't be captured if you attempt to leave. You must trust me and your husband. You will not mistake my signal."

"They will come in two groups, my Lady. The first will attack de Brye's men at the ferry. Even if you hear the fighting, you must wait for the signal. That is when the second group, led by your husband, will arrive." Rolfe insisted, "Please, it is hard to wait, I know. But you must."

Catheryn grasped her man's arm. "What about the others? How will we protect the men who are good and true and loyal but forced to—"

Shaking his head, Rolfe answered, "I do not know, but we must ensure your safety first. You are our lady."

There came a crash of thunder from outside, and the men left without waiting for any further questions or providing her any more information. She was again alone in the dark, with only the roaring thunder for company. This time, however, the noise mattered little, she was preoccupied with other thoughts. How long would she have to wait? Moments would seem like days. She held her makeshift rock weapon to her chest. She hoped she would be free long before it became necessary to test her will to survive.

ᚾ

Rain dripped down his nasal plate, and Gerard felt as if he were reliving the attack on Brezden. Except this time the lightning did not accent a towering keep. Instead, it lit only nearby sections of the forest, the river, and the path along the water.

He waited. They all waited. A scout had spotted a ferry making its way down the river toward the cave. When it arrived, they would attack. While de Brye and his men were busy handling the ferry, Gerard and his men would take the traitors by surprise. The waiting was torturous, though. His mind played games with his heart. Had de Brye harmed Catheryn? Had he tortured her? Was he just about to do so?

"Cease, Gerard."

William's softly issued command broke into his thoughts, and he gave the Earl a blank look. "Cease what?"

"You are dwelling again. It will do you no good to ponder things you cannot find answers for."

"Who's to say——?"

William's low laugh rankled. "You may be able to hide your moods from others, but not from me. I know you well. From the time you were but a page for my father I have been able to read every line of your face. While you trained to read, write, and follow orders at my father's keep, I was at King Henry's court learning to read men and their expressions. And yours are plain."

This was not news to Gerard. William indeed got inside of men's thoughts, which was why he was so respected and feared. So instead of seeking to hide his thoughts, Gerard asked, "Do you think she still lives?"

William sighed and shook his head. "Now you waste my time with questions I cannot answer. Maybe we should attack now, just to give you something worthwhile to think about. It is night after all. There will be no more fears of waiting too long."

A shiver ran down Gerard's spine, and his stomach clenched with the thought of her death. No. He would not find Catheryn dead.

He would not.

A sound other than the storm broke the night, and it caused both men to smile. A vessel approached.

"Now," Gerard repeated.

His mind cleared and all thought focused on one thing——

rescuing his wife. Lifting his sword high in the air, he silently rallied the men behind him.

❦

"Come, sweeting. It is time to journey to our new home."

De Brye's voice trailed down the corridor that opened into the cavern where she'd been kept, and Catheryn's pulse pounded loud and fast. She grasped the rock and waited. The hour was nigh, it seemed Rolfe's companion and her husband had not arrived in time.

Keeping her direct gaze away from the torch he carried, she was able to slowly accustom her eyes to the light. Never again would she welcome darkness. She would have to save herself. It was a blessing that her enemy had come alone.

Leaning over her, de Brye stroked her cheek. "The moment I was promised has arrived."

"No one promised you anything," Catheryn spat. She wanted to keep him off guard until she could choose the perfect moment to strike.

He ran his hand down the front of her gown. "Oh, but you are wrong. Your mother gave you to me with her dying breath."

Catheryn bit back her outrage. "And who caused her to die?"

Laughing, de Brye turned to her feet to unlock the chain. "It was the only way she said I could have you. I simply obliged the lady."

As soon as he bent to released her, Catheryn lifted her rock and slammed it against the side of his head. Quickly, before he could fall across her, she rolled away and stood.

As de Brye fell, he dropped the torch onto the wet stone floor. The cavern was once again enveloped in darkness. Not waiting to see if he still breathed, Catheryn forced her scattered thoughts to gather. De Brye had fallen forward, toward the center of the cavern. Reaching behind her, she groped for the wall, and a moment later her fingers brushed the cool, damp stone.

Breathing a sigh of relief, she turned away from de Brye's body and felt her way along the wall toward the entrance of her cavern cell. Slowly, but steadily, she would leave this evilness behind.

At the door of the rock chamber, she prayed she could find her way in the dark through the tunnel and to the mouth of the cave. In her joy at learning of Gerard's arrival, she'd not thought to ask Rolfe or his companion the way. Her breath quickened. They wouldn't have told her. She remembered now their order to wait for a signal. But she'd had no choice.

At a shout of rage behind her, she picked up her pace. *De Brye!* Trailing one hand on the wall at all times, she kept moving. It was too late for signals. There was no time for anything but flight. One thought kept her moving. One thought kept her from looking behind her to see where de Brye was. The thought of her husband's arms.

Suddenly, a shrill whistle split the darkness. Certain that the sound was her overdue signal, hoping she was not following an echo that would lead to her capture, she rushed toward it. But she heard de Brye coming up behind her. She could hear his labored breathing and could almost feel his hands around her neck, smell his fetid breath as he gasped for air. She thanked the stars that his torch had gone out and that he was as blind as she.

"You will not escape me!"

She ignored the threat and kept moving.

"You will regret this act, sweeting. More than you can imagine."

She would regret it only if he caught her. And he would

not.

"Your men will die too," de Brye promised.

Her heart tripped, but Catheryn's feet remained steady. She would not answer him. He spoke in an effort to frighten her, to make her give away her position, but she'd not let his words have any ill effect upon her again. Her lungs threatened to burst with the effort she was making in staying out of his reach.

"And your husband. I will permit him to watch me violate and mutilate you before I cut his throat." The image caused her to stumble. Regaining her footing, she forced the horrific picture from her mind. "I am adept with a knife. I can keep you alive for days before you bleed to death."

Catheryn fought to remember her vow to herself. Covering her mouth with her free hand, she swore she would not cry. She would not cower before him.

"You will beg for death the same way Reveur's first wife did!"

Catheryn had known from the little Gerard told her and what she'd overheard that his first wife Edyth had perished at de Brye's hands, but until this moment she'd not pictured the terrors the woman faced before meeting her end. Empathy for the poor Edyth made her vision blur.

"She begged for the life of her son too. But it was too late."

His ragged, panting voice was closer, and the nearness gave Catheryn a renewed burst of courage. That courage lent speed and strength to her steps. Following the wall of the tunnel around a corner, she headed toward sudden shouts and a beacon of light. Even if this group was comprised of de Brye's men, their wild cries meant that Gerard's force had engaged them in battle.

But she heard no sound of clashing swords.

"Stop her!" de Brye screamed. The men were clearly his. The blood rushing through her veins froze, but what she saw in the glare of lightning from the mouth of the cave unthawed that ice. Only some of the men followed de Brye's order. The others rushed outside and fled.

Dodging, she avoided one man. Another's hand grazed her arm, but she jerked away. They would *not* catch her. De Brye's curses sounded close in her ear.

Reaching the mouth of the cave, two of de Brye's minions stood shoulder to shoulder in the entrance. If she died while trying to escape, surely it would be an easier death than one at de Brye's hands. She plunged blindly between them, twisting from one pair of hands, and then another. She bent low and kept moving. Faster than the two of them she was free.

She raced out and down the path along the riverbank, following the first bend then the second. Then the sight that met Catheryn's terrified gaze took her breath away and stopped her flight. Gasping for breath, she watched in horror as the world around her came to a stop. The sachet's dream was again becoming a reality.

Battle-clad warriors astride Satan's own destriers raced through the storm toward her. Mail, as black as the starless sky, covered each battle-hardened warrior from helmed head to leather-booted foot. Unrelenting, the mighty warhorses with their terrifying riders charged ever closer. Ironclad hooves pounded in perfect unison with the heavy thudding of her heart. Swords, pikes, and axes raised, the men rushed nearer.

Fighting to calm her racing heart, Catheryn forced her trembling limbs to still. The dream. It had not foretold her *death*, it had been a harbinger of hope and rescue.

He was here.

Her dream knight was here, and all she had to do was hold her ground and trust him not to see her trampled beneath those charging hooves coming straight at her, or murdered by the madman at her back.

There was nowhere for her to dodge, though. De Brye and his men were behind her, thick brush was on her right and the raging river on the left. Her only chance for safety, for hope, for life, lay in absorption of that brutal force bearing down on her, and in the man leading the charge. With a hushed voice, she prayed, "Lord, give me strength."

The leader of the pack slowed his horse but did not stop. Leaning to the side in his saddle, he pierced her with his glimmering sapphire gaze. She could see the deep blue in the light of the torches that the other riders carried.

But Catheryn's gaze flicked to the line of beasts charging toward her. Her knees weakened. De Brye would not have the chance to kill her. She would be destroyed by the strength and weight of these warhorses bearing down on her. Her legs threatened to fold, but lifting her head for one last look at her husband, she stared in amazement. A smile, almost as bright as the streak of lightning that flared above him, lit his face.

He wrapped the reins of his mount around one wrist and held out his arm. Raindrops rolled down his mail armor, and another thunderbolt lit the sky. The line of horses crashed closer. Catheryn held her breath, lifted her arms and—

Gasped as Gerard's strong arm jerked her from the ground. His horse was slowing even now.

His remaining warriors rushed by. Their shouts of challenge drowned out the roar of the thunder. Fighting for air to fill her lungs, Catheryn struggled to wrap her arms around Gerard's neck as she clung to him. She was safe. Her heart threatened to burst with love for this man who had again ridden out of her dreams to save her from a nightmare.

✍

Gerard yanked on his reins with one hand, bringing his horse to an unsteady halt. He had not expected to literally snatch Catheryn from de Brye's grasp, not in this manner. But he wasn't about to question the manner of her salvation. He was simply happy to have her safe. He would never let her go again.

Tightening his grasp on her, he shouted over the din of battle, "Hang on!"

Pulling his one foot from the stirrup, he hoisted Catheryn high enough for her to use the piece of leather and metal for support. His destrier was fitted for battle. The high saddle was meant to hold him firmly on his horse while he fought, and there was nowhere for another rider to sit comfortably. Not in front, nor behind. And he was not putting her down until they were safely away. He turned his horse and headed away from the battle, back toward the clearing where he'd left a small band of reinforcements—several squires and mounts with fresh horses.

William's voice stopped him. "Gerard! De Brye and his men—"

"Can be brought to Brezden."

Without turning, Gerard waited for William's angry reply. But it was not forthcoming. Instead the Earl said, "So be it." Then William issued one of his most bloodthirsty battle cries and Gerard knew he was charging into the fight.

Catheryn buried her face in his neck a moment before lifting her head to look at him. "You seek revenge for what de Brye did to your wife and child. You cannot let him escape you again. *Go.*"

He found it odd that revenge suddenly did not seem as important as her safety. "He will never escape. His time will come, and you will be somewhere safe."

"But—"

"No. Catheryn, do not argue this with me. *Please*." When she fell silent, he asked, "Are you unhurt?"

Her bitter laugh sent a chill down his spine. "I am alive. I am whole. Is that not enough?"

They arrived at the clearing. Gerard lowered Catheryn to the ground and joined her there. A flash of lightning lit her face. There'd been times he'd thought never to see her again. Pulling her close, he rested his lips against her forehead. "More than enough."

Tearing his helmet from his head, he tossed it to a waiting squire, then he pulled his wife back into his arms. "Catheryn—" His throat closed up, and he could say no more.

She returned his embrace. "What took you so long?"

Her feeble attempt at humor made him laugh. "Well, I was attending this bathing party, and the days slipped away."

She trembled against him. Was it from laughter or tears? What exactly had she suffered? It didn't matter, because he would make everything right. "Catheryn, you are safe. Fear not," he promised. "All will be well." But whom was he seeking to comfort—her, or himself?

Her choked laugh told him that both emotions ruled her. "If you ever say that again, I will tear out your tongue."

The fierceness of her words surprised him. Then he realized that every time he had promised that all would be well—it was not.

Cupping her chin, he slanted his mouth over hers. Never had a kiss tasted sweeter. Never had a woman's touch reduced him to tears. But he knew by the tightening in his throat and the painful twisting in his gut that it was about to happen now.

What was wrong with him? Abruptly breaking the kiss, he turned away.

A squire waited with the reins of another mount for Catheryn. Gerard took them from the lad's hands and said, "Come. Let us return home."

"Gerard?"

He wanted to ignore the question in her tone. Instead, he turned to look at her.

Guilt made him ashamed. Hurt filled her gaze. Hurt that he had put there by breaking away so suddenly. He wished not to linger here. He would rather explore these feelings and emotions in the safety of the keep.

Reaching out, he grasped her hand and pulled her forward. He held her close. Seeking words, he finally whispered, "Catheryn, I seek not to hurt you. I only wish to leave this place. To return to Brezden and hold you without the barrier of mail and clothing between us."

He felt her sigh and she patted his shoulder. "You lie, Gerard. It is more than that. Something is wrong, I can feel it. But I too wish to return home. Let us pray that Earl William lives up to his promise and brings de Brye back to us in chains."

Chapter Twenty-One

Gerard paced the hall. A runner had come with news that William and Walter approached Brezden with de Brye and the blackguard's men in chains.

Soon they would enter the keep. Soon Gerard would be able to put the past behind him. He would finally fulfill his promise to Edyth. After doing so, he would be free to turn his full attention to the years ahead and to the woman resting in his chamber—Catheryn. The woman who was his future.

When nothing but tomorrow loomed before them, he would be able to tell her what his heart had known since the moment he'd first seen her.

"Gerard?" Catheryn touched his arm. "They have arrived?"

An irrational fear for her safety overtook him. Spinning, he seized her arms. "Return to bed. I do not want you down here."

"It is my right to be here." Anger reddened her face. "This is my keep. My people were harmed by de Brye's hand."

"Your keep? Your people?" Pulling her toward the stairs, he felt his voice roughen. "Tell me, Lady Reveur, have you no husband to carry these responsibilities? You have no

rights other than what I give you. Can you not trust me to—
"

"Other than what you give me? This is my battle too. You are not the only one who has been harmed by de Brye. I seek my own revenge, and I deserve to see it paid."

He imagined de Brye breaking free and somehow managing some last act of impossible evil. An evil that would take his wife, his love from him. "I will not stand here and argue with you. If you do not return to our chamber on your own, I will—"

She tore out of his hold and finished his threat. "Place me under guard? Lock me in a cell? Where have I heard those words before? Just what sort of man do you plan to be? What sort of husband?"

A loud commotion in the bailey announced the arrival of the prisoners. Pointing up the stairs, Gerard growled at Catheryn, "Now!"

Her complexion paled, but she argued no further. Gerard breathed a sigh of relief when she turned and headed up the stairs. Had she remained in the hall, his thoughts would have revolved around her and her safety instead de Brye and his death.

Within a few heartbeats, the huge doors to the hall burst open and men poured through. Some entered of their own accord, while others entered at the point of a blade. All came to a stop before him.

From the corner of his eye, Gerard saw Catheryn's maid Agnes slink down the steps and try to hide herself in the shadows. There existed no doubt that his wife had sent the woman to spy. He called the maid forward.

"Agnes." The guilt on the woman's face was almost laughable and Gerard ignored it. He motioned to the group of men he did not recognize and hoped that some of them were Catheryn's missing guards. "Are any of these men from Brezden?"

The woman quickly scanned the crowd. "Yes, some are, my lord."

"Good. Take our men away from here. See that their needs are cared for, but do not let any of them out of your sight until I call for you. Take some of my soldiers to protect you."

The look that crossed the maid's face told him that she suspected his true purpose, her removal from the hall, but that did not concern him, he would soon be left with only his own men and ten of de Brye's.

Gerard quickly noticed that a prisoner Walter held at sword-point was the one who had helped his wife escape. He had heard the story from Catheryn on their return to the keep, and he would see to it that the man was repaid tenfold for his bravery. He would be released and set free, and all of this would be done in secret. That precaution should be enough to keep what remained of his family safe from retaliation until something could be done for them.

Gerard turned his gaze back to the other prisoners. Only one looked directly at him. That stare glittered with hate and rage.

Stepping up to the man, Gerard understood why Edyth thought she'd seen Satan. These pale, ice-blue eyes shimmered with an eerie fanatical glow. If that were not enough to freeze the blood, the smile most certainly was. Never before had Gerard seen such a cold, cruel smirk.

Gerard turned and addressed his friend. "Earl William, all of these prisoners stand guilty of treason against King Stephen and you. Willingly do I release all but one to your justice."

Lounging idly in a chair, William yawned as if he had not

a care in the world. "They are not fit to dirty my cells. Hang them in the morning."

"But, my Lord, you cannot!"

Gerard spun to see who had shouted the insane denial. As he feared, it was the man who'd helped Catheryn. Striding forward, Gerard quickly landed a hard punch on the fool's chin. Then, leaning down to help Walter pick the now unconscious man off the floor, Gerard whispered, "Hide this imbecile."

In a loud voice, he said, "This man can die now." He nodded to his captain. "Sir Walter, take him to the gallows and see it done."

After Walter dragged the man from the hall, Gerard returned to the dais.

William spoke up from where he sat. "What about the prisoner you refuse to release?"

The very man's voice rose in answer. "You will make no decisions concerning me."

Gerard faced de Brye. "And why is that? Are you above justice? Are you not to be condemned for your crimes?"

The man's sinister smile broadened. "Of what crimes do you speak?"

Gerard felt his blood heat. It rolled and boiled in his veins. Edyth's dying words echoed in his ears, the look of fright on Catheryn's face as she ran away from that cave tripped through his mind. But he forced the sounds and sights from him. Battles were lost because men were ruled by emotion. He'd not allow pain or rage to cloud his judgment. This execution would be lawfully handled.

"What crimes do I speak of?" He nodded toward William. "We can start with the crime of treason—against your overlord and your king."

De Brye laughed. "I owe no fealty to William of Aumale.

And Stephen of Blois is a pretender to the crown that rightfully belongs to the Empress Matilda."

The man had condemned himself right there, but ignoring that statement, Gerard moved on. "Then we can add the crime of murder. You did push the Lady of Brezden down the stairs of this very keep. You admitted it to—"

De Brye interrupted, shrugging. His eyes burned with growing fervor. "She said it was the only way I could have her daughter. I simply fulfilled the lady's wish."

Gerard had expected disavowals, but it seemed de Brye was not so clever. "And the Lord of Brezden?" Had de Brye been involved in that too?

"Ah, well, that was a necessary occurrence, a planned accident to ensure Pike's cooperation." De Brye looked past Gerard at William. "I am sorry you never received the lady's missives, but your help was really unnecessary."

William sat up. "Letters?"

"I told you as much," Catheryn answered from the stairs. Her voice rose. "But you would not believe me."

Gerard bit off a groan. "Be gone from here, wife."

She shook her head. "No. I will not leave."

Facing Gerard, de Brye sneered. "Are there any other crimes you wish to place upon me? Charges concerning rape? Other murders?" His smile turned even more ghastly. "She was a tasty morsel, Gerard. I was truly saddened that it had to end so quickly. But the babe…" He lifted one shoulder. "The babe was no sport."

"Gerard!"

William began to intercede, but Gerard waved him back. Obviously, de Brye sought to goad him into losing control. Gerard took a deep breath, seeking to clear the red haze drifting before his eyes. He would not fly at de Brye in a rage. When he snapped the man's neck, the monster would be put down lawfully and clear-headedly.

De Brye did not give up. "Your current wife is a rather choice piece of flesh too. How did it feel when you discovered you weren't her first?"

"That isn't true!" Catheryn shouted at de Brye. She then looked at Gerard. "Why are you doing nothing? Why do you stand there and let this devil lie about me?"

This was another reason Gerard had not wanted her present. It was difficult enough that he fought to control his own temper, how was he to deal with hers too? She had a right to be angry, every right to want de Brye's blood. He would see that her honor, and the deeds committed against her and her family were avenged, but not simply when she demanded it.

For him to retain his own honor, this had to be done fairly and justly—otherwise he was no better than the cur before him.

Keeping his voice as level as possible, he ordered, "Catheryn, close your mouth."

De Brye continued, clearly seeking death. "Is it satisfying to know you married a common whore? I myself prefer a fine lady, a lady such as your first wife. Although, I suppose a slut does have her purposes."

Gerard heard Catheryn hiss. He knew she was building a fine fire with that breath, like a dragon ready to battle. William must have known it too because the Earl leapt from his chair and locked a hand around her wrist. He dragged Catheryn forcefully to the dais, took a seat and held her at his side.

De Brye repeated what he had first said. "You will make no decisions concerning me. If I hang, so does your wife."

"And why is that?" Gerard growled.

"You cannot hang one traitor without hanging the other."

"My wife is no traitor. That flimsy evidence you planted in the tunnel is damning only to you. The dead man placed for William to find along with the missive to the Empress could not have been arranged by my wife."

"No? You are certain of that?"

"Yes. She never left my sight." Gerard took a step closer to de Brye and repeated, "Ever."

De Brye looked toward William. "I demand fairness, not this mockery of a trial."

Gerard was amazed. The man was either very bold or extremely insane. "We are handling this justly, but how can you talk of fairness?"

"I have ever been fair. I only kill when the need arises. You, on the other hand, kill whenever the urge strikes you."

Gerard frowned. What was the man talking about? He was no murderer, and he took little pleasure in the deaths of any but his enemies on an honorable field of battle.

At his silence, de Brye continued. His lips curled as he spoke. "While your memory is shoddy, I remember the day clearly. You, Baron Reveur, were so filled with bloodlust that you removed my brother's head from his body when he knelt before you, vanquished."

There had only been one man he had killed in that manner. And that man had knelt before him with a dagger hidden in his tunic. "So that is why you butchered my wife and son? Because your brother pretended to surrender and then—"

De Brye laughed, interrupting him, and the hairs on the back of Gerard's neck rose. "I have only begun to make you pay." He pointed at Catheryn. "She has helped to fulfill my dreams by wedding you. Now, none can refute the evidence pointing to her betrayal. I am gladdened to know she will finally be mine—in hell."

314

Catheryn tried to take a step forward, but William yanked her back. He leaned forward in his chair. "What evidence do you speak of?" He looked around the hall. "I see nothing that implicates Lady Catheryn in any treachery."

De Brye pinned Gerard with a gaze of accusation. "You saw the letter on that dead man. You cannot deny this bitch's missive to the Empress."

Gerard shook his head. "I do not know of what you speak. I saw only an act of forgery."

De Brye stared at the ceiling and shouted, "What now?" He tipped his head like a man listening intently before nodding and muttering, "Yes, yes, I know."

Gerard turned to look at the Earl. Was their prisoner truly insane? William shrugged, and then shook his head.

"He has a sword!"

Gerard spun at Catheryn's shouted warning, but it was too late. De Brye had already disarmed the man guarding him and did indeed have a sword. He held the blade steady, and the point was directed straight at Gerard's chest.

Stepping clear of his stunned guard, de Brye turned to William. "I will not die a common criminal at the end of a rope." He waved his sword in the air. "I demand a trial by combat."

"You demand?" William sounded incredulous.

His blade whipped expertly before him, and de Brye sliced open Gerard's tunic without grazing the flesh beneath. "Yes, *demand*. If I die, all will end here. If I live, the Lady Catheryn hangs."

The man thought to threaten Catheryn with death? No. Never again. De Brye wished to fight him? The challenge brought a smile to Gerard's lips. De Brye would never threaten, harm, or kill another woman or child again. This was what he had long been waiting for. Insane or not, the man needed to be sent to his maker.

Unsheathing his sword, he nodded. "I accept the challenge."

☙

Catheryn nearly swooned. Fear for her husband clawed at her soul with icy talons of horror.

William rose and pulled her to the far end of the hall. She realized that Gerard did not need to be distracted by thoughts, or the sight, of her. Yet she wished to be not so far away. She could not bear to imagine this battle instead of see it.

The guards pulled the remaining prisoners out of the hall. While there would be no help for de Brye, there would be none for Gerard either.

The two circled each other like wild animals. De Brye struck the first blow. His blade rang loud against Gerard's, and then the fight was joined in earnest. Catheryn cringed with each strike. Every blow felt like a stab at her heart. De Brye claimed to be an expert with a blade. What if he was? Would Gerard be capable of besting the devil?

Back and forth across the floor they fought. Attack and retreat, repeated swings and jabs with long, heavy blades designed for one purpose alone—to bring death. "Come, Reveur, kill me if you are able."

De Brye's words were laced with gasps for breath but sweat drenched Gerard's hair and ran down his face. Catheryn could not stand still. Wrapping one arm across her stomach, she shifted from one foot to the other. She sucked in a quick breath when Gerard backed into a stool and was caught off balance. Seemingly it was her husband's final moment, and she watched in mute terror as he lifted his blade to ward off the downward arc of de Brye's—

To her amazement, Gerard laughed and regained his

316

footing. He spun to the left, and de Brye screamed in rage. Grasping his weapon with both hands, the monster lifted it above his head and rushed forward. Twisting, Gerard lowered his sword and held it out, clearly all part of his plan.

The blade cut into de Brye's side. Blood ran from the wound, yet the devil did not slow. He did not even pause in his attack.

Instead, he spun around and brought his blade down across his opponent's arm. Again, blood ran. This time it was Gerard's.

Fear built in Catheryn's throat. She groaned with the effort to contain her scream, but William jerked on her arm.

"Do not watch. Do not make a sound." The softly spoken words were heavy with threat.

Catheryn bit her bottom lip. Nothing from Heaven or Hell could force her to close her eyes.

The fighting slowed as the men tired. Life and death would be a matter of who made a mistake—or who did not. Silently Catheryn prayed for her husband's life. She begged for God to spare the life of the man she loved. No matter what he did or said, she loved him. She always would.

The men circled the hall. The clashing of their swords reverberated off the walls, and winded gasps for air filled any momentary silences. Soon Gerard's back was to her, and Catheryn stared at de Brye. His eyes were glazed and shimmered with unspeakable evil. An evil no mortal seemed able to quench.

An icy claw tore at her chest. Breathing became impossible as she realized what she must do. She could not force her lungs to fill with air. Gerard would be angry at what she was about to attempt, but this needed to stop. Trial by combat was not what de Brye deserved. He was a sick animal who deserved only to be put out of his misery.

Catheryn ripped her arm from William's grasp. She ignored his curse and avoided his attempt to recapture her, bolting across the hall. She paused only long enough to retrieve a sword left on the floor by one of the guards, then took a place alongside her husband.

Without taking his focus off de Brye, Gerard asked, "What are you doing?"

"I have as much a say in this as you do."

Gerard fended off de Brye's sword thrust. "Have you completely lost your wits?"

"Only when people insist on making decisions for me." She circled along with the men, keeping de Brye in front of her at all times.

De Brye laughed. "Fear not, Reveur, I will teach her how to obey orders."

Catheryn narrowed her eyes, tightened her grip on the weapon in her hand, and jabbed the tip into de Brye's knee. "Shut up." She'd been aiming for his groin, but the weight of the weapon naturally lowered her aim.

The man stumbled, his eyes wide in shock. "You will pay for that!"

"Catheryn, this is foolish. Go—"

"No!" She wasn't listening to more of his orders. "Stop ordering me about as if I am one of your guards."

"This is absurd!"

As far as she was concerned, this whole trial by blade was absurd. "Then end it, Gerard. Let us be done with this madman."

Gerard sighed. "Yes, my Lady, if that is your wish."

She swallowed her own sigh. "If we are in agreement, then yes, yes it is."

De Brye suddenly lunged at her, his sword cutting a swath of fiery pain across Catheryn's shoulder that spread like wildfire. It tore a scream of agony from her throat. Her weapon clanged to the floor, and she tripped, falling alongside of it.

Instantly, with a shout of rage, Gerard ran de Brye through. The blade pierced his chest, but when it was withdrawn de Brye fell atop Catheryn. His evil smirk still curved his lips, and he stared into her eyes promising, "This day you will join me in hell."

❧

Gerard dropped his sword. It clattered to the floor as bile choked him. Blood drenched Catheryn's shoulder and chest. Fear chilled him as much as the air on his heated and sweaty flesh, and de Brye's words echoed in his ears.

"No!"

The shout tore from his chest. It tore hoarsely from his lips. No. Not again. She was not dead. She could not be.

He shoved de Brye's body off his wife and found her motionless. Without pausing to see if the devil were truly dead, Gerard took Catheryn in his arms and carried her toward the stairs. He saw the expression of horror on Earl William's face. That same expression echoed in Gerard's soul.

"Find her maid," he told the Earl. "And find Mistress Margaret." Then, without waiting to see if William did as he asked, he carried Catheryn up the stairs to their chamber and laid her upon their bed.

Removing Catheryn's clothes, he threw the bloodied garments on the floor. He was sickened by the sight of what he'd caused. It had been foolish to accept de Brye's challenge, foolish and unnecessary. Had he thought of his wife instead of himself, he'd have turned all of the traitors over to William, including de Brye. He'd have washed his hands of the devil, and taken care of his tomorrows, not his yesterdays. He'd have acted like the man he wanted to be, a husband and a lover.

Retrieving a pitcher of water and some linens from alongside the bath, he carried them to the bed. His hands shook. He sat next to Catheryn on the mattress and wiped the blood from her face. Then he stopped and stared at his wife. She was pale. Too pale.

Guilt kicked him in the gut. She'd been right. He had forced her into rashness by ordering her about with little regard to her thoughts or feelings. And now…Gerard closed his eyes against the force of the blow and bent to the task at hand. For the moment he could do nothing about the past. He could only worry about this moment. This breath. Catheryn.

Where was the wound? There was so much blood. He worked feverishly trying to locate the source.

"My Lord." Agnes entered the chamber with Mistress Margaret and her bag of remedies. Never had two older women been so welcome.

Gerard held up his rag. "I cannot find the injury."

Both women looked at each other before Agnes stuck her head outside the chamber door and shouted for Earl William.

At the same time, Mistress Margaret waddled to the bed. She took the cloth from Gerard. "My Lord, I need you to move out of my way." Glancing about the room, the woman suggested, "Why do you not tend the fire and bring me more light?"

Agnes offered, "You could also bring us more water."

"I am not leaving." It did not take a great deal of cleverness to see that they were seeking to remove him from Catheryn's side.

Again, the women looked at each other. Then Agnes

turned an overly innocent gaze upon him. "We would never presume to tell you to leave. We need the water and light, my Lord."

William entered the chamber. His gaze flew from the bed, to Gerard, and then to the older women. "What can I do?"

Agnes nodded to Gerard. She said nothing.

Shaking his head, William grabbed the front of Gerard's tunic. "Come here."

"I am not leaving." Nothing was going to make him leave Catheryn's side ever again, especially not William. So much harm had already been caused by that man already.

"I am not asking you to." His friend pointed to his wounded arm. "I want to see if this needs stitches."

"Oh." Gerard had forgotten he'd been sliced by de Brye's sword. He tried unsuccessfully to shrug off William's hold. "It is nothing."

The Earl pulled him to a bench on the other side of the room. "Humor me."

Gerard sunk down onto the bench. The room swam before him. It was hard to breathe. A weight the size of Brezden itself rested on his chest.

William unlaced the mailed sleeve and freed it from Gerard's hauberk, dropped it to the floor, then pulled up the linen sleeve beneath.

Gerard remained still, saying nothing as the Earl wiped away the blood. These were familiar actions. Many times, they'd taken turns tending each other's battle wounds. But Gerard doubted William could heal the bleeding gash in his heart. A chill rushed through him, and he shuddered.

"You are ill." William's voice was gruff.

"I am fine."

Soon William confirmed what Gerard already knew, though only after applying a salve from Mistress Margaret.

"This requires no stitches."

Gerard nodded and started to rise. Strangely, the floor rushed up to meet him and he almost fell. He sat back down. Quickly.

William's soft chuckle raced across his ears. "You are ill," the Earl repeated.

"No," Gerard insisted, "I am fine."

The Earl rested a hand on Gerard's shoulder. "No, my friend, you are sick at heart. It is a disease that befalls many men."

Gerard remained silent.

"Have you told *her* of this fatal disease?" When Gerard still didn't answer, William sighed. "I will not tease you. Have you told your wife that you love her?"

Shaking his head, Gerard muttered, "No." He'd told her he knew nothing of love. He'd claimed it wasn't important.

"You can tell her when she wakes up," Mistress Margaret called from the bed.

"Wakes up?" As if torn from a terrible dream, Gerard bolted from the bench.

Agnes laughed. "Her wound is nothing but a cut on the top of her shoulder."

Gerard was confused. "The blood."

Both older women shook their heads. "The blood was yours and de Brye's. Very little was Catheryn's."

Crossing the chamber and leaning over the bed, Gerard placed his fingers on her chest, over her heart. He stared into her face and thanked God for what they suggested.

"She sleeps, my lord. She only sleeps." Agnes's whisper was broken by tears. "And this is finally over."

Gerard turned to Mistress Margaret. The lady nodded in agreement, adding, "She just needs sleep, my Lord. I would say she's had a few hard days. Nothing a good, restful slumber cannot cure. Then this can truly be over."

He sank down onto the bed. "Thank you, God." His voice, barely above a whisper, was as broken as Agnes's had been. He hardly noticed as William hustled the women from the chamber and closed the door behind them.

Chapter Twenty-Two

More stars than he could count dotted the dark sky.

Gerard leaned against the window ledge for support. A heavy weariness had settled about his shoulders halfway through the day.

As the sun set, that weariness seeped into his blood and his soul. Catheryn slept the sleep of the dead.

He glanced at the woman on the bed. There was no tossing or turning, and no sound broke her unending slumber. She'd been that way since last night. After much harassment on his part, Mistress Margaret had finally told him that Catheryn might stay asleep for a long time.

Gerard rubbed his temples, but it did little to ease the pain, a dull ache that was echoed in his heart. Crossing the room, he sat on the edge of the bed. Jewel crawled into his lap. The growing kitten was as lost as he, and just like him, the animal had not left the chamber for more than a few moments since he'd brought Catheryn up.

De Brye was truly dead. Edyth's murder had been avenged, Gerard consoled himself. She could rest in peace. And perhaps he could finally set aside his grief.

He'd cared deeply for Edyth and would have remained faithful to her until the day he died. He'd once wondered what had been missing from his first marriage and now, he knew. Where Edyth had been dutiful and put him at ease, she'd never looked at him the way Catheryn did. He smiled just thinking about the shimmer in his second wife's eyes and the heat of her gaze when she saw him enter a room.

Catheryn would never be dutiful, but he had no right to expect her to be, or to behave as one of his vassals. She wasn't a vassal, she was his wife, his partner, his very breath—and deserved to be treated as such.

Edyth had put him at ease by ensuring all was right and perfect within the walls of his keep. The food on his table was above reproach. His home was warm and clean. Minor disputes between the servants never reached his ears, as Edyth saw to them, leaving him free to tend more important matters. She ensured that he had all the privacy or quiet that he needed or wanted.

Catheryn put him at ease by teasing him, making him laugh, or stealing his mind with kisses. She threw herself into his arms regardless of who was about. She shamelessly chided him before all. In doing so, she made it possible for him to simply be himself. Once the day's tasks were completed, and he was within Brezden's walls, he didn't have to be "the lord" any longer, he was free to set aside the title and simply be Gerard—a husband, a lover. And that made him more at ease than he ever could have imagined.

He loved them both, to be honest. But with Catheryn he never had to wonder for one minute what she was thinking or feeling. He didn't lie awake at night staring at her trying to determine if she loved him, or wanted him, or desired him. He knew she did— almost as much as he loved, wanted, and desired her.

Gerard picked up the tattered yarrow dream sachet and smiled sadly. He had once thought the bag a young girl's charm. He had once thought dreams useless, childish, a waste of time. How wrong he'd been. This sachet could foretell true love—and it had. Maybe it had other powers as well.

He touched Catheryn's cheek. He'd dreamed about her being whole, awake, and loving him. He still did dream that. Day and night, he dreamed. She'd once told him that dreams could come true if you believed, so with every fiber of his being he believed. Stretching out next to her on the bed, Gerard whispered in her ear, "Catheryn, love, wake up."

⌘

Battle-clad warriors astride Satan's own destriers raced through the fog toward her. Mail as black as the starless sky covered each battle-hardened warrior from helmed head to leather-booted foot. Paralyzed and unprotected, Lady Catheryn could only tremble at their onslaught.

Unrelenting, the mighty warhorses with their deadly mounts charged ever closer. Ironclad hooves pounded in perfect unison with the heavy thudding of her heart. Swords, pikes, and axes raised, the men rushed nearer, and the leader of this demonic army ensnared her gaze. Dark, sapphire eyes held no sign of mercy. There would be no quarter given if captured by this unforgiving force.

The cloying smell of death permeated the air, broken only by the acrid scent of smoke and destruction. The vile stench seared her nostrils. She shuddered with revulsion. Would death claim her as its hapless victim this night?

Fighting to calm a racing heart, Catheryn forced her trembling limbs to still. She would not cower before her enemies, nor would she kneel in the cold mud and beg for mercy. With a hushed voice, she prayed, "Lord, give me strength."

The leader of the pack of death-hungry wolves stopped before her as the remaining warriors raced past. A thunderbolt lit the sky. Raindrops rolled down the mailed arm reaching for her. These tears from Heaven shimmered over an emerald-and-gold ring on the hand that grasped her shoulder with a bruising hold.

No. That wasn't right.

He didn't grasp her shoulder in a bruising hold. No. He had reached down to save her from the hell dogging her heels. That hand reached out to offer safety and love. Love she returned.

Gerard.

"Catheryn, love, wake up."

In her dream, Gerard called to her. She remembered hearing his worried voice many times of late. Then lips were touching her forehead, warm and soft. His voice was soft too, inviting her again to wake up. But she felt safe where she was. Safe from de Brye. Safe from the darkness.

Arms gathered her close. Hands gently cupped her head. "Ah, love, it is lonely without you. Come back to me. I am sorry I forced you into such rashness and vow to never again treat you as anyone less than my equal, my partner in this life."

Silken threads held her securely in a cocoon of warmth and light. She had no wish to leave.

The lips kissed her again, and she felt a warm raindrop fall upon her cheek. She tipped her head, and the drop slid slowly down her skin and across her lips. The rain tasted of salt. Tears?

"Catheryn, I love you. I will wait."

He loved her? Gerard *loved* her? Catheryn's heart swelled with a longing to see him. To touch him. To know if his words were true. Clawing her way through the soft, clinging threads, Catheryn sought her way out of the dream.

Opening her heavy eyelids, she gazed in wonder at the man holding her. She'd not been mistaken. It was Gerard. His tear-reddened eyes shimmered in the flickering candlelight.

"Hello, love."

Catheryn traced his lips with a finger. "I am dreaming?"

He shook his head. "No. You are not dreaming."

"I thought I heard—"

He stopped her with a kiss, a slow, gentle kiss that tugged at her heart and warmed her soul.

Gerard lifted his head and met her gaze. "You heard only me. No one but me."

A memory of a fight tugged at her mind. Her breath caught in her throat. "Is…de Brye…? Is he…?" She trailed off.

Stroking her cheek, Gerard answered. "He is dead. His men are gone as well, every one of them. Your man Rolfe was quick to point them out. The entrance to the cave has been sealed."

"Brezden's men. The children, Sarah and Matthew? Are they safe? What—?"

He placed a finger gently against her lips, stopping her questions. "Our men are safe. Their wounds have been treated and all of them will mend with time. Agnes and Mistress Margaret are caring for the children until you can determine their fate." He moved his hand back to her cheek and announced another piece of news she found surprisingly welcome. "Mistress Margaret and the smithy seem to be forming a bond. With a little encouragement from you, we might have a family for the children with people who are familiar to them."

Catheryn nodded in agreement. That would be the perfect solution.

She moved to stretch then stiffened with the pain of someone too long abed. Something wasn't right. "How long have I been asleep? What happened?"

"Just a day." He searched her face with his eyes. "Do you

not remember?"

Frowning, Catheryn begged her sluggish mind to work. "You brought me back to Brezden. De Brye and his men were here. There was a sword fight."

"Anything else?"

Catheryn pulled at her bottom lip with her teeth. Her husband didn't appear angry now. Had he been at the time?

At her hesitation, he said, "Catheryn, love, we have much to discuss. There will be many times in future that we argue, but right now we are in our chamber, in our room of truce. No words of anger or accusation have any power here—or anywhere else."

She shook her head, remembering. "I took up a sword to join your fight."

"Yes." He laughed softly. "The next time I seek to fight someone in such a manner, I will first make certain you agree with the decision. That way we won't have to worry about you doing anything rash because you disagree."

"It was rash. I knew it was foolish."

"Yes, it was." Gerard agreed. "But I goaded you into it by not listening to your opinion and ordering you away. That will not happen again. It is unfair to you, and far too dangerous for both of us." He laughed again, then rolled away and walked to a chest on the other side of the room. Glancing over his shoulder he added, "Close your eyes."

She did so and waited. Within a heartbeat, she heard the herbs and rushes strewn across the floor crunching under the fall of his returning steps. Then Gerard took her hand in his and placed a kiss on her palm. Closing her fingers, he whispered, "Always remember that no matter what your eyes may show you, no matter what your ears may hear, what I tell and show you in this chamber tonight is the truth." He brushed her cheek with the back of his hand. "There is no one else I would rather spend my life with. No other woman I want to share my dreams with."

The events of the last few days flitted in and out of her still ragged memory. "Why? Why would you wish to burden yourself with —?"

"Burden? You are no burden to me." He cut her off with a kiss and knelt by the side of the bed. "I can think of no one as brave, or as honorable, as you, Catheryn. Many another person would have broken under de Brye. It would have been an easy thing to give him all he asked. You never did. And who else would throw themselves at a charging destrier, trusting me to snatch her from death at the last moment?"

She shook her head. "I am not brave. I simply love my husband. And my dreams always said you would let no harm befall me. I just did not know how to read them."

"Well, you are no worse at that than I, and your slow-witted husband cherishes both your love and you. Never again will he laugh at your dreams. Dreams, when you believe hard enough, come true."

His voice shook with emotion, and unbidden tears gathered behind Catheryn's closed eyes in response. He took her other hand and, after softly kissing that palm, placed something in it, then closed her fingers around the object.

"Open your eyes," he begged. He held her hand closed for another moment while he stared into her gaze with a promise that took her breath away. "This I give as token of my love for you."

He released her hand and waited. Opening her fingers Catheryn stared at the ring she held. An emerald sparkled from its golden band. Her building tears now slipped down her cheeks.

Holding out his hand, Gerard showed her another ring. It was identical. Identical to the ring she still held, identical to the one her knight had worn in her dreams.

Gerard took the ring from her palm and slipped it on her finger. "This circle of gold represents our marriage. Unending. Always united. The green of the emerald is to remind you that my love will be as constant as the spring that arrives every year without fail."

Taking the ring from his palm, she slipped it onto his finger. Her voice shook as she repeated his words back to him. "This I give in token of my love for you. The circle of gold represents our marriage. Unending. Always united. The green of the emerald is to remind you that my love will be as constant as the spring that arrives every year without fail."

Leaning forward, Gerard kissed the tears from her cheeks. "You are and always will be my one true love."

Catheryn reached up and lightly touched his cheek. "You are and always will be *my* one true love, my dream knight."

The End

THANK YOU!

Dear Reader:

Thank you for reading "Dream Knight". I hope you enjoyed Catheryn and Gerard's story and the innocent little yarrow infused spell that brought them together. Catheryn's sisters are currently discovering herbal love spells of their own that I will be sharing with you soon.

If you did enjoy this story, please consider posting a review, as reviews help other readers find books, and I sincerely appreciate them, no matter how brief.

To discover more of my stories, read excerpts or reviews, find my social media links, or to simply drop me a line (I LOVE hearing from readers), visit my website at: www.denise-lynn.com

Again ~ THANK YOU ever so much!

Printed in Great Britain
by Amazon

26273646R00192